By the same author:

In the Tildy series:
TILDY
POORHOUSE WOMAN
NURSING WOMAN
POINTING WOMAN
RADICAL WOMAN
WIDOW WOMAN
INVINCIBLE WOMAN

THE BITTER DAWNING
THE HARSH NOONTIDE
THE HEALING NIGHTFALL

THE SUMMER OF THE FANCY MAN
THE SISTERHOOD
THE DREAMERS
THE IMPERIALISTS

SARA FRASER

GANG WOMAN

WARNER BOOKS

A *Warner* Book

First published in Great Britain in 1989
by Futura
Reprinted 1990
Published by Warner in 1992
This edition published by Warner in 1994
Reprinted 1997

*All characters in this publication are fictitious
and any resemblance to real persons, living or dead,
is purely coincidental.*

ISBN 0 7515 0292 8

Typeset by Leaper & Gard Ltd, Bristol, England
Printed in England by Clays Ltd, St Ives plc

Warner Books
A Division of
Little, Brown and Company (UK)
Brettenham House
Lancaster Place
London WC2E 7EN

Introduction

In the England of 1823 pauper women and children were rented out like beasts of burden to the highest bidder to slave their days away in the 'gangs'.

Brutality, hardship and poverty were the rewards they received, and no one cared about the suffering they endured.

Tildy Crawford was a member of one such 'gang', and this is the story of her lonely fight to survive.

Chapter One

Redditch, Parish of Tardebigge, Worcestershire, June 1823

For more than two weeks the heatwave had gripped the town of Redditch and its environs, the sun mercilessly baking the narrow courts and alleys of the slum quarters, turning the cramped hovels into stinking ovens of wretchedness. Even the coming of darkness brought little or no relief, for no breezes cooled the air, and the heat stored by ground and walls during the hours or daylight was released through the hours of night.

Tildy Crawford lay naked upon her narrow bed in unquiet sleep, her slender yet full-breasted and shapely body palely illuminated by the moonlight shafting through the cracked panes of the tiny window. Barely two feet from her, Davy, her child, tossed and turned in his crude cot, and then cried out in sharp distress. Tildy awoke with a start and for a few seconds her eyes stared up uncomprehendingly at the sharply-angled roof trusses and tiles which were the ceiling of her attic room. Then the child cried out again and the young woman came to instant fearful awareness.

'Davy? Davy, what ails you, Honey?' She bent over the whimpering child, her hand stroking his black curly hair.

'Mammy, my head hurts me, and I keep feeling cold then hot,' he whimpered.

Her fingers moved to his brow and alarm mounted in her as she felt the heat pulsating from his skin.

'Were you playing out in the sun today, Honey?' she questioned anxiously. 'Did the sun burn you?'

He solemnly shook his head. 'No Mammy.' In the moonlight his delicately moulded features appeared almost skull-like, his eyes like deep-shadowed empty sockets, and Tildy's fear sharpened.

'Dear God, don't let him be ill,' she prayed silently. 'Let it just be too much heat which ails him.'

'Are you thirsty?' she questioned. 'Would you like a drink of water?'

He nodded, and taking a horn tumbler from the shelf above her bed, Tildy dipped it into the wooden pail of pump-water which she kept in the corner of her minute room. Gently she lifted his small body to a sitting position and with her arm supporting him held the tumbler to his dry lips. The child sipped at the tepid liquid, and then, without warning, vomited.

Tildy held his straining body and, while the sour smell of bile flooded her nostrils, fought down the rush of panic which momentarily threatened to overwhelm her. When his retching ceased she stripped the soiled night-shift from him, and used a dampened flannel to sponge and cleanse him. Then dressed his slender body in a clean night-shift and laid him in her own bed. She stayed by his side, soothing his whimpers with soft cuddles and caresses, and murmuring reassurances to him until he drifted once more into a restless sleep. She rose and peered out of the eastward-facing window, searching for some sign of the dawn paling the skies along the horizon. The roofs of the surrounding buildings were silver in the moonlight, and nothing stirred in the square beneath her.

'I'll wait 'til daylight, and if he's no better, then I'll go for the doctor,' she decided. Anxiously she turned to stare down at her son. 'Don't take him from me, God, please don't,' she whispered aloud, 'for he's all I have in this world. I beg you, don't take him from me . . .'

The manservant, a coat covering his night-shirt, glowered at this dark-haired young woman who had come with the dawn to pound on the front door of Doctor Alexander Pratt's house.

'What the bloody Hell does you think youm about?' he demanded heatedly. 'To come creating such a rucus at this hour? 'Tis barely four o' the clock.'

Tildy was uncaring of his anger. 'Is the doctor at home?' she questioned anxiously. 'My child is ill.'

The man softened a trifle. 'What's up wi' it?'

'He's burning with fever, and he keeps on being sick, and his head hurts badly,' Tildy told him hurriedly. 'Please can you call the doctor for me? I fear my babby's sorely ill.'

The man's bovine features mirrored his uncertainty. The spectacle of such a beautiful young woman in so much distress evoked his sympathies, but she was poorly clad, and his master, Doctor Pratt, did not normally attend on the poor of the town.

As if she sensed the reason for the servant's hesitance the young woman held out coins on her outstretched palm.

'I've money to pay with. It's not charity I'm asking for, but help.'

Still the man hesitated, fearful of his master's uncertain temper. 'What's your name, young 'ooman, and wheer does you dwell?'

'My name is Crawford, and I live at Mother Readman's in the Silver Square.'

Involuntarily the man's head jerked back and he frowned, and Tildy felt a sense of despair. The Silver Square was considered by respectable people to be the worst slum in the town, and its inhabitants to be beyond redemption, hopelessly sunken in idle wickedness, debauchery and degradation.

'Will you fetch the doctor to me?' she asked once more, and waited for the inevitable rebuff.

The man sighed heavily. 'I doubt he'll come wi' you, girl. The last time he went up the square he got pelted by a pack o' drunks theer. He swore then that he'd ne'er treat anybody else from theer as long as he drew breath. I reckon it might be best if you tried to get one o' the other doctors in the town.'

'I already have,' Tildy told him. 'Doctor Taylor and his son are both away, and the apothecary is bedridden himself.'

'That's a shame.' The man sounded genuinely sorry for Tildy's predicament, but said no more, and she turned to leave.

'No, hold hard.' His hand reached out as if to detain her physically. He drew a deep breath, and asked her, 'How much money has you got wi' you, young 'ooman?'

'I've three shillings.' Again she showed him the coins.

'Hand 'um here,' he instructed. 'You looks very clean and respectable, for all you lives at Mother Readman's. So I'm going to wake my master and show him the money you'se brung wi' you. Mayhap he'll take his fee in advance and come wi' you. It's worth a try anyhow.'

Before Tildy could voice her thanks he had taken the coins from her hand and closed the heavy door with its huge brass lionhead knocker in her face.

During what seemed to her an endless time of waiting Tildy stared up at the clear sky, and could already feel the faint warmth of the early sun upon her bare head and arms.

'It's going to be another scorcher,' she thought despondently, and waves of fearful worries washed over her as she thought of what that heat would entail for her tiny son, already entrapped by the flames of fever.

At last the door re-opened, and the manservant told her, 'My master says he'll come when he's able.'

'When will that be?' Tildy wanted to know.

'When he's able, girl. When he's able,' the man answered impatiently, and re-closed the door.

'I needs must be thankful for small mercies,' Tildy told herself ironically, and hurried back towards the Silver Square.

Despite his dislike for the inhabitants of the Silver Square Alexander Pratt was thorough in his examination of little

Davy, and was gentle in manner to the frightened child.

Tildy stood watching the sallow-faced, lanky-bodied doctor, her hands nervously clutching and twisting the skirt of her shabby black dress.

At length the man straightened and turned to her.

'Now tell me, young woman . . . has the child . . . had the smallpox?' He spoke in clipped, staccato bursts.

She nodded. 'Yes, Sir, and I have had it myself. We took the vaccination when we were at the poorhouse in Webheath and had the mild attack then.' Even now, distraught as she was, her voice was low and pleasant-timbred, with a soft rustic burr interlacing its tones.

Pratt nodded, pursing his lips in a reflective manner, and his dour expression allied to his dark clothing and tall black hat imparted a funereal aspect to him, making him appear like some harbinger of doom in Tildy's fear-heightened imaginings.

'What is it, Doctor? What is it that's ailing my babby?' she beseeched anxiously, and the man frowned and gestured her to silence.

'If you will . . . be good enough . . . to hold your tongue . . . and allow me to speak . . . then the sooner I'll be able to tell you . . . young woman.' He went on to bark a series of questions concerning the child's previous symptoms at her, and Tildy answered as best she could.

Once satisfied he nodded curtly, and again bent over the child, peering into the small open mouth with great concentration, and carefully counting the pulse rate at wrist, neck and temple. At length he straightened once more.

'The boy is labouring under a nervous fever . . . However, his life . . . does not appear . . . to be endangered . . . I shall prescribe . . . a course of treatment for him . . . which you . . . must exactly follow.' He shook his forefinger admonishingly before Tildy's face. 'Exactly! Do you understand that, young woman? Exactly!'

She nodded vigorously. 'You may depend upon me doing that, Sir.'

Taking a large white handkerchief from his pocket, he

patted at the rivulets of sweat running down his face while telling her: 'The source of the fever . . . is the unwholesome air . . . of this dammed place . . . And you may be sure . . . of one thing . . . young woman . . . and that is . . . unless you remove your child . . . from this foul den . . . of malignant putridity . . . then he'll not reach manhood . . . On that, you may rest assured . . . He'll not reach manhood . . . Now, can you read?'

She nodded absently, her mind grappling with what he had just told her.

'Very well . . . come to my house . . . at noontime . . . shall leave written instructions . . . as to medicine and treatment . . . with my manservant . . . And mind what I say . . . you must follow my instructions . . . to the letter . . . To the letter, young woman . . . Good-day to you.'

With that he was gone, leaving a sorely troubled young woman behind him.

'Mammy? Mammy, my head's burning again and hurting me.'

The querulous whining the the child brought Tildy out of her reverie and she forced a smile. 'I'll bathe it with some nice cool water, Honey. That'll take the soreness and burning away.'

She sat on the edge of the cot and used a flannel which she continually dipped in the wooden pail of water to soothe the boy's discomfort. As she did so she thought on what the doctor had said, and a sensation of helplessness stole over her.

'Take Davy from here? God knows if I could, I would. But where can we go that is healthy? Who would give us shelter anywhere else? How would we live? It's all I can do to get us through each week as it is. Why, without Mother Readman's kindness, I fear we'd be in even sorer straits than we are now . . .'

From the narrow passageway beyond the door there came the sounds of heavy shuffling footsteps and a wheezing of breath, and Tildy called softly, 'Is that you, Mother Readman?'

The door opened and a monstrously tall and bloated

female figure swathed in layers of black clothing squeezed into the cramped space between bed and cot.

'Just a minute . . .' The newcomer jerked out the words between gasps for air. 'I needs . . . to catch . . . me breath.'

Tildy jumped to her feet. 'Set you down here on the bed,' she invited, but the fat woman waved aside the invitation and grinned self-mockingly, showing stubs of brown teeth.

'I'd ne'er manage to get back on me feet iffen I did that, girl,' she panted.

Tildy smiled with genuine warmth at Mother Readman, proprietress of the lodging house, and the acknowledged monarch of the Silver Square and its satellite, the Silver Street, the long narrow crooked alley which connected the square to the outer world. She was a tallow-complexioned, brawl-scarred harridan who yet possessed immense kindliness of heart, and although ready and able to fight like a pugilist, was gentle and tender to those for whom she had affection.

When her panting had eased she asked, 'What about the babby?'

Tildy related all that the doctor had said, and the older woman's eyes, almost buried in puffballs of fat, were saddened. She sighed, and nodded, causing her several chins to wobble and scratched with stubby fingers among her grizzled mass of grey hair beneath the floppy, grimy mobcap.

'Ahr, he's right, God blast it! This place is a slaughter-house for the little 'uns. There arn't above one in five birthed here that lives more nor a few years at the outside.' She paused, and again sighed heavily. 'Trouble is, Tildy, wheer else can you goo wi' the nipper? You'se got no money, and no place o' settlement in any other parish. And at least when the trade's good there's work to be got in this town.'

'Yes, when trade's good,' Tildy remarked dispiritedly.

Like the majority of the local people Tildy was employed in the local trade, needle-making, of which article Redditch town and its its district was the world's principal producer. But the trade was subject to periodic fluctuations, and just recently had entered something of a recession, causing the Needle Masters to cut their costs by laying off the majority of their labour force. Tildy was one of those unfortunates, and was now existing on what Outdoor Relief the Parish Overseers to the Poor allowed her.

Charlotte Readman had caught the girl's tone, and now she grinned fondly. 'Ne'er mind, Tildy, at least youm looking bonny again, having a rest from that bleedin' Lye Wash like you am.'

Matilda Crawford was indeed a beautiful woman. Her long dark hair was thick and glossy, her pale skin clear and smooth, and her eyes a luminous brown. All this, coupled with her shapely, full-breasted body, was a sight to turn men's heads and fill their eyes with desire. Many men did desire Tildy, and many men offered her their protection, but she refused all of them, preferring to care for her child by herself, and make her own way through life by her own efforts.

The child whimpered for attention, and both women turned to tend to him. As she once more laid the cool flannel on his burning forehead, Tildy prayed silently, 'Help me, God. Help me to find a safe and healthy place for my child to live in . . . '

Chapter Two

The central buildings of hilly Redditch town were ranged around a large triangular common, on the south-west corner of which stood the squat cupolaed Chapel of St Stephen. The chapel almost fronted the main crossroads of the town, the roads running north towards Birmingham, south towards Evesham, westwards to Bromsgrove, and eastwards towards the neighbouring parish of Ipsley in Warwickshire County. The northern road traversed the common then plunged steeply down the Fish Hill to the broad valley of the Arrow River.

Fish Hill was lined on both sides with cottages, houses, workshops and Needle Mills. In the heat of midday a small group of men came climbing the steep slope towards the centre of the town, sweating under the heavy bundles they carried on their backs, and exchanging brief comments in a language so ancient that its origins were buried in time's mysteries.

When the group reached the first plateau of the common the leader, a tall, broad-shouldered, grave-faced man, signalled a halt, and thankfully his companions let their bundles fall and sat upon them to rest their weary legs. The leader let his own bundle fall but did not sit down, instead he went on alone in the direction of the Chapel of St Stephen. There were few people about, only a party of shrill-voiced urchins playing, and a dark-gowned, bare-headed young woman hurrying across the common. The tall man removed his shallow-crowned, broad-brimmed hat and accosted the woman.

'Excuse me, good lady, can you tell me if there iss a

lodging-house hereaboutss?'

Tildy halted and turned to face her questioner. As he repeated his question she wondered momentarily at the sibilants and the rolling R's of his unfamiliar accent, then, preoccupied as she was, told him.

'Yes, there are two.'

'Will you direct me to them, good lady?'

She hesitated, then offered. 'I can show you the way, but you'll have to wait while I do my errand.'

He nodded gravely. 'Yesss, good lady, I will wait.'

She nodded absently in return, 'I'll not be long then,' and went hurrying on to Doctor Pratt's house, which stood opposite the Unicorn Inn on the top of the western arm of the crossroads, which like the northern also plunged steeply downwards.

The manservant answered her knocking, and handed her a slip of paper covered with the spidery handwriting of the Doctor. Tildy briefly scanned the contents, and experienced a sense of dismay at what she read.

'Here, girl, take this.' The manservant handed her a small rag-wrapped packet. 'I've snuck this out from the Doctor's cabinet for you. There's the Vomiting Julep Powder, and all the stuff you'll need to mix the Blistering Plasters. But don't you go telling nobody what I'se done, or the Doctor 'ull be having my guts for garters.'

'No, I won't tell, and thank you for your kindness,' Tildy assured him gratefully, for she had no money to buy any of the items.

'That's alright, girl.' The man grinned at her. 'We must all try to help each other in hard times like these be, mustn't us . . . But remember,' he winked and held his finger against his lips, 'no names, no pack drill.'

Warmed by his goodwill Tildy walked back towards the common, and saw with a sense of disquiet that the man who was waiting for her had now been joined by four or five companions. She studied their appearance as she neared them. They were all big, powerful-looking men, their faces browned by weather and heavily stubbled, their clothing rough-cut and travel-stained, their heads shaggy beneath their wide-brimmed hats. She wondered if they might be travelling navvies, but they carried none of the tools that navvies took with them, and their large bundles were wrapped in stained, dirty sheepskins.

As if he sensed her disquiet the leader chuckled and told her, 'There iss no need to distrust uss, good lady. We are honest men.'

One of his companions laughed aloud, and said something to the others in his strange-sounding tongue and the leader turned and berated him angrily, then spoke again to Tildy.

'We are Welshmen, good lady. Drovers from the Tregaron parish in the Cardigan country. We are here to look for shearing work before we go back to our own land. We have driven a herd of cattle to Birmingham market you see, and the people there told us there would be work at the shearing in these parts.'

There was a quality in his strong-featured face and steady eyes that evoked Tildy's trust, and she smiled apologetically. 'I meant no rudeness, Master Welshman, and as to the shearing work, I doubt you'll be finding any in this town. We make needles here. But there's farms aplenty all round the town, so you may make enquiries at them with little effort.'

He was not handsome, but when he smiled as he did now, showing good teeth, there was something about his face attractive to Tildy.

'Then you will show uss the lodging house now, if it pleases you, good lady. We'll rest awhile before we travel to the farms.'

Side by side Tildy and the leader walked past the chapel and eastwards in the direction of Red Lion Street where Silver Street debouched under an archway at the side of the Red Lion Inn, and the rest of the group followed behind.

'My name iss Oriel Evans,' the tall man told Tildy. 'My friends with me do not have the English tongue, but I know it well, and I have often been jolly with my English friends in London when we have droved the cattle to the Smithfield market there.'

Tildy, preoccupied by her worry for little Davy, only nodded absently, and the Welshman asked perceptively, 'There iss something troubling you I think, good lady?'

'My child is ill,' Tildy answered. 'He's taken a fever. That's why I've been to fetch these from the doctor.' She lifted the small packet and showed him.

Oriel Evans was instantly sympathetic. 'I'm sorry for your troubles, good lady. It iss hard for a mother when her child iss ill.' He hesitated for a moment, then asked diffidently, 'What treatments does the doctor say you should give the child?'

'Vomits and Blister Plasters,' she said unhappily. 'It seems cruel to torment him further with such harsh treatments. But the doctor must know best, I suppose, and all the books I have read about medicines recommend blistering as a true benefit in Nervous Fevers.'

'Tchaaa!' the Welshman ejaculated in disgust. 'It iss in my mind that doctors kill more people than they ever cure. In my country we don't have much to do with doctors. In the mountains we have to cure our own sick.' Again he hesitated, looking sideways at Tildy's drawn features, then offered, 'I am known ass a Healing Man in my own country around Tregaron, good lady. If you would wish it, then I'll look at your child for you, and see if there iss a kinder way to cure him than vomits and blisters.'

Tildy was instantly tempted to take up his offer. In her world it was rare for poor people ever to have a doctor prescribe for them. They simply could not afford the necessary fees, and so they relied instead on local wise-women and cunning men who were reputed to be skilled in treating the sick. Her great love for her child had impelled her to spend her last remaining shillings on calling in Doctor Pratt, but the present course of treatment he had instructed her to administer was filling her with dread. She had seen what terrible sores and ulcers could be created by the blistering plasters, and the debilation caused in a sick person by the constant administration of vomiting doses, and she was fearful of the further suffering such treatments would cause her beloved child. If this stranger was really a Healing Man, then perhaps he could indeed prescribe a kinder, gentler method of curing her Davy.

By now they had reached the Red Lion Inn and the archway that led into the long, narrow, fetid alley known as the Silver Street. Tildy halted and faced the Welshman.

'The lodging-house lies in the square at the end of this street.' She pointed through the archway. 'It's where I live myself. Mother Readman keeps it, she is a good woman and honest, you'll not be cheated by her. But I think it only fair to warn you that this neighbourhood bears a bad name in the district. We who live there are classed as rogues and vagabonds by many people in these parts. so if you choose not to go there with me, I shall well understand.'

His strong teeth glistened in his tanned face, and he chuckled drily. 'Good lady, I told you we were honest men, but none of us are saints, nor simpletons either. The droving sometimes takes us into places where the people are worse than animals. I don't think we shall come to any harm here. You can lead on.'

'Very well.' Tildy nodded gravely. 'so long as you have understood what I have told you. We get some rough customers in the Silver Square, and strangers can be given a hard ride of it at times. I think it only right that you tell your friends of this.'

Oriel Evans, still grinning broadly, turned and spoke rapidly to his companions, and when one of them made a voluble reply, they all burst into laughter.

Evans turned back to Tildy. 'He says that if these rough customers are only a tenth ass pretty ass you, good lady, then to meet with them will be a pleasure.'

Not displeased by the implied compliment Tildy led the group along the alley and into the large square at its end. Before she took them inside the tall, four-storied lodging house she spoke again to Oriel Evans. 'Master Evans, when you've settled with Mother Readman, I'd like for you to have a look at my child, and thank you for offering to do so.'

He regarded her solemnly. 'I pray that God will give me the means to aid your little one, good lady.'

After settling terms for a night's lodgings with Mother Readman, Oriel Evans mounted the flights of dark rickety stairs to the top of the house. Despite his rather dour appearance he was possessed of a poetical fancy, and now he could not help but fantasize as to how a beautiful, fresh young woman such as Tildy Crawford came to be living here surrounded by filth and degradation. 'She is truly a flower growing on a dungheap,' he smiled to himself.

She answered the door to his knock and invited him to enter her tiny room. Compared to what he had already seen of the rest of the house it was an oasis of cleanliness, and it touched his heart to see how she had tried to brighten its cramped austerity with tiny clusters of sweet-smelling wild flowers and herbs. Although her abysmal poverty was evident in the lack of any possessions that he could see, the flowers demonstrated that her material poverty had not created spiritual poverty or deadened her soul to beauty.

'This is my Davy.' She smiled lovingly at the sick child who lay, wide eyes fixed on this strange man.

'Good afternoon, young gentleman,' Evans gently greeted the child. 'I'm come here to make you better. But first I need to have a close look at you.'

Davy lay still and silent while the man deftly drew the small nightshift from his hot, dry skin, and equally deftly ran large hands over his delicately formed head, throat and limbs.

Aftera short period of reflection Evans told Tildy, 'In my language we call this fever *gwres cos haf*, the heat of the Summer Marsh.' He smiled reassuringly at her. 'I can cure the boy, Mistress Crawford, without needing to torment him with Blisters and Vomits.' He glanced briefly at the cramped surrounds. 'But it would be better if we had more room to work in, just for an hour or so. And I will need both hot and cold water, and stone bottles and a sheet and a blanket. The other things I can find myself.'

Tildy thought briefly. 'If it's only for an hour, then we

could use the kitchen. There won't be anyone in there until nightfall I shouldn't think, and Mother Readman won't mind.'

'Good!' Oriel Evans patted her shoulder. 'Then you prepare what I have asked for, and bring everything to the kitchen. You can wrap the young gentleman in his own blanket to bring him down. He'll take no harm from being moved. I will meet you there shortly.'

The kitchen was big and gloomy, its walls greased by countless bodies, the ceiling low and smoke-blackened. A great wooden table stood in the centre and rough wooden benches were against the walls.

When they met there Tildy had a big iron pot full of water simmering over the fire in the great inglenook which dominated one wall. No matter how warm the weather Mother Readman always insisted on keeping her cooking fire lit, and the air was stiflingly hot in the room, the smells of stale bodies and stale cooking thick in throat and nostrils. Oriel Evans' companions had gone drinking in the alehouses, and only Tildy, little Davy and he were in the room.

The Welshman produced a small sack of onions and two small canvas tie-backs. 'We shall need these as well, good lady,' he told Tildy. 'Go you now and wet the sheet under the pump, then wring it out.'

While she did this he busied himself in chopping the onions into small pieces with his horn-handled knife, tears running from his eyes as the acrid juices spurted. He filled the two small bags with the chopped onions, and then gently inserted Davy's feet into the bags, making sure that the onion chunks covered them completely, before tying the tops around the slender ankles.

'There now, young gentleman, what a fine new pair of boots you are wearing,' he joked, and the child tried to smile, but could only produce a nervous twitching of the lips.

Next Evans took the night-shift off the boy and once again carefully scrutinized the well-formed little body. 'It iss good, Mistress Tildy,' he smiled at her, 'that there iss no spots or rash has come out. So we'll have this young gentleman well on the road within the hour. Do you lay the sheet on the table there.'

Tildy obeyed, and the Welshman laid little Davy down on the sheet, the bags like crude pillows on his feet, and gently wrapped the damp folds around him, soothing the child's frightened whimpers with soft words crooned in his own language. Next he took the blanket and wrapped it loosely around the child, and lastly filled the stone bottles with hot water from the pot and corked them before placing them against Davy's body.

'Now we must wait,' he told Tildy. 'Soon the young gentleman will begin to sweat like a pit pony, and the badness will come out from his body. We'll let it come for about half an hour, then all we need to do is to give him a good rub down with a towel and put him back in his own bed. The bags on his feet must stay until the morn.'

He fumbled in his bundle which lay beneath the table and produced a handful of dried leaves. 'Here, take these.' He handed them to Tildy. 'These are from the Verbena plant. You must make a decoction from this and give the child a cupful to drink every three hours from now until he iss better again. That will be tomorrow afternoon. Be sure of it. You will see with your own eyes that I speak the truth.'

His confidence was such that Tildy found herself believing him implicitly.

'How do I make this decoction?' she wanted to know.

'It is very easy.' Evans smiled. 'Put half of what I have given you into a quart of cold water. Cover it, and leave it stand for two hours. Then you must put it on the fire and bring it slowly to boiling. Let it boil for half a minute only. That iss very important. It must only boil for half a minute. No longer, or it will destroy the strength in it. Then all you need to do is strain it, leave it to cool, and give him a cupful every three hours. Do you have that now?'

'I do,' she told him.

By now Davy's small face was becoming a bright shiny red and sweat was beading his smooth skin. Tildy bent over him anxiously.

'Are you alright, Honey? Does it pain you?'

He shook his head slowly, his eyes huge, and his expression very solemn, and Tildy's love for him swelled within her heart and caused a lump to form in her throat. Tears stinging in her eyes, she went to pat away the sweat with a piece of clean rag, but the Welshman stopped her.

'No, leave it be. You must not touch it in case you drive it back into his body. You must let the bad humours come out without any hindrance.'

They sat on the benches on opposing sides of the great table and stared at the child; smiling to reassure him as his eyes switched from face to face. The sweat was now streaming from him, and his thick black curls were wet with it.

Evans chuckled with satisfaction. 'It goes well. It goes very well. Look you, Mistress Tildy, start making the decoction why don't you. I'll look to the boy.'

Later, when Davy was once more in his own bed, appearing greatly soothed and dozing easily, Tildy tried to thank the Welshman, but he waved her words aside.

'It wass nothing, Mistress Tildy. I wass glad to be of help to you and your fine son. Go you now and watch him getting better. I am going to find my friends and be jolly with them for a few hours. Tomorrow iss plenty soon enough to go looking for work, I think.' He patted her shoulder. 'This place iss not good for children. He should be living in the clean air of the country.'

She went back to her tiny attic and sat on her narrow bed looking down at her sleeping child. Although still flushed and sweaty he lay peacefully, breathing evenly and seemed to be in no discomfort.

'Thank you, God, for sending the Welshman here,' Tildy thought gratefully, her vivid imagination picturing how Davy would now be if he had been subjected to violent vomiting and the burning Blister Pads. Highly intelligent as she was, she could not help but doubt the efficacy of many of the medical practices she had witnessed during her lifetime, and was greatly interested in any alternative treatments.

'I think I could learn much from the Welshman,' she told herself.

Tired and made drowsy by the heat she leaned her head upon her coarse pillow and still thinking about Oriel Evans, fell asleep. In her dreams it seemed she could still hear his voice repeating over and over again . . . 'Your fine son should be living in the clean air of the country . . . the clean air of the country . . . the clean air . . . the clean air . . . the clean air . . .' In her dream she was looking down at a deserted Silver Square and then she saw her Davy come from a doorway, running as if pursued by some unseen danger. Then, from all round the square, from doorways, windows, entries, swirls of thick vapour billowed out, growing ever thicker, its writhing tentacles stretching out, reaching towards Davy. In her dream she tried to shout down to her child. to warn him of the danger that she knew the vapour held for him. But strain as she would no sound came from her lips, and sobbing helplessly she watched the vapour envelop her child and smother him in its opaque mists.

She came awake with a start, the horror of the dream still holding her in its thrall.

'It's true!' she thought, with a sickening sense of dismay. 'This place will kill him. I must get him away to a healthy clean spot where he can grow tall and strong . . . I must get him away from here . . . I must . . . I must . . .'

Chapter Three

Three days after Tildy's meeting with the Welshman, in the small vestry room of St Stephen's Chapel, the governing body of the parish, the Select Vestry, gathered together for a special meeting. In the chair was John Clayton, curate to Reverend the Lord Aston, the Vicar of Tardebigge Parish. He was a young man of remarkable ugliness, and equally remarkable power of physique, and the strength of his muscular arms was repeatedly called into service to intervene between the Vestrymen as the meeting became increasingly acrimonious and actual physical combat threatened between the disputing Vestrymen.

The reason for this special meeting was the proposed levy of an extra Poor Rate to replenish the coffers that had been all but emptied by the recent demands made upon them due to the unexpected recession in the needle trade. The reason for the bitter disputation between the Vestrymen was that two of them were farmers, two were Needle Masters, and two were shopkeeper and coal merchant respectively.

Behind his serious demeanour John Clayton was highly diverted by the proceedings, and could not help but compare the antagonists to the Gadarene Swine, all greedy to suck the largest amounts from the trough.

Now, once again, Clayton's gavel thundered down upon the table top and his stentorian voice bellowed for silence as voiced hurled insults and challenges. 'Gentlemen! Gentlemen?! If you cannot conduct yourselves as gentlemen then I shall be forced to declare this meeting closed, and refer the whole affair to my Lord Aston, and through him, have it brought to the attention of the Earl.'

His threat served to impose a sullen hush, for the Earl of Plymouth was the great local landowner and magnate, and the Reverend the Lord Aston his trusted right hand in this district, and if they so wished they could bring down ruin upon any of those present.

'Master Davis,' Clayton spoke to the Vestry Clerk who was seated to one side of the room, his tall thin body perched on a tall thin stool at a tall thin desk, 'Would you leave us please, and return when I call for you.'

Joseph Davis's long thin nose twitched visibly as he settled his tall thin black hat on his narrow head and stalked from the room, radiating his affront at being so dismissed from the gathering, for he considered himself to be a person of great consequence in the parish, and more than worthy to be privy to any doings of its ruling body.

When the door had closed behind his black-clad back, Clayton addressed the meeting. 'Gentlemen, I have that to say which it ill behoves our clerk to hear, since it might be taken to be a criticism of his betters.'

Clayton's tone was neutral, but his eyes held contempt as they glanced in turn at each man present. William Smallwood, Needle Master, burly and blunt-spoken. Henry Milward, Needle Master, portly and pompous. The red-faced, leather-gaitered farmers, George Holyoake and Charles Whadcoat. The grocer, whose nose betrayed his love of brandy, Ingram Monnox, and Josiah Cutler, dark-visaged and lean-bodied, his skin engrained with the coal dust that he spent his days amongst.

Clayton coughed before continuing, 'Between you, gentlemen, you hold the posts of Chapel Wardens, Overseers to the Poor, and Way Wardens of this parish, and although I fully sympathize with the fact that these positions carry no salary, and each of you gives freely of his own time to render inestimable service to this parish and its inhabitants, yet I feel constrained to remind you that this Select Vestry is virtually self-appointed and self-perpetuating.'

'What are you getting at, Parson Clayton?' William

Smallwood demanded aggressively. 'Spake out plain and open, and don't go beating around the bloody bushes.'

Clayton's own quick temper rose in answer to this aggression. 'I will be plain and open, Master Smallwood, do not doubt that fact for one instant. Each and every one of you chooses to serve as a Select Vestryman, and each and every one of you draws every advantage from that position that he can contrive to gain.' His voice rose above the instant rumblings of resentment. 'My master, the Lord Aston, in his capacity of magistrate would most certainly look askance at some of the dealings that have been carried out at the behest of this vestry.' Quick sidelong glances passed between the men, and Clayton noted these but made no comment; instead he smiled pleasantly. 'My Lord Aston, and indeed, the Earl himself, are unhappy about the continual increase in the Poor Rate of this parish during these last two years. The Earl has even been heard to wonder aloud if certain of our parish officers may not be abusing the trust he places in them . . .' A hubbub of indignant protest greeted this last sentence, but to Clayton's shrewd ears that indignation was tinged by fear.

And rightly so, he thought. Each and all of you are corrupt in your own interests.

His thoughts ranged over the instances of corruption that he knew of personally, such as the two farmers underpaying their labourers so that their wages would have to be made up from the parish Poor Rate under the Speenhamland system which was practised here. The shopkeeper and the coal dealer issuing relief tokens for food and fuel on behalf of the parish, which could only be exchanged for goods at their own establishments. The Needle Masters having housing erected for their workers which were too lacking in any amenities to be rated, yet with rents set so high that the parish was forced to make an allowance to the occupants to enable them to pay those rents.

Yes gentlemen, Clayton silently castigated them, you are indeed swine guzzling yourselves fatter and fatter at the trough . . . But what can I do to prevent you? He asked himself, and answered in the same instant with a sense of angry impotence. Nothing! Nothing at all, for the whole nation is equally riddled with corruption, and those who should be above reproach, the ruling classes, are the most corrupt of all . . .

His bitter ruminations were broken into by a knocking at the door, and he roused himself to call, 'Is that you, Master Davis?'

'Yes Sir, there's a Master Borth come here to speak with you. He says that he's expected.'

'One moment,' Clayton shouted, and explained to the Vestrymen, 'I have taken the liberty of sending for this Master Borth, gentlemen, so that you may hear his proposals at first hand. They may well prove to be a partial answer to our Poor Rate problem. You may enter, Master Borth,' he called, and the door opened to admit a man dressed in a peaked military-style forage cap, wide-skirted blue corduroy coat and breeches, and riding boots.

The man paused for a moment, his hard, shrewd eyes scanning the faces of those around the table, then he removed his cap from his shaven bullet-head, and said bluffly, 'My name is Jeremiah Borth, your Honours, and I thank you for receiving me.'

'Pray take this seat, Master Borth.' Clayton indicted a chair set against the wall at the far side of the room.

William Smallwood leant to whisper in Henry Milward's ear, 'This bugger looks like a dammed pug to me.'

Milward nodded agreement, for the newcomer's stocky body looked powerful, and his weatherbeaten face was broken-nosed and ridged around eyes and mouth with thick scar tissue.

As Borth settled himself, George Holyoake suddenly snapped his fingers and exclaimed, 'By Christ, I knows who you be now, Master Borth. Youm the prizefighter they used to call the Battling Brummie.'

'That's just so, your Honour.' The newcomer's tobacco-stained teeth showed fleetingly between his puffy lips. 'But I arn't one o' the Fancy any more. I'm too long in the tooth for it now.'

Smallwood leant to Milward. 'There Henry, didn't I tell you he was a dammed pug. Ugly looking-customer, arn't he.'

'Now, Master Borth we are busy men, so please state your proposals to the Vestry,' Clayton requested.

'Certainly, your Honour. What I'm proposing, gentlemen, is to rent from you your able-bodied female paupers and any kids they might have whom able to do a hand's-turn o' work.'

Inevitably it was William Smallwood who immediately demurred. 'That's not possible. Our paupers are already put out to employment wherever possible. Morris, our Poor'us Master, keeps 'um well occupied.'

Borth's shaven head nodded, and he grinned. 'I'm pleased to hear that, your Honour, but with all respect to you, you arn't rightly understood me. It arn't the Poor'us women that I'm wanting, but the ones on the Outdoor Relief. I knows that your men on the Outdoor Relief already does Yard-land work on your roads and suchlike . . .' There was a suggestion of a sneer in his voice. Yard-land men, as they were termed, were notorious for their laziness, and the difficulties that anyone who tried to make them work faced. '. . . but to my knowledge, your Honours, you arn't bin able to put your females out to any sort o' useful toil. So they'm just a burden on the parish, arn't they?'

Emphatic nods and murmurs of agreement greeted this last statement.

Satisfied that he was gaining their interest, Borth went on. 'What I'm proposing, your Honours, is to take part o' that burden from the parish, from now until mid part o' November at least. I knows that in this district most o' the females and kids be normally employed at the needles. I knows as well that at present the trade's real bad, and that's why so many am drawing relief. But by November the trade should ha' picked up again, shouldn't it? So my proposals arn't agoing to cause any inconvenience to you manufacturing gentlemen, because the females and kids 'ull be available to you when you needs 'um.'

The two Needle Masters exchanged glances, and Smallwood said, 'No, Master Borth, that being the case, I would not think so.'

'Nooo, o' course not!' the man answered expansively. 'As for you farming gentlemen . . . Well now, you needs all the labouring hands you can get ahold of during the harvest seasons, don't you. But there's all sorts o' work that it arn't easy to ha' done by the piece, arn't there. And you has lots o' trouble trying to oversee that work, don't you, 'specially when you'se got such a powerful lot of urgent matters to be aseeing to . . . And don't your labourers try and sting you for every penny that they can get from you at this time, because the artful buggers knows that youm in a tight bind and can't do wi'out 'um.'

Holyoake and Whadcoat were quick to voice agreement with the aggrieved airs of those who considered themselves to be very hard done by.

'Well now, if I comes to your Honours and offers to gi' you a lower piece-price, and I guarantees the work 'ull be well and quickly done, otherwise you needn't pay me . . . Well now, you'd be gaining, 'udden't you?'

'What youm saying, Master Borth, is that you wants to form travelling work gangs from our Outdoor Refief females and their childer,' George Holyoake stated, and Borth reacted with apparent pleasure.

'Exactly so, your Honour! Exactly so. You'se got it in a nutshell, so to spake.'

'But this arn't no new invention, Master Borth,' Holyoake challenged. 'We farmers hereabouts always get gangs coming out from the town during the harvesting.'

''O course you does, your Honour.' Borth's battered features radiated goodwill. 'I knows that well. But them gangs don't allus gi' satisfaction, does they. They'd sooner play nor work, 'udden't they. And they'm powerful greedy, and most on 'um powerful light-fingered, arn't they.'

'That's true enough,' Holyoake granted.

'Well, my gangs 'ull be none o' them things.' For an instant a merciless brutality glimmered through Borth's mask of pleasantness. 'And they'll cost you a sight less in the long run than they does at present. That, I'll guarantee.'

Ingram Monnox, the grocer, had been trying to think of any possible benefits which might accrue to him if this man were allowed to form his work-gangs, and had so far failed to find any. When, as an Overseer to the Poor, he issued his food tickets, he was able to give low measures of inferior goods for the highest prices. If large numbers of paupers were now to be earning cash, he would end a loser. For the women would demand full weight and better products for their money, or take their business elsewhere, and his profit margins would be accordingly reduced.

'Tell me, Master Borth,' he enquired pettishly, 'if we should accept your proposals, why should the women work for you anyway? They can go independently, as they do now, to seek work at the harvests.'

Borth had been anticipating such objections. He had made detailed enquiries as to the make-up of the Vestry, and had expected that the shopkeeper might prove hostile. He looked briefly about him, trying to evaluate the moods of the other men present. The two farmers he counted as allies. The Needle Masters on balance tilted in his favour. The coal merchant he could disregard to some extent, because at this season of the year his trade would not be affected either way. The clergyman? Borth was unsure. But in his experience the men of the cloth were more concerned with saving souls than filling the bellies of the poor. Now, he grinned at Monnox.

'Why, as to that, your Honour, it's easy answered . . . The farmers can turn 'um away, and then any female who refuses to work on the gangs can be refused her Outdoor Relief.'

Monnox dismissed this with a contemptuous snort. 'If they was to be refused what they regards as their entitlement by us, then they'd be straight off to the magistrates and lay complaint against us, saying that we was using them cruelly, and giving them inhuman treatment. They'se done it afore, my bucko, and the Justices ordered us to grant the buggers their tickets; and there was naught we could do about it but to give the buggers their demands.'

The ex-boxer betrayed no sign of offence at the grocer's insulting manner, although inwardly he seethed with rage. Maintaining his pleasant mask, he replied quietly, 'There's an easy way round that problem, your Honour. All you, the Gentlemen o' the Vestry, needs to do, is to appoint me as the Assistant Overseer to the Poor o' this Parish. You presents to the Justices the pressing need you has for such an officer at this time, and they'll gi' their consent quick enough.'

The quicker-witted of the Vestrymen instantly grasped the connotations of this proposal, and William Smallwood slapped his thigh and voiced his appreciation.

'By God, that's a good 'un, that is, Master Borth. If we was to so appoint you, then you'd be a full-time salaried officer of the parish. You'd have the legal powers to override any decision as to Relief made by the Overseers of the Poor. Because they'm only unpaid and serving for six months at a time in this parish.

'The magistrates 'ud have to give you the benefit o' their support, especially since they'm the ones who has to approve your being put in that position in the first place . . .' As an afterthought he added, '. . . On our recommendation, o' course.'

'Exactly so, your Honour.' Borth beamed radiantly at the Needle Master. 'It's easy to see why youm such a successful man o' business, Master Smallwood. You grasps the whole picture straight off, so you does.' He addressed the table at large, 'Why, if any pauper went running to the magistrates wi' complaints about cruel and inhuman treatment, she'd not get far wi' it, 'ud she. Especially when the Assistant Overseer to the Poor showed that she was wilfully refusing to take the lawful employment that that same officer had gone to great trouble to find for her.' His eyes gleamed slyly, as he went on persuasively, 'I appreciates the difficulties you local gentlemen faces if you tries refusing Relief to anybody. After all, you has to live here wi' your families, and some o' these paupers don't care about offering abuse to your loved ones iffen you refuses them their relief.

'But, wi' me as the Assistant Overseer, then it's me who'll be refusing the Relief. And it's me the paupers 'ull be blaming for it. And it's me who'll be taking the abuse and threats from 'um. You gentlemen won't be held responsible any more, 'ull you . . .'

He had made a good point with those last sentences and appreciative comments sounded.

Aware that he had been routed on that point Monnox sought desperately to throw in another attack. 'But by so appointing you, Master Borth, the Parish 'ud then have the expense of your salary. What 'ud that cost us in the long run? And who'se to say that some of the farmers won't take on the women that don't belong to your gangs?'

Borth spread his hands as if supplicating understanding. 'I can't believe that any farmer 'ud be silly enough to have work done for a guinea, that he could have done better and quicker for half that sum . . . And as to my salary,' he grinned broadly, 'set it at what you will, gentlemen. For I've no intention of taking any money from the Parish Chest. Like I said afore, it's me that's agoing to be paying the Parish rent money for the women and kids. I'll take my salary from what I gets for the work they does.' He inwardly smiled as he saw the impression his words had created.

'How do you intend to oversee your gangs, Master Borth?' the beefy-faced Charles Whadcoat wanted to know.

'I'll bring in my own men for that, your Honour. Unless any of you gentlemen have someone that you want particularly to recommend for the work.'

John Clayton now intervened for the first time. 'What I am concerned about, Master Borth, is the amount these women and children could be expected to earn? If the wages are set too low, then the Parish would still have to make the sum up to the amount these women and children could be expected to earn? If the wages are set too low, then the Parish would still have to make the sum up to the amount stipulated by the Speenhamland system. That is the law.'

Sensing victory, Borth was careful to keep any note of triumph from his voice. Very seriously he told the clergyman, 'I'd make sure that the law was satisfied, your Honour. 'm not a hard-hearted man. I've a woman and childer or me own, so I'd not ill-use any other man's woman or child.

'I can assure you o' one thing, your Honour, and that is, if you agree to my proposals, why, then we'll all be the gainers, and not only us but all the ratepayers in this parish. Because there'll be no call for any extra Poor Rate to be levied.'

Clayton nodded, and asked the meeting, 'Are there any other questions you wish to ask at this time, gentlemen?'

None were forthcoming, and Clayton told Borth, 'You may leave us now, Master Borth, Please to attend on us outside until we call you again.'

Within the hour Borth was informed that his proposals had been accepted, and that within three days he would be also confirmed in his appointment as the Assistant Overseer to the Poor of the Tardebigge Parish . . .

Chapter Four

Monday was the day ordained by the Select Vestry for dealing with the applications for Outdoor Relief, and from an early hour men, women and children collected on the Green outside St Stephen's Chapel. The heatwave still gripped the district, and the hot sunshine, coupled with the expectations of forthcoming money and food tickets created something of a festive atmosphere among the gathering crowd.

Joseph Cashmore, the taciturn, burly-bodied constable carrying his long-staved, crowned staff of office joined the crowd, and his appearance was greeted with good-natured jeering. He smiled grimly.

'I reckon most on you 'ull be wailing a different tune afore this day is done,' he told those nearest to him.

'Why so, Master Cashmore?' a bent-bodied, elderly man queried.

'Oh you'll be alright, George Cole,' the constable answered. 'Youm too old to work. But these younger 'uns has got a terrible shock acoming to 'um.'

'What d'you mean?', 'What's the matter wi' the younger 'uns?', 'What sort o' shock?' questioners badgered him.

'Be they agoing to increase our allowances agen?' one wag wanted to know.

Cashmore refused to enlarge upon the matter any further and took up his customary station before the big double doors of the chapel.

A few minutes later Joseph Davis, Clerk to the Vestry, made his appearance, carrying beneath his arm the big leather-bound ledger in which the Relief accounts were entered. He frowned as the crowd's chaffing was directed at him.

'Here he comes, good King Wenceslas.'

'The man wi' the biggest heart in Worcestershire.'

'Ahr, the biggest heart in the country, and the bloody stoniest.'

'Come on, Shylock. We can't be all day waiting for you. We'se got more important matters to attend to.'

'That's right, you heathens, you just keep on amaking mock o' me,' Davis shouted angrily. 'But I'll be having the last laugh this day. You'll see.'

'Now, the more thoughtful among the crowd began to exchange concerned looks and whispers. Tildy, standing with Sarah Farr, one of her workmates, a haggard-featured, gaunt-bodied woman who looked far older than her thirty-odd years, shared that sense of foreboding. And it deepened when Joseph Davis shouted, 'You'd all best know now that theer's bin an Assistant Overseer to the Poor appointed by the Select Vestry. Master Borth is his name, and he'll be dealing wi' your applications today.' His narrow head bobbed on his long thin neck as he sneered openly. 'You'll not be finding Master Borth as easy to gull wi' your sorrowful tales as some others I could name. No, not by a long chalk you wun't.'

A rustling of disquiet went through the crowd, which by now numbered over a hundred, the majority of them women, many of them with infants in their arms and young children hanging on their skirts.

'Wheer is this Borth, then?'someone shouted, and Davis pointed along the Green.

'Theer he comes now.'

Flanked by two tough-looking men, Jeremiah Borth strode into the crowd, which parted before the trio to make way.

'Have you told 'um who I be, Master Davis?' he questioned.

'I have, Master Borth.'

'Right then.' The ex-prizefighter turned to the constable. 'I don't reckon you'll be needed here, Master Cashmore.' He smiled affably.' I reckon me and me mates here am capable of handling anybody who tries to kick up a row.'

Cashmore's face was dour beneath the broad brim of his hat. 'I don't doubt that fact, Master Borth,' he agreed, 'but iffen I'm here then there arn't agoing to be such a likelihood of anybody creating a ruckus. The parson don't want any upset if it can be avoided.'

Borth's affability did not falter. 'Right then, Master Cashmore, an' it so pleases you to stay, then stay and welcome. Let's get inside and make a start shall us, Master Davis?'

The clerk produced a great iron key and unlocked the chapel doors, and led Borth and his two companions inside, leaving Cashmore as sentinel before the entrance.

'Come on then, form your line,' Cashmore bellowed, and obediently the crowd surged to obey him.

Tildy, with Sarah Farr, was at the head of the queue, and Cashmore, who knew Tildy and had considerable respect for her, told the two women in a low voice, 'You'd best remember that this newcomer, Borth, has got the full backing o' the Vestry. It's him that's calling the tune about Poor Relief now. So you mind what youm about, Tildy Crawford, and try and keep that tongue o' yourn atween your teeth.' He stared meaningfully at Tildy who, fiery-spirited and proud-stomached as she was, had clashed before with the local authorities.

Tildy met his eyes squarely. 'I'll behave to Master Borth as civilly as he behaves towards me, Master Cashmore,' she stated quietly, but very firmly, and he jerked his head for her to enter.

She went through the doors and into the Vestry room to stand in front of the long table behind which Borth, flanked by his two friends, lounged in a chair. Joseph Davis was perched on his high stool, looking very disgruntled because Jeremiah Borth had the great ledger open on the table in front of him, and he, Davis, had been relegated to being a mere onlooker of the proceedings.

'What's your name, girl?' Borth's bloodshot eyes gleamed appreciatively as he examined Tildy's fresh beauty. Her dark, glossy hair was coiled on her head and she wore no mobcap or shawl, but only a simple, shabby yet neat, dark gown, beneath the hem of which could be glimpsed wooden-soled clogs and a flash of trim ankles in white cotton stockings.

'My name is Matilda Crawford.' Her cheeks reddened s the three men stared hungrily at her, and one whispered a comment which caused the others to snigger lewdly.

Jeremia Borth's thick forefinger ran down the open page of the ledger. 'You bin drawing two shillings a week for yourself, and an extra ninepence for your kid. You normally works at the Fountain Mill for Henry Milward as an in-worker, but you got laid off a month since.'

He paused, as if awaiting confirmation, and she nodded.

'That's so, Master Borth.'

'That kid o' yourn, is it a bastard?' he asked bluntly, and Tildy flushed hotly.

'No, he's not a bastard,' she replied indignantly. 'He was born in wedlock.'

'Well, wheer's his bloody feyther now then? Run off, has he? Give leg-bail and left you on the Parish?' The man was brutally indifferent to any distress to her feelings that he might cause.

'My husband is in the prison-hulks. He's waiting on transportation.' Tildy was angry at herself for the way she was flushing so uncontrollably, and allowing this man to see what embarrassment he was creating in her.

The trio exchanged sly winks, and grinning broadly, Borth exclaimed with mock surprise. 'By the Christ! A bloody gaolbird, is he? And here's you looking so clean and respectable . . . How many years has he got?'

Although her fiery temper was close to igniting, Tildy fought to control it, for losing control had brought her much grief and trouble in the past. 'I think it to be fourteen years.'

'What d'you mean, you think? Don't you know?'

Borth's manner seemed to be deliberately provocative, as if he wished to goad her into an outburst. 'I would ha' thought that a loving, dutiful wife 'ud ha' known how long her husband was agoing to be enjoying himself in Botany Bay, wi' all the rest o' the jolly boys out theer.'

Tildy drew a deep breath, 'I parted from my husband more than two years since,' she answered, and then could not restrain herself any longer, and burst out angrily. 'But what all this has to do with you I cannot see. All I am here for is to apply for my lawful rights. If there was work to be had I would not be before you now. I don't enjoy having to beg for the few measly shillings you allow me.'

Borth laughed delightedly. 'Take care, lads, she bites!' he crowed, and his friends roared their pleasure.

Tildy's sense of humiliation was such that she was near to tears of impotent fury and shame. It was only the thought of her child that kept her standing before the table. She desperately needed the pitiful allowance from the parish for his sake, so swallowed her outraged pride and remained still, her small hands so fiercely bunched into fists that the fingernails threatened to break the skin of her palms.

Borth's laughter quietened. 'So, my wench, if there was work to be had, then you'd take it? Is that what youm atelling me?'

'It is,' she gritted out between tightened lips.

He grinned mockingly at her. 'Well then youm in luck, my wench. For there is work to be had, and plenty of it. More than enough for you and all the rest of them lazy bleeders out theer. From tomorrow you'll be working for the Parish. You'll be here at six o' the clock tomorrow morn ready to sweat some o' that fat from your bones.' He spoke to his friends, 'I'll take this 'un in my gang, lads. I reckon she'll need watching. Got a bit o' gutter-devil in her, arn't she. Needs a strong hand.'

'Needs a strong prick, more likely,' one of the men grunted, and all three again burst into raucous laughter.

Borth waved in dismissal. 'Off you goo then, Matilda Crawford. And mind and be here to time in the morn, or you'll get no money from the Parish.'

When she did not move, the man scowled. 'What's the matter wi' you, girl? Be you fucking deaf? I'se told you what you'se got to do.'

'What is this work?' Tildy demanded. 'And where is it? I've got a sick child to care for. He can't be left for long.'

'That arn't my problem.' Borth's own temper erupted suddenly, and he bellowed, 'Gerrof from here, girl, or you'll get my bloody fist in your chops. I arn't agoing to bandy words wi' a bloody pauper, I've better things to be doing wi' my time. Now gerrof!'

Despite his menace Tildy still stood defiantly. 'I've a right to know what's expected of me,' she argued stubbornly.

'Paupers arn't got no fuckin' rights.' The ex-prizefighter rose to his feet and made as if to move around the table. 'I'se heard enough from you this day, you saucy bitch!'

Joseph Davis suddenly left his stool, and taking Tildy by her arms dragged her out of the room despite her struggles to stay.

'Have sense, girl! Have sense!' he whispered urgently into her ear.

In the entrance hall the clerk asked 'Are you calmer now?'

Realizing the futility of further struggle Tildy nodded, and the man released her arms. For once the normally pompous self-righteousness of the clerk seemed to have deserted him, and his pinched features were almost shamfaced, as he told her, 'The Vestry has give him consent to form farm work-gangs from the women and kids whom claiming Outdoor Relief, Crawford. Anybody who wun't join the gangs gets their Relief stopped.' He held a hand up before her face to forestall any rejoinder. 'No, wait and hear me out, girl, for your own good. It arn't no use you agoing to the magistrates, or anybody else to complain, because they'm giving Borth their full support.'

'I can find my own work with the farmers for the harvests,' Tildy stated confidently. 'It's what I intended dong anyway if the Fountain was still closed to me.'

Davis shook his head. 'I doubt you'll find any work, my wench. Nigh om every farmer in this parish, and in Ipsley parish as well, has agreed terms wi' Borth.' With grudging admiration he observed, 'The bugger's as artful as a cart-load o' monkeys. He's got the farmers to agree not to take on any woman who'se bin claiming the Outdoor Relief unless that woman brings a note from the Vestry to say that her's got their permission to apply for work.'

'Then I'll get such a note from the Vestry,' Tildy stated forcefully.

'Now just you stop and think for a minute, girl,' Davis exhorted her.

'What's there to think about?' Tildy's fiery spirit was still aflame.

'Well, the Vestry got no intention of issuing any such notes to any woman who'se bin on Parish Relief,' the clerk informed her. 'They'se all got to goo wi' the gangs. Borth is paying a rent to the Vestry for every head he counts.'

'If that's the case then I'll not make any further claim for relief. They cannot refuse me a note to say I'm not claiming, can they. That wouldn't be lawful.'

The man smiled bleakly at her naivety. 'You arn't listened to what I'se said, has you. If you seeks for work from the farmers, then you must have a note from the Vestry, because without such a note no farmer in these two parishes 'ull give you work.'

'But how will the farmers know if the woman has been claiming relief or not?' Tildy still argued, her stubborness making her wilfully obtuse.

Davis hissed with impatience. 'It doon't matter them not knowing, girl. Because you'se got a note from the Vestry you wun't be given work anyway. You'se got no choice in the matter, my wench. Borth has sewed it all up as tight as a duck's arse. You either goes wi' the gangs, or you gets nothing and bloody well starves for all the Vestry could care.' He paused to see what effect his words had had, then told her brusquely, 'Now you'd best be off, Crawford, and not risk upsetting that bugger in theer any further. Because if you does, then you'll only be biting off your own nose to spite your face.'

For this moment, at any rate, Tildy accepted her defeat, and turning from him she went from the chapel. She passed Sarah Farr in the entrance and exchanged a brief word of farewell.

Outside in the hot sun Tildy made her way back towards the Silver Square. As she passed the squat, castellated Town Lock-up which stood at the junction of Red Lion Street and the road that led down past the stinking Big Pool, a hard-faced, thick-set man in a calico shirt, sleeveless leather waistcoat and knee-breeches, wearing an old military forage cap on his greying head came from one of the small shops opposite and intercepted Tildy.

'Now then, my duck, why so long-faced?' he questioned.

'Hello Josh.' Tildy smiled at him.

Josh Dyson was a hardener in the Fountain Mill, and a very good and close friend to her. A widower and ex-soldier, he was also a Radical, strongly opposed to the system of government that existed in England, and it was only the fact that he was the most skilful hardener in the district that prevented him from being driven out of the town by those in power for his forthright strictures against them, and what they represented.

Briefly Tildy related what had occurred and he cursed loudly, then said, 'Listen Tildy, you don't have to put up wi' such insult from the bloody Vestry and its bully-boys. Why don't you come and live wi' me, and let me care for you and little Davy?' He saw the guarded look come into her eyes, and grinned ruefully. 'Alright Tildy. Alright. I knows what the answer is, there's no need to tell me. God strike me if I'se ever met such an independent, obstinate cratur as you in all me born days.'

Tildy could only shrug, and tell him gently, 'I am what I am, Josh. I can't help being this way.'

'Ah well,' he sighed sadly. 'You knows wheer I am, if you ever needs me.'

'I do that, Josh. And thank you for it.' She continued on her way, leaving him staring regretfully after her slender back.

Tildy's own thoughts were a confused jumble. Although she cared deeply for Josh Dyson it was as a friend that she wanted him, not as a lover. Tildy had yet to meet the man that she could give her heart to, and share her life with. Her husband, Tom Crawford, she had only ever felt contempt for.

Her mind went back across the years. Left orphaned as a child, she and her small brother had been taken in by her father's sister and her raving religious maniac of a husband. Before he was eight years old her brother had been sent to work as a bonded apprentice to the dreaded cotton mills of the North Country, together with a cartload of other pauper children, and Tildy had never heard from or of him since. She could only assume that like so many of those other pitiful child-slaves he had long since died.

She herself had been kept in the isolated country cottage of her aunt as an unpaid drudge. On her eighteenth birthday Tildy had escaped from her bondage and had travelled to the nearest town, Redditch, in search of work. The Michaelmas Hiring Fair was in full swing when she arrived there, and she had found service in the household of the vicar of Ipsley parish. But on the very day that she engaged into that service, her fellow servant, Thomas Crawford, had taken advantage of her youth and naivety to get her drunk, and when she lay senseless to rape her. Pregnant, she had been virtually forced into marrying the man, and her life had become a torment of hardship and violence at his hands, until events had set her free from him.

The experience had left its scars on her mind, and now she wished only to live her life independently, and raise her beloved child. Still not twenty-two years of age, naturally she hoped that some day she would meet the man with whom she could share a lifelong loving partnership, but that day had not yet dawned, and until it did so Tildy was prepared to fight her own way through the harsh existence that was her lot in life. That she had survived so far, and maintained her own high standards of morality, was owing mainly to her natural intelligence and stubborn courage.

Back at the lodging-house she went directly to her room, and smiled with relief and pleasure to see little Davy sat up in his cot playing with his treasured wooden soldier. a gaily uniformed Hussar with a pelisse and busby fashioned from real cloth and fur, and painted fierce black eyes and mustachios.

Although still pale and wan, the child was now completely free of fever and regaining strength hourly. Tildy felt a surge of gratitude towards the Welshman who had cured her boy, and wished that she had some means within her power of rewarding him for doing so. A mischievous smile quirked her lips as she thought of one reward she could give him, and then she chided herself light-heartedly for such sinful thoughts. 'Shame on you! Respectable women shouldn't think of such things.'

'Mammy, I'm hungry,' Davy informed her, and she promised, 'I'll fetch you some bread and milk, Honey, in just a few minutes. Play with Sergeant Tom now, like a good boy.'

As she went downstairs with her empty tin pannikin Tildy's worries assailed her afresh. She had no money for milk or for bread.

'God curse my temper!' she thought ruefully. 'If I'd kept my mouth shut I could have asked Borth for a few pence in advance.'

Even as she thought this, the realization dawned that she had already in her subconscious mind accepted that she would be working in the gangs.

'What other choice do I have?' she questioned bitterly, and answered herself in the same breath, 'None! None at all!'

Ben Waring, the main cheese and milk dealer in the town, had his premises on the road beyond the Big Pool that led down towards Bredon and the Ipsley parish. His dairy and cowsheds lay just behind the old cottage that served as his shop. He liked pretty women, and was only too happy to give Tildy credit for her pannikin of fresh creamy milk.

'That's a penny ha'penny you owes my, my pretty

flower,' he joked with a broad wink. 'And iffen you'd prefer to gi' me a kiss instead, then you can have it for naught.'

'I heard that, Waring.' His wife came from the rear of the cottage,a fitting mate for her ruddy-faced, plump-bellied husband. She chuckled heartily and mock-cuffed her man's head. 'Iffen this maid was to kiss you, you'd have a bloody stoppage of the heart, you silly old sod.'

He laughed and shouted, 'At least I'd be dying happy, udden't I!'

Tildy went smiling from the building warmed by the obvious affection the couple had for each other, and could not help but envy their happiness together, in such glaring contrast to the misery of her own marriage.

'Ne'er mind it. It's done with now, thank God,' she consoled herself, and thrust all thoughts of her husband from her mind.

Mother Readman was in the big gloomy kitchen, enthroned on her great chair before the inglenook fire-place, sweat coursing down her huge tallow-skinned face. Sitting on a low stool by her side was the parish bastard, Apollonia, a waif of fourteen years that Mother Readman sheltered and protected. The girl's precocious and insatiable sexual appetite caused Mother Readman much concern, and only a month past Apollonia had given birth to a still-born baby, whose father could have been any of a score of transients who had passed through the lodging-house. Wizen-faced and stick-thin once more, Apollonia reminded Tildy irresistibly of some ancient elf. But the child possessed a kind heart, and loved Mother Readman with a fierce possessiveness, a love that she also gave to little Davy and to Tildy herself.

Tildy borrowed bread from Mother Readman, and busied herself in breaking the dark heavy lump into small pieces in the wooden bowl she kept for Davy's food. As she worked she related the morning's happenings to the other two.

Mother Readman heard the full story before commenting, 'He's a fly bastard this Borth, arn't he. Mind you, he's from the right place for that. All them Brummagems thinks themselves to be fly coves.' She chuckled hoarsely. 'But they'd do well to remember our old Redditch saying, that iffen you wants to find a cunt in the country, then you must needs bring one wi' you.'

Tildy could not help but smile, then she sighed resignedly. 'Ahh well, I'll be with the work-gangs tomorrow, and there's naught else for it. Will you look to little Davy for me, Apollonia? I'll settle with you for doing so when I next get some money.'

'O' course I 'ull, Tildy. You doon't have to ask.' The girl's rotting front teeth were black and green in the gloom, but still there was something appealing about her grimed gamine face haloed by the great shock of frizzed hair.

'At least he's out of the fever now,' Tildy murmured, almost to herself.

Mother Readman looked concerned. 'Listen Tildy,' she began hesitantly, 'you knows well that I loves having you and your babby here wi' me. But I 'udden't count meself as a true friend if I didn't spake out plain what's in me mind. That babby has got over this fever, but 'ull he get over the next 'un? I've seen him start to look more and more pulled down lately. And it's living here in the Silver Square that's adoing that to him. This place arn't healthy for grown men and women, God only knows, but for the childer it's a bloody slaughter-house. If you was to take up Josh Dyson's offer, then I'd bet he'd get a little cottage out from the town wheer the air is healthy for the three on you to live in.'

Troubled doubts flooded through Tildy's mind as she heard these words. 'Am I being too selfish?' she asked herself. 'Am I keeping my Davy here, in this place of danger for him, just because of my own foolish fancies? Josh Dyson would be good to him, that I'm sure of. Could I not settle for that?'

Aloud, she replied, 'I just don't know, Mother Readman . . . I just don't know what I should do . . .'

Chapter Five

'The wench has gone, Feyther. That's why there's no breakfast ready.' The youth stood in the outer doorway of the farmhouse kitchen, his ruddy face twitching nervously.

'Gone? What d'you mean, gone?' Arthur Winterton came to his feet so abruptly that the wooden armchair on which he had been sitting at the table crashed backwards onto the stone-flagged floor. In three strides he had covered the intervening space, and grabbing his son by the front of the shirt he shook him bodily. 'What d'you mean, gone?'

'He means what he says. Sally's run off in the night.' Arthur Winterton's elder son, Tobias, entered the kitchen through the inner door, and seated himself on one of the benches that flanked the huge wooden table. 'So just let Jem be, can't you. T'is no fault of his that her's run.'

Arthur Winterton's great shaggy head swung to glare furiously at his eldest son.

Tobias met the glare without flinching. ''Tis no use you giving me hard looks, Feyther, it arn't my fault she's gone neither.'

Arthur Winterton brutally thrust Jem from him, and the boy stumbled and only saved himself from falling headlong by grabbing the door frame. As his father stepped towards him Tobias Winterton rose to his feet and stepped over the bench to stand clear of the table, hands hanging loosely at his side, but his body tensed.

Arthur Winterton stood well over six feet in height, with a barrel-like chest and shoulders. His eldest son could not match him in height, but still he was well-muscled, carrying none of the fat which layered his father's body, and with a hard, flat stomach instead of Arthur Winterton's protruberant belly.

'Be you saying that it's my fault her's run?' the older man growled.

'I arn't said nothing about that,' his eldest son answered levelly, 'but run she had. So who'se to look to the house, and to our Annie?'

'Maddy 'ull manage, wi' one o' the other wenches to help her when needful,' Arthur Winterton replied, and Tobias laughed aloud.

'God s'trewth, Feyther!' he ejaculated scornfully. 'But there's times you comes out wi' terrible nonsense. It's too much for Maddy, and there arn't one o' the others that's capable of looking to herself properly, ne'er mind caring for a house and an idiot girl.'

His father's brutal features suffused darkly as his passion mounted. 'Don't you make mock o' me, boy,' he warned. 'Because big as you are, you'll needs ate a lot more loaves afore you can match me in a fight.'

'Ohhh yes, that's it, Feyther.' Contempt twisted the younger man's lips and throbbed in his voice. 'That's your answer for everything that upsets you, arn't it. Use your fists on it. Well if you weren't so quick and heavy with them, we'd not have the trouble we do in keeping servants here. Sally was trying her best 'til you started at her with the bloody whip. I don't blame her for running. You near flayed the bloody skin from her back.'

The older man's face purpled and he bellowed, 'That's enough! Just shut your mouth right now, afore I does it for you. I'm the master here, and it's my right and my duty to punish insolence and idleness in my servants. That wench deserved every whipping I give her, and more besides. Her was a saucy little bitch.' The great shaggy head nodded violently. 'Ahrr, and doon't you goo thinking that I doon't know the reason her got so above herself neither. I seen you agoin into the barn wi' her late at nights when you thought the rest on us was all abed. What was you promising her for opening her legs for you? Promising to marry her, was you? Is that why her's took up and run, is her acarrying your bastard? Is it you that's chased her off because you'se babbied her, you dirty-living bleeder?'

Now it was the younger man's turn to flush hotly as his temper mounted, and he rejoined angrily, 'What took place between me and that girl had naught to do wi' her running away. She wasn't pregnant by me. In fact, if it hadn't been for me she'd have run long since to get away from you and the treatment you gave her.' He hesitated a moment, and then added, 'You'll do well to draw breath and think on your own actions afore you go spreading tales about me giving women bastards. Sally told me a few things about you that you'd not like to come out into the open.'

'You saucy bastard!' Arthur Winterton bawled, and rushed at his son with fists raised.

The younger man, taken by surprise by the sudden onslaught, tried to avoid his father's blows, but was caught high on the forehead and stumbled sideways and tripped across the bench. Before he could recover the older man's heavy boot thudded into his groin and with a strangled scream Tobias doubled into a foetus position. Again and again the boots thudded into his body, and then, mercifully, he was kicked in the side of the head and black oblivion released him from further pain.

In the doorway the boy, Jem, watched with sick horror, too terrified to move or even to cry out, and he could only stand trembling violently until his father had spent his rage and stamped out of the room. Then, with shaking hands, the boy tried to rouse his brother to consciousness.

Arthur Winterton, his ungovernable temper still rampant, strode across his fields. His farm was a large one and, rarely for these parts, he owned it. His meadows stretched from the ancient Icknield Street to the banks of the River Arrow, and lay two miles eastward of Redditch town as the crow flew. Beoley hamlet and crossroads lay directly north of his land, and Ipsley hamlet directly south. His forefathers had been in this area since Saxon times, and Arthur Winterton's proud boast was that his ancestors had been thanes of Mercia when the ancestors of the local present-day magnates had been mere serfs. He gave precedence to no man, and feared no man, regarding himself as the equal of any lord or bishop in the land.

Now, as he strode along, his eyes absorbed all around him, annotating, considering, decision-taking. He welcomed this present spell of hot weather. His wheat was ripening well, and the grasses and clovers of his hay fields would cut dry and need little tedding and turning before being stacked. His acres of turnips could be hoed and singled more easily, and the heat had brought forward his other green crops so an early start at their horse- and hand-hoeing could be made. Also, his first early potatoes were now ready to raise, and his cabbages could be transplanted since the fine weather had made it possible for his labourers to work the extra hours necessary to prepare well the land to receive them.

He frowned as another problem loomed in his mind. He possessed a sizeable flock of sheep, and they were now due to be washed in preparation for their shearing and dipping. Tobias normally took charge of the washing operation.

Arthur Winterton's frown became a savage scowl. 'The young bugger might be too hurt to work today arter the hammering I'se give him, and I'm damm short o' men as it is, God damn and blast it! And I'm to waste more o' me time finding another wench to take the place o' that runaway slut, God damn and blast her!' He turned on his heel and went stamping back towards the clustered buildings of his farmstead.

Ebenezer Morris, Master of the Tardebigge Parish Poorhouse in the hamlet of Webheath, some two miles west of Redditch, pursed his thin lips and sipped his gin as he listened to what Arthur Winterton had to say. The two men were seated facing each other across the parlour table of the large decaying building, the nearly empty bottle between them.

'So, Sally Jukes has run away, has her, Master Winterton?' The Poorhouse Master's pinched mean features displayed uneasiness.

'God damn and blast it, man, haven't I been telling you that for nigh on half an hour already!' Winterton shouted, his uncertain temper, inflamed by gin and heat, simmering close to the surface. 'What I'm wanting to know is if youm agoing to sign another bugger out to me?'

Morris eyed him warily, knowing the farmer's propensity for violence. 'Well now, it arn't that simple, Master Winterton,' he essayed. 'I mean, there arn't any who'd be suited for you, I shouldn't think.'

'Look man, all I needs is some slut who can look to a house, do a bit o' cooking and washing, and see to me daughter.'

The farmer lifted his glass and tossed its contents down his thick throat, then refilled it from the bottle draining the last dregs of spirit and tossed that down his throat also. Now that the first bottle was emptied Winterton took a full one from the pocket of his brown, full-skirted riding coat and banged it down upon the table.

'Here, Master Morris, take some more gin, it might make you a bit readier to do me this small service I'm asking of you. And arter all, I'm doing this parish a favour taking one o' their Poor'us sluts off their hands, arn't I? It makes one less mouth to feed out of the Poor Rate.'

'Yes, that's allus a blessing to the Parish,' Morris acknowledged. 'But . . .' he let the final word hang on the air.

'But what?' Winterton demanded.

The Poorhouse Master's eyes lingered hungrily on the as yet unopened gin bottle, his greed battling with his fear of the other man.

'Spake out, damm you,' Winterton ordered, 'and don't be fritted to say what's in your mind. I'll not raise a hand to you . . . Here!' He uncorked the fresh bottle and filled the Master's empty glass. 'Get this down you. Mayhap it'll gi' you the courage to tell me straight out what's preventing you from signing another slut to me.'

Morris took a big gulp of the fiery spirit, his protruberant Adam's apple bobbing in his long scrawny throat. Then gathering his courage, he gabbled breathlessly,

'Right then, Master Winterton, let's be plain spoken wi' each other. Over the past three years you'se had two lads and two wenches signed out to you from this poor'us, the last being Sally Jukes, and they'se each and every one on 'um become runaways.

'The Vestry took me to task when that third 'un run, because the bugger got to Bedford, and then bloody well took badly and died theer, and the Vestry had to pay for bringing him back here to be buried.

'Now you tells me that Sally Jukes has done a bunk. What does you think the Vestry 'ull say to me if she should goo and get bloody well copped for vagrancy or whoring in some other bloody parish, and then they has to pay for her to be carted back here to her place o' settlement? They'll have my guts for garters, Master Winterton. I might even lose my position here.'

'They can't blame you if some pauper slut runs away from her lawful master,' Winterton objected.

Morris dragged in a deep breath and screwed his courage up another notch. 'In this case they 'ull blame me, Master Winterton. They'll blame me for letting you have another pauper from here arter what happened wi' the others.'

'Why so?' the farmer demanded.

'I'll tell you why so. Because you'se got the name of being a hard man to work for. It's well known that you has trouble keeping your farm servants for their full contract. And it's well known that none of the other parish vestries hereabouts 'ull direct their poor'us paupers or their Yardland men to goo and work for you if they can help it, because them same paupers kicks up merry bloody hell if they'm so directed.'

The broad brutal features of the other man darkened ominously, but he replied evenly enough, 'The buggers don't want to do a fair day's work, that's why they don't want to come to me. They'm idle, good-for-nothing bastards, that's all.'

Fearful of provoking the man too far, Morris was quick to mollify him. 'I should think every right-thinking person in this parish 'ull agree with you there, Master. The paupers hereabouts don't want to bloody work. They'd sooner sit on their arses and let the parish feed 'um, that's a fact, that is.'

Winterton grinned, but there was no mirth in that grin, it was more a ferocious snarl. 'And it's a fact also that you arn't agoing to sign out a woman from here to work for me, arn't it, Master Morris.'

It was a statement, not a question, and the Poorhouse Master nodded unhappily. 'It's more nor I dare do, Master Winterton. Mayhap in a few months, or weeks even, if there's no trouble comes over Sally Jukes. I might be able to help you then.'

'That's no good to me, man,' Winterton growled, 'I needs a woman now. I'se got the shearing within the sennight, and I must needs find a company for that, and I must start to get my hay in, so I needs every pair of hands I can muster in the fields, and we'll all be needing to be fed, wun't us. This heat 'ull bring thunder and storm afore much longer, that's as sure as sunrise, that is, and I needs my hay stacked afore that happens. I swear I wish I'd broke that bitch's neck afore she'd run off, for leaving me in this pickle.'

Morris could only shrug his narrow shoulders in mute commiseration, and he visibly winced with disappointment when without another word Winterton replaced the cork in the gin bottle, put the bottle in his pocket, and left . . .

Chapter Six

From long before dawn Tobias Winterton had been preparing for the washing of the sheep. At a place in the river where the bottom was hard and gravelly and the grassy banks sloped gently to the water's edge, he and his helpers had created a pool some three feet in depth by damming the flow of the water with doors held firm against the flow by posts driven deep into the river's bed. The gaps and cracks between the doors and the river bottom sealed with wedges of turf. On each bank temporary folds were created by nets stretched between uprights.

The lambs had been separated from the rest of the flock and were kept penned at the farmstead, making the ewes troublesome to drive into the net fold as they bleated incessantly, searching for their lost lambs.

When the flock was finally collected the sun was well risen and the men already heated by exertion.

Tobias issued his final instructions: 'You, Jem, and young Tommy will be the catchers. Sim, you'll be the first washer. Joseph, you'll be the second, and Gilbert will be third.'

'This is a bad business, this is,' old Gilbert Tongue, the shepherd, as brown and gnarled as an ancient oak, grumbled querulously, and Tobias grinned at him.

'Listen Gilbert, you says the same thing every year, and every year you gets the same answer . . . Washed wool sells at a higher price.'

'Ahrr, that's as maybe, but washed wool weighs less, don't it. So wheers the bloody gain? And you knows as well as I does that arter washing the sheep be twice as likely to catch cold.'

'You must tell me Dad that,' Tobias grunted. 'For it's him as wants 'um washed.' He pointed upwards at the sun. 'Anyway, it's going to be another hot 'un today, so they'll not catch cold.'

The old man cackled with wheezy laughter, and gestured towards Tobias' badly bruised head and face. 'Oh no, young Toby. I arn't agoing to risk telling your Dad any damn thing at all this day. I likes me yed the way it is. I don't need it looking like yourn.'

Tobias grinned ruefully. 'I can't say as how I'll blame you for not risking what I got yesterday, old 'un.'

The old man cackled with laughter, and Tobias told him, 'Right then, that's settled for another year, arn't it. You'se had your say, and I'se had mine. So let's get to work, shall we.'

He stripped down to his old leather breeches, removed his boots and stockings, then waded into the pool, gasping at the first shock of the cold water against his skin. The other three men only cast aside their smocks and rolled up their shirt-sleeves before following him into the water, old Gilbert cursing vilely as he did so.

The three men arranged themselves in a slanting line cross the river, one behind the other. The burly Sim nearest the bank, purple-complexioned Joseph in the centre behind him, and old Gilbert at the rear opposite the slope of the far bank which had been covered with a thick layer of clean straw.

The two youths caught and dragged the first ewe into the pond, handing it over to Sim. He deftly turned the frantically bleating, struggling animal on to its back, holding its head above the water by gripping the woolly cheek with his left hand, his right hand grasping the animal's foreleg. He pushed and pulled the beast against the current, and the dirt and filth loosened from the fleece floating away on the swift-flowing surface and over the dam spill. As the catchers dragged another ewe into the pond Sim passed the first behind him to Joseph, who treated it in the same manner, then passed it on to old Gilbert.

The old man's gnarled hands burrowed through the thick fleece, his fingers seeking for growths on the skin, and any obdurate filth and dirt, then, satisfied, he completed the cleansing process by dipping the animal's head beneath the water two or three times. Tobias took the animal from the shepherd and with an ease that demonstrated his immense physical strength, swung it out of the water and on to the straw bed of the far bank.

For some moments the soaked, streaming fleece was so heavy with water that the ewe could not stand. But presently it was able to rise to its feet and shake itself, then wander up into the waiting netfold, where it immediately began cropping at the grass, uncaring of its successors' pitiful bleatings and strugglings.

As the men warmed to the work the tempo quickened, and the two youths were hard put to maintain the flow of sheep into the pool.

Sweat streaming down his face despite the cold water up to his waist, Tobias gloried in the exhilaration of his own strength and fitness. The blood pumping into his muscles, distending the veins, swelling the arteries, engorging and expanding the flesh until he resembled a gleaming living statue of some mythological athlete.

The gang of forty women and children led by Jeremiah Borth crossed the river where the water ran quick and shallow over a ridging of gravel, their long skirts lifted and bunched around their thighs, their legs white in the sunlight.

Jeremiah Borth stood watching them cross, his eyes greedily devouring the spectacle of the younger women's soft rounded thighs. Particularly he noted Tildy Crawford's shapely legs, and his lust quickened as he thought of what was hidden by her dark gown and apron of sacking.

'By Christ, but she's well fit to be ridden. I'll have to see what can be done in that direction,' he promised himself.

In the next meadow he could see the men working at the washing pool, and he waved his arm at the gang.

'Cummon, my beauties. Let's goo down and see if Arthur Winterton's si' that lot.'

As they neared the pool they could clearly see Tobias Winterton's magnificent physique, and some of the women commented loudly on it.

'Jesus! I'd like to wrap me legs around that 'un,' Bella Perks, a well-built young matron, exclaimed.

'Ahrr, but is he as well made under his britches, Bella? That's what you got to ask yourself!' another woman gibed, and amidst raucous laughter, Bella made lewd sucking noises, and told them, 'Iffen he arn't, then this 'ud soon make him grow to what's needful. This manure can bring any plant to size.'

Tildy laughed with the rest at this rude sally. She was no prude, and could enjoy healthy Rabelaisian humour. What offended her sensibilities was when men deliberately made sexual innuendo, and insulted the main context of any conversation they might have with a woman.

Their noisy approach caught Tobias' attention, and he told his companions, 'I'll see what this lot want.'

Wiping the sweat from his eyes with a piece of rag he waded from the water and went to meet the oncomers. The sight of his injured face evoked more ribaldries and laughter from the women.

'Looks like he was copped in the wrong bed.'

'It warn't yourn, was it Bella?'

'Did that happen when you threw your legs around him, Bella?'

'Wheer was his yed when you did that then?'

The well-built Bella was unabashed. 'Well it's easy to see that we warn't face to face, arn't it.'

'No, but you could ha' bin lips to lips, couldn't you.'

Tobias laughed at their joking, and the sight of his white teeth in the sun-bronzed face created frissons in several of the women's hearts.

Tildy admitted to herself that despite having one side of his features bruised and swollen, still he was good to look at, and handsome enough to suit even the most demanding of tastes.

'What can I do for you, Master?' he asked Borth.

'I'm looking for Arthur Winterton,' the Overseer told him. 'Me name is Jeremiah Borth. I'm the Assistant Overseer to the Poor for Tardebigge Parish. Me and Arthur Winterton settled terms yesterday.'

'Oh yes.' Tobias nodded thoughtfully. 'I recollect me Dad did say something about a work-gang coming, when he got in last night.'

Arthur Winterton had returned home ery late, drunk and rambling-mouthed, and Tobias had paid little attention to those ramblings.

'Right then, wheer's this bloody turnip field that wants weeding and singling? My beauties am bosting to get to work.'

Borth's manner was bluff and hearty, but Tobias sensed the hidden darknesses of the man's nature, and his eyes went sympathetically to the women and children, few of whom looked hardy enough for long hours of gruelling toil in the fields.

'The turnips are half a mile beyond the house,' he told Borth brusquely. 'What about tools? It's normal around here for the gangs to bring their own.'

The Overseer's eyes hardened as he detected the latent hostility in Tobias' tone, but he answered with his customary affability of manner. 'Your Dad said he'd tools aplenty for us to use. And iffen there arn't enough to goo round, then these buggers must needs use their hands to do the business.'

The younger man nodded, feeling confirmed in his evaluation of the Overseer. 'Alright then, Master Borth. I'll come up to the house wi' you and see what I can sort out in the way of hoes and that. Then I'll take you on up to the field and show you what wants doing. Jem, you give Gilbert a hand wi' the washing until I come back,' Tobias instructed his brother, and then led Borth and the gang towards the cluster of farmhouse and outbuildings.

'Your Dad reckoned there's nigh on eighty acres o' turnips?' The overseer sought confirmation, and Tobias nodded.

'What other crops have you got?'

'About the same o' wheat. Then we've barley, oats, carrots, vetches, clovers, pulses and potatoes. So there's plenty of work to be had over the next couple or three months.'

'It's a big farm,' Borth observed casually, and again Tobias nodded, and informed the other with more than a hint of pride, 'Nigh on six hundred acres all told, Master Borth. Been in our family for centuries, some of it has. My Dad reckons that our family was powerful lords in these parts afore the Norman Conquest come.'

'Yes, he told me that yesterday, when the drink had got his tongue.' Borth's voice held a sneer. Thoughtfully he evaluated the fallow land that they were now crossing. Although city-born he had spent much time in country areas, and was knowledgeable about farming. He saw by the extent and types of the weeds flourishing upon the fallows that in this respect at least the farm was being badly managed. The ditches also were rank and overgrown, and the fences and hedgerows ramshackle and broken in many places.

Tobias followed the direction of the man's staring, and said defensively, 'We'se had to let a few things slip this year. We'se had servant troubles. That's one o' the snags of living so close to Redditch. The labourers in these parts 'ud sooner work at the needles and fish-hooks, if they can get suited. When the trade's good they can earn more than we can afford to pay 'um. And o' course, in the wintertime we only really has enough work for our own bond hands to do, so I can't really blame them who goes to the town to earn their money.'

Borth only grinned knowingly, but made no reply, and momentarily Tobias experienced irritation that he should have felt the compulsion to explain anything at all to this stranger. His thoughts turned to his father, and bitter anger surged through him. Doubtless the older man was still lying in his bed, snoring and grunting like the drunken pig he was.

Local people thought Arthur Winterton to be a wealthy

man, and a successful farmer, but Tobias knew very differently. The family were near to bankruptcy and the farm itself mortgaged to the hilt to the Jewish moneylenders in Birmingham. Arthur Winterton, like so many of his peers, was over-fond of the drink, but what was worse, when in drink he was a compulsive gambler, and a very reckless and stupid gambler at that. He would wager on anything, the fighting cocks, the racing horses, the cards, the dice, even on raindrops trickling down a window.

Tobias hated his father, and had lately begun to hate his own life on the farm. Although he sweated and toiled all the hours he could, yet the seemingly inexorable slide to ruin only gathered momentum. He wished with all his heart to leave this farm, and to go out into the world to make his own life, but his love for his sister Anne, and his brother Jem, held him here. He was their sole protection against their brutal father, and as long as they stood in need of that protection, he accepted that he could never leave them.

By now they had reached the farmstead, and as they entered the yard, bounded by its outbuildings, Tobias could hear a loud, distressed lowing coming from the shed in which the dairy cows were stalled. He frowned angrily, cursing beneath his breath. 'They haven't been milked again, damn that idle slut Susy, and damn that drunken bastard as well for not being up and seeing things get done.'

For a moment he hesitated, debating his course of action. Then became aware that Borth was eyeing him quizically, and not wishing to demonstrate yet another area in which the farm was being badly managed, he decided to leave the matter of the unmilked cows for the time being, and to get this man and his gang on to the turnip fields.

From one of the outhouses he issued out hoes, weedhooks and crotches to the women. Some of them smiled at him suggestively as they took their tools, but his anger was seething over the unmilked cows and he did not return their smiles, or answer the equally suggestive remarks two or three of them made to him. However, one young woman took her tools without either smile or word, and perversely Tobias felt constrained to speak to her.

'You doon't look as though youm accustomed to this sort o' work?'

She looked at him gravely, and he felt an almost physical shock or recognition of her beauty.

'I'm well used to hard work, Master,' she told him, and he found her soft voice pleasing to his ear.

'What's your name, Missy?'

'It's Missus,' she answered softly. 'Missus Matilda Crawford.'

A sharp pang of chagrin struck through him. 'Youm married then,' he stated. 'But o' course, you'd have to be married 'udden't you. A maid so pretty is bound to have a husband.'

'I've a child as well, Master.' Tildy could not resist teasing him a little after she had seen the reaction her first piece of information had created.

'Come on, Tildy Crawford, let's be having you,' Jeremiah Borth shouted irritably. An irritation engendered by seeing her talking, however briefly, with such a handsome young man.

She nodded a farewell to Tobias and walked away to join the rest of the gang. The young man watched her, noting the rounded hips swaying beneath the thin black cloth, and envied the husband who shared her bed.

'Ahr well, I'd wish good luck to Master Crawford,' he thought with wry amusement, 'but with a wife as tasty as her, he's already had more than his fair share o' luck.'

He led the way to the turnip fields and indicated to Borth what needed to be done.

'What price did you agree wi' me Dad?' he wanted to know, and the Overseer frowned slightly.

'Two shillings the acre for the weeding.'

'What about the singling?' Tobias was very curious. Two shillings the acre was a poor price for weeding, even though one woman should be able to clean half an acre in a ten-hour day. But singling the plants was a slower and more tedious process, and even a good labouring man would be hard to put to manage half an acre a day.

'The same price,' Borth said, and added, 'Your feyther drives a hard bargain.'

Tobias nodded slowly, and his eyes were shadowed with doubt as he glanced back over his shoulder at the women and children.

'In all truth, Master Borth, if they'm to do the job properly, I can't see that lot earning a deal o' money at these prices. It 'ud tax the strongest man, ne'er mind women and kids.'

He was not being entirely altruistic in his concern. The weeding and singling needed to be well done, otherwise the crops would suffer. To him it seemed a false economy to put the price so low, that in order to earn a living wage the work would have to be hastily and carelessly done.

Borth looked out across the turnip rows and saw how foul with weeds they were. He exclaimed with sarcastic admiration, 'Fuck me, if your Dad arn't drove a harder bargain that I thought he'd done.' Then he grinned brutally at the young man. 'Still, it arn't me who'll be breaking me back clearing this lot. It's them buggers behind us who'll be suffering, not me.'

As he made his way back to the farmhouse Tobias Winterton found his thoughts troubling him. Already, despite the early hour, the sun was fiercely hot and the air still and turgid. He had been raised to farmwork and could remember the terrible exhaustions of body he had endured as a young child, driven to toil beyond his strength by his own father. He dreaded to think how those children he had left behind him would fare at the hands of such a man as Jeremiah Borth.

'At these prices he'll need to drive them like galley-slaves to make the work pay.' He had a visual image of dark-haired Tildy Crawford, and wondered how she would cope with what lay ahead of her. 'It's a shame to see a soft pretty cratur like her having to slave her life away.' Then he grinned and mentally castigated himself. 'Stop thinking like a noddly-yed, you stupid bleeder. Don't all of us in the farming line have to work like slaves to earn our crust. Why should she have it any different from the rest on us just because she's pretty to look at . . . Ahrr, but it's still a pity that she has to,' he chuckled in his mind.

'Susy? Susy, are you up there?' Tobias' shouts resounded up the stairwell and roused Arthur Winterton to bleary-eyed consciousness. He belched, and broke wind loudly, and the vile stench he released caused the young woman in the bed beside him to complain aggrievedly.

'You dirty sod! Youm like to choke me!'

'Susy? I want you.' The clumping of heavy hobnailed boots progressed up the stairs and along the bare planks of the corridor.

'Your Toby's going up to the attics,' the young woman informed Arthur Winterton needlessly, and added with a touch of malice, 'Shall I call and tell him I'm in here wi' you?'

'Hold your tongue,' Winterton warned savagely, and groaned as blinding pain lanced through his head. 'Fuck the drink! And fuck Tobias, and fuck you and all, you bloody cow!'

'That's what you bin adoing all night, arn't it,' the woman said cheekily. 'Fucking me! Or at least, trying to. You'se had a bit o' trouble getting it up lately, arn't you. You oughten to drink so much, it gives you the droop.'

'Shut your bloody mouth, you bitch!' Angrily Winterton thrust himself upright, and then groaned as the sudden movement brought fresh agonies in his skull. 'Stir that fat arse o' yourn afore he comes knocking at this door, 'ull you.'

For a moment it seemed that she would protest, then she thought better of it, knowing the man's capacity for violence. Slipping from the bed she quickly pulled her grimy shift and gown down over her plump nakedness and pulled heavy boots on to her dirty feet. She listened at the door until she heard Tobias' shouts echoing from the top of the house, then quickly went downstairs and out across the yard to the cowshed.

Finding no one in the attic, Tobias was passing his father's door again when the older man shouted him to enter. The foul smell inside the room engulfed him, and he felt a surge of revulsion for the physical grossness of his father. As soon as he looked at the big four-poster bed Tobias knew where Susy had been. The indentations left by her head on the dirty greasy pillows were plain to see, and his keen sense of smell detected the lingering odours of unwashed female flesh.

'Has that bugger from Redditch brought his gang yet?' Arthur Winterton grunted, and Tobias answered with equal surliness.

'He has. I've put him on to the Four Acre.'

'How long has he bin come?' the older man wanted to know, and bellowed angrily when told. 'What? Only half an hour since? What in Hell's name does he reckon he's about? The bloody day's near wasted.'

Tobias forebore taxing his father with his own wasting of valuable time. Instead he merely pointed out, 'Well, he's took the fields by the piece, arn't he, Feyther. So he most likely thinks that it's up to him what time he starts to in the morn.'

'Oh no it arn't, my bucko!' Winterton shook his great shaggy grey head, and scowled as the vigorous movement brought fresh agonies. 'It arn't up to him at all. Iffen he don't make early starts then he'll not get the bloody job done soon enough to suit me.'

'Well then you goo out and tell him so.' Tobias lost patience. 'For I've too much on my own plate this day to have time to argue the toss wi' any bloody gang master. The bloody cows arn't bin milked yet. What's Susy bin about?'

'How should I know?' the older man blustered. 'It's up to you to make sure the slut does her work. Youm my steward. I've got more important matters to attend to.'

An angry rejoinder came to Tobias' lips, but he bit it back, knowing the futility of further bickering. Without another word he went back out into the corridor, slamming the door shut behind him. For a few moments he stood in the gloomy passageway, fists tight-clenched, struggling to control the almost overwhelming desire to physically assault the other man.

Although up to this point in time every violent clash between them had ended in his being badly beaten, still Tobias had no fear of his father. His hatred and loathing for Arthur Winterton was so strong, so intense, that it drove out fear, and every defeat at his father's hands only served to strengthen his resolve to stand against the brutal treatment and bullying that the older man inflicted upon all his dependents, and indeed, anyone else unfortunate enough to cross his purpose.

When he had calmed down Tobias went further along the corridor and opened a door at its end, calling softly as he did so.

'Are you awake Annie? It's me, Toby.'

The sparsely furnished, whitewashed room was small and austere. Tobias smiled sadly at the sight that met his eyes.

A small, fat-bodied girl with the flattened features, pug nose and oval, upward-sloping eyes of a Mongol, dressed only in a white night-shift, was sitting on the narrow bed, engrossed in moving a large goose-feather around and around the quilted counterpane. Tobias gently fondled her shoulder, and the girl looked up at him, an expression of fear clouding her eyes.

'Now, don't you be feared, sweetheart, it's only me, Toby. I've come to bring you out to the river with me. You can have a picnic there on the bank.' He took the girl's small hands in his and gently raised her. 'Come now, sweetheart, I'll wash your hands and face.'

Docilely she stood motionless while he poured water from a pewter jug into a bowl of the same metal, and with a flannel bathed the pale skin of her face, neck, hands and arms and feet. Then he dried her and taking a small brush cleaned her teeth with the powder of woodash and salt kept in its painted wooden box.

From its hook behind the door he lifted the checked gingham dress and helped her to draw it down over her head. He slipped her feet into her wooden-soled clogs, and was thankful that he didn't need to brush her hair which was neatly plaited into a single long pigtail hanging down her back almost to her large hips.

The toilette completed, he kissed her forehead. 'There now, it's done. You look like a princess,' he told her.

She only stared uncomprehendingly at him, her eyes empty and vacuous. Tobias sighed heavily, and stroked her cheek with his fingers. At times she would know him, and would smile and try to talk with him; at other times, she was like this.

'They say God has a reason for everything upon this earth,' he murmured, 'but I can't see any good reason for making you like this, my sweetheart. It's more like the work of the Devil.'

Taking her hand he led her past his father's door, and as he passed he shouted, 'I'm taking our Annie with me, Feyther.'

A muffled grunt was the only reply, and Tobias smiled mirthlessly. 'Ah well, what else could I expect from a pig, but a grunt.'

The mirthless smile touched his lips again when in the yard he heard Susy singing lustily inside the cowshed. He halted and told Annie, 'Stand here and wait for me, Honey. I'll not be more than a minute.'

Inside the dark, low-roofed shed redolent with the smell of cowdung and hay, Susy was sitting on a low three-legged stool, her head pushed against the side of the limpid-eyed, tail-swinging beast she was milking. Her practised hands encircling and pressing the teats of the full udder, bringing the steaming spurts of warm milk splashing into the wooden pail so quickly as to resemble a continuous stream.

Despite the young woman's laziness Tobias did not dislike her. Although slovenly she was attractive in her plump rosiness, and possessed a cheeky, likeable sense of humour. She heard his approach, and turned her head to greet him.

'How hist, my handsome?' She grinned cheerily. 'Come

to gi' me my roasting, have you?' She winked salaciously. 'I know I was late abed, Master Toby, but I bin dreaming about you all night, and you fare wore me out so you did. I had to lay in awhiles to get me strength back. So it's your fault, arn't it, that I was late. You oughter let me sleep, instead of having your wicked way wi' me all night long.'

Her saucy gaiety disarmed him, and his anger dissolved in a wry inward chuckle. He tried to tell her sternly, 'You be to your time in future, Susy. I don't want these beasts made distressful.'

But there was no real force in his voice, and she knew that she had evaded any retribution.

'I'll be to time from now on, Master Toby. Honest I 'ull.' And now she smiled invitingly, running the tip of her pink tongue over her full moist lips in sensual invitation. 'And now what can I be doing for you, my handsome?'

'I want a can of milk for Annie,' he told her, trying to maintain a stern air.

'You shall have it this instant, my Master.' She sprang to her feet and with a mischievous parody of submissive obedience ran to fill a small tin can with the thick creamy liquid from the wooden pail. She handed the can to him, then slowly ran her hands down over her full breasts and thighs.

'Be you sure there's naught I can do for you personal, Master Toby?' she questioned huskily.

Despite her unwashed grimy face she exuded sexuality, and Tobias was momentarily tempted by the sight of her firm rounded breasts almost spilling out from the low-cut bodice. He was a hot-blooded man with a strong sexual drive, and like most countrymen had enjoyed numerous tumbles in the hay with willing girls. Then he thought of where she had spent the night, and his desire became repulsion.

'I'll have to go, Susy,' he told her, not unkindly. 'Annie is waiting.'

She shrugged her rounded shoulders. 'Oh well, suit yourself, my handsome.' She put her tongue out at him cheekily. ''Tis your loss.'

'Yes Susy,' he agreed with a tinge of regret. 'T'is my loss.'

For the first couple of hours the novelty of being out in the fields in the sunlight and fresh clean air imparted a holiday atmosphere to the gang, but then, as the heat of the day increased, sapping energies and dulling senses, and the effort of wielding the short-handled hoes began to cause joints and back muscles to ache agonizingly, the light-hearted mood of the women eroded rapidly.

Tildy's own back was aching unbearably. She was singling the turnip plants, bent almost double over the ridges where the slender shoots grew some three inches in height, using the head of the hoe to push the unwanted plants out of the earth, and then drawing the loosened soil back into its place. The sun beating down on her bare head causing the blood to pound through Tildy's temples and brought on a dull throbbing ache behind her eyes.

Great care had to be taken to leave the singled plant untouched and undamaged. The weeds were very troublesome, growing in the furrows and on the ridges themselves, couch-grass, wild mustard, knot-grass and wild radish and red shank, their roots tough and difficult to cut.

The women were nearly all singling the plants, while the children for the most part were employed in gathering the cut weeds and discarded turnip shoots into piles around the edges of the crop, and handweeding in the furrows, the thistles piercing their soft hands and fingers, the roots blistering their skin, causing some of the younger children to whimper and wail with pain.

At first Jeremiah Borth had merely lounged in the shade of a hedgerow tree, watching the gang work. But as their pace began to slacken he started patrolling along the lines of toilers with a long thin stick in his meaty hand that he used with increasing frequency to cut at the backs and buttocks of the slowest workers, shouting genially as he did so.

'Quicken up, my beauty! Quicken up!'

Initially it was only the small children and the young

boys and girls who received these stinging visitations, the women merely getting verbal castigations.

Bella Parks was wielding a hoe on the ridge next to Tildy, and heavily built as she was, the heat was taking a heavy toll of her strength. Abruptly she jerked out, 'Fuck this for a game o' soldiers,' and threw her hoe to the ground.

Borth saw her straighten her back, and bawled, 'Oi you, gerron wi' your work.'

Bella swung to face him, her face flushed and sweaty, the reddish dust thick on hands and bare arms. Borth came along the toiling line to reach her, and as he passed the women and children surreptitiously paused from their labours to stare after his broad back.

Bella Parks stood motionless, hands on hips, her large breasts rising and falling as she panted for breath.

'I said gerron wi' your work!' the Overseer's voice was rising with temper, but still the woman made no move to comply.

'Be you fucking deaf?' Borth bellowed furiously. 'Can't you hear what I'm atelling you, you fucking cow?'

Her own broad features worked with a gathering anger. 'I'm only taking a breathe,' she shouted back. ''Tis bloody sore work, this is. A body's got a right to take a breathe in this heat. And I'm thirsty as well. I wants a drink o' summat.'

By now the man had reached her, yet still she stood, hands on hips, facing him defiantly.

All the lines of women and children had now come to a standstill, and all eyes were avidly watching this confrontation.

'Be you agoing to pick up that hoe and set to?' Borth growled.

Bella Parks' face was sullen and resentful. 'I needs a drink. Me throat's parched.'

'I'll tell you when youm able to stop for a drink,' Borth stated flatly.

'You can't treat me like some bloody slave,' Bella Parks protested angrily. 'I'm a free-born Englishwoman, I am, not some bloody foreigner.'

'Youm a fucking free-born pauper,' the Overseer sneered with brutal contempt, 'and if you don't pick up that hoe and set to this bloody minute, then youm in a peck o' trouble.' He paused, then ordered, 'Now pick it up and set to.'

Very deliberately Bella Parks raised her fingers in front of his face, and forked them in a lewd gesture. 'That's what you can do to yourself, you Brummagem bastard!' she hissed.

Tildy drew a sharp breath of apprehension, for it seemed that the man was about to physically launch himself at Bella Parks. Her thoughts raced through her mind. 'What shall I do if he attacks Bella? I can't just stand here and let him beat her.' Unconsciously her own body tensed and her hands gripped the short shaft of the hoe ever more tightly. 'I can't let him beat her. It's not right for a man to beat a woman.'

Despite her own fears of Borth's obvious physical strength, Tildy's own resolve hardened to intervene in support of Bella Parks should it come to an actual bodily assault. But, to her amazement Jeremiah Borth's mood miraculously metamorphosed, and instead of attacking Bella Parks, his mouth opened, his head went back, and he roared with laughter.

Bella Parks' own mouth gaped in astonishment, and she stared wildly around at the onlookers as if seeking an explanation of this man's bizarre behaviour.

That explanation was quickly vouchsafed by Borth himself, when his laughter abruptly stilled, and he told Bella Parks, 'Right then, my beauty, you'se done me a favour. Now everybody 'ull see what happens to them as wun't work for me. Youm finished in this bloody parish. You'll never get any sort o' Relief again. And if you finds any sort o' work to support yourself, then it 'ull be a fucking miracle. I'll guarantee that.'

The woman's broad features showed puzzlement. 'What does you mean by that?' she demanded, and now he smiled and told her genially.

'Exactly what I'se said, my beauty. So shift your arse off

this field and fuck off away from here altogether.' He raised his voice in a stentorian shout which carried to everyone in the gang. 'Listen well, all on you. Bella Parks is finished in this parish. She gets naught from the parish in relief, and she'll get no work from any employer. I'll see to that.If she don't work for me, then she works for nobody. I'm buggering her off now, and if any o' you lot wants to goo wi' her, then now's your chance. Does you understand me? Now's your chance to goo if you arn't ready to work for me. You'se got one minute to think on it.'

From his waistcoat pocket he produced a brass-cased hunter watch and held it high above his head, where the sun's rays flashed on its glass-covered face. 'One minute, my beauties, one minute to make your minds up whether to goo, or to stay.'

He brought the watch down to his eye level, and silently counted off the seconds, then bellowed, 'That's it! The minute is up. Them who wants can goo wi' this stupid cow right now. Them who'se staying, get set to . . . And quicken up, or I'll be warming your hides wi' me stick.'

For a brief span of time no one moved, all seemed held motionless by an invisible bondage.

Bella Parks looked around her, then grinned, and shouted triumphantly, 'Theer now, that shows you summat don't it, you Brummagem bastard. You can't do what you likes here. You can't treat us like a load o' nigger slaves.'

Borth scratched his flattened nose reflectively, then turned to Tildy. 'Does you need this work to feed you and your babby, girl?'

Wordlessly Tildy nodded. Inwardly she was torn in two conflicting directions. One part of her mind clamoured to thrown down her hoe and stand defiantly in support of Bella Parks's demand to be allowed to take a drink, and rest her aching back for a few moments. The other, more rational part of Tildy's mind merely reiterated the price she and her child would have to pay if she did act so.

'Get set to then, girl. Or you'se bloody well lost it,' Borth ordered flatly, and with one despairing glance at

Bella Parks, Tildy bent low over the ridge of turnips and began to push against the soil with her hoe.

'Damn my poverty,' Tildy raged silently, 'Damn this necessity to let bullies like him lord it over me. Damn and blast it!'

The Overseer grinned triumphantly in his turn at Bella Parks, as one by one the rest of the women and children resumed their toiling. Silently he jerked his thumb over his shoulder, and swearing vilely Bella Parks shuffled from the field.

The gang had been labouring for almost six hours before Jeremiah Borth called halt. Painfully Tildy straightened her back, biting her lips as her overstrained spinal muslces contracted and cramped. Slowly she made her way along the cleared furrows towards the hedgerow where the gang had left their meagre provisions.

Borth glanced at his watch. 'It's nigh on three o'clock,' he bawled. 'You'se got half an hour to ate your grub.'

Wearily the women slumped to the ground, their children gathering around them. For the most part all they had to fill their stomachs were lumps of bread and raw onions, with bottles of water to wash the dust from their parched mouths and throats. Sinking down in the sparse shade of the hedgerow Tildy gratefully drank from her own bottle of tepid water, and hungrily devoured her lump of dark bread and sharp-tasting onion. There was little talk among the gang, all their energies and high spirits had been drained by the pounding sun and relentless toil. Even the children were subdued, but some of them whined and complained querulously, until threats and sharp slaps from their overwrought mothers hushed them into fearful silence.

'What does you reckon to it then, Tildy?' Sarah Farr, her ravaged features caked with sweaty red dust, wanted to know.

Tildy shook her head. 'I'm finding it sore hard, Sarah.' She glanced around the gang, noting that some of the older women and the more frail-built of the younger appeared near to exhaustion. 'I don't see how some of these wenches can last the day out, if Borth keeps driving us so hard.'

'No, nor me neither,' the older woman agreed, and added resentfully, 'The bastard's a real slave-driver, arn't he.'

Tildy nodded, and for a brief instant her own fiery spirit flared. 'It's wrong!' she ejaculated fiercely. 'It's wrong that women and children should be driven so!'

'Shhhh!' Sarah Farr warned. 'Here's Borth acoming.'

The Overseer sauntered into the midst of the huddled women and children, and smiled bluffly at them. 'I know it's hard going wi' you today, girls. But tomorrow you'll be better used to it, and we'll make an earlier start, then you'll not need to grind so hard to finish your stint.' He looked about him, but no eyes met his, only sullen, downcast faces. He chuckled merrily and pointed towards the field gate. 'Look yonder theer, girls. I'se arranged a little treat for you, and it's out o' me own pocket it comes.'

A man leading a horse had entered the field and was ambling along the side of the hedgerow towards them. When he neared the gang they could see the two wooden kegs slung across the horse's back.

'That's best ale, girls, and it's all for you lot. You can have a drop on it now, just to taste how good it is, and arter you'se finished your stint it 'ull be waiting for you.'

His eyes sought and found Tildy's, and he grinned with a sly amusement. 'Theer now, Jeremiah Borth arn't quite so hard-hearted as you took him for, is he, my beauty. In fact, to them he takes a fancy for he can prove real kind-hearted.'

She did not return his grin, but only told him quietly, 'It's the carrot you're showing us now, Master Borth, but speaking for myself, I'd sooner forgo the carrot and see less of the stick.'

He regarded her speculatively for some moments, and then, equally quietly, replied, 'I hope I'll not be having trouble from you, young 'ooman. I'd take no pleasure from bosting the yed of a pretty cratur like you.'

He walked away, and Sarah Farr stared at Tildy with visible alarm. 'You wants to watch what youm saying to that bastard, Tildy. He's a bad 'un to cross, that's easy seen.'

Tildy herself was uncomfortably aware of her own apprehension of the Overseer, yet her stubborn courage would not allow her to admit or give in to that emotion.

'It's true what I said, Sarah. That drink he's offering us is the carrot, but he wields too big a stick for my taste.'

'That's as maybe,' Sarah Farr said impatiently, 'but you ought to have sense enough by now to only think them things, and leave them unsaid. You'se allus bin the same Tildy, ever since I'se known you. You gives voice to things that the rest on us has the sense to keep silence on. It's got you into trouble afore now, and it 'ull goo on getting you into trouble until you learns sense.'

Tildy opened her mouth to reply, then realizing the futility of argument closed it without speaking, but inwardly vowed that despite all the trouble it might bring upon her head, she would never, ever accept submissively the blatant injustices inflicted upon the poor of her country . . .

Chapter Seven

Five days had passed, and the gang were becoming more used to the work in the turnip fields. The heatwave had cooled a little, clouds passing over the land in clusters, and during the nights occasionally shedding light showers of rain that laid the worst of the dust without rendering the soil too wet to be worked. But although this cooling brought relief in one aspect to the gang, the fact that they were becoming more adept at the work became an added burden to be borne, because Jeremiah Borth demanded more and more speed from them, driving them mercilessly.

Each morning at four o'clock they gathered on the Green and trudged half-asleep to Winterton's farm where, with only two short breaks, they would toil until nine or even ten o'clock in the evening, and then make their weary passage homewards. Resentful and sullen, every one of them was tempted again and again to thrown down their tools, but the example of Bella Parks restrained them.

She had been trudging the lanes in a fruitless search for work. They knew that she had applied to the Vestry for Outdoor Relief, or failing that, admittance to the Webheath Poorhouse, and had been refused on both counts. In desperation, since she had no family to support her, and was herself the sole support of her three children, she had gone to the magistrate, Reverend the Lord Aston, to complain of her treatment and demand redress. He had only threatened to commit her and her children to the Worcester Bridewell as vagrants, and had had her ejected from his property by his servants. Now she existed miserably on the scant charity of her neighbours, and feared that her children might be taken from her by force by the Parish Officers and put into the Poorhouse as Parish Bastards.

The subject of Bella Parks was brought into the conversation during the second break of the day by Sarah Farr.

'I seen the poor cratur last night, Tildy.' Her gaunt face held genuine pity. 'Her's bloody nigh drove to madness wi' worry, so her is. She arn't got a penny piece to her name, and owes all over the shop.'

Tildy was equally pitying, but could only shrug helplessly. 'Well, if it had been me who saw her, I've not a penny piece meself that I could have given her.'

'Nor I hadn't neither,' Sarah Farr informed her glumly. 'I'm ateing on tick meself these last three days.' She lowered her voice to a hoarse whisper. 'Mind you, Tildy, she's more nor likely got a few bob in her pocket by now. When I saw her, her was on her way to the Barley Mow down Studley.' She named an inn in a nearby village. 'Theer's a gang o' foreigners bin drinking in theer these last couple o' nights, so her was told. They'm Welshmen, come for the shearing, so they say.'

'I think I know them,' Tildy informed her friend. 'If it's the same gang, they stayed at Mother Readman's one night.' Gratitude towards Oriel Evans flooded through her. 'Their ganger-man is a fine person. It was him who cured my Davy of the fever.'

The other woman abruptly cackled with laughter. 'It warn't for a fever cure that Bella was alooking for 'um.' She winked lewdly.'No . . . She was hoping to earn a few bob from 'um. Arter all, men away from their own womenfolk am always hungry for a bit of loving, arn't they.'

'Poor Bella,' Tildy almost whispered, 'she's always tried to keep herself straight, for all her loose talk. It must be bitter hard for her, to be driven to whoring.'

'What choice has her got, Tildy?' Sarah Farr spread her hands, palms uppermost as if in supplication, and her voice hardened. 'The bastards wun't gi' her naught in Relief, and her kids has to be fed. The poor wench is fritted to death that the Overseers 'ull take the kids from her, as it is.'

'But if the constables take her up for whoring she'll get put in the Bridewell, and her kids will go to the Poorhouse then of a certainty, God help her!' Tildy's tone became bitter. 'And I wish He'd curse them who've driven her to this.'

'It don't sound as though He's cursed that Brummagem bastard yet though, does it?' Sarah Farr jerked her head at Jeremiah Borth, who was bawling for a resumption of work.

The sun had set when Borth finally called a halt to the work, and a soft breeze cooled the twilight air. With a weary slowness the gang shuffled towards the farmstead, their relief at having finished for the day overshadowed by the knowledge that in scant hours they would again be pitting their aching, sweating bodies against the tough weeds and heavy clays of the land.

'Cheer up, girls,' Jeremiah Borth bade them jovially. 'Think of the wages youm earning. When the Golden Eagle flies over and shits, you'll all have money in your birtches then.'

'How bloody little, I wonder?' Sarah Farr commented morosely, and Tildy shook her head, causing the long neckshade of the cloth sunbonnet she was wearing to swing from side to side. 'Surely it's got to be more than the Relief money?' she half-questioned, and a woman directly behind her snorted angrily.

'It wun't surprise me if it don't turn out to be the same amount. But when be we going to get paid anyway, that's what I'd like to know?'

'Christ! I hope it's more than the parish gives us,' Tildy exclaimed. 'I've got to pay to have my Davy looked after, and then buy extra food to bring with me to eat here, or I wouldn't have strength for the work. If we don't earn a reasonable wage, than I'll be getting deeper into debt for working like a slave.' She walked in silence for a few paces more, then stated decidedly, 'I'm going to ask Borth when he's intending paying us, and how much it'll be.'

Sarah Farr stared at her in alarm. 'I don't know as how that's a good thing for you to be doing, Tildy.'

'Why not?' Tildy challenged. 'We've a right to know what wages we can expect, and when we'll be getting them.'

'That's as maybe, but you knows what a funny-tempered bugger he is, girl. If you catches him on the wrong side he might just tell you to sod off, like he did to Bella Parks . . . Nooo,' Sarah Farr finished with a judicious air, 'you'd best wait until we gets our money, and then you'll see what's what.'

Tildy's demon of stubbornness roused itself and gripped her. 'No! I'll not wait, Sarah. When we hand our tools in, then I'll tackle him about it. We've the right to know.'

The older woman recognized the mood, and shrugged her skinny shoulders. 'Alright then, girl, have it your way. But don't you go bringing me into it. Youm on your own in this.'

'That's nothing new for me,' Tildy rejoined, with a tinge of bitterness in her tone, then lapsed into silence for the remainder of the trek to the farmstead.

At the toolshed Tobias Winterton was waiting to count the implements and check that none were broken or damaged. He watched the weary procession approaching and a pang of pity struck through him as he noted the obvious exhaustion of some of the weaker women and children. When Jeremiah Borth came up to him, Tobias nodded towards the gang. 'They looks worn out, Master Borth. Youm driving them over-hard, I fear.'

The Overseer's scarred lips twisted in a spasm of contempt. 'These lazy buggers has to be drove hard to get a fair day's work out on 'um.'

'Mayhap some of them ar lazy, but not all have the strength for the work. My meaning was that the weaker ones shouldn't be forced to do more than they're able,' Tobias argued.

'Then you'd best gi' me a higher price for the work, my master, and I'll ease off on 'um,' the Overseer riposted, and the younger man flushed as the barb struck home.

'It's not me who fixes the piece-prices on this farm, Master Borth,' he pointed out.

'No. I knows that fact well enough,' Borth sneered openly. 'But that's the way o' the world, arn't it, my bucko. It's the organ grinder who runs the show, not his monkey.'

Before Tobias could reply the Overseer turned away from him and bawled, 'Come on, you buggers, step up lively. I wants to be done afore bleedin' midnight. Them wi' broke tools, come to the front.'

It was part of his agreement with Arthur Winterton that the gang master replaced all tools broken or damaged by his gang. An arrangement which suited Borth very well as an added source of profit. He would deduct the cost of the replacement from the user's wages, and add a little extra on the price for himself to pocket.

Tonight only one woman stepped to the front and proffered a weed-hook, the small sickle-like blade of which had been snapped in two.

Borth grinned as he took the pieces from her thin hands. 'How the bleeding hell did you manage to do this?' he exclaimed in mock wonder, and his small eyes travelled up and down her skinny, under-nourished body. 'Jesus! I'se sin more fucking muscles on a piece o' twine,' he scoffed. 'What's your name?'

'Mary-Ellen James.' The careworn face was woebegone, and her lips trembled when he told her jeeringly, 'Well, Mary Ellen James, that's agoing to cost you a few pennies, arn't it.'

'But it warn't my fault.' Tears fell from her eyes. 'I left it down for a couple o' minutes, and when I went to use it agen I found it was laying like that. Somebody else had bin using it. It was them who broke it.'

'Well let that be a bloody lesson to you then, my wench.' The Overseer laughed uproariously. 'The next time you goes for a shit, then take your tools wi' you.'

When she would have protested further he cut her short. 'Gerron out of it, you whining cow, or you wun't be getting any wages at all, only my boot up your bloody arse.'

Tildy seethed inwardly as she watched and heard, and her determination to ask the man about her wages steeled rigidly.

Tobias Winterton smiled at her as she stepped up to the door of the shed and handed her hoe. 'And how are you finding the work, Missus Crawford?'

'Sore hard, as you well know,' she snapped, and was instantly sorry that her anger against Jeremiah Borth had been directed at someone who had done nothing to offend her. 'I'm sorry to bite at you like that,' she apologized almost in her next breath. 'I'm out of sorts today.'

He grinned understandingly. 'I can't say as how I blame you for that, Missus Crawford. Working for that man there cannot be very pleasant.' He nodded towards Borth who was strutting up and down the queue of women and children.

He seemed about to say something more, but was interrupted by the next woman stepping up to him, and Tildy, unable to restrain herself any longer went to speak with the Overseer.

'Master Borth, can I have a word with you?'

The man stared at her lasciviously. 'A tasty morsel like you can allus have words wi' Jeremiah Borth, my duck. What's it about?'

All eyes were intent upon the couple. Ears strained to catch what passed between them.

'It's about our wages,' Tildy began.

'What about 'um?' Borth cut in with an instant aggressive reaction, but Tildy refused to back down to that aggression.

'I want to know when we'll be getting them, and how much they'll be?'

For a second or two he only stared at her, as though not fully comprehending what she had said.

Tildy repeated herself. 'How much are we getting, and when, Master Borth?'

He pushed his peaked cap back on his shaven head and scratched his low forehead. Then readjusted his cap and told her, 'You'll be getting what I give you, Crawford, and you'll get it when I chooses to give it you. Does that answer your question?'

Tildy drew a deep breath, and summoning her courage picked up the verbally proffered gauntlet. 'No, Master Borth! That doesn't serve for an answer. I want to know when we are getting our money, and how much it will be?'

Among the gang nudges and whispers and nervous giggles were exchanged, and by the shed door Tobias Winterton was engrossed by the interchange.

Jeremiah Borth scowled at the gang, his hard eyes moving from face to face, as if daring anyone to meet them. No one did. Instead, as his eyes caught theirs, they looked down, shuffling their feet, their hands toying nervously with the tools they carried. Once satisfied that Tildy stood alone in her defiance, the Overseer glared threateningly at her.

'Does you know summat, Crawford. I'd ha' bet on it! I'd ha' bet me last shilling that it 'ud be you who'd try and cause trouble. I had you marked for such from the fust second I clapped eyes on you.'

'I'm not trying to cause any trouble,' Tildy told him in a steady voice. 'I'm only asking you to tell me what I've a right to know.'

'I've said it afore, and I'll say it again.' Borth's features were a mask of brutal contempt. 'Fucking paupers arn't got no rights.' Then he raised his voice and shouted, 'Listen well, all on you. I was intending to pay you summat tomorrow out on me own pocket. Because no money 'ull be coming from Master Winterton until the turnips be all done wi' weeding and singling. This job's bin took on the piece, which means we don't get paid t'il all the work is finished. Like I said, I was prepared to pay you summat in advance out o' me own pocket. But I'll be fucked if I'll do that if I'm to be blaggarded by bitches like this 'un here. There's another four days o' work at least afore this job 'ull be done. So it's up to you lot. The sooner you gets it done, the sooner you gets paid, and anybody who doesn't like it can fucking well lump it. Now? Has anybody got anything to to say about that?'

With this last challenge he stopped speaking and waited

for their reaction. Although most of them were bitterly resentful none spoke out, or even dared to meet his eyes. He nodded, satisfied that he had mastery over them. Then, with an abrupt change of demeanour he grinned and told them affably, 'Good! I see you knows which side your bread is buttered on. Seeing as that's the case, then Jeremiah Borth is not the sort o' chap to thrash willing horses. I'll see if I can scrape a few bob together, so that I can give you summat on account tomorrow.'

His words were greeted with visible and audible relief. Tildy herself experienced that same relief, but could hardly believe that she had won her point so easily. Within seconds her doubts were realized as Borth said to her in a conversational tone, 'O' course you realize that you wun't get paid anything tomorrow, don't you, Crawford. You'll needs wait until the job's done afore you gets your wages. Perhaps that 'ull teach you not to blaggard your betters.' He stepped away from her to shout at the gang. 'Come on now, you lot, let's get these bloody tools handed in.'

They hastened to obey, shuffling up to the shed door in quick succession, some casting sidelong glances at Tildy, but none of them daring to speak or even nod commiseratingly at her.

She stood motionless, a terrible desolation of loneliness assailing her, so that she wanted to weep. She was sickeningly aware of her own impotence to combat the Overseer's tyranny, and although she was experiencing a sense of betrayal in that none of the gang had come to her support, yet she could not find it in her heart to condemn them for their failure. After all, none of them had asked her to intercede with Borth.

'No, no one made me do it,' she accepted with a bitter chagrin directed against herself, and inwardly damned her own concept of justice which had once again impelled her into a struggle which she could not hope to win.

Now she turned to the only source of help that had never failed to come to her aid. Her own fierce pride. And with that to sustain her she held back her tears and kept her head high.

'You'll not break me,' she silently repeated over and over again, using the words as a talisman to give her added strength of will. 'You'll not break me, Borth. You'll not break me . . . You'll not break me . . .'

'You'd best make haste, or you'll be walking back home by yourself, Missus Crawford.'

It was Tobias Winterton's voice that brought Tildy back to an awareness of her surroundings, to find that the gang had already left the farmstead to begin their homeward journey.

She grimaced regretfully. 'At this time I prefer walking by myself, Master Winterton.'

He nodded understandingly. 'I wouldn't blame you for that, Missus Crawford. You've no real friends in that bunch, that's easy seen. They let you shoot the bullets for 'um, and then gave you no support when you needed it.'

She stared at him with suspicion, wondering at the motivation behind his outwardly sympathetic façade. Then he surprised her by his sensitive perception.

'I see that you're wondering what it is I'm trying to get from you, Missus Crawford.' He smiled wryly and shook his head. 'I'm not seeking anything from you, so don't misjudge me. I only wanted to tell you that I admire how you tackled that bruiser. There's not many who'd have the guts to do that, women nor men neither.'

By now the rearmost of the gang were disappearing from sight, and Tildy nodded to him in farewell. 'I'll needs be on my way, Master Winterton. It's getting very late, and I've a fair distance to walk.'

He studied her face in the gloom, and found himself powerfully affected by her beauty. On impulse, he offered, 'I'll go a part of the way with you, Mrs Crawford. It's not safe for a woman to walk these roads alone at night at present. There's some wicket buggers on the prowl. A girl from Mappleborough village was jumped on by some cove just the other night. If some of the village lads hadn't happened to come along and chase him off, she'd have been grievous treated.'

Tildy nodded. 'Yes, I heard about that.' She appeared

to be searching for words, before continuing, 'I know you'll think me vain and silly for what I'm going to say, Master Winterton,' she looked him squarely in the eyes, 'but say it, I will. Some men find me attractive, and because my husband and me have been long parted, they think I might be ripe for sporting with. But I'm a respectable woman, Master Winterton.' She glanced up at the rapidly darkening sky. 'I don't relish the thought of walking alone until they've taken up the man who attacked that girl, so I'd be glad of your company. But there is no reward offered for you walking me back. No reward of any sort . . . I hope that is plain spoke.'

Unconsciously a note of aggression had entered her voice, and he chuckled amusedly. 'There's no call for you to have a go at me, Mrs Crawford. I know you're a respectable woman, and I'm not planning to offer you any offence. But to speak equally plain, I'd like us to be friends, if that's possible. Come now, we'd best be on our way.'

For a while they walked in silence along the narrow, deeply rutted Icknield Street. A thoroughfare that had been ancient when the first Roman legionaries marched its length to reinforce the garrisons of the northern frontier. Then Tobias broke the silence.

'Are you and your husband parted for good, Mrs Crawford?'

'Yes. We were not happy together.' Tildy was reluctant to say more, but with a gentle persistence he gradually drew from her the story of her violent, loveless marriage, and her present impoverished circumstances. As he listened he became increasingly enthusiastic about offering her the position left vacant by the runaway Sally Jukes.

But already he had sensed Tildy's pride and independence of spirit, and so he did not rush in, but instead told her of his own life, and the difficulties he faced in caring for his younger brother and sister. Finding her an intelligent and warm-hearted recipient of these confidences, he opened his heart more and more, relating his desires to travel and to educate himself, and to find a way of life and work that would satisfy his half-understood yearnings.

For her part Tildy found that she had much in common with this young man, and experienced a growing liking for his open simplicity and patent honesty.

When the reached the lower slopes of the Beoley Lane which led up through Bredon and into the centre of Redditch town, she indicated the dim lights shining from some of the windows of the cottages that bordered the lane.

'I shall be quite safe from here on, Master Winterton. So please don't trouble to come further. I'm very grateful to you for giving me your company, and making the walk back so pleasant.'

The words to offer her a home and work at the farm trembled on his lips, but for some reason he found unaccountable to himself he left them unsaid. It was as if some subconscious force in his mind was telling him that this was not the time to speak. So, he merely half-bowed and with a simple, 'God speed, Mrs Crawford,' he retraced his steps.

'Good night, Master Winterton, and thank you again for your company,' she called after him as the darkness swallowed his figure, and then continued on her way up the long sloping lane.

Her dreams that night were a strange mixture of crystalline images and vague shadows. She seemed to be at the farmstead, talking and laughing with Tobias Winterton, and then while still at the farmstead, she was alone but aware of an unseen menacing presence which threatened danger to herself and her child, but which, struggle though she might, she could neither see nor identify.

When she awoke early next morning, it was the memory of the laughter which was uppermost, and the threatening presence only a vague whisper in her mind . . .

Chapter Eight

The gang were having their first break of the day when Arthur and Tobias Winterton came to the field. Jeremiah Borth swaggered to meet them.

'Well now, Master Winterton, what do you think to the progress?' He indicated the great stretch of weeded and singled crops.

The older Winterton gave grudging acknowledgement. 'Youm doing well enough, Master Borth.'

'A lot better than well enough, I reckon, Master Winterton,' the overseer boasted. 'I've got this gang working like prime navvies. We'll have this finished in two more days.'

'I'm glad to hear that,' Arthur Winterton grunted, 'because I needs your gang for other things. In fact I wants some on 'um now for the haymaking.'

Borth looked up at the sky which was patterned with clumps of large grey-white cumuli. 'Yes, it 'ud pay you to start your haymaking right away.' He pointed to the clouds. 'See how ragged them edges be up theer. That's nearly always a sure sign of rain acoming, arn't it.'

The big farmer frowned. 'I don't need any advice about the weather from a townie, Master Borth. I can read the signs.'

'Oh, I don't doubt that, Master,' the Overseer hastened to placate him, but there was still a hint of a sneer in his tone. ''Tis well known hereabouts that youm a positive oracle regarding the weather.'

The farmer's heavy face darkened ominously as he detected the sneer, but knowing that he needed this man's gang at this time, he kept his resentment concealed. 'I'se got men mowing this morning, Master Borth. so I'd like half a dozen o' your women to do the forking and raking for 'um. Preferably them who had worked at the haymaking afore.'

A wary gleam came into Borth's eyes. 'Well o' course I'll let you have 'um, Master. But we arn't discussed a price, has we.'

'I'll pay by the day,' the farmer stated, and seeing Borth was about to protest, went on, 'Don't worry, I'll see you don't lose by it.'

'Alright then,' Borth accepted. 'I'll pick 'um out for you.'

He would have turned away, but Tobias stopped him. 'Hold hard, Master Borth.' He spoke to his father, 'Youm forgetting about a woman for the house, Feyther.'

'Oh yes.' Arthur Winterton nodded. 'That's summat else I wants to ask you about, Master Borth. I needs a woman to look arter the house and to see to my daughter. I thought I'd ask the gang theer and see if any o' them might be suited for the work.'

The Overseer appeared doubtful. 'I don't know about that, Master. These women be all contracted out to my by the Vestry. I pays rent for 'um.'

'You don't own them,' Tobias challenged. 'What we're looking for is a servant to suit us. She'll be contracted by us, not the Vestry.'

'It arn't that simple,' the Overseer stated flatly. 'I'se made an agreement wi' the Tardebigge Vestry about these women, and under the terms o' that agreement I does own 'um, in a manner o' spaking. They only works when and where I says they does.' He allowed his listeners a few moments to absorb this information, then asked, 'Has you got anybody particular in mind for the work?'

'Yes. The Crawford woman,' Tobias answered.

A broad grin spread across Borth's battered features, and he winked lewdly.

Tobias' anger kindled at the man's attitude. 'Well then?' he snapped.

'Well what, Master?' Borth rejoined.

'Is it alright for us to offer her the work?' Tobias heatedly questioned.

Borth made a show of giving serious consideration, then slowly shook his head, and said with mock regret, 'No, it arn't alright. I'm sorry to have to say, Master. It arn't convenient.'

Tobias' temper broke through. 'Be damned to convenient! We need a woman for the house, and if she wants the work, then we'll take her.'

Borth's expression hardened, and slowly he shook his bullet head. 'Oh no you wun't, Master. It's me who says what these women does, and nobody else.'

'I reckon we'd best ask Tildy Crawford herself what she wants to do,' Tobias tried a different tack. 'If she agrees, then I can't see what you can do to stop her coming to work for us.'

Borth had his own plans for Tildy, and his determination matched that of Tobias Winterton. He spoke to Arthur Winterton. 'I reckon your son is a bit too big for his britches, Master Winterton, to be forcing this quarrel on to me like this. Now I've got great respect for you personally, and because o' that I'm going to tell you what could happen here. This gang is working well because I'se whipped 'um into line. This Crawford woman is a troublemaker, forever being insolent to her betters. Now I'se put her in her rightful place, and I intends to keep her theer, that way she serves as a good example to the rest o' the buggers. But if they now sees her getting a good position in your house, arter the trouble she's tried to cause in the gang, well then, all the good work I'se put in 'ull be set to naught, wun't it. They'll think that being saucy and disobedient 'ull serve them as well. There'll be no controlling the buggers! So sooner than have that, I'd prefer to take my gang off from your land here and now.'

Jeremiah Borth had totally misjudged the older Winterton, and his shock showed clearly as the farmer gritted out, 'Who does you think youm threatening, you Brummagem cunt? You can take your dammed gang from here any time you've a mind to. I don't tolerate any man trying to rule me, and especially when he's some jumped-up-jack in-office who got his position by crawling up the arses of them thieving Vestry bastards. My forebears were lords o' this land when yourn were serf scum, and as far as I'm concerned I'm still the Lord o' this land, and youm still a serf.' He looked towards the huddled clump of women and children some twenty yards distant, and roared, 'Crawford? Tildy Crawford? Get yourself here to me.'

Tildy had been sitting with Sarah Farr, and had paid little attention to the three men. Now, surprised, she stared at the trio and did not move until Arthur Winterton shouted again.

'Come over here, Crawford.'

'You best get theer,' Sarah Farr advised nervously. 'That old sod is a bad 'un to cross. I'se heard tales about him afore.'

Feeling nervous herself about what this unexpected summons might mean for her, Tildy rose gracefully and walked to join the men.

As she reached them, Tobias smiled reassuringly. 'Don't be feared, Mrs Crawford. There's naught going to go amiss for you.'

Jeremiah Borth's thoughts were racing. Despite his outward show of arrogant confidence, he knew that his power in the parish was not as absolute as it might appear to outside eyes. For his present scheme to continue and earn him substantial profit he needed the co-operation and acquiescence of the local farmers in the two parishes of Ipsley and Tardebigge. A man like Arthur Winterton would undoubtedly have great influence among his fellow farmers.

Physically, Borth was not afraid of either Arthur or Tobias Winterton, and was confident that if it should come to a physical confrontation he would be able to beat either, or even both of them together. But such a confrontation would in all likelihood eventually cost him dearly, and perhaps lose him his present position.

'Box clever now, bucko,' he told himself, 'box clever . . . You can settle any scores later, but for now . . . box clever . . .'

He abruptly changed course and hastened to soothe Arthur Winterton. 'You misunderstands me, Master, I 'udden't dream o' taking my gang from here.' He forced himself to grin at Tildy, and tell her bluffly. 'Youm a lucky wench. These gentlemen am going to offer you a position in their house, and if you wants to take it up, why then, I'm willing to release you from the gang.'

Tildy gazed at him in open surprise, and he was aware that Tobias was looking at him with open contempt, but he kept the grin on his face, while inwardly promising, 'Sneer now, you young bastard. Sneer now. My turn 'ull come by and by. I'll promise you that. My turn 'ull come.'

Tildy's lucent brown eyes turned to Tobias, and he hastened to tell her. 'We need another woman to help in the house and look to my sister. You would live in, and you could bring your child to live here as well. You'll find us good masters, you and the babby would not want for anything. He'd grow strong and healthy here.'

Tildy looked over the young man's shoulders towards the western skyline where the hills of Redditch shimmered in the sunlight. She drew the sweet clean air, redolent of earth and growing plants, into her lungs, contrasting it with the foul stenches of the Silver Square.

'I've nothing to lose by coming here,' she told herself, 'and much to gain for my Davy.' Without any further thought she nodded at Tobias Winterton. 'I'll come. When do you want me to start?'

The young man's white teeth gleamed in his delight. 'Right now, Tildy Crawford. Right this minute.' He swung to face the Overseer. 'If that's alright by you, Master Borth?' he challenged.

Borth itched to smash the other man to the ground, but he kept the affable grin on his face. 'O' course it's all alright wi' me. I was out of order afore, I admits that. I've no wish to quarrel wi' you or your feyther, least of all on account of a pauper slut.' For a brief instant his hatred of the young man flashed in his bloodshot eyes, then he told Arthur Winterton, 'I'll sort out the wenches for the haymaking, Master,' and walked away.

Arthur Winterton scowled at his son. 'Don't forget this 'ooman is your choice, my bucko. If her don't serve for the work, it's your yed the blame 'ull fall on.'

Tobias, happy that he had gained his wish, grinned easily. 'That's fair enough, Feyther. And thank you for supporting me like you did.'

The older man's scowl deepened. 'It warn't you I was concerned wi' supporting, it was my own name I was thinking of. I couldn't stand and let some arsehole of a Parish jack-in-office try and dictate terms to me. There arn't a man alive that I'd let tell me what I can or can't do . . . Now take this young 'ooman up to the house, and set her to her duties.'

For the first time he spoke directly to Tildy. 'Do your work well, girl, and you'll have no cause to complain about your life here. But be plain on one thing . . . Then who thinks to live off me wi'out pulling their weight soon has another think coming. They sorely rues the day they ever tried it on wi' me. Just remember that.' He gestured to his son. 'Gerron then, boy. Time's wasting. I wants you back at the hay just as soon as you'se set this 'un here to her duties.'

'Don't be feared of him,' Tobias told Tildy as they walked towards the farmstead. 'Mostly his bark is worse than his bite.'

Tildy's eyes strayed to the swollen bruises on her companion's face, and aware of this, he laughed ruefully. 'Well, let's say rather that sometimes his bark is worse than his bite, but when he does bite he's got awful strong teeth and jaws. But if you does your work well, then you'll have naught to fear from him. I'll promise you that.'

'I hope so,' Tildy asserted spiritedly, 'because I'll not let any man ill-use me or my child without fighting back, and that I'll promise . . .'

The farmhouse was a building that had grown haphazardly through many centuries, successive generations adding to it, until now it stood big and rambling, a warren of rooms and passages. The kitchen was in the oldest part of the house, its walls constructed from massive stone blocks, and its roof also of high-vaulted stonework.

Tobias smiled at Tildy's expression of surprise as they entered the kitchen. 'They do say that this part of the house was once a chapel when the monks from Bordesley Abbey had their grange here.'

Tildy admired the slender carved pilasters of the Gothic-arched windows set high in the walls. 'Yes, I could believe that it was such.' Her gaze fell upon the hugely wide and long table in the centre of the room, and she exclaimed, 'But this is a rare-looking table, Master Winterton!'

'Look, afore anything else, let's get one matter agreed.' The young man pointed at his own chest. 'My name is Tobias, or Toby for short, and that's how you shall address me in future, and I shall address you as Tildy. Is that a bargain?'

She smilingly acquiesced, and he went on, 'Good! That's settled, and now I'll tell you summat about this old thing, shall I.' He looked down proudly at the massively thick table-top which had a series of large deep round concavities scooped in its surface all round its edges. 'My Feyther says that this table was the very one used by our ancestor who was a thane of Mercia long afore the Normans came. These holes were used as platters. We ates the very same way.' He paused for a moment, then with a smile of pleasure told her, 'I think it's wondrous in a way. Us ateing at the very same table that our warrior forefathers ate from all those centuries past, taking our food from the very same boards.'

Staring down at those scooped depressions in the dark smooth wood Tildy found her own imagination stirring, and for a brief instant she pictured the Saxon warriors and their womenfolk sitting feasting, as harpers played to them and serfs attended to their every wish.

Tobias sighed regretfully. 'I sometimes think what a pity it is that I warn't born in them times. Life's awful dull in these modern days.'

Tildy thought of her own turbulent life, and could not help but say wryly, 'I can't really call life dull, Tobias. There's times I wish I could do such.'

'Ahr well,' he dismissed his regrets, 'let's get on wi' what we'em here for. Now, the larder is back theer. You'll find the pickle and brine barrels theer, and the flour-chests and suchlike. The scullery is theer. It's got a good sweet-water pump and a fine stone trough in it, and the brewhouse and the wash-house both leads off from the scullery. You can see the cooking range yourself.'

'Indeed I can,' Tildy murmured, for the iron and brick range in its inglenook covered one entire end wall.

'The baking oven is in the side of the ingle theer, and you'll find pots and skillets here . . .'

She followed him around the great room as he indicated all the areas, implements and foodstuffs it contained. She noted the general dirty greasiness of everything, and Tobias was sensitive to her unspoken disapproval.

'It all needs a good seeing to, I know, Tildy. But since Sally went there's only bin Maddy Thomas to look to the house, and it's too much for one woman to cope with. And Maddy arn't what you'd call over-particular at the best o' times.'

'Will I be working under this Maddy Thomas?' Tildy wanted to know, and he laughed and shook his head.

'Lord love you, no! You'll have to be telling Maddy what to do. But she's alright, you'll find. She's a good-natured soul. She'll bless you for coming here and taking the worry from her shoulders.'

'Where is she now?' Tildy asked.

'I'm buggered if I know,' he shrugged. 'She ought to be here. Anyway, you knows wheer everything is to be found now, don't you. We wun't be in until past eight this even to ate, so you'll have time and to spare to get the meal ready by then.'

'How many are you? And what d'you want me to prepare for your meal?' Tildy was feeling a little apprehensive.

'Oh there's me, and me brother Jem, and his mate, young Tommy. Our Feyther, and our Anne, and Gilbert the shepherd, and six hinds and the dairymaid, and two women field hands, then you and Maddy.'

Tildy gulped, 'Jesus! That's a good number.'

'Don't worry, Maddy 'ull certain sure be back presently,' Tobias encouraged her. 'And there's plenty of provisions in store. I'll say this much for me Feyther, he don't stint on the grub. So make sure you gets plenty ready. There's beef and mutton both in the larder. And plenty o' pig meat theer.' He pointed to the dried flitches of bacon and hams hanging from iron rods in the top of the inglenook.

A short, stocky woman wearing a sun-bonnet and sack apron came into the kitchen.

'Here's Maddy come now,' Tobias greeted the newcomer. 'Now Maddy, this is Tildy Crawford. Her's come to see to the house and that. You'll be working wi' her from now on.' He turned to Tildy. 'I must get back to the fields, Tildy, so I'll see you at eight o' the clock.'

With that he was gone, leaving the two women alone.

Tildy looked curiously at her companion, and with equal curiosity Maddy Thomas returned the scrutiny.

Tildy judged her to be about twenty-five or -six, with a pleasant-featured, rosy plumpness that was physically appealing, and wide-spaced, remarkably beautiful violet-hued eyes. Tildy liked what she saw, and so it seemed did Maddy Thomas, for she grinned and said in a chuckling voice, 'Fuck me, but I'm glad to see you here, Tildy Crawford.'

Tildy experienced a quickening of warmth for the young woman, and she in turn smiled, and replied, 'Well, I'm glad to be here, Maddy Thomas, and I hope we shall be friends.'

'I'm sure we 'ull.' Maddy's teeth were small and white, and Tildy thought that she must be very attractive to men, and wondered why she wore no wedding ring.

'Come on, let's get the cooking started,' Maddy said. 'We can talk whiles we works.'

Tildy marvelled at how easily they fell into a camaraderie, and how easily she was able to relate her antecedents to her new-found friend. On her part Maddy was equally forthcoming, and told Tildy of her life in Studley village, where she was part of a large family, and had a child of her own who remained at the family home.

'We would ha' got wed, me and Tommy Biddle,' she named her child's father, 'but the silly bastard got took up one time too many for poaching, and now he's out in Botany Bay.' She chuckled richly. 'I wonder what the bugger is poaching out theer, Tildy. I'se heard tell that theer's some stands as tall as a man and hops everywheer, and carries their babbies in pouches in their bellies.'

'They're called kangaroos, Maddy. I read of them once in a book, and there were pictures of them also.'

'Can you read and write then, Tildy?' The plump rosy fetures were openly impressed.

'Yes, I taught myself mostly, but I was helped by a lady I was servant to at the time, as well.'

'I'd love to be able to read and write,' Maddy said wistfully. 'I ne'er even went to a Dame's school, though theer was two o' them in our village. We ne'er had enough pennies in our family to send any of us to school.'

'If you like, I'll teach you to do both,' Tildy offered, and was surprised at the eagerness with which her companion accepted.

'When can we make a start at it, Tildy? When?' Maddy begged to know.

'Why, this very night if you've a mind to. After I've fetched my Davy from Redditch.'

'I'll goo wi' you to fetch him, Tildy. Two's safer than one, what wi' that bloke attacking women.'

It was Tildy's turn to accept gratefully. 'Yes, I'd like that, Maddy. I'd like your company . . .'

At eight o'clock the meal was placed on the table. A big iron pot full of steaming, floury boiled potatoes, another pot with cabbage, and a great jug of gravy. Huge round loaves of wheaten bread, and a big half-wheel of hard yellow cheese. Three long rotund roly-polies made from flour, suet, bacon chunks and herbs, and directly in front of the master's place at the head of the table, a massive joint of roast beef ready for carving on its pewter dish. From the brewhouse jugs of home-brewed beer had been carried, and a keg of sharp-tasting cider. To Tildy's eyes the table presented a spectacle of rude plenty that she had never seen before.

Her fellow workers gathered to the feast, the six male hinds in grey or blue smocks she would come to know were ploughmen, cattleman and hedger. The old shepherd, Gilbert Tongue, Susy the dairymaid, young Jem and Tommy and two dour-faced, strong-bodied women field-hands, and lastly Tobias and Arthur Winterton.

Dirty, sweaty and smelly from their work, the company seated themselves on the benches flanking the table. Arthur Winterton took his station at the head, and with a surly expression wielded the long-pronged, bone-handled fork and carving knife.

'Tobias, Sim, Gilbert, Susy, Betsy, Maggie . . .' As he grunted each name Arthur Winterton deftly flicked the thick slices of juicy meat from the fork prongs into the hollows scooped out in front of them.

When all had been given meat, Arthur Winterton seated himself in his big wooden armchair. The iron pots were pushed towards him and he ladled out potatoes and cabbage into his own hollow, then poured gravy over the steaming pile. The pots travelled down the table as each helped themselves, and then, when all had been served, Arthur Winterton grunted, 'Get to it then.'

Voraciously the company fell upon the food, chewing noisily, smacking their lips, tearing chunks from the loaves of bread, slurping beer from their leather tankards, knives and spoons clattering as they gorged.

Tildy and Maddy stood at each side of the table, ready to fetch more beer and bread, or anything else that Arthur Winterton might call for. They had already eaten thick slices of fried bread and bacon, and if they wanted more would satisfy themselves from the remnants of the meal when the rest had finished.

Tildy sensed someone staring at her, and met Tobias' eyes. He smiled and winked, and she felt a mingling of embarrassment and pleasure. The embarrassment caused by the fact that the sight of his handsome face and taut, muscular body had sent a *frisson* of sexual desire coursing through her. Flustered, she broke the eye contact, and taking a jug from the table went to refill it from the trestled barrel in the brewhouse.

Maddy followed her out, and Tildy asked her, 'Why does no one speak?'

'It's because the Master's not in good humour. Nobody dares spake when he's in a bad mood. He's like to let fly at anybody who says summat he don't agree wi'. Mind, it arn't always like this. When he's in good fettle they talks. And there's times then when I wishes the old bugger was in bad humour, because some o' the things they comes out wi' 'ud put a blush on the face of a bloody tanner whore.'

'The Master, is he quick to use his fists?' Tildy asked, and the other girl laughed grimly.

'Oh he's quick and heavy wi' his hands alright. And he arn't slow to take the whip to the lads and women neither. That's why Sally done a bunk. He near flayed the skin from her back.' Seeing the concern in Tildy's expression, she said reassuringly, 'To be fair to the old sod, Sally was deserving of the bloody whip at times. She could be a real cow when her felt like. Her used to be real spiteful to poor simple Annie, and the master wun't stand anybody being nasty to the wench, even though he can't abear having her near him himself. That's why she never ates wi' the rest on us, but must keep to her room. Her's sleeping now . . .' Maddy lowered her voice to a conspiratorial whisper, 'At night times I always gives her a good big dose o' Godfrey's Cordial. That keeps her nice and quiet.'

Tildy nodded understandingly. Godfrey's Cordial was a medicinal mixture of sassafras, treacle and tincture of opium, widely used as a sedative and sleeping potion. But in ignorant hands it could be very dangerous, and many babies and old people died from overdoses of the potion.

Suddenly a hubbub of talk and laughter sounded from the kitchen, and Maddy tossed her head in satisfaction.

'Theer now, the Master's buggered off. You can allus

tell when he's gone, because then everybody starts trying to talk at once.'

She lifted the filled jug of beer to her lips with both hands and took a long drink from it, her glottle jerking up and down in her smooth, plump throat, then belched contentedly and wiped the froth from her upper lip.

'I does like a drop o' beer, Tildy. Come on, we'll goo and fetch your babby. We can clear up and wash the table down when we gets back.'

'Doon't you be forgetting wheer we lives now, 'ull you Tildy?'

Flanked by stick-thin Apollonia, Mother Readman came to the door of her lodging-house to bid Tildy farewell. And remember, theer's allus bed and board for you and the babby here, it youm in need of it.'

Tildy was genuinely saddened to be leaving her two friends, and tears glistened in her eyes as she kissed them both, then with a last murmured goodbye walked away from the Silver Square.

The loungers against the walls and in the doorways and windows of the fetid Silver Street stared curiously at the two women as they passed, but no one moved to interfere with their progress. Once they had reached the arch that was the gateway into Red Lion Street, Maddy Thomas gusted a sigh of relief.

'Jesus! I'm glad to get out o' theer, Tildy. Them buggers looks as if they'd slit your throat as soon as look at you.'

Tildy smiled wryly. 'Yes, they're rough enough, to be sure. But truth to tell, I've never been offered insult or injury while I've been living there. Mind you, having Mother Readman for my friend was probably what kept me safe.'

Little Davy, slung papoose-style with tied shawls on Tildy's back, his curly head resting against her shoulder, was sleeping soundly. Tildy had reluctantly given him a dose of Godfey's Cordial, so that the journey would not fret or distress him. Her scant possessions were tied into a small bundle, and Maddy Thomas was carrying that.

As they passed the Kings Arms at Bredon fork, and began the descent of the Beoley Lane, Tildy sighted Jeremiah Borth coming up the slope towards them followed by the straggling line of gang-women and children.

'Theer's the bastard you was working for.' Maddy frowned towards the burly figure in his blue corduroy coat and breeches, his peaked military cap pulled down low on his shaven head. 'Jesus! He looks a tough 'un, don't he. I'd not fancy meeting him in an entry of a dark night.'

Seeing him brought Tildy unhappy remembrance of her empty purse, and the money that she owed Mother Readman for rent and food, and to Ben Waring for milk and cheese.

'He owes me for a week's work,' she told her new friend. 'I'm going to see him about it now.'

When he saw Tildy crossing the lane to intercept him, Borth grinned cruelly. 'What's this then, Tildy Crawford? Be you wanting to come back to the gang?'

'No, Master Borth,' she answered civilly. 'What I'm wanting is to be paid for the week's work I did for you. I've debts to settle up, so when can I expect to get my wages, please?'

He came to a standstill, and with one hand lifted his cap and rubbed his scalp with affected puzzlement. 'Wages? What wages be they?'

Tildy refused to bite, and merely repeated levelly, 'You owe me for a week's work at the turnip singling, Master Borth, and I'd like to know when you intend to pay me for it?'

He replaced his cap, and now his eyes showed contemptuous dismissal. 'I owes you fuck-all. You left afore the work's bin done,' he hissed, 'so just get out of my path.'

Maddy, alarmed by his manner, tugged Tildy's sleeve. 'Come on, Tildy, let's go from here,' she urged anxiously, but Tildy stubbornly stood her ground.

'You owe me for a week's work, Master Borth, and I

need that money to pay my debts.'

The first of the straggling gang had now come up to them, and Borth snarled, 'Don't stand theer gawping, gerron off home wi' you.'

Obediently the women and children shuffled on a few more paces, but then slowed and stopped to turn and stare, while the oncoming gang members hastened their steps to find out what was happening.

Borth stepped towards Tildy and brought his head to within inches of her face, so that his stinking breath gusted into her nostrils.

'I'se told you once to clear my path, Crawford,' he warned, 'so do it right now, or be ready to pay the price.'

'No! It's you who must pay the price, Borth.' Tildy's fiery temper ignited, driving out all her fear of the man.

'You gobby cow!' he spat out, and raised his clenched fist as if to strike her.

She glared at him without flinching. 'Yes, go on, hit me,' she dared him, 'and I'll go straight to the constable and have you took up for assault.'

Momentarily disconcerted by her boldness, the man blustered, 'Does you really believe that the constable 'ud pay any heed to a bloody pauper slut like you?'

'But I'm not a parish pauper now, am I,' she countered fiercely. 'I'm a housekeeper to one of the biggest farmers in these two parishes now, arn't I? And if my master hears that you've been beating his housekeeper, then it'll be him that goes to the constable. And the constable will certain sure pay heed to Arthur Winterton, won't he, Borth?'

For long moments they stood glaring into each other's eyes. Then, suddenly the Overseer thrust his hand into his pocket and pulled out a half-crown coin. 'Here's your fucking wages, slut!' He threw it on to the ground and the heavy coin bounced and rang and rolled along the rutted surface. 'Now gerrout o' my way.' He swung his arm and struck Tildy on her shoulder, sending her stumbling sideways, then he strode on.

For a brief instant it seemed that Tildy was readying herself to spring on his back, but before she could move

Maddy grabbed her arm and hung on grimly.

'No Tildy! Leave it now! Leave it! You'll get the babby hurt.'

Remorse assailed Tildy as she suddenly realized that she had indeed risked Davy's safety, and her body sagged.

Maddy picked up the coin and then, dragging Tildy bodily with her, hurried on down the lane away from the staring gang. After a few score paces Tildy gasped out, 'Stop Maddy. I'll needs set down for a minute.'

The reaction to the clash had struck her and her hands were shaking uncontrollably, while her body was racked with a sudden nausea. She slumped down on a cottage garden wall and drew long shuddering breaths, her face white and clammy.

Maddy gazed at the seated girl with mingled admiration and concern. 'Jesus! But youm a proper spitfire, arn't you, Tildy,' she breathed in awed tones. 'Youm a really 'un, you am. A real bloody spitfire. I doon't know wheer you got the courage from to stand up to that bastard like you did.'

'Nor do I, Maddy,' Tildy smiled wanly, 'nor do I.'

'If looks could ha' killed, you'd have bin struck stone dead.' Maddy's plump rosy face mirrored her anxiety. 'You'se made a bad enemy theer, Tildy. You'll needs to watch your back when that bugger's about.'

By now Tildy was recovering fast, the colour returning to her cheeks and the trembling of her hands steadying. She got to her feet and checked that Davy was still sleeping soundly. 'I'm glad now that I gave him the syrup of poppies. He'd have been sore feared else.' She looked about her at the fast gathering darkness. 'Come Maddy, let's get on. I don't relish walking far in this.'

'Nor me neither, not wi' that loony on the prowl,' her friend agreed fervently.

They went on side by side, hands clasped to give each other support and comfort; and it was with a distinct sense of relief that Tildy saw the light shining from the kitchen windows of the farmhouse.

'Be you going to tell the master what happened between

you and the Overseer?' Maddy queried as they entered the farmyard, and Tildy shook her head in negation.

'I've learned long since that it's better to fight your own battles in this life, Maddy. People don't relish being involved in another's troubles.'

'Oh I 'udden't say that was the case all the time,' Maddy grinned knowingly. 'I should think meself that Master Toby 'ud like nothing better than to fight your battles for you. Judging from the way he was staring at you at suppertime.'

'Don't talk silly, Maddy,' Tildy admonished, thankful that the darkness hid the mounting flush of her throat and cheeks. 'Don't you say anything about what's happened either.'

'The other woman's grin widened. 'Alright, I wun't,' she promised, 'but I wish that Toby 'ud look at me like that. I'd bloody soon run to him wi' my troubles, and that's a fact.'

Tildy made no answer, but inwardly acknowledged that the temptation to do just that was assailing her more strongly than she liked.'No!' she told herself angrily. 'The last thing you need is to let yourself come to care for Tobias Winterton. You must travel alone, Tildy. You must travel alone.'

Only Susy, the dairymaid, was seated at the huge table when the two women came into the lamp-lit kitchen. 'Everybody's gone to their beds,' she informed them, and lifted one of the beer jugs in invitation. 'Come and have a sup o' this, and let's have a bit of a cank afore we sleeps.'

Tildy manoeuvred Davy into her arms, and seated herself opposite the other woman, thankful to rest for a while. 'I can't stay too long. I'd like to get him to his bed.'

'Bless him.' Susy regarded the sleeping child fondly. 'He's a real bonny bairn, Tildy. He'll make a real handsome cockerel afore too many years have passed, judging from the look of him.' She grinned tipsily, and Tildy realized that she was half-drunk. 'Was his dad a gyppo, Tildy, only he's got the bloody colouring for it, arn't he?'

The woman's good humour was such that Tildy could take no offence, even though to imply that a woman had slept with a gypsy man was tantamount to an insult in respectable circles.

'No. His Dad was a Christian. He comes from the Sidemoor in Bromsgrove parish.'

'Wheers he at now then?' Susy probed.

'He's in the prison hulks, as far as I know. Waiting for transportation.' Tildy kept her voice neutral.

'Fuck me, I'm sorry, Tildy.' Susy was instantly contrite. 'I meant no harm in asking.'

'You've done me no harm,' Tildy told her quietly. 'Me and Davy's dad never got on. Our marriage was a bad one, and he went off and left us both long afore he was taken to the hulks. I weep no tears for his loss.'

'Well that's alright then.' Susy smiled in relief. 'So long as it arn't grieving you, my duck, then that's probably the best place for him. What I always says meself, is that men be like rainstorms. Iffen you waits awhile then there's allus another 'un come along to get you wet in the night.' She winked, and chuckled lewdly. 'If you gets my meaning.'

Maddy took a swig of beer and stared down at the table, still covered with the remnants of the meal, then swore, 'Bollocks to it! We'll clane this lot in the morn. Cummon Tildy, we'll get up the wooden hill to Bedfordshire.' She grinned at Susy. 'Be you sleeping in our bed tonight, or has you got other plans?'

The slovenly young woman drank deeply from the beer jug, then shook her frowsty head drunkenly. 'I'll be sharing wi' you, my ducks. The old bastard's gone out on the piss agen, and I don't feel like having him trying to shove it up me all night, and not managing to get it in.' She saw Tildy's shocked expression, and laughed uproariously. 'I don't mind missing me sleep if I'm getting what's needful, Tildy, but I'm buggered if I likes to lose it for naught.'

A surge of foreboding filled Tildy's mind, and she suddenly had grave doubts as to whether she had acted wisely in coming here to live at this farmhouse.

Maddy Thomas recognized how her new-found friend was feeling, and tried to quell those doubts. 'Theer's no call for you to be worried about the menfolk here, my duck. On, some on 'um 'ull try it on wi' you, o' course. That's only natural, that is, especially when a man comes alongside a pretty wench like you be. But nobody here 'ull harm you, or your babby.'

Susy, although half-drunk, also recognized Tildy's concern, and she also tried to assuage those fears. 'Maddy's telling you the truth, Tildy. You'se got no call to worrit your yed about the men here. I sleeps wi' old Arthur sometimes, because it suits me to do so. But it's me own choice when I lets him have a bit.' She cackled with raucous laughter. 'Or at least, lets him try and have a bit. He arn't bin able to manage it for some time now, I'll tell you. I reckon that's why he's so bloody arsey these days.'

Again she erupted with laughter, and Tildy relaxed and laughed also, then turned to Maddy. 'Shall we get to bed then? I'm sorely tired.'

By the light of a candle the three women made their way along the cavernous passages and stairways of the rambling house. All the farm servants slept in the big lofts at the top of the building; the men in one large room, the women in another.

Tildy peered round her new living quarters, the flickering candlelight casting wavering shadows over the ancient black beams and roof timbers, and the cracked lime-washed wall plaster. There were two great beds with rough linen sheets and wool blankets and hard-looking bolsters for pillows. In one of the beds the two female field hands now snored in guttural concert. Tildy and her two companions were to share the second bed, and Davy would sleep beside her in its vast expanse.

'Jesus, I've never seen such a big bed,' she breathed in wonderment, and Maddy whispered, 'They do say it's as old as the house is, Tildy. I reckon wi' a bit of a squeeze you could sleep a dozen of our size in it.'

'The po's over theer if you needs it,' Susy indicated a big

wooden bucket in the corner of the room, 'but I'll needs use it fust.'

Without any modesty the dairymaid drew up her skirts and squatted over the bucket, urinating noisily into it. Her action caused Tildy no distaste. Natural bodily functions were often performed openly in her stratum of society, and although her own innate fastidiousness would not permit her to relieve herself in plain view of others, the fact that certain of those others might do so did not offend her.

Quickly they undressed, and naked climbed into the big bed. Tildy snuggled Davy close to her warmth, and tired out by her eventful day was asleep almost as soon as her head touched the hard bolster. Her two companions whispered desultorily, and then they also slept, and the only sounds were the snoring of the fieldhands and the creaks and groans of the ancient house settling itself for the night.

At four o'clock next morning with the sun barely risen, Tildy and Maddy rose from the bed, and after hurried ablutions in the scullery began their day's work.

The massive table was levered on to its side, sluiced and scrubbed, the food scraps thrown into the pig-bucket. The flagstone floor was mopped and dried, the fire which had been banked down the previous night resurrected, and the iron cauldron containing porridge suspended on its chains above the flames to heat. From one of the hanging flitches of bacon Tildy cut thick slices and put them to fry in a huge iron skillet, while Maddy portioned out bread, cheese, onions and small personal kegs of beer for the hands to take with them to the fields.

As the two women worked Maddy gave Tildy an account of what they were expected to do each day. 'We sees to the pigs and the poultry. Then once a week we washes all the linen and clothes. Any bits that needs mending we can do when and how we has to. We bakes three times a week, because old Arthur is most particular about his bread being fresh, he can't abide a stale loaf.

'Now theer's two on us agen, they'll expect us to help

out at other things whenever needful. Like we can give Susy a hand wi' the butter and cheese making. See, old Plum-face Joe is the cattleman by rights, but there arn't a lot he needs to do wi' 'um in the summer, so Susy puts 'um out to grass and brings 'um in for the milking, and she looks that they got sufficient watering in the meadows. On some farms I bin on, the dairymaid looks to the poultry and sees to the food and bedding o' the reapers at harvest-time, but we does things a bit different here.

'They arn't a bad bunch o' souls to work wi', taking 'um all round. Of course, we has our ups and downs, but that's only natural where'er you be, arn't it?'

By now the rich scents of the sizzling fat bacon were wafting through the house, and as if that were a reveille the rest of the farm servants began to come into the kitchen, frowsty headed and yawning, surly with sleepiness.

Only Tobias Winterton went into the scullery and dowsed his head and upper body beneath the pump there. None of the others washed themselves, and the smell of stale sweat hung heavy in the air, mingling with the scents of frying bacon, bubbling onion porridge, and apple wood burning in the range.

The young man stared keenly at Tildy as he took his seat at the table, and she was glad that she had washed herself and brushed her glossy hair, so that in comparison to the other females she looked fresh and clean.

Tildy lifted the iron cauldron of porridge from its hooked chain and placed it on the table. The hands ladled the greyish mess into their hollows and ate heartily, interspersing spoonfuls of porridge with bites from the thick wedges of bread and bacon that Tildy also served to them. To drink there were again jugs of cider and small-beer, and also a bowl full of whey milk for those who wanted either to drink it or mix it with their porridge.

Again Tildy found herself marvelling at the plentiful supply of food and drink, contrasting it with the short commons she had known as a worker in the needle mills of Redditch town.

As breakfast progressed Tobias issued his instructions

for the day's tasks. 'We've got the shearing gang coming this morn. You'll stay with them, Gilbert, like always, and have young Jem and Tommy wi' you until midday. I wants you to give them a bit o' practice wi' the shears.

'Sim and Edward, you take your teams up to the old glebe and finish that bit o' drilling off, then make a start on shifting the cabbages.

'The rest on you can keep on wi' the hay. You'd best let the old mare rest for the first yoking I think, Joseph – her warn't looking too grand yesterday. Use the new black 'un in her place. If the old 'un looks better later, then use her for the second yoking.

'If possible, I wants the main crop cut by tonight. I'll be joining you just as soon as I can get the shearers started, and we'll take extra hands from Borth's gang.

'Susy, try and finish sorting that batch o' chickens for the mart on Saturday, 'ull you. It might be a good idea to clear 'um all this weeks, rather than sell 'um in two lots.

'Now Tildy, has you ever rolled fleeces?'

She nodded. 'Yes, but it was years ago.'

'Well, I shouldn't think you'se forgot how to do it, has you?' He grinned, and she smiled back, her colour heightened as she saw from the corner of her eye Maddy's knowing smile.

'Right then,' Tobias instructed her, 'when the lads come over to the hay this afternoon, you can goo on the fleece-rolling. Come to the straw barn at noontime.

'Right then, that's it, let's be having you all.'

Obediently the hands rose from the table, collected their small kegs and provisions from Maddy, and went to their various duties.

Tobias lingered to tell the two women, 'You'll needs prepare some broth and potatoes for the shearers to ate at dinner and supper times. There'll be six on 'um. You can fetch it with you when you comes to the barn at noontime, Tildy. Meanwhiles, bring a keg of ale over in a couple o' minutes as well. Them Welshmen likes their drink whiles they'm grafting.'

As he sauntered away Tildy said to Maddy, 'He did say

Welshmen, didn't he? I think I know that gang.'

'Be there any pretty 'uns among 'um?' Maddy questioned, only half-jokingly. 'I'se never had a Welshman, but I've heard tell that they'm regular rams in the bed. I wouldn't mind trying one to find out the truth on it.'

Tildy chuckled as she mentally reviewed the rough, unkempt gang of men. 'Well, I wouldn't call any of them pretty, Maddy,' she informed her friend, then the memory of Oriel Evans' strong features came into her mind, bringing with it the flooding of gratitude for the debt she owed him. 'But I would say that they are proper men. Definitely proper men, alright . . .'

The big straw barn had been made ready for the shearing. The clipping-floor had been prepared between the two doors next to the chaff-house at one end of the building. Clean straw spread some three inches thick and the large canvas barn-sheet spread over the straw, its edges nailed to the floor, creating a soft platform for men and animals.

The rest of the barn floor and up to a yard height on the walls had also been swept, and fresh straw spread on which the sheep were now penned in by netting, waiting to be fetched to the clippers. Their bleating filled the air, sounding like distressed infants waiting to be fed.

The gang of Welshmen were already inside the barn when Tildy brought in the keg of ale, carrying its heavy load on her shoulders. As they saw her they voiced audible surprise and Oriel Evans left the gang and came to take the keg from her and place it on the floor. He straightened and held out his hand.

'Hello Mistress Tildy, it iss a surprise to find you here. But a very nice surprise for me.'

She smiled warmly at him, and took his proffered hand. 'I'm very pleased to see you also, Master Evans. I only came here to work yesterday myself. I'm helping in the house.'

His strong features radiated his pleasure at finding her once more. 'I've thought of you often, these last days, and wondered how the young gentleman wass getting on?'

'Oh he's quite well now, thanks to you. I've brought him with me to live here.'

'That iss very very good,' he observed gravely. 'The air iss clean and sweet here. He'll grow strong breathing it into his lungs.'

'Hey Taffy, if you'd be good enough to leave go of my housekeeper, we've still got things to sort out. So stop wasting my time, 'ull you.'

It was Tobias Winterton who shouted, and Tildy flushed as she realized that she was still clasping the Welshman's strong hand.

'. . . and you, Tildy, arn't you got any bloody work in the house to be getting on with?' The young man seemed unusually irritable, so Tildy merely nodded to Oriel Evans.

'I'd best be off, Master Evans. I'll see you later, we can talk some more then.'

As she left the barn she was conscious that two pairs of eyes were locked on her. Although not a vain or self-deluding woman, she was well aware of the fact that many men found her beautiful, and were quick to profess love for her. She had sensed the cause of Tobias Winterton's unusual irritability. 'He was jealous of my talking to Oriel Evans,' she thought. The knowledge imparted mixed reactions. A sense of gratification that such a handsome young man as Tobias should be so strongly attracted to her, – and after all, she also was strongly attracted to him – yet there was at the same time considerable disquiet that he should have so quickly developed such an apparent degree of possessiveness. Which was a hard thing for a woman to have to endure. She suddenly became impatient with herself. 'Stop this silly fancifying. You're worse than some mooning virgin maid. You should be ashamed to be thinking so daft.'

With that she tried to concentrate her mind on the mundane tasks which awaited her in the house, but still Tobias Winterton's irritable outburst echoed in her thoughts.

In the barn Tobias Winterton's eyes held hard glints as

he visually measured the Welshman. 'How did you come to know my servant, Taffy?'

Oriel Evans did not like the other man's tone, but for the sake of peace he decided to ignore the thinly-viled aggression. 'We stayed one night at the lodging house Mistress Tildy was living in. Her boy wass ill with the fever, and I helped to bring that fever out from him. That iss how I know her, there hass been nothing else between uss.'

Tobias nodded slowly. 'I'm glad to hear that.' He made a visible effort to speak civilly. 'Well then, Taffy, what do you think to 'um?' He indicated the penned sheep.

Oriel Evans leaned over the strung netting and with apparent ease took hold of and lifted out one of the beasts. After its initial struggles it stood quietly while his knowing fingers explored its fleece and flesh. After a while he replaced it in the penned area, then told Tobias Winterton, 'They'll be cross-breds, won't they. I should think Cotswold ewes with Leicester rams. Bit lacking in the forequarters are the Cotswold, but crossing with the Leicester improves that part of them. We should get six and a half to seven and a half pound weight o' fleece from them if that one is anything to go by.'

The younger man was impressed, despite his instinctive antipathy towards this big Welshman. 'You know your animals, Taffy. If you can shear them as quick and well, then I'll be more than suited.'

Oriel Evans grinned, and spoke to his gang in their own language; and one of them jerked his thumb at Tobias and said something which caused their laughter to erupt. Tobias' expression was uncertain, as if he was unsure of whether to take offence or not, and Oriel Evans quietened his men with a wave of his hand, then, still grinning told Tobias, 'Don't go thinking he wass making mock of you, Master. He wass not.'

Tobias was still hovering on the verges of aggression, and Oriel Evans was by now becoming ready to resent this. But, knowing that he and his men could earn good money here in the next two days, he smothered his own fast-burgeoning dislike of this arrogantly-acting young Englishman, and explained, 'I told them what you said about my knowing my business with the sheep, and he asked how could you ever doubt it, because it iss so well known by the *Saeson*, the English, that we Welshmen have connections with all sheep.'

'Connections?' Tobias repeated, uncomprehendingly, and the Welshman chuckled.

'Yes, connections . . . Carnal connections, Mr Englishman, like men have with women.' He again turned and spoke to the others in his own tongue, and again laughter greeted his words.

Tobias was rent by inner conflict. He was mortified with himself for giving way to the sudden attack of jealousy that had caused him to speak sharply to Tildy without any justification. 'I don't know what's come over me. I must be looking a real fool to her now, and to these Taffies.' He was honest enough with himself to admit that his antipathy towards this particular Welshman was rooted in his jealousy. 'It's bloody madness!' he castigated himself. 'I hardly know the woman, and yet I'm acting as if I was her husband, and she was a faithless wife. This man's done naught against me, and if he's speaking the truth only did a good turn to Tildy. I'd best start acting like a man, and not a bloody fool.' With this resolve he nodded at Oriel Evans and said quietly, 'Well I'd best leave you to get on with the clipping then, Master Evans. There'll be food brought out to you at noontime. I'd like the lads there,' he pointed towards Jem and Tommy, 'to try their hands at shearing as well. You can add whatever they manage to do to your own score.'

Oriel Evans had a shrewd idea what had caused the younger man's aggressive attitude, and now that Winterton seemed to be trying to make amends, he was ready to meet him halfway.

'Very well, young Master.Just one thing afore you go, who will be doing the rolling? I don't want to waste one of my own men on it.'

'The lads will do it between them until noon, then one

of the women will come over.'

'That's fair enough.' Oriel Evans was satisfied, and told his men, 'Come on then, boys, let's earn some money . . .'

When Tildy returned from the barn she found that Maddy had brought Anne Winterton and little Davy down into the kitchen. Both were seated at the great table, the hollows before them filled with steaming onion porridge, and Davy was prattling artlessly to the girl, who was sat staring at him with a bemused smile.

For a while Tildy stood in the doorway regarding the scene. She studied Anne Winterton intently, and drawing on her own previous experience of caring for insane people, instinctively judged the girl to be a gentle, harmless retard.

Davy was so engrossed with his new-found audience that it was some considerable time before he became aware of Tildy's presence. When he did so he crowed delightedly, 'Mammy! Mammy, come and see Annie. Come and see her. She's going to play with me. We're going to play, arn't we Annie.'

The girl's vacuous blue eyes displayed a puzzled pleasure, as though while she did not fully comprehend what the child was saying, nevertheless it pleased her.

'Hark to the little soul, bless him!' Maddy bustled in from the scullery, and beamed fondly at the child. 'O' course you an' Annie shall play together, my Honey,' she told him, and to Tildy said, 'It'll do the poor cratur a power o' good having your nipper here, Tildy. They'm both infants together. Though I'll swear she's not as bright as him, God help her.'

'I'm going to let Annie play with Sergeant Tom,' Davy informed his mother, referring to his wooden soldier. 'She'll like playing with him, won't you Annie?'

The girl's bemused smile touched Tildy's heart, and she experienced a deep pity for her. 'What a damned shame,' she murmured to Maddy. 'What a crying shame that she should be so afflicted.'

Maddy Thomas frowned and lowered her voice to a

conspiratorial whisper. 'It's more than a shame, it's a bloody judgement, Tildy. It's her bloody feyther's fault that her's like this.'

'How is it?' Such a statement quite naturally made Tildy anxious to hear more.

'Wellll, they do say . . .' Maddy's head went left to right, her eyes searching for any potential eavesdropper. 'They do say that her mother was real poorly, but Arthur Winterton 'udden't let her be, but must needs keep on forcing her to have connections wi' him. And then, when her was acarrying Annie, why then the old bugger served her so badly, and did such terrible things to her, as turned the babby in her womb into this poor benighted soul.' She nodded portentously, then fell silent, until Tildy, driven by curiosity, urged in her own conspiratorial whisper, 'What, Maddy? Tell me. What were the things he did to her Mam?'

Maddy sighed with vexation. 'I only wish I bloody well knew, my duck. It fair drives me mad, not knowing. But then, nobody else seems to know for sure what it was that happened. It's a secret that the family has kept to themselves. But folks do say that it was definite that it was Old Arthur's fault, the wicked old bastard!'

Sharp disappointment struck Tildy, and she felt somehow cheated that such an enthralling story had been so tantalizingly curtailed. But even as she was experiencing this, so simultaneously came the realization of how she was reacting, and she laughed at herself. 'By Christ, Maddy, I'm as bad as any old Goodbody Gossip, arn't I.'

Maddy chuckled richly. 'And me as well, my duck. And me as well.'

For most of the morning Tildy was baking bread. Filling the brick-lined baking-oven with faggots of wood, and when they had burned away, raking out the ashes and using a small wooden flat-bladed shovel to put the rounds of risen dough into the heated interior. While waiting for the bread to bake, she and Maddy performed the myriad of other tasks that needed doing. Tildy found that she was enjoying herself working with the other woman, and enjoying the work itself.

Maddy smiled at her at one point, and observed, 'I reckon you'll be happy here, wun't you, Tildy?'

'I hope so,' Tildy told her wistfully, 'because truth to tell, Maddy, I've found precious little of happiness so far in my life.' She made the statement without any sense of self-pity, but merely as a simple fact.

Women of Tildy's class were not brought up to regard happiness as an inalienable right due to them. They were taught from childhood to obey their betters and to expect little or nothing for themselves. To endure without complaint, and accept without resentment whatever was meted out to them by life, which was normally hard work, hard times, and hard treatment. But human nature being what it is, many covertly, and a minority overtly, rejected that teaching and expectation. Tildy was one of that minority.

The final batch of bread was brought out from the oven, and Tildy regarded the big golden-brown loaves with satisfaction as their warm fragrance filled the air.

'Youm a fine hand at the baking, Tildy,' Maddy praised, and Tildy glowed at the compliment.

The yard door was half open, and Tildy glanced through it, and drew in a sharp intake of breath as she saw the woman walking across the yard.

The newcomer was tiny and wiry-bodied, wearing a black gown and despite the warmth of the day a heavy black shawl around her thin shoulders. A wide-brimmed straw hat shielded her stringy grey hair from the sun, and her thin face was deeply-lined and brown with age and weather. She came up to the door and thrust it fully open with one claw-like hand. Her eyes were dark and bright like a bird's, and had a strange piercing quality.

Maddy turned from the hearth pots where the broth and potatoes for the midday meal were cooking, and cried out in shock, 'Why, it's Esther Smith! What brings you here, Esther?'

Tildy knew the old woman also, for at one time she had

gone to her seeking aid. Esther Smith was a witch-woman, considered by many to be the most deeply-versed and powerful practitioner of the occult arts in the entire district. There were other professed witches, wisewomen and cunning men in the area, but this tiny birdlike creature was the most feared and respected of them all, for popular belief had it that she was a black witch, able to cast the evil eye on those who offended her.

Despite this being the age of progress, superstitions and belief in magic forces still held away in the minds of millions, and even the most rational and educated of individuals could still be awed and intimidated by women such as Esther Smith when the sun had set and clouds scudded across dark skies, while the winds howled and dogs cowered, and strange unearthly cries echoed in black-shadowed wooods.

The witch-woman ignored Maddy's question. Her black piercing eyes looked on Tildy. 'I knows you, doon't I, young 'ooman. You come to me in your trouble, didn't you.'

Tildy nodded wordlessly, conflicting emotions battling within her as her memories came in vivid procession.

Isolated black fangs of teeth glistened in the almost lipless mouth. 'And I told you true, didn't I, young 'ooman. The grey horse brought an ending to your troubles, didn't it?'

Tildy's head nodded in reluctant acquiescence, as despite all her own wishes to be rational, she was forced to acknowledge the truth of the old woman's words.

The hag cackled briefly with satisfaction, and then her cunning eyes swung to Maddy. 'And you Maddy Thomas, you birthed a bastard, didn't you. You should have heeded me, girl. The powers warned you what 'ud happen if you opened your legs for that man, didn't they?'

Wide-eyed and pale-faced, Maddy nervously agreed, 'They did, Esther. They did.'

'Ahrrr, I knows they did so.' The skull-like head bobbed on the withered neck. 'They warned you he'd be carried away across the deep ocean, didn't they. But you wenches be all fools when you gets the itching for a man's loving. 'Tis no use whatever to lift the veils and tell you what's to be. You wun't heed it, 'ull you, but needs must goo gallivanting on to your ruination.' The clawed hands lifted and waved in dismissal. 'But then, that's the way things has allus bin, and that's the way things allus will be. You might as well wish for the moon, as wish for sense in the yed of a lovesick maid.' Her eyes went from one to the other of the two young faces, and again her harsh cackling laughter sounded. 'Theer's no call for you to fear my coming here this day, you daft besoms. I'm only looking for a bit o' bread and cheese.'

Both girls visibly relaxed, and despite her self-disgust at being so influenced by her own superstitions and fancies, Tildy could only ruefully accept that in matters of the occult, her emotions would always prove stronger than any logic.

Maddy hastened to fetch a hunk of cheese and to cut a thick chunk of bread. 'Do you want cider or beer to drink, Esther?' she invited.

'I'll take a sup o' beer.' The old woman seated herself at the table and sucked noisily from the pewter tankard as soon as Maddy filled it, then started to tear at the bread and cheese with her hooked fingers, chewing with difficulty because of her rotted teeth and smacking her lips loudly.

The clumping of heavy boots sounded from the staircase and approached along the passageway leading to the inner door, and Maddy grinned at Tildy and whispered, 'It'll be the Master, I'll be bound. He was drunk as a bob-owler last night, I'll bet, and he'll be as miserable as sin wi' it this morn. You wait and see.'

The towering bulk of Arthur Winterton filled the kitchen doorway and his bleared eyes glared into the room from beneath his thick bushy eyebrows. Heavily stubbled, wearing only shirt, breeches and boots, his shaggy hair uncombed and flying out wildly around his head, the stench of the previous night's ale, brandy and tobacco reeking on his breath, he was a fear-invoking spectacle.

He scowled at Esther Smith. 'What's this evil old bitch doing in my house, ateing my food and drinking my drink?' he growled hoarsely.

The old crone ignored him, and went on eating and drinking with every sign of relish.

Maddy Thomas gulped nervously, 'I thought it no harm to gi' the poor old cratur a bite and sup, Master.'

His eyes reddened, and without another word he walked up behind the old crone, plucked her from the bench by the scruff of her neck and the rear of her gown, and carried her bodily to the outer door. As if she were weightless he tossed her out into the yard. She hit the cobbles and rolled across the muck shrieking in pain and outrage.

Tildy's jaw dropped, she was so stunned by this casual display of brutality.

Winterton dusted the palms of his huge hands against each other, as if ridding them of dirt, and then, as if nothing untoward had occurred seated himself in his big armchair and ordered Tildy, 'Get me a jug o' cider, girl, and half a dozen eggs.'

For a moment or two she stood unmoving, and Maddy hissed in alarm, 'Do as the Master says, Tildy. For the love o' God, fetch the things.'

Still trying to come to terms with what she had just witnessed, Tildy fetched a jug of cider and six brown-shelled eggs and placed them before Winterton.

He did not look at her or acknowledge her service, only cracked the raw eggs and emptied the whites and yolks into the cider, then lifted the quart jug to his lips and gulped the mixture down in long swallows. Slamming the jug back onto the table, he belched loudly and rose to his feet.

From the yard outside the cracked voice of Esther Smith screeched, 'My curse is on you and yourn, Arthur Winterton! You'll rue what you done to me this morn. My curse upon you and yourn. You'll suffer for this, you bastard! You'll suffer! My curse upon this house and everything in it.'

The farmer's brutal features twisted in contempt, and he bellowed, 'Gerroff my land, Witch, afore I breaks your bleedin' back for you.'

Then, with another resounding belch he left the table and his boots clumped along the passage and up the stairs once more.

Tildy hurried through the outer door and into the yard, but Esther Smith had gone. Tildy ran to the yard entrance, looking down the track, but still could see no sign of the old woman. It was as if she had vanished into thin air. A shiver of fear chilled Tildy and she walked rapidly backwards and forwards along the track, her eyes searching high and low.

'She can't have gone from sight so quickly?' she wondered aloud. 'How can she have vanished like this?'

Maddy came running after her. 'Wheer is she, Tildy? Wheer's old Esther gone?'

Tildy shrugged helplessly. 'I don't know where she's gone, Maddy. She's just vanished.'

They exchanged looks of superstitious fear.

'Her really is a witch, arn't her, Tildy?' Maddy's rosy face had gone pale. 'No mortal 'ooman could ha' gone from sight like this. Oh God! What 'ull happen to us now?' Maddy moaned the last words, and instinctively crossed herself. 'Old Esther's put her curse on this place, arn't her. What 'ull befall us now?'

Tildy's own fear made her snap angrily at her friend. 'Don't talk so bloody silly, Maddy. Nothing can happen to us. It was just the old hag's temper, that's all. She's got no powers to lay curses on us.' She repeated the statement in a vain attempt to quell her own dread: 'She's got no powers of cursing, Maddy. She's just a mad old woman, that's all she is. A mad old woman.'

'Then if that's all her is, Tildy, tell me how has her managed to vanish like she had?' Maddy demanded to know, and Tildy could only sigh unhappily, and shake her own head. 'I don't know, Maddy. I just don't know.'

After a final brief fruitless search for the missing woman the two girls returned to the kitchen. The incident had affected Tildy more than she cared to admit, and she felt depressed and irritable. Maddy also was deeply worried by the curse and went about her work with a miserable frown on her normally smiling face.

An hour had passed when Arthur Winterton reappeared in the kitchen. Now he had shaved and was dressed to go out in his brown broadcloth coat with brass buttons, white cravat and buff waistcoat, leather gaiters above his boots and a black low-crowned top-hat on his head.

'I'll be back by seven o'the clock,' he told them, 'so have my meat cooked for then.'

Both women nodded silently, and he regarded them keenly for some seconds, then swore explosively, 'God-damn and blast you both for stupid fools! I knows whats ailing you. Youm believing that that filthy old bat is really a witch-woman, arn't you? Well let me tell you summat, you stupid cows, I care not a friar's fart for all the bloody so-called witch-women and cunning men in the fucking kingdom, and I cares even less for their soddin' charms and curses. So both on you get that fact planted in your yeds.' He went to walk away, then stopped and turned to them once more. 'And another thing. Don't you go telling any of the other bloody mawkins on this farm anything about what happened here wi' Esther Smith, or they'll be walking about wi' faces longer than a soddin' wet week, as well. Iffen either on you so much as whispers a single word about Esther Smith and her curses to anybody else, then I'll flay the bloody hides off you, and that arn't a bloody old hag's raving, my ladies, that's Arthur Winterton's solemn promise, that is. So don't be forgetting it.'

He slammed out of the house leaving two subdued young women behind him.

Their subdued mood did not last long however, and soon they were chatting and giggling together once more.

When noon came Maddy helped Tildy to carry the big iron pot of broth and potatoes and the fresh loaves of bread across to the straw barn.

The shearers were sweaty and grimy, and the greasy damp smell of clipped fleeces pervaded the barn. All the men had discarded their outer clothing and were working in shirt sleeves. Some stood and bent low to shear the sheep, others were on their knees, and Tildy stood marvelling at their dexterity as they positioned the animals in different ways to enable the big broad-bladed shears to strip the thick wool, leaving neat parallel ridges that created patterns on the shorn sheep that were pleasing to the eye in their uniformity.

A smooth plain deal door had been set on low trestles some three feet from the wall and near to the shearers, and here young Jem Winterton was rolling the fleeces, taking each fleece as it was separated from the sheep, lifting it carefully and unbroken from the shearing platform, then spreading it upon the board upon its clipped side with the neck end farthest from him.

Tildy moved to his side. 'Shall I take over now then, Jem?'

He grinned and nodded. 'If you likes, Tildy. I'm fair clemmed, so I am. That food smells good.'

'Then you'd best eat some of it.' Tildy smiled, and turned her attention to the spread fleece on the board before her. She examined it carefully yet rapidly, searching for whins, burrs, straws and thorns, and any lumps of dung which might have escaped the attention of the sheep washers. She pulled off whatever she found, then folded in both sides, putting the loose locks in the middle, and made the breadth of the folded fleece some twenty-four inches. She then rolled the fleece tightly and neatly from the tail towards the neck, and when she reached the neck put her knee upon the fleece to hold it while drawing out and twisting the neck wool with both hands to form a rope long enough to go around the roll. When she had sufficient length she passed the makeshift rope round the roll, winding it tight and making it fast, then laid the silver-lustred bundle with the other rolled fleeces on a canvas sheet laid between the table and the barn wall.

As the shearers finished off their animals, so Tildy took the fleeces and repeated the previous operation. Her hands quickly became greasy from the natural oils in the wool, and she knew that by the end of the day's work her skin would feel remarkably soft and supple.

As each shearer finished he joined his companions sitting around the iron pot of broth and potatoes, from which they ate communally. Soon only the boy, Tommy, was left working, trying to clip a fractious animal that continually struggled to break free and escape. The beast's hide was gashed and bleeding in several places from the boy's clumsy workmanship, and old Gilbert Tongue stood to one side berating the hapless youth, but making no attempt to aid him.

Oriel Evans would have risen to help the lad, but the old shepherd waved him back. 'No, leave the bugger do it himself, Taffy. He's got to learn.'

Again the animal cried out in pain and struggled furiously as the shears gashed its skin, and in wiping the sweat streaming down into his eyes the boy smeared the animal's blood across his face so that he resembled a head-shot casualty of war. He seemed near to tears as the old man cursed and cuffed him, and young Jem went to his friend's aid.

'Leave the bugger!' old Gilbert swore vilely 'The fucking numbskull arn't no more use than a fucking mawkin, God blast his fucking eyes!'

Jem ignored the man and laid hands on the sheep, which reared and bucked, and Jem cried out in pain as young Tommy accidentally jabbed the points of the shears deep into his friend's palm.

'Theer now, look what you'se done, you stupid, useless bastard!' The shepherd grabbed the boy's shirt collar and shook him violently, buffeting the blood-covered face with one horny hand, then took the shears from him, and with an expert ease secured the animal and finished clipping the fleece, and released the bleating beast to join its shorn fellows.

'Now gerroff away from me, you useless little bastard!' old Gilbert bawled furiously, and sent Tommy reeling with a kick on his buttocks.

Oriel Evans protested against this brutality, but the old man turned on him fiercely.

'You mind your own affairs, Taffy. this bugger's showed us up, so he has. Showed us up in front of a load o' bleedin' foreigners! If you judged us all by that sod, then you'd goo away thinking that we doon't know our business here.'

The Welshman laughed wryly. 'Yess, you have reason to be angry with him, old man. But then, did not all of uss have to learn to clip the hard way? I spilt many a pint of the poor beasts' blood, when I wass learning the shearing.'

Tommy went from the barn rubbing his injured buttocks with both hands, his face working as he tried to keep back the tears which threatened to spill from his eyes.

Tildy came and took Jem's hand. 'Let me see the damage, Jem.'

There were two deep punctures in the dirty greasy skin of his palm from which blood was oozing.

'You'd best come with me to the house, Jem, and I'll wash and bind your hand.'

Old Gilbert, still incensed, scoffed at her words. 'Gerrof wi' you, girl. He's had naught but a bloody pricking.' He lifted the shears. 'I'll grease these and put 'um away. Them pricks 'ull heal in no time at all, if I does that straight off.'

He went to where his box lay which contained his ointments and tinctures for treating his sick and injured sheep, and from it lifted a small wooden tumbler which was filled with an odorous dark-green ointment. He spread the ointment thickly on the blades of the shears, rubbing it well into the area of the points, then wrapped the shears in a scrap of dirty rag and placed them in the box.

'Theer, that's it,' he said satisfiedly. 'That'll settle them punctures. Now, let's be having a bit o' grub, shall us.'

The belief that by greasing the object which had caused a wound would cure that wound without any other intervention was widely accepted, and Tildy herself had seen it practised many times in her life. But still she persisted, 'It will still do no harm to let me wash and bind his hand, will it?'

The old man waved her away. 'Leave the lad have his bit o' grub in peace, 'ull you, girl. Youm fussing and farting around like a bloody old hen, so you am. Theer's no call for anything more to be done.' He appealed to the Welshman, ''Ull you tell this silly wench, Taffy?'

Oriel Evans regarded Tildy with an affectionate smile, and supported her. 'It would not do any harm to clean the lad's hand, I think.'

It was young Jem who settled the argument. 'I wants to ate summat, Tildy. I'm nigh on starvin' wi' hunger. And me and Tommy has to goo down to the hay field as soon as we'se ate, so I arn't got time to mess around wi' me hand. I'll wash it well when we'se finished for the day. That'll be time enough.'

Reluctantly Tildy accepted defeat, but with an uneasy forboding, even though she herself half-believed in the efficacy of the greasing of the shears.

'Alright then, Jem. I can't force you to come back to the house. But mind that you give your hand a real good washing just as soon as you can.'

'Alright Tildy, alright, now leave me be, 'ull you,' the youth told her impatiently, and applied himself to the food with a voracious greed.

While the men ate Tildy sat by Oriel Evans' side and listened while he talked to her of his life as a drover, and his home in Wales. She was content, knowing that Davy was playing happily in the farmhouse with Anne Winterton, and so was able to give her whole attention to the Welshman.

He had never married, he told her, but lived with his aged mother and four brothers on a tiny hill farm close to the town of Tregaron. '. . . Of course, it iss poor land, Tildy, not rich and fertile like here. Good only for the sheep really. We could not live by the farming alone. That iss why I follow the droving trade, and my brothers also. Two of them are in London at present, and the other two are at home with Mam. We never leave her alone there.'

'Did you never wish to marry?' she questioned, and his dark eyes were gentle and tinged with sadness.

'Oh yess. I wass in love once. But the girl's family moved away to the south to find work in the iron trade there, and she wanted to go with them. She wass very young, you see, and it wass a great adventure to her to move south. She thought that living with me on the farm would be too dull a life.'

'Could you not have gone south with her?' Tildy was curious about the girl, thinking her foolish to have spurned such a good and gentle man as this one appeared to be.

Oriel Evans shook his head and smiled sadly. 'Oh yess. I suppose if I had gone south, then in the end she would have married me. But I could not live my life in such a place. Around Merthyr Tydfil it iss like your English Black Country, all noise and smoke and flames and filth. I could not endure to live there. I like the peace of the mountains, and the clean rain and the pure air to breathe. You would like my land, I think, Tildy. Some strangers think it harsh and bleak, but when you learn to look clearly at it, then you can see that it iss very beautiful. We have produced many famous bards there since the ancient times, and their poems sing of its beauty, and the beauty of its daughters.'

He began to recite lines of a poem in his own tongue, and Tildy was enthralled by his melodious tones, and felt that she could listen without ever tiring of hearing.

'That is a poem by Dafydd Ap Gwilym.' He smiled. 'He was a great bard and he lies buried at a ruined abbey close to my home.'

'What does it mean in English?' Tildy wanted to know.

Oriel Evans shrugged. 'It iss difficult to give a true translation, Tildy.'

'Try,' she demanded.

Again he shrugged, then told her, 'Very well, but I shan't be able to do poor Dafydd justice.' He paused, frowning slightly in concentration, then intoned softly. 'Your forehead is like a lily, slender you stand as if under a web of gold! I have loved you a long time, and with all my strength. Oh Blessed Mary! How shall I be delivered?' He stopped and stared at her quizically. 'Well? How shall I be delivered, Tildy?'

Tildy understood the dual intent of his question, and to

her chagrin experienced the heat of a blush spreading upwards from her throat. Flustered, she jumped to her feet. 'I've an errand I must do before we start back to work,' she blurted, and hurried out from the barn. In one of the outhouses adjoining the building she hid herself, not fully understanding why she was behaving so, but obeying deep-rooted instincts. 'I'm acting like a booby,' she admitted, but still made no move to return to the barn until the sounds of shearing began again. Then she went back inside to the trestle table, avoiding Oriel Evans' questing eyes, and deliberately immersing herself in her work.

When she fetched a fleece from him she gave him no opportunity to detain her with him, but only nodded and turned away.

Then, when in his turn he ignored her, she perversely experienced pique that he should do so, then inwardly smiled at her own reaction. 'By the Christ, I grow sillier as I grow older,' she decided, and mentally shrugged. 'Still, I am what I am, and there's naught that can change me, and them that don't like me can always leave me alone . . .' She chuckled silently. 'But there's times that I wish they wouldn't . . .'

Chapter Nine

When Jem and young Tommy came to the hay meadow the mowing gang were still at their midday rest. Some dozing, others eating, drinking and talking.

Tobias was walking along the swathes of mown hay that had been left lying since the previous day, stooping low at intervals to feel the dryness of the cut grasses and clovers. Jem ran to join him and side by side the two brothers walked on.

'You and Tommy had better help the women to ted this lot, Jem,' Tobias instructed, and then noted the youth's crestfallen expression, and grinned. 'Alright then, boy, you'd better come scything with me, and let Tommy help the women by himself.'

Jem's face brightened and he nodded in eager assent.

Tobias regarded him fondly and reached out a hand to ruffle the youth's thick hair. 'Youm near a man in years now, Jem, so it's only fitting that you should be doing men's work.' He stopped and stared out over the wide expanse that still remained to be mowed. 'The grass is thinner up by the top end theer, Jem, so I reckon that with six of us on the scythes we should manage another four acres afore nightfall.'

'I'd best run back and get my scythe, Toby,' the youth said, and Tobias winked at him.

'There's no need. I brought one along for you.' He noted the piece of dirty rag wrapped around his brother's hand. 'What's you done there?'

'Tommy jabbed me with the shears,' Jem told him. 'It was an accident, and me own fault really.'

'Well make sure you doon't jab yourself with the scythe then, my bucko. That'll make too big a hole to wrap wi' a bit of rag.'

They lapsed into silences for a few paces, then Tobias asked with a forced diffidence, 'Who was it come to take the rolling from you?'

'The new wench, Tildy.' Jem grinned mischievously. 'Why does you ask, our Toby? Has you taken a fancy for her? She's really pretty, arn't her.'

Embarrassed by his brother's teasing, Tobias only mumbled gruffly, 'Pretty is as pretty does. All I'm interested in her for is to see that she does her work well. That's all.' He shielded his eyes with his hand and glanced up at the glaring sun. 'Well, they'se had a good hour or more to rest. We'll get 'um moving again.'

Made sluggish by food, drink and heat the workforce took up their tools and made ready to resume their gruelling labours.

Counting himself and Jem, Tobias now had six scythe-men and he divided them into three pairs, each pair taking a different adjoining strip of land. Before starting to reap each man resharpened his scythe blade, using the long rounded whetstones they carried in pouches slung in the small of their backs. Setting the points of the long curved blades upon the earth and holding them upright with their left hands while whetstones in right hands they worked downwards from snaith to point, alternating from side to side of the cutting edge with each stroke of the stone.

'Tommy, you take the women and start tedding that lot,' Tobias ordered, indicating the fallen swathes.

Chivvied on by the boy, the women took their wooden-toothed rakes and forks and began to toss and thin out and turn the fallen hay, so that sun and air could reach every part of it.

The scythemen took up positions at staggered intervals and advanced steadily, swinging their scythes from right to left, blades horizontal to the ground, the ripe grasses and clovers tumbling to lie in neat swathes at the left-hand sides of the reapers, their juices spurting invisibly to flood the air with rich, fecund fragrance.

Tobias loved reaping the hay, becoming half-intoxicated with sun and scents and the sensation of his body's absolute mastery of the scythe. His energy seemed to increase as the work progressed, and he moved faster and faster across the broad acres until he left his fellows trailing far behind him.

Above his head larks sang, and nearer the earth winged insects hummed and bumbled through the waving seas of soft-bladed, woolly-headed vernal grass. Mental pictures of Tildy Crawford came into his mind, and despite his efforts to be rid of their disturbing influence, persisted and strengthened until he surrendered to their dominance and let his imagination run riot picturing himself entwined with her in love's embrace.

'I want her,' he admitted. 'Dear God above, how much I want her.'

Ahead of him the white scuts of bolting rabbits flickered through the verdant mass, and once his keen nose detected the rank, harsh reek of a polecat. Briefly he glanced around him, staring out across the broad acres that were his heritage, and bitterness came to sour his mood.

'This should all belong to me some day. This should be mine, and mine alone. But with that drunken, useless hound for feyther, I'll not inherit any of it. He'll gamble it all away.'

He reached the highest point of the field, and slowed and stopped, then up-ended his scythe to sharpen its cutting edge. As the whetstone rasped ringingly against the steel Tobias stared down across the land towards the farmstead, and saw a horseman trotting up the approach lane towards the buildings. Despite the distance his keen eyes recognized the tall figure of his father, and could detect that Arthur Winterton was swaying erratically in the saddle. His lips twisted in disgust.

'He's drunk again. The old bastard is drunk at this hour of the day. Is it any wonder that we're heading towards ruination? No matter how hard I labour, that drunken pig will drag us all down with him.' He wiped the sweat from his brows with the back of his hand. 'I wish to God the horse would buck him off and break his bloody neck for him. It's what I'd like to do myself, break his bloody neck!'

The young man dragged breath sharply as he suddenly realized that that was what he was truly wishing for: his father's death. And with that realization came the inevitable acknowledgement: 'I'd kill him myself, if I thought that I could get away with it.' Momentarily he quailed at the enormity of the sin. 'It's truly evil even to think of such a thing,' he told himself, yet still the notion exercised an ever increasing attraction for him. 'If he were dead then all this would be mine. I could care for Jem and Annie and make their lives happy . . . And I could take a wife for myself, and raise children of my own. I'd be happy myself then, I know I would. I'd not want to leave here then. Not if I had the land, and a wife . . . a wife like Tildy Crawford . . .'

The hunger to see her came upon him, and for a moment he was tempted to cast aside his scythe and go to the barn where he knew she was working. He battled against that temptation. 'You bloody fool,' he jeered at himself. 'Youm fair besotted wi' that wench, arn't you?' He forced himself to continue reaping, but now, instead of pleasure the work had become an onerous imposition which kept him from where he wished to be, at the side of Tildy Crawford.

Mentally he was beset by a dichotomy, one part of his mind confessing his yearning for the young woman, the other half arguing furiously against that yearning.

'She's a married woman wi' another man's child at her side. Married to a bloody jailbird at that. You knows naught about her character really, does you?'

'I know that she's decent and honest and clean-living, that's plain to see . . .'

'Youm blinded by a stupid passion for her. She's a pauper, a bloody slumrat!'

'That's no fault of hers, being poor.'

'How do you know it's not? You knows nothing about her except that she's beautiful to look at, and has a pleasing way with her. She could be a hedge-whore for all you knows of her . . .'

'No! She's no whore. That's obvious . . .'

'Why so? Why so, is it obvious?'

'Alright then, I'll find out about her. I'll ride into Redditch this very night, and I'll find out about her.'

With that decision made Tobias was able to quell the clamorous thoughts and give his attention once more to the work before him . . .

Chapter Ten

Two final snips of the shears and the fleece fell free. Oriel Evans released the ewe and straightened, grimacing at the ache of strained spinal muscles. The netting fold was empty and around him his friends were finishing off their final animals of the day.

Against the wall the silvery rolled fleeces rose high and spread to fill up the intervening space up to the trestle board. The Welshman watched Tildy Crawford as she tied another fleeces and found her very beautiful, with her cheeks flushed from exertion, and the tendrils of dark glossy hair falling about her face as she deftly knotted the drawn-out strands of wool and then moved to lay the tied fleece atop the others.

He took up the fleece at his feet and went with it to the table-board. Tildy took it from him without speaking and began to check it for any remaining burrs or lumps of dirt.

He smiled at her. 'I'm glad to be done for the day. It iss hard work, the shearing, no matter how used to it a man may be.'

She answered without looking at him, 'I wish I was done for the day myself, Oriel. But after this I must go to the house and help Maddy with the chores.' There was no note of complaint in her voice, merely a factual statement.

'There's a pity. I wass hoping that you might care to walk down to the alehouse with me and take a glass of something.' The Welshman sounded truly regretful.

Tildy looked searchingly at him. She was very strongly attracted to this man, and admitted to herself that the prospect of spending time in his company did appeal to her. With some regret she told him, 'I doubt that I'll have any time to go to the alehouse with you, Oriel, but mayhap we could share a glass before you leave this place. When do you think that you'll be finished with the shearing?'

'By tomorrow night.'

'And then you'll go from this parish?' To her own amazement Tildy felt a distinct sense of loss as she considered that prospect.

His expression was solemn. 'Well, it iss not for me only to decide that, Tildy. My friends may want to go.'

'And you will go with them if they so decide?'

He shook his head. 'No, Tildy. I shall go with them if I decide.' He paused for a moment, then went on, 'I will speak frankly to you, girl. Before I met you I would have followed the wishes of my friends. We always take a show of hands if we are not sure as to our next movements, and what the majority wishes, then that is what we do. But now, now I have met you, then if my friends decide to move on, I am not certain if I shall go with them. That will depend on you.'

'On me?' Her colour heightened.

He smiled, and nodded. 'Yess, on you. I think I am falling in love with you, girl.'

Embarrassed, she gestured in protest. 'That is a nonsense, Oriel. You hardly know me. And anyway, it is not right that you should entertain any such feelings towards me. I am a married woman.'

It was his turn to make a gesture of protest. 'How can you believe yourself to still be married, Tildy, when you have been separated for so long from your husband, and you will never see him again in this life?'

'Whether I see him again or not doesn't signify. I am still married to him.'

He regarded her shrewdly, then said quietly, 'You use that as a shield, Tildy. A shield to hide behind because you are afraid to share your life with a man.'

'No Oriel,' she told him with absolute certainty throbbing in her voice. 'I am not afraid to share my life with a man. But I am afraid to make a mistake in choosing that man. I know that we do not have any right to expect a deal of happiness in this life. But I do believe that we have the right to try and avoid misery.'

'How can the love of a good man bring you misery, Tildy?'

'The love of a good man would not bring me misery, but if I did not return his love, then would that fact not bring him misery?' she riposted.

'Not necessarily,' the Welshman argued. 'Mayhap his love would be so strong that eventually you would come to love him equally in return. His love would awaken a corresponding love in your own heart for him.'

Another man came to the table with a fleece, and Tildy was grateful for the chance to break off the conversation. Oriel Evans was perceptive enough to leave matters where they lay for the time being and said to Tildy, 'We'll talk some more tomorrow.' He left her to finish her work.

As she tied the last few fleeces Tildy thought on what the Welshman had said to her. 'Do I really use my unhappy marriage as a shield? And if I do, then is that a bad thing after all? It's my own life, to do with what I choose. No man has the right to expect me to love him, just because he fancies that he loves me.' The memories of past and present loneliness came bleakly upon her and she sighed heavily. 'God knows, but I would give a great deal to meet some man that would truly love and cherish me, and be such a man that I could love and cherish in return. But how can that ever be, when I am already married in God's house to Tom Crawford?' Despite her fiery spirit, and her high intelligence Tildy was a child of her times and in the bottom of her heart believed in a wrathful, all-seeing Deity, even though at times when her temper was high she challenged that Deity, and defied Him. She was also of a moral nature. Apart from her forced sexual congresses with her husband she had only ever slept with men on two other occasions, and on both those occasions she had cared greatly for the man, and had known that he loved her in return. But she had suffered torments of guilt after making love with them, and knew that until the death of her husband released her from her marriage vows, then she would continue to feel that guilt no matter how much she might love and want any future sexual partner. She was hot-blooded, and had strong sexual needs, but for her own self-respect she smothered those needs and when driven beyond endurance attempted to assuage her hungers herself in the loneliness of her bed.

The last fleece was tied and stored with the others and with a heartfelt sigh of relief Tildy took off her sack-apron and made her way back to the kitchen.

This evening the Welshmen were ranged around the great table and Maddy, her rosy face glowing hotly, bustled about to bring the men their food and drink, admonishing them as she did so. 'Come now lads, ate up quick because the servants 'ull be back in shortly wanting their own grub.'

As she leaned over the table to place the iron pot of stew in its centre the rounded tops of her full breasts strained against the low neckline of her bodice and the men stared hungrily at the plump whiteness and muttered to each other. When she went to move away the man nearest to her reached out and fondled her buttocks, then tried to pull her down beside him.

'You cheeky sod!' Maddy flared and slapped him resoundingly across his hairy cheek. A roar of laughter went up from his companions and grinning himself, he rubbed his smarting cheek and released his grip, while saying something to her in his own tongue.

'What's you asaying, you cheeky bugger?' Maddy demanded angrily.

'He iss telling you that he meant no insult, and that in his country the girls would be highly complimented by what he did,' Oriel Evans explained laughingly.

'Well, you tell him from me, that in my country the girls regards what he did as a bleedin' liberty. And you can tell him as well and the rest o' these sods, that in future they'm to keep their hands to themselves. I'm a respectable girl, I am. If they wants a bit o' easy meat, well then there's plenty o' that sort to be found in Redditch.' She tossed her head scornfully, and her floppy mob-cap threatened to fall off. 'Mind you, it doon't pay foreigners like you lot to try taking any liberties up in Redditch theer. The bloody Pointer lads 'ull bloody soon sort you lot out if you should happen to try it on wi' the wrong wench, and that's no lie.'

She came out into the scullery where Tildy was washing her arms, neck and face.

'Theer, that's told them bloody foreigners what I reckons to 'um. To spake the truth, Tildy, I can't abear any bloody foreigners, and I doon't think it right that any of 'um should be let come into this country at all. I mean to say, just look at that bloody lot in theer.' She jerked her thumb over her shoulder in the direction of the kitchen. 'They comes here spakin' their heathen language that no Christian can understand and they 'udden't think twice about raping us all in our beds if we'd a mind to let 'um.' As she spoke her indignation fuelled upon itself and her large breasts rose and fell with such force that they threatened to spill from her bodice.

Tildy dried herself on a strip of rough towelling, and made no reply.

Maddy pressured her friend. 'Well? What does you reckon to 'um, Tildy?'

Tildy smiled wryly. 'If you must know, Maddy, I think that there are good and bad people to be found in every nation. And truth to tell I can only ever feel grateful towards Oriel Evans for what he did for Davy.'

Tildy hung the towel up to dry and then asked, 'Where's my Davy? Is he sleeping?'

Maddy smiled fondly. 'He's bin sleeping these last two hours, him and Annie both. I'se put 'um both in Annie's bed.' She chuckled at Tildy's expression of mingled surprise and doubt. 'Now don't be worrying your yed about 'um sleeping in the same bed, my duck. They'm two infants together, and I couldn't have prised 'um apart wi' a crowbar. Why, you'd think they was blood-kin the way they bin wi' each other this day. You goo up and take a look at 'um and then see if you wants to part 'um.'

Tildy went through the kitchen aware of Oriel Evans'

questing look but deliberately keeping her head averted from him. In Annie's small room three heads were ranged upon the pillows: the girl's, Davy's and the fiercely mustachioed Sergeant Tom's. A smile curved Tildy's full lips and her heart welled with love for her sleeping child, lying so peacefully, breathing gently, his left arm on top of the counterpane, hand clasping the hand of the idiot girl. Quietly she moved to the head of the bed and with an infinite gentleness pressed a kiss upon her child's forehead.

At the door she turned for a last lingering look, her thoughts tinged with a faint sadness. 'Is this the only playmate I can find for you, Davy, this idiot girl?' Even as she gave utterance to this her mind recognized the injustice. 'Idiot she might be, but there's no harm in her. The poor benighted soul hasn't got a bad bone in her body. Davy could have a lot worse choice of playmate than her.'

By the time she returned downstairs the Welshmen had already wolfed their food and were crowding into the scullery to wash their hands and faces in preparation for their nightly visit to the alehouses in the surrounding villages. Maddy, still smarting from the advances made to her, was baiting them.

'Off on the drink now, are you, my bold buckos. I'll lay odds that you wun't be gooing up into Redditch for your fun though, 'ull you. The Pointer Lads am a bit too handy wi' their fists for you lot to risk drinking in their company, arn't they. No, the Pointer Lads arn't over-fond of any bloody foreigners coming into their pubs and thinking they can rule the roost.'

One or two of the Welshmen who could understand the English tongue better than their friends appeared to be ready to resent this human gadfly, but a few quiet words from Oriel Evans prevented any verbal retaliation, much to Maddy's annoyance.

Tildy started to clear away the remnants left by the Welshmen on the great table, and to wash out those hollows they had taken their food from. Oriel Evans was still sitting at the table, and he watched her working, but said nothing.

Perversely, Tildy felt constrained to speak to him because of that silence. 'Was your food alright?'

'Yess, it wass very good, I thank you,' he answered briefly and again fell silent.

She finished her task and took the collected scraps of food outside to throw them into the large wooden barrel which was kept in the yard for the pig-swill. Twilight had fallen and Tildy could hear the sounds of voices coming up the lane towards the farmstead. She waited to see who was approaching and within a few moments the burly figure of Jeremiah Borth appeared. He grinned bluffly when he saw her.

'Well now, if it arn't the lovely Mrs Crawford awaiting to welcome me. Is the young master around?'

'No, he's not here,' she told him, and would have returned into the kitchen, but he lifted a hand and beckoned her.

'Doon't run away from me, my duck. I want's a word wi' you.'

'Well I've no wish to talk with you, Master Borth,' she answered coolly.

Now the leading members of the gang were following into the farmyard and taking their stations before the door of the toolshed. Borth turned and shouted at them, 'Just wait quiet until I comes.' Then spoke again to Tildy, 'I shouldn't be too hasty in buggering me off, my wench. Because you never knows when you might need my friendship.'

Tildy's first impulse was to leave him, but some instinct made her ask, 'What makes you think I would ever need your friendship, Master Borth?'

He winked at her. 'Well now, that 'ud be telling, 'udden't it. And if I was to tell you all I knows, why then, you'd be as wise as me, 'udden't you, and that 'udden't serve at all.' He grinned and winked again. 'No, Tildy Crawford, all I'll say is that it might pay you to spake civil to me, because you never knows when you might be needing to come and work wi' the gang agen.'

Again her first impulse was to walk away from him, but

still some instinct prevented her from doing this. Instead she said civilly enough, 'I don't think I'll be needing to work with the gangs again, Master Borth. I'm well suited here.'

'Ohhh I arn't doubting that fact, Tildy. And I'm sure that Master Winterton is happy wi' your work. I'll allow you that, my wench, you was always a good worker. Nooo . . .' He shook his head. 'No, it'll be no fault o' yourn if you should find yourself out of work agen. But,' once more the grin and the wink, 'I'se heard a bit of interesting news, girl. So, like I said afore, you might find it to be in your best interests to let bygones be bygones between you and me. I'll always give you work wi' me, Tildy, when it becomes necessary for you to ask.'

He seemed about to say something more, but noticed from the corner of his eye the arrival of Tobias Winterton in the yard, and with a final wink at Tildy sauntered off.

Tildy stood for a moment or two, staring blankly down into the greasy mess of the wooden barrel, puzzling about the import of what the man had said. Then she became aware of Tobias Winterton at her side.

'What are you doing, Tildy, searching for gold? I doubt you'll find any in this lot.'

She smiled at him, and dismissed the vague premonitions that Borth had implanted in her mind. She looked at the young man's sun-bronzed face and fair sun-bleached hair with a distinct feeling of pleasure. 'By the Christ, you really are a handsome devil,' she silently acknowledged. 'You could turn the head of any woman if you'd a mind to . . . including mine.' She smiled inwardly, then said aloud, 'No, it's not gold I'm looking for. Are you ready to eat now?'

'In a little while. I want to check the tools in first'. With that he left her and went to join Borth at the shed door.

The farm servants now started to arrive, and Tildy hurried back into the house to make ready for them.

The gang of Welshmen left as the newcomers came into the kitchen, but Oriel Evans remained behind, seated on one of the inglenook benches, a short-stemmed clay pipe clenched in his strong teeth from which clouds of rank-smelling smoke belched at intervals.

Weary from their gruelling labours, their hands and arms stained with the juices of the hay, their clothing impregnated with its heady smells, the labourers ate their food and drank their drink, exchanging few words.

Arthur Winterton was absent from the table, and Tobias asked, 'Has anyone seen my Dad?'

'He went out this morn, then come back just arter the noontime, then went out agen,' Maddy informed him. 'He told me earlier to have his meat cooked for seven o' the clock, but he ne'er come back for it.'

Tobias frowned unhappily, but made no reply.

Once they had eaten, most of those present left the lamp-lit kitchen and went to their beds, knowing that they would be rising before dawn to recommence work. Tobias joined Oriel Evans in the inglenook, taking the bench opposite the Welshman. He also filled and lit a pipe of tobacco, and for a time, while Tildy and Maddy cleared and cleaned the table the two men sat in a companiable enough silence puffing out clouds of blue-grey smoke.

Surreptitiously Tobias watched the Welshman, and noted how his eyes followed her every movement. Despite his resolution of the morning the young man could not restrain his jealousy, but struggled not to display it openly. But his resolve was sorely tested whenever Tildy exchanged a smile or a brief word with the Welshman. Shamed by what he considered to be his weakness, Tobias tried to be pleasant to the other man.

'Old Gilbert tells me that you and your men are fine shearers, Master Evans.'

The other man's dark eyes held a gleam of gratification as he nodded in acceptance of the compliment. 'I'm happy to hear that the old man approves of our work. He himself iss a very fine shearer. Even at hiss age he iss still faster than any of uss.'

Tobias leaned forward to gently tap the ashes from the bowl of his pipe into the grate, then rose to his feet.

'Tildy?' he called, and she poked her tousled head

around the door jamb of the scullery where she and Maddy were washing the pots and pans. 'I've got to go on an errand. Don't you or Maddy bother to wait up for my Dad. I doubt that he'll need any food when he comes in.'

She smiled and nodded, and bidding the Welshman goodnight, Tobias went out into the yard and crossed to the stables. Even in the darkness it needed only a few minutes for him to saddle his horse and lead it out into the yard. There he mounted and trotted away down the lane. The moon was high and large and cast a good light across the land. Tobias was able to cover the ground at a fast canter towards Redditch, and in a comparatively brief time he had reached the outlying houses of that town and was riding up the sloping Beoley Lane towards its centre.

The two women finished their chores and came back into the kitchen to find that Oriel Evans had also gone from the room. Tildy was disappointed; she had hoped to talk some more with the man, and perhaps to persuade him to tell her of the cities he had visited, and the people he had known. Tildy hungered for knowledge and was bitterly conscious of her own ignorance, even though in comparison to most other women of her class she was able to read and write with an equal facility.

Lighting a stub of candle from the fire she and Maddy made their way to their bedroom. Susy the dairymaid and the two fieldhands wee already snoring and Maddy giggled.

'Hark to the nightingales, Tildy. They sings a fine lullaby, doon't they?'

'Don't they just,' Tildy agreed sarcastically.

Maddy was soon snoring too, but Tildy could not sleep, try though she might to relax and settle for the night. The moon shafting through the small windows created patterns of light and shadow across the cracked plaster of the walls and those patterns constantly shifted and changed as straying clouds drifted across the moon. For what seemed to her to be interminable stretches of time Tildy tossed and turned restlessly and then, with an exclamation of self-irritation, she rose from the bed and went to stare out of the window. The countryside was an enchanted land beneath the moonlight, its woods mysterious, its meadows fairy playgrounds. On impulse Tildy pulled her gown over her head, slipped her feet into her clogs and went from the room, down the stairs and out from the house. The night air was cool and sweet to breathe and Tildy drank deeply of it as she wandered in the direction of the hayfields. The fragrance of the new-mown hay enveloped her as her feet swept through the fallen swathes, and to her moon-induced fancies the rows of haycocks were sentinels guarding the fallen grasses. She halted and let her gaze wander along the rows travelling upwards to the highest point of the field.

Although there was not even the suggestion of a breeze, it seemed to her that the land was pullulating with a myriad of life forms. Life forms which she could not see, but were made tangible by the rustlings and shiftings and whisperings that pervaded the air.

'There could be goblins and elves and fairies all around me,' she thought with a half-smile, 'Watching me. Wondering if I am also a creature like them.' Delighted by this notion, she raised her arms and extended them wide in silent invitation, and slowly spun around and around as if dancing to a melody.

'If you are here, you creatures of the night, then show yourselves,' she whispered. 'Show yourselves to me, for I'll not harm you. Please, show yourselves to me.' Intoxicated by the magic of the night she closed her eyes and danced on through the haycocks, her feet moving with an uncanny sureness between the mounds and across the rutted ground. 'Come to me, you fairy people. Show yourselves to me. Come to me.'

Her feet slowed and with a final turn she came to a standstill, her lips smiling, her heart singing within her, and opened her eyes.

The black figure erupted from the ground before her, and Tildy screamed in terror.

'Don't be feared! Don't be feared, Tildy, it's me! Oriel.

Oriel Evans. Don't be feared.'

Relief coursed through her, to be followed immediately by quick anger. 'Why did you do that? Why did you jump out at me so? You could have killed me with the shock of it,' she demanded heatedly.

'I didn't jump out at you,' he replied indignantly, 'and as for giving people shocks, how do you think I felt? Sitting quietly up here, minding my own business, and then next thing some dancing dervish comes spinning down on me. No wonder I jumped up. I thought you were the *Bwgan Drwg*, the evil goblin!'

'But you must have heard or seen me?' she accused.

'No, Tildy, I wass dreaming. A herd of cattle could have been running across the field for all I would have known, I wass so far away in mind.'

By now the worst effects of the shock had lessened, and she was rapidly becoming calmer. She laughed jerkily. 'By the Christ, Oriel, you really scared me. I thought I was going to faint clean away.'

Genuine regret was in his eyes and tone. 'I'm truly sorry, Tildy. The last thing in thiss world that I would want iss to cause you any distress.' He bent over and lifted his wide-brimmed hat from the ground, then straightened and stared keenly at her. 'Are you alright now, *cariad?* Have you forgiven me?'

She smiled at him, and teased, 'I'm considering it.'

In the silver light she was unbearably beautiful to his eyes, and driven by an irresistible compulsion he reached out, drew her to him and pressed his lips on hers.

Taken by surprise, Tildy's first impulse was to push him away and her hands went against his broad shoulders, but the feel of the hard muscles beneath the rough cloth of his jacket, and the taste and pressure of his mouth and body against her own brought all her long-suppressed needs surging upwards from their depths. Her fingers closed into tight fists, then opened and searched and clung. Her arms moved of their own volition to enfold his shoulders and from deep within her throat there sounded a soft moan of hungry desire.

Now his hands moved upon her body, firm yet gentle, caressing her hips. He sank down upon the heaped hay, drawing her with him, and she came unresisting. Her desire was by now an aching void, an unbearable wanting, and she lay still while he drew the clothes from her body and cast his own aside. His body was a glowing paleness, his muscles etched in sharp relief and as he came down upon her nakedness and she felt the heat of him upon her, she gasped with delight and her hands went to his taut buttocks and her fingers dug deep into the hard roundness as she strained against him. His maleness throbbed against the soft skin of her belly, and his mouth sought her erect nipples in turn, sucking, kissing, tongueing, then moved down lower and lower, and she felt the moistness of his lips upon the insides of her thighs and a shiver of exquisite pleasure ran through her as that moistness mingled with the moistness of her intimate body. He took her hand and guided it to his maleness and she welcomed its hard pulsing length and, driven beyond any semblance of control, took it within her, panting as he drove deeper and deeper inside her and raising her hips to thrust against his thrusts. Their breathing became a gasping, shuddering as their desire mounted higher and higher and higher and their bodies pounded together and strained to merge closer and closer, to achieve a complete union, to become one flesh. Tildy existed in a timeless ecstasy that drove all else from her consciousness, an ecstacy that heightened until it dragged from her a long drawn cry and a shattering climax of physical delight beneath the impact of which she half swooned and as the man cried out in his own climax and collapsed upon her, so she also fell back and lay drained and satiated beneath him.

'Oh *cariad, cariad,*' he panted over and over again. 'You're mine now, my *cariad.* You're mine. You're mine.

The words he spoke made no actual impression upon Tildy's mind at that moment. The physical reactions to their lovemaking still held her in thrall, the sheer relief and bodily contentment engendered by the satisfaction and assuagement of her long-repressed bodily needs filled her consciousness, and she was happy to lie beneath him, to feel his maleness still within her, to feel the silken smoothness of his skin under her trailing fingers.

'We'll go back to my country, *cariad.* Little Davy will be able to grow tall and strong there. To live as a free man should live. I'll make a drover of him. He can travel with me, and when we come back home to you, then I'll be able to teach him the ways of the mountains. We'll be happy there, you will see, *cariad.* We'll be happy.'

Now the import of his words began to penetrate Tildy's love-drugged senses, and her first reaction was a sense of alarm. 'What is it you're saying?' she questioned, and slipped out from beneath him to lie on her side facing him. 'What are you saying?'

He smiled happily at her, his face youthful in the moonlight. 'I'm saying that you are now my wife, Tildy.' He saw the instant doubt in her expression, and hastened to add, 'Oh I know that you are not my wife in chapel or church, but in my heart you are. And I don't give a damn for chapel or church. It iss what iss in our hearts that counts. That iss the only thing that matters. The feelings we have in our hearts. And if it worries you that people will say that we are not truly man and wife, well, don't be concerned by it. Because we can tell them that we have been married here in England, and no one will ever be any the wiser.'

A sense of utter confusion assailed Tildy, and to give herself time to think she began to dress.

Oriel Evans came into a seated position, staring at her in bewilderment as he saw the expression on her face. 'What iss the matter, *cariad*? What have I done to make you like this?'

She forced a smile. 'Nothing, Oriel. You've done nothing. It's only that you have taken me by surprise, talking like this.'

'But why are you surprised?' he demanded in bewilderment. 'I told you before that I wass falling in love with you. How can it be a surprise that I want you to be a wife to me? Why did you make love with me if you did not want to be my wife?'

'But I can't be your wife, Oriel,' she told him with a burgeoning sense of desperation, 'I am married to Tom Crawford.'

'But that iss of no importance, *cariad*. That man iss no longer a part of your life. I am your man now.'

The need to escape, to be by herself so that she could think, overwhelmed Tildy, and she jumped to her feet. 'I must go,' she blurted out, and when he went to rise, held out her hand as if to keep him seated by physical pressure. 'No, Oriel! Stay there. Please, if you do truly care for me, then let me go alone. I must have time to think. I'm so confused at this moment, that nothing I could say to you would make any sense.'

Again he made as if to rise, and this time she pushed down on his shoulder to keep him seated. 'No! Stay there and let me go alone. Please, Oriel, let me go alone.'

With a bad grace he grumbled assent, and slipping her feet into her clogs Tildy ran down along the rows of haycocks. When she reached the lane she turned away from the farmstead and towards the Icknield Street. She ran and ran as if trying to outdistance her own troubled thoughts until gasping for breath, her legs weary and trembling she came to a halt and slumped down on the steep bank against the hedgerow. Now she began to castigate herself bitterly.

'You've acted the whore! Behaved like any sixpenny drab, and unlike them you've no excuse for doing it. You're not in want. Your belly is filled with food. You've clothes on your back, shoes on your feet and a roof above your head. You're worse than them!'

Another part of her mind offered excuses for her behaviour. 'You like the man, and he is a good man who truly loves you, and would take you for wife if he could. He saved Davy's life, and is ready to accept him as his own son. So what have you done that is so wrong? Everyone needs some love in their life. You cannot be expected to play the nun for ever. Why should you not accept this man's love, and take pleasure from his body? You owe no loyalty to Tom Crawford. He is an evil man, who brutally misused you and Davy, and deserted you without a second's thought when it suited him to do so.'

As her breathing eased and the trembling of her muscles ceased so her rampaging thoughts calmed also, and she was able to consider what had happened more rationally.

'What's done is done, and truth to tell I took pleasure from it.' She drew a long breath and came to a decision. 'But there'll be no repeat of it. I want my Davy to grow up able to respect his mother because she is deserving of respect, not because it is considered a duty of sons to respect their parents. He'll not be able to respect me if I make love with men that I hardly know just because my hunger for loving sometimes becomes an unbearable burden to me. I'll not have anyone able to point the finger at me as a loose-living woman, and have justice in doing so.

'No, I'll not have that. Tomorrow I'll tell Oriel how I feel, and tell him also that while Tom Crawford lives, then all we can ever be to each other is good friends.'

This resolution brought her some degree of peace of mind, if not of happiness, and with that she went to rise and retrace her steps back towards the farm. But had only taken a few steps when she heard the sounds of horse's hooves coming at a fast pace along the Icknield Street behind her. Remembering the stories of a prowler attacking women in the area Tildy left the roadway and hid herself in the shadows of the hedgerow.

It was a solitary horseman, riding at a fast canter, and in the brightness of the moonlight she was able to clearly see and recognize Tobias Winterton. Her first impulse was to call out to him but she smothered that impulse, realizing that her presence here at this hour would entail explanation, and that that explanation would of necessity entail her lying to him.

'I've committed sufficient stupidities for this night,' she decided, and remained hidden until he had passed and the sounds of his progress had died away before she left the shelter of the hedgerow and continued on.

Tobias Winterton was a happy man as he rode homewards. He had done as he had intended and travelled to Redditch to make enquiries from friends he had there concerning Tildy Crawford. What they had told him of her had greatly pleased him. She was regarded as a rebellious hothead, who acted towards her betters and social superiors without the respect they considered due to them. She had lived in the roughest quarters of the town, and had friends who were considered unfit to mix in respectable society. Her husband was a ne'er-do-well, who was now in his rightful place, the convict hulks. The work she found to do in the needle mills was of menial nature, and when not in work she joined the ranks of the paupers applying for Parish Relief from the Poor Rate. And yet, with all this, she was still considered to be an honest, good-living woman, against whom no contempt could justly be directed. She kept herself and her child clean and fed and clothed to the best of her ability, and did no harm to anyone, but only asked to be left alone to live her own life, and to care for her child, a child that was acknowledged to be exceptionally well-loved and cared for.

All this had made pleasant listening for Tobias, but above all he had found joy in being told that despite the many offers and opportunities of protection from men that her physical beauty had brought her, Tildy Crawford had lived a highly moral life. Naturally at times there had been rumours that this man or that was enjoying her favours, but his informants had assured Tobias that all these rumours seemed to be completely unfounded.

The young man reached the lane leading to the farmstead and mindful of its deep ruts slowed his mount to a walk. As the beast ambled slowly on Tobias stared about him at the bright countryside, acknowledging that in this moonlight it presented a picture of rare beauty. In the sunken lane he was hidden by shadows yet could see clearly the slopes of the rising ground stretching away to each side of him. Suddenly he cursed softly to himself, and reined in his mount. There above him, coming down the slope of the hayfields, he had spotted the figure of a man walking alone.

'Bloody poacher, I'll wager.'

Tobias had very mixed feelings about the practice of poaching, and considered that if a man had hungry children at home, and no money to buy food, then that man was fully justified in taking whatever game he could to feed his children with. The poachers that Tobias hated, however, were those professionals who robbed the landowner of expensively reared game to sell to the poulterers in Birmingham or even far-off London. These professionals were not averse to sheep and cattle-stealing, and in the past Tobias had lost some fine animals to them.

The man was walking at an angle away from Tobias, and quietly he urged his mount onwards, letting the animal pick its own way over the rutted track, knowing that his quarry was too far distant to hear any isolated strike of a horseshoe against a stone.

Before very long Tobias realized that the man was heading directly towards the farmstead. 'By Christ, if it's stealing you have in mind then you're taking risks, my buck. The geese and dogs will kick up a hell of a racket when they hear you coming.'

Then, abruptly, the man ahead turned and stared directly into the shadowed lane, and started to walk quickly in Tobias's direction. The young man watched, and as the other drew nearer suddenly recognized him as Oriel Evans. The Welshman climbed over a low place in the hedgerow and stood waiting on its bank for Tobias to come up with him. When they were abreast, Tobias reined in his horse and asked, 'Well now, Taffy, what brings you abroad so late?'

'Don't worry, young master, it iss not poaching or rustling of the animals. I could not sleep, that iss all.'

Tobias was somewhat taken aback by what looked to be an uncanny perception on the other's part. But he made no attempt to hide what he was feeling. 'I don't take kindly to any man wandering over my land at night, Taffy. Particularly when that man is a stranger.'

He stared curiously at the Welshman, sensing that he was agitated for some reason, and challenged, 'Is anything the matter with you, Taffy? You seem aereated about something. What have you been up to?'

Oriel Evans resented the younger man's accusatory tone. Normally he would have been able to disregard Tobias' manner, and indeed empathise with the younger man to some degree, because he himself disliked having strangers wandering over his own acres back in Wales. But tonight, worried and irritated as he was by Tildy's abrupt departure, he was in no mood to shrug anything aside.

'I've already told you once that I could not sleep,' he snapped curtly, 'and I don't like being treated ass if I wass some bloody tramper. I have land and beasts of my own back in Wales, Winterton, and I am a master drover, not a bloody herdsman. And as a master drover I am trusted to deal in larger sums of money than you have ever had in your britches pocket. So don't keep on badgering me because I have chosen to take a walk by night. I do what I please, and when it pleases me.'

All Tobias' innate dislike of the Welshman rose to the surface. 'No Taffy, you don't do as you please on my land, and particularly not when you're in my employ.'

'But it iss not your land, is it, good boy. It iss your father's land, and he iss the man who iss paying us to shear his sheep.' Evans' voice was jeering.

It was not so much the jeering tone, as the fact that the man was speaking the truth that stung Tobias Winterton to fury. 'I act as my Dad's steward, and it's me that runs the farm, and decides who or who shall not work here,' he gritted out.

'Ohhh yess, good boy. I can believe that,' Evans sneered openly. 'It iss easy to see by the state of your fallows and ditches that you are running thiss farm.'

'What d'you mean by that?' Tobias demanded grimly.

'I mean that thiss place needs a man to run it, not a bloody infant who'se not yet grown into a man's britches.'

For a moment the younger man's temper threatened to explode, but he fought to control it, knowing that at this time the Welshman and his gang were badly needed to finish the shearing.

'Have a care that you don't try me too far, Taffy,' he warned, and would have left it there, but by now the volatile Celtic temperament of Oriel Evans was in the ascendant, and the Welshman was thirsting for trouble.

'I've got my bellyful with you, good boy,' he growled, 'and if you open your mouth once more to me, then I'll be closing it for you in double quick time.'

Tobias Winterton swung down from his saddle, and with a sharp slap on its rump sent his horse trotting onwards up the lane towards the farmstead. Then he stepped to confront the other man. 'Come on then, Taffy,' he challenged angrily, 'let's see if you're as handy with your fists as you are with your mouth.'

Tildy heard the sounds of men grunting and gasping, and the scuffling of feet and the thudding of fists on flesh and bone as she rounded the bend in the lane and saw in the moonlight the two dark figures coming together, parting, circling with fists weaving, then coming together again with dull impact and muffled outcries of pain.

Even at a distance her instinct told her who the combatants were, and she shouted out as she ran towards them, 'Stop this. For pity's sake, stop!'

Heedless of her own safety, she interposed herself between them, and both men fell back a pace when they realized who she was.

'Are you both mad?' she demanded. 'Why are you fighting like this? What's happened between you?'

Tobias stared at her in wild-eyed bewilderment. 'Tildy? What brings you here?'

'No matter what brings me here,' she retorted spiritedly. 'You're lucky the whole household isn't here, the bloody racket you're making.'

'Leave us be, girl, and get to your bed. Thiss iss no concern of yours,' Oriel Evans told her roughly, but Tildy held her ground between them.

'Of course it's my concern, because I am a friend to you both. And just look at yourselves, can't you. You're both bleeding.'

In the moonlight black smears of blood liberally plastered both their faces.

'Go from here, Tildy,' Tobias ordered, but stubbornly she stayed, and told them both, 'I'll not go and leave you to half-kill each other. I'm staying, and I'll push between you if you start fighting again.'

'You'll be sorely hurt if you do so,' Tobias warned.

'I don't care!' she flashed back. 'I'm not leaving here until you both come to your senses.'

For long long seconds he three stood locked in an impasse, neither man wishing to turn away from the other, and Tildy determined to stand between them come what may. Then the older, wiser head of Oriel Evans prevailed. 'Alright then, girl. I'll leave it lay. For now at least,' he qualified, and spoke directly to Tobias, 'We can settle this matter some other time, good boy.'

'I'll look forwards to that,' Tobias promised grimly.

Oriel Evans nodded to Tildy, 'I'll see you tomorrow, *cariad*,' and turned on his heel and strode away.

Tobias Winterton would have spoken to Tildy, but she waved his words aside. 'No Toby! I don't want to hear anything more this night. I'm going to my bed.'

With that she also turned and hurried away, leaving a very disconsolate young man staring miserably after her.

Chapter Eleven

'Wheer was you last night, Tildy?' Maddy Thomas stared curiously at her friend's face, noting its drawn tiredness and the dark smudges beneath the lucent brown eyes.

For a brief instant Tildy was tempted to confide in the other woman, then thought better of it. 'I was in bed asleep of course.' She carried on filling the bread oven with the bundles of faggots she had fetched in from the woodshed.

Maddy grinned slyly. 'Oh yes, you was in bed alright, but for a good part o' the night you was out of it, weren't you. I woke up and you was gone.'

'I had to go to the privy,' Tildy said shortly, and the other girl laughed aloud.

'Jesus! How many times did you need to goo theer, my duck? I must ha' woke up three times at least, and you was never by me side when I did.'

Tildy sighed and faced her friend squarely. 'Look Maddy, I was out for most of the night, I'll admit. But I can't tell you what happened, or why I was gone, not yet I can't anyway.'

Maddy was instantly agog with curiosity. 'Oh come on, Tildy. I'm your friend. You can tell me anything, and I'll not breathe a word on it to anybody, cross me heart and hope to die if I should.' She suited action to words by making the sign of the cross upon her large left breast.

The sound of heavy boots on the stairs saved Tildy from further evasions. 'Leave it now, Maddy, please. I promise I'll tell you all about it when I can.'

With that Maddy had to rest content, but her disgruntled expression showed her displeasure.

It was Tobias Winterton's boots that they had heard, and now he came into the kitchen. Maddy's eyes avidly locked on to the fresh cuts and bruises on his face, and she darted speculative looks between him and Tildy, but said nothing more, only placed his breakfast of bread and salt bacon before him on the table, together with a freshly drawn jug of ale. He stared at Tildy, but she kept her eyes averted and busied herself at the bread oven.

One by one the rest of the servants came to the table and after their hasty breakfast Tobias issued the instructions for the work of the day. He finished by telling Tildy, 'You'll stay in the house today, Tildy. Maddy can go to the barn at noon and take over the fleece-rolling from young Tommy.'

Tildy nodded, but said nothing in return, aware of Maddy's questing looks. Arthur Winterton now came into the kitchen, precipitating a general scramble for the door among his servants and in scant seconds the kitchen was empty but for himself, Tobias and the two housewomen. He cast a bleared eye on Tobias' face, and grunted, 'What's you bin up to?'

'Nothing,' the young man snapped, and with a final despondent look at Tildy went out into the yard.

Maddy hastened to bring the old man his jug of cider and six eggs, and he followed his usual practice, breaking the eggs and mixing their contents with the drink, then swallowing the mixture in a series of noisy gulps, punctuated by resounding belches.

He had barely finished when Jeremiah Borth came through the yard door.

'Good morning to you, Master Winterton.' The Overseer grinned bluffly and waved his hand genially at the two women. 'And good morning to you ladies also.' He saw that Arthur Winterton was dressed for the outdoors in brown broadcloth coat, breeches, leather gaiters and heavy hobnailed boots. 'I'm glad to see that youm ready for the off, Master Winterton. I was feared that you might have forgotten our bit o' business.'

The older man scowled at him. 'Arthur Winterton never forgets any of his business, Borth. Anybody roundabouts here can tell you that. Have you brought your rhino wi' you?'

The Overseer chuckled merrily, and took a small pouch from his pocket which clunked metallically when he shook it in front of the farmer's face. 'Never you fret, Master. There's enough here for my purpose.'

The old man rose to his feet, standing a full head taller than the stocky Overseer. 'Maddy, get my hat,' he growled, and she ran to fetch his low-crowned black top hat. Taking it from her he crammed it on to his shaggy head, pulling it low down so that its brim was directly above his eyebrows. 'Come on then, Borth, we'em wasting time here.'

Immediately the two men had gone, Tildy asked, 'What d'you reckon they're about, Maddy?'

Her friend pondered for a moment, her plump features screwed up in concentration. 'It'll be dog-fighting, I'll wager. I know that the master keeps a couple o' the beasts up in Redditch wi' a cove theer who trains the buggers for him. My brother called in here to see me yesterday when you was out at the barn, and now I thinks on it, he mentioned summat about a big match coming off today up in Redditch, between a dog from Brummagem and one o' the local beasts. I'll lay odds that's wheer them two buggers are going.' She sniffed loudly. ''Tis a pity the old bastard can't pay us a bit more and waste less on the gambling. I feels real sorry for young Toby. He works like a bloody slave day in and day out to make the farm pay, and that old sod takes all the money, and pisses it up the wall. And what he can't piss up the wall he loses gambling.'

Now Borth's words came back to Tildy's mind, and she asked, 'Does he lose much money gambling then, old Arthur?'

Maddy nodded vigorously. 'They do say that the old bugger loses a bloody fortune.'

Using a live coal from the cooking fire, Tildy set the faggots in the bread oven ablaze and closed its iron door. Turning back to her friend she said wistfully, 'If I'd money like that I'd not throw it on the wind.'

'What would you do with it then, Tildy? Would you buy fine clothes and jewels?' Maddy questioned eagerly. 'I knows that I 'ud. I'd be dressed like a queen, me, and have my own carriage to ride in.'

Tildy shook her head. 'No Maddy, I'm not hungering for those things. I'd have Davy educated, and make a gentleman of him.'

'But if you made him a gentleman, Tildy, then mayhap he'd expect you to dress like a lady,' Maddy pointed out shrewdly. 'There was a man and wife in Studley who come into some property, and they had their son educated as a gentleman. And the ungrateful young bugger 'udden't walk the road wi' 'um arter that. He thought they was too far beneath him, and only ignorant yokels.'

'Then that's their own fault for not seeing what type of man he was. True gentlemen are born, the trappings only blind people to what lays beneath,' Tildy told her, somewhat tartly. 'My idea of a gentleman is not a fine Corinthian, or a powdered dandy. To me a gentleman is someone who is well-educated, and well mannered, and who treats all with the same courtesy whether they be rich or poor. He should be kind and give to those in need, and be ready to speak out against injustice and oppression.'

'Bravo! That iss very well said, *cariad*. I agree with what you are saying with all my heart.'

It was Oriel Evans, who had come to stand by the kitchen door unseen by the two women while Tildy spoke.

Flustered by his unexpected appearance Tildy blushed deeply, and Maddy grinned slyly when she saw that blush, and teased the Welshman. 'Theer now, look what you'se done to this maid. Her's glowing like the Beoley Beacon, so her is. Shame on you, Master Welshman! Shame on you!'

'Will you stop talking such nonsense, Maddy.' Tildy's embarrassment caused her to speak sharply, and the other woman rejoined huffily, 'There's no call for you to bite me yed off, I was only funning.'

'Well I'm in no mood for it,' Tildy said tartly, and even as she spoke was regretting her words, but before she could say anything in amendment Maddy Thomas snapped out,

'Forgive me for bloody well breathing,' and went from the room.

Paradoxically the remorse she felt for hurting her friend's feelings now caused Tildy to turn on the Welshman. 'There now, look what you've made me do! 'Tis your fault that she's gone off in a huff like that.'

Oriel Evans was himself under strain. The events of the previous night had left him with very confused feelings, and he had come looking for Tildy because of his anxieties over her reactions to their lovemaking. Now, stung by the injustice of her attack, he reacted without pausing for thought. 'She's upset because you are acting like a shrew. You had no call to speak to her like you did. And you have no cause to blame me for it either.'

Impelled by subconscious forces which at that moment she could not control, Tildy told him, 'Then if I am a shrew, you'd best go and let me alone, hadn't you, Master?'

The Welshman was a man who possessed a touchy sense of pride. It had taken him long years to get over the loss of his first love. That girl's rejection of him had hurt him very badly, and since then he had vowed repeatedly that he would never again allow any woman to wound and humiliate him in that manner. At this moment in time it appeared to him that this was what Tildy Crawford was trying to do to him, and so his pride forced him to react. 'Yes, girl, I think that iss what I had best do . . . Let you alone.' Without another word he stamped out into the yard, and Tildy's overwrought emotions exploded, and slumping down on to a bench she burst into tears.

After a couple of hours' work in the hayfield Tobias had once again far outstripped his fellow scythemen. But today he took no pleasure from that fact, and no joy in reaping. Depression lowered his spirits, a depression engendered by Tildy Crawford's attitude towards him at breakfast time. Miserably he pondered on the possible reasons for her undoubted coolness, and tried to comfort himself.

'It's just a woman's megrims that's all. Mayhap it's her bad time of the month. A lot of wenches get bad-tempered then, don't they?'

But try though he might to accept this as the reason, still his doubts plagued him. He stopped and upended his scythe and began to sharpen its long blade with his rounded whetstone. While stone rasped on steel his eyes flickered along the rows of haycocks, drawing pleasure from their symmetry. Then he frowned in puzzlement as he noted a gap in the ordered rows. 'Why have they left a gap there? The grass is real thick in that area.'

He finished the sharpening and wandered over to look more closely at the haycocks. When he neared the spot he saw that the gap had been caused by an existing haycock being flattened. At first he grinned when he saw how the grasses had been pressed down as if by heavy objects rolling on it. 'Somebody's been tumbling a wench on that.' He knew from personal experience, having himself made love to willing girls on haycocks. He bent to lift the fallen heap and re-stack it, and as he did so saw a gleam of whiteness amongst the greenery.

It was a short-stemmed clay pipe, with a curiously-shaped design on the outside of its bowl. Tobias drew breath sharply as he recognized where he had seen such a pipe before.

'It's that bloody Welshman's. He was smoking it last night. It was him who was up here with a wench. That's where he was coming from when I saw him.' The next instant a certainty invaded the young man's mind, a certainty that created a feeling of sickening emptiness within him. 'It was Tildy he was with! That's why she was in the lane last night. She'd been up here with him. She'd been here laying on her back for that Welsh bastard, opening her legs for him like a bloody tanner-whore!' Vivid images came crowding into Tobias Winterton's mind. Images which filled him with a nauseated fury. 'I'll kill the fucking whore and her bloody fancy man! I'll kill them both.' He sank down upon his knees, pulverizing the clay pipe in his strong hands, his breath coming in short ragged gaspings, and over and over again the refrain re-echoed in his mind, 'I'll kill thé bastards! I'll kill them! I'll kill them both!'

Chapter Twelve

It was late afternoon when Oriel Evans came again to the house in search of Tildy. She was alone and, although she had apologized to Maddy and made her peace with the girl, was still ashamed of her own behaviour of the morning. She greeted the Welshman gravely, and said to him, 'I want to apologize for how I behaved towards you and Maddy this morning, Oriel. I acted like a booby.'

He smiled warmly at her. 'There iss no need to apologize to me, *cariad.* We can all act stupidly at times. I wass foolish myself.'

Tildy had given much thought to what had occurred between herself and this man the previous night, and although able to rationalize what had happened, still could not rid herself of the sense of guilt for having made love.

The Welshman's sensitivity enabled him to recognize the reason for her reserved manner, and now he told her gently, 'I will speak frankly with you, Tildy, about last night. I meant what I said. I truly love you, and want you to go back to my own country with me. I will cherish and protect you and your son, *cariad.*' When she would have interrupted, he said quickly, 'No, say nothing yet, *cariad.* Only hear me out, I beg of you. I know that you will feel a guilt because you are still married to your husband. But you must not let that sense of guilt rule your life, girl. The man could be dead even now as we talk. And if he lives you owe him nothing. I know how he treated you. He is a worthless animal, girl. Don't allow such a man to ruin the rest of your life for you. Free yourself from him. Come with me to a new land and make a new life for yourself there with me. If you find that you do not want to live in Wales, well then we can go elsewhere, to America or Canada. I can make a living wherever there are animals and land. And I have money enough to buy a small farm in either of those countries.'

He paused and studied her face, trying to evaluate what impression his words were having. Tildy's eyes were downcast, and she stood motionless, her feature expressionless. But inwardly her thoughts and emotions were a seething turmoil. Both mentally and physically this man attracted her far more strongly than her independent spirit wished to acknowledge or accept. The proposals he was now making had immense appeal to her adventurous nature. To travel, to see new countries, new people, experience new ways of living, and above all else to cast off the shackles of her present existence.

'Why do I not say yes to him?' she demanded of herself. 'Why cannot I seize this chance he offers me to start afresh with my life? In all truth I've nothing to lose, and everything to gain. I know in my deepest soul that I can trust this man, and believe his words and promises. I know that he will serve me honourably and treat my son as he would his own bloodchild. We could make a good life together, and I know that I would find it easy to respect him, and take pleasure from his body and his mind. Why cannot I say yes, and have done with all this?'

'Well, *canad*? Will you come with me? Will you let me love and care for you and little Davy?'

Tears stung in her eyes and when she looked fully at him, he was blurred in her sight. Slowly she shook her head. 'I'm sorry, Oriel. I'm truly, truly sorry.'

A spasm of actual pain twisted his strong features. Then he forced a smile and told her, 'The shearing is finished now, *cariad*, and my friends have voted to move on elsewhere. I shall go with them. But while I'm gone do not forget me. Because I am going to come back to you, and when I do, I shall ask you again what I have asked you now.'

With an infinite tenderness he used his fingers to wipe

away the tears that now trickled from her eyes, then gently kissed her on her lips, and said huskily, '*Nes welwn ni ein gilydd to, cariad* . . . Until we see each other again, my dearest.'

As his footsteps receded Tildy's tears fell freely and the anguished sense of loss struck to her heart.

Chapter Thirteen

Arthur Winterton counted out the last of the coins into Oriel Evans' hand. A process which left his own money-pouch nearly empty.

'Many thanks,' the Welshman nodded, 'and now I'll bid you a goodbye, Master Winterton.'

The farmer looked at the neatly stacked rolled fleeces and consoled himself with the thought of the potential profits they represented. He had gambled heavily and lost at the dog-fighting earlier that day, and his sour mood was only partially sweetened by the thought of money to come. 'You've worked well, Taffy,' he told the other man grudgingly. 'If you and your men wish it, I could find you other work here.'

The other man shook his head. 'We have taken a vote, and the lads wish to move on. But we might be coming back this way later in the summer, and if that iss the case, then I'll call in and see if you have anything for uss then.'

Bundles on their backs, the gang walked down the winding lane and were soon lost to view.

Left alone in the barn Arthur Winterton stood staring blankly at the silver, greasy-smelling fleeces, and his thoughts were gloomy. His debts were beginning to appear an unscalable mountain, and all his desperate attempts to clear them by gambling only sent them soaring higher. Bitterly he cursed his luck. Today it had been particularly foul. His favourite fighting dog, with which he had hoped to recoup his fortunes, had been winning, and as the bloody fight progressed Winterton had doubled his bets. Then, for no good reason that he could see, his dog had suddenly weakened and gone under to die a terrible death, with its throat literally torn out by the teeth of the other animal.

The farmer cursed aloud, 'Goddamn my luck! Nothing I've touched has gone right for me these last months. It's like there was an evil spell on me.'

Unbidden the memory of old Esther Smith's screeching voice pushed into his mind, and for a brief instant Arthur Winterton wondered if it could be possible that she had managed to influence the fates against him during the dog-fight.

'No! That can't be!' He tried to scoff at his own superstitious imaginings. 'Bugger me, Arthur, youm getting lardy-yedded in your old age, even to give room for such notions.'

Yet try to scoff though he might, still the uncomfortable thoughts persisted, and in an effort to dismiss them from his mind he left the barn and walked through the fields to inspect his land. The late afternoon sky had clouded over, and there was a turgid humidity in the air.

'Wun't surprise me if we gets a storm afore too long,' he told himself, and directed his footsteps towards the hayfields. 'I hope Toby has started building the big stack. If the storm does break I don't want too much hay left lying out in the small cocks.'

As he came into the field where the haymaking was in progress Arthur Winterton's mood darkened further. No raised and tented rick-cloth used to cover a haystack in the process of construction was to be seen, and the horse and cart stood motionless and unloaded. The people in the meadow were working hard, and far ahead of the other scythemen Tobias was reaping with a demonical energy, the grasses and clovers falling in long swathes to his left-hand side in an almost continuous motion. But Arthur Winterton's irritability was not mollified by the sight of so much hard labour, and he strode towards his eldest son, ignoring the greetings of the nervous labourers, a nervousness engendered by their sighting of his thunderous expression.

Tobias was oblivious of his father's approach. Consumed by his passions he attacked the grasses with a savage energy, wielding the heavy scythe blade against the yielding stalks as if he were slashing into the body of an enemy, and exalting as that enemy fell before him.

'Tobias? Why arn't you made a start on building the stack?' the older man shouted as he came up to his son.

The younger man ignored him.

'Tobias, be you bleedin' deaf?' Arthur Winterton was now directly behind his son, but still the younger man acted as though he was unaware of anything other than the grasses tumbling before him.

'Doon't you act the bloody goat wi' me!' the elder Winterton roared and grabbed Tobias' right shoulder with one huge hand and spun the young man round to face him by sheer force.

Tobias' eyes were wild and strained, and his father stared at him in amazement. 'What in hell's name ails you, boy?' he demanded angrily.

The young man stared at his father as if he were a stranger, and his lips moved but no words came from them, only an incomprehensible muttering.

'What's the matter wi' you?' Arthur Winterton shook his son roughly. 'Can't you bloody well spake, you young hound? What's the matter wi' you? Answer me! Answer, blast you!'

Abruptly a frightening change twisted the younger man's features. His face was glowing from exertion and sheened by sweat darkened in hue, and his upper lip curled as he snarled like a savage beast.

A terrible memory assailed Arthur Winterton. A memory he had long-buried in the recesses of his mind, and he released his grip on his son's shoulder and fell back a pace.

'Don't you know me, boy?' His voice shook, as that terrible memory impacted upon his nerves. 'It's me, boy. It's your feyther.'

An animal-like growl rumbled deep from the younger man's throat and his eyes reddened, and the ferocity of his expression was such that even the normally fearless Arthur Winterton felt fear, and he fell back further paces.

By now the other people in the field had seen what was happening, and they stood motionless, their eyes locked on the two men.

Then, as abruptly as the first, another metamorphosis came over Tobias Winterton's features. The beast-like snarl disappeared to be replaced by an expression of utter bewilderment, and he asked his father, 'What's the matter, Feyther? Why do you look at me so?'

Still gripped by his memories, Arthur Winterton could only shake his head and mutter, 'Nothing, boy. Nothing's the matter.' For a moment or two he struggled to regain his composure, and then turned to bellow at the motionless workers, 'What be you lot looking at? Gerron wi' your work, afore I kicks your arses for you.'

Immediately they resumed their gruelling labours, and satisfied that their attention was now directed elsewhere, Arthur Winterton turned once more to his son. 'Are you feeling alright now, boy?' His tone was curiously gentle, a fact which caused Tobias to regard him with surprise.

'Of course I'm alright, Feyther. Why do you ask that?'

The older man waved his hand in the air. 'Oh, it don't signify. Pay it no mind.' His entire manner was subdued, and now openly puzzled his son asked, 'Is ought the matter? Has anything happened to our Annie, or our Jem?'

'No. They'm alright.' The older man drew a long rasping breath, and then something nearer his normal manner reappeared, and he questioned, 'Why arn't you started to build the bloody stack? Can't you see what the bloody sky looks like? Are you blind?'

Tobias looked up at the lowering greyness, noting the gathering thunder-clouds. 'It looks like we'm in for a storm.'

Now the father he knew came back. 'Is that all you can tell me, you fucking mawkin, that it looks like a storm rising?' Arthur Winterton roared. 'You should ha' sin that hours since. You'd best stop cutting right now, and get what's cut into the small cocks afore the bloody weather breaks and the hay gets soaked right through. Doon't stand theer gawping at me, boy. Gerron wi' it.'

Tobias hastened to obey, shouting orders to the scythemen, and Arthur Winterton strode away. But despite the bold front he presented, inwardly he was very badly shaken by what had occurred . . .

'It's come back to haunt us agen,' he thought with a sensation of dread. 'It's come agen, God help us all. It's come agen.'

In the farmhouse kitchen Maddy Thomas used a big horn spoon to taste the meat broth bubbling in the iron pot slung over the fire, and smacked her lips in noisy appreciation. 'By Christ, but that tastes good, Tildy. Youm a bloody good cook, my wench.'

Although Tildy was gratified by the compliment, she felt too heavy-hearted to raise more than a faint smile of acknowledgement, and Maddy clicked her tongue sympathetically. 'Youm upset because the Taffy's left, arn't you, my duck. But you needn't fret yourself, because he'll be back. Theer arn't a doubt about that. He'll come back to you.'

Tildy could not resist this opportunity to unburden herself to a friendly listener. 'Truth to tell, Maddy, I don't know whether I want him to come back or not,' she began hesitantly. 'He holds a strong attraction for me, I'll admit. But yet, when he asked me to go with him this afternoon, I couldn't bring myself to say yes.' She looked at her friend beseechingly. 'If what I feel for him is really love, then I would have gone with him, wouldn't I?'

The other woman shrugged her plump shoulders. 'I arn't able to answer you that, Tildy. I always reckoned that I was in love wi' Tommy Snipe, and I cried buckets when the constables carted him off to the Warwick Assizes. Yet when I thinks about it now,' again she shrugged, 'well I don't know if I was acrying for him, or crying for meself left wi' his babby in me belly, and me Dad ranting and raving at me for bringing another mouth into the house to be fed.'

Her rosy face suddenly brightened and she chuckled richly. 'Does you know what the cheeky bastard wanted me to do, Tildy? I walked all the way to bloody Warwick Gaol to visit the bugger, and me wi' a belly bulging o'out me apron, and bloody Tommy Snipe had the gall to tell me that he wanted me to get transported as well, so that we could be together in bloody Botany Bay.' Her laughter erupted and rang through the room. 'Could you just imagine it, Tildy, me aliving out theer amongst all them bloody convicts and savages and soddin' kangaroos?' She thrust out her hands in rejection. 'Not bloody likely, my bucko! I told the cheeky sod. I likes Old England for all its bloody faults. I arn't got no wish to goo and dwell in foreign parts. Bloody Ipsley parish is foreign enough for me, and as soon as I can, I'll be back home living in Studley agen, among my own sort o' people. Like I told you afore, Tildy, I can't abear bloody foreigners.' She hesitated and then qualified that last statement. 'Well, some of 'um be alright. I mean to say, I thinks the world o' you, and youm a foreigner really, arn't you. I mean, you was born right the other side o' Redditch, warn't you.'

Tildy laughed herself at the artless simplicity of the girl, and felt her own sombre mood lighten. 'Oh yes, Maddy. I'm a real foreigner, I am.'

'Ah well, you can't help wheer you was birthed, can you,' Maddy commiserated. 'Arter all, we can't all be birthed in Studley, can us.'

'There'd not be room enough there for us to stand shoulder to shoulder if we were,' Tildy smiled.

The advent of Arthur Winterton brought the conversation to an abrupt end.

The big man's manner was curiously subdued, and he slumped down into his great armchair at the head of the table without uttering a word to either of the women.

Maddy's inquisitiveness overcame her natural timidity of her employer, and she asked, 'Am you feeling alright, Master?'

He scowled at her. 'Why does you ask me that, girl?'

'You seems different from normal, that's all.'

'Doon't you concern yourself about me, girl. Just get on wi' what I pays you to do.'

Maddy tossed her head defiantly, but was not bold enough to risk provoking the man by answering him back. Instead she walked behind him and made a rude gesture with her fingers to the back of his head. Tildy spluttered with laughter, and the man glared at her. 'What's you sniggering at?'

'Nothing, Master. It was only something that I thought about, that's all.'

Behind his back Maddy Thomas was now pulling grotesque faces at him, and unable to keep her own face straight Tildy turned and hurried into the scullery, where she grabbed up a piece of rough towelling to smother her mirth.

After serving her employer with food and drink Maddy joined Tildy there, and the two exchanged whispers and giggles until the sounds of the fieldhands returning brought them into the kitchen once more.

Tobias was later in coming than the others, and when he did arrive made no effort to speak to Tildy. Instead he ignored her, and quickly wolfed his food and disappeared once more without saying anything to anybody.

Tildy was relieved rather than upset by his apparent indifference to her, telling herself that she had already made a sufficient fool of herself with Oriel Evans, and did not wish any other involvement with any man – at least for the foreseeable future.

What did strike her as extremely strange, however, was the worried look in Arthur Winterton's eyes as his eldest son disappeared into the darkness of the night.

'Why does he look so concerned?' she wondered. 'He doesn't appear to give a damn about any of his children normally. So why should he look so worried now?'

Chapter Fourteen

More than a week had passed since the departure of the Welshman, and although Tildy thought often of Oriel Evans and wondered where he was, she found that his absence did not cause her unhappiness. Working as she did from dawn until dusk and beyond, sometimes only being able to lie in her bed for four or five hours of the night, her work was too demanding for her to pine after romance. Yet although she laboured hard and long she was feeling in better physical health than she had done for many years. The plentiful wholesome food and the clean air brought strength to her body and a bloom to her cheeks, and the fact that her Davy was also beginning to thrive in his new life filled her with a joyful contentment. At times she would pause and stand watching her son exploring his fascinating new universe, and think to herself, 'If I should have to leave here this very day, it would still have been worth coming. Even this short time has done wonders for my babby.'

Her personal relationships here at the farmstead also gave her cause for satisfaction. She and Maddy Thomas were now fast friends, and the rest of the farm-servants seemed to have accepted her as one of themselves, and treated her with an easy camaraderie. Her relationship with the Winterton family itself was also satisfactory on the whole. Jem treated her almost as an elder sister, poor simple Annie was the devoted and adored playmate of Davy, and Arthur Winterton treated her as he did all of his other servants, no worse, no better, and that suited her, for she had no wish to be singled out for any different treatment that would set her apart from them.

But Tobias sometimes troubled her thoughts. Ever since the night she had interposed herself between him and the Welshman, the young man had only spoken to her out of necessity. On the surface he seemed indifferent to her presence, and ignored it. But Tildy was always conscious of his covert watchfulness and his eyes upon her whenever he thought that she was unaware of his regard. Naturally Tildy was not happy about this state of affairs, but fatalistically accepted that there was little or nothing she could do to rectify it without risking exacerbating the situation. If Tobias wished to continue on in this manner, then Tildy was prepared to let him so do. Alternatively, if he were to give any indication of wishing to be friends with her once more, then she was more than willing to meet him halfway.

The wash-house was thick with the steam from the great copper in which Tildy was boiling the household linen, and its water seethed and bubbled as she plied the wooden dolly to stir and punch the dirt from the sheets and bolster covers. A big wooden tub was placed on the floor beside the bricked-in copper, and once satisfied that the cloths were clean Tildy laid the dolly aside and taking a thick wooden staff levered out the streaming lengths of linen from the boiling water and dropped them into the tub.

'Maddy,' she called to her friend, 'Maddy, will you come and give me a hand for a minute?'

A few seconds later the figure of her friend came through the thick steam. They lifted the heavy tub between them and carried it along the short passageway which connected the wash-house to the orchard which lay on the opposite side of the main house to the farmyard.

Several rope washing-lines were tied between the trunks of the apple trees, and after rinsing the sheets in the rainwater butt which stood beneath the roof drainpipe and wringing them out the women pegged them along these lines. When they had done, Tildy wiped the sweat from her brows with the back of her arm.

'Phew! It's hot work this. I'm glad we don't have to wash every day.'

'You and me both, my duck,' her friend agreed fervently.

The sheets started to move, swaying gently in the soft warm breeze, and Tildy sighed thankfully. 'They'll not be long in drying, at any rate.' Her gaze moved idly along the white expanses, and then she frowned and pointed at a tree on the outer edge of the orchard.

'Look there, Maddy. What's that dangling from that branch there?'

Her friend stared in the direction that Tildy indicated. 'It looks like it could be a kid's doll, Tildy.'

Tildy walked towards the small object and when she reached it her face puckered in puzzlement. It actually was a small crudely-shaped doll fashioned from hard-baked clay, and a length of cord had been tied around its neck to suspend it from the branch in a grotesque parody of a hung human being.

Tildy reached up to take hold of it, and then jerked back her hand as Maddy suddenly shouted, 'No, Tildy! Don't touch it!'

The two women stood side by side staring uncertainly at the small figure as it swayed gently in the breeze, turning slowly in semi-circles as it moved.

Unaccountable dread filled Tildy as she saw that the crude figure had what looked to be human hair glued to its scalp and roughly moulded features to form a sinister caricature of a human face.

'Look theer, Tildy,' Maddy whispered nervously as she pointed to the thorns embedded in the figure's face, head and body. 'I knows what it is now. I'se seen summat like it afore.'

Tildy nodded, and her mouth felt dry. 'It's a curse doll, isn't it, Maddy?' Despite the warmth of the sun she suddenly shivered. 'And it's meant for somebody in this house, isn't it?'

'Jesus Christ, Tildy,' Maddy's voice was a frightened moan, 'doon't say that. For pity's sake doon't say that.'

Struggling as she was against giving way to her own superstitious fears, Tildy spoke sharply to her friend, 'It's a stupid nonsense, it can't harm anyone, so stop behaving like an idiot!' Driven by the need to overcome her own fear of the hanging doll she suddenly snatched at its body and broke it free of the cord which held it. But as her hand closed about it and the brittle clay crumbled, the thorns dug deep into her palm and with a cry of pain she hurled the broken doll to the ground, and sucked at the blood already welling from the tiny punctures in her skin.

'Theer, I told you not to touch it, didn't I!' Maddy's voice was a high-pitched screech. 'I told you not to!'

'For the love of God be quiet for a minute, can't you.' Tildy's own nerves were becoming stretched and she was fast losing patience with the other woman. But Maddy refused to be silenced.

'It's old Esther Smith's doing, this is. I'll bet a penny to a pound o' snuff on it. It's old Esther who'se done this. She cursed this place and all in it, didn't her. And now she's begun casting her spells agen us all.' A frightened sob tore from her throat. 'Lord Jesus protect us!'

In the face of her friend's distress Tildy softened. 'There now, Honey, don't be feared. We've done naught against old Esther ourselves, have we. It's not us that she wants to harm, but the Master and his kin.'

Maddy was not to be so easily reassured. 'What can we do, Tildy? Tell me, what can we do?'

By now Tildy's first shock of unreasoning fear was lessening fast and her more logical mind reasserting itself.

'I can't believe that a silly clay doll like this can ever harm anybody, Maddy. It's only a mad old woman's fancies, that's all. And besides, we don't even know for sure that it was old Esther who put this here, do we? It could have been anybody. And the more I think on it, I'm inclined to believe that it was some young jackanapes who did it for a prank.

'This is the year of 1823, Maddy, we live in modern times. We're not in the Middle Ages any longer, when people believed in witchcraft and suchlike. This is the modern age. We know that there are no such creatures as wicked witches or dragons, or fairies or goblins. Such things are only found in old wives' tales. They don't really exist.'

Maddy Thomas' normally rosy face was pale, and miserably she blurted out, 'What youm asaying might all be true, Tildy. But it doon't make any difference what you says, I still believes that old Esther is a black witch, and I still believes her's got the power to put the evil eye on anybody her chooses to. The next instant the girl screamed in fear and pointed with one wildly trembling hand. 'Look theer, Tildy. Look theer! Oh God, save us!'

The scream caused Tildy to physically jump, and her heart pounded as she glimpsed a small, bent, dark figure scurrying across the field on the other side of the orchard hedge. The sun was shining directly towards her, half-dazzling her eyes, and she shielded them with both hands in a vain effort to get a clear view of the retreating figure. Beside her Maddy begged, 'Can you see who it is, Tildy? Me sight arn't a lot o' use at this distance. Can you see who it is?'

Tildy sighed and shook her head. 'No Maddy, the sun's too glaring.' She looked down at the broken doll, its head was lying apart from the rest of it, but was still intact and its mishapen face seemed to be glowering up at her in malignant threat.

'Don't be so stupid!' she told herself. 'It's only a trick of the light. You're becoming as daft as this silly besom here with you.'

She stared out across the fields again, but now the dark figure had disappeared, and despite her logic, Tildy breathed a heartfelt sigh of relief that it had done so.

'What shall we do, Tildy? What shall we do?' Maddy pleaded.

Tildy shrugged helplessly. 'I don't know what we can do, Maddy.'

'We can tell the others, and see what they reckons about it,' Maddy suggested, but Tildy negated that suggestion.

'Don't forget what the Master said, about what he'd do to us if we breathed a word about what happened between him and old Esther in the kitchen that day,' she reminded.

'Well, shall we only tell the Master then?' Maddy persisted.

Tildy pursed her lips reflectively, then again shook her head. 'I don't think that a good idea, Maddy, knowing his temper God only knows what he'd do. He might well break old Esther's neck for her, and in all fairness, we don't know that she did this, do we. So we can't really risk getting her into more trouble with the Master, without any real proof that she's done this. And even if she did do it, I can't believe it warrants a broken neck.' She hesitated a moment, then came to a decision. 'We'll keep this to ourselves, Maddy.'

Stooping, she picked up the pieces of the broken doll and tossed them into the hedgerow. Then, with Maddy at her heels she went to the rain butt and washed her hands in its cold water.

'Come on, we'll get the wash finished,' she told her friend, 'and put all this nonsense out of our heads . . .'

Chapter Fifteen

Jacob Sarney, wool merchant and factor, always travelled with his own packers and pack-sheets, scales and weights, in his own massively constructed, broad-wheeled, high-sided, canvas-topped waggon drawn by a team of eight horses.

It was late afternnon when his waggon lurched from the Icknield Street into the Winterton Farm lane, but Sarney was not concerned by the comparative lateness of his arrival. It being the month of June, there were still sufficient hours of daylight left for him to be able to complete his business and be on the road towards his next destination before nightfall. Arthur Winterton himself came to meet the waggon, and Jacob Sarney, perched beside the driver on the high front seat, called out in greeting.

'How now, Arthur, have you got good quality for me this year?'

The farmer nodded dourly. 'Don't you always get such from me, Jacob.'

'That's very true, my friend, 'the merchant agreed. 'That's one thing I always gives you full credit for. Your wool's always well cleansed, and good value.'

'T'is a pity that you can't gi' a fair price for it, and gi' me the chance to gi' you full credit for that. Instead o' cheating me for every penny you can,' Winterton observed.

There was truth enough in the gibe to cause the merchant to glance sharply at the big man, and wonder if he had noticed the two overweight packs of wool that he had not been paid the full price for the previous year.

Arthur Winterton was not the type of man that Jacob Sarney would relish being caught cheating by, and now he made a mental note to resist any such temptation this year, and instead to deal with an absolute honesty.

Panting with the effort he clambered down from the high seat, his hugely fat stomach banging painfully against the protruding wheel-hub as he did so.

'Now then, Arthur, I tek it the stuff's in the barn theer, as usual.' The accents of his native city of Leeds betrayed his origins.

'That's right,' Winterton's yellow teeth showed in a brief grimace which might have been a smile, 'and as usual I expect you'll be wanting to sup my gin while your men make ready, wun't you?'

'Now then, Arthur, that enna fair. Look what I've brought you.' From the big leather satchel slung over his shoulder he produced a large dark-green glass bottle. 'Finest Hollands!' He flourished the bottle beneath Arthur Winterton's nose. 'The very finest! Cost me a bloody small fortune, this did.' His broad pink face beamed. 'But I'll not begrudge sharing it to the bloody dregs wi' an old and valued friend like yourself.'

This time Arthur Winterton actually did give a sardonic grin. 'I'll needs remember the old saying then wun't I, Jacob. That when supping wi' the Devil I'll needs use a long spoon. Come on into the house.'

Side by side the short fat merchant and the tall farmer went across the farmyard and into the kitchen door, while the merchant's men swarmed into the barn to make preparation for the weighing of the fleeces.

The supper meal was cooking on the range and a strong appetizing smell of roasting beef caused the merchant to sniff in keen anticipation. 'Still keeping a good table then, Arthur, if my nose don't deceive me.'

'Ahr, and you'll doubtless do dull justice to it afore you leaves, Jacob.'

Tildy was busy at the range, and Arthur Winterton told her, 'Bring us a couple o' glasses, girl. Then make yourself scarce for an hour. Young Jem's over in the barn wi'

Master Sarney's men, so you can goo and see if you can make yourself useful over theer until we'em done here.' As she silently obeyed the merchant stared at her with open desire, and when she had gone said, 'By the Christ, Arthur, that's a sweet armful you got there.'

'Ne'er mind about wenches now, Jacob,' Winterton told the other man impatiently. 'Let's crack this bugger open, and start talking prices.'

Maddy had taken little Davy and Annie down to the river to search for watercresses, and Tildy wished that she could join them there, but dare not disobey Arthur Winterton's instructions, so went reluctantly into the barn.

Jem smiled in welcome, and when Tildy told him that his father had sent her to help pointed to a heap of straw. 'You just set yourself down on that, Tildy, and rest your bones. There's no need for you to do anything, theer's enough on us here already.'

Never loath to rest for a while after the hard labours of washday, Tildy did as she was bid and watched the merchant's men preparing for the work.

Three ropes had been slung over the huge roof beams of the barn, and from one of them hung the big beam-scales with their broad square shallow weighing-pans. The other two ropes were attached to the top corners of the canvas packs. These packs were doubled sheets of thin canvas, forming oblong rectangles about eight feet long and five feet broad. The resulting envelopes were opened along the upper edge, so that the pack formed a huge bag suspended by the two ropes so that the lower edge remained on the barn floor. Two of the merchant's men climbed into the bag, and as the fleeces were weighed in twenty-eight-pound lots and brought to them, laid the fleeces in alternate layers on the bottom of the bag and trampled the wool down hard,building the layers progressively upwards until the pack contained two hundred and eighty pounds weight. As soon as this poundage was reached the two men came out of the pack and applied iron hand-clamps and skewers to hold the edges firmly against each other while the men used strong twine and long pack-needles to sew them securely. Their skilled expertise made it all appear very easy, but Tildy knew how difficult such work could be, and did not envy them their task.

Jem Winterton stood by the scales, recording each twenty-eight pounds of weight, or tod, by cutting a deep notch in a long tally-stick he held in his hand.

Tildy smiled fondly as she saw his intent face, and how when deeply concentrating on what he did his tongue poked out between his lips like a small child's, and then wondered why he was so frequently shrugging his shoulders, and moving his head from side to side with grimaces of pain. Feeling concerned, Tildy moved to stand beside him, and when a lull in the process of weighing gave her opportunity, questioned, 'What's the matter, Jem?

Even as she spoke another spasm affected the youth, and when he faced towards her he was forced to turn the upper part of his body instead of merely his head.

'It's me neck and shoulders, Tildy, they'm that stiff I can hardly use 'um. And it's hurting me jaws even to spake, and I can hardly swallow spit.' His eyes mirrored acute fear. 'I feels real funny, Tildy. What can be the matter wi' me?'

She tried to ally his fear. 'Mayhap it's only a fit o' rheumaticks, Jem. I think you'd best come to the house, and I'll put a hot poultice on your neck. That'll ease it for you.'

'But me Dad's told me to mark off the tods, 'the youth protested nervously. 'I darsn't leave off now.'

The merchant's men started weighing out the fleeces again, and the youth was forced to stop speaking and mark the count.

Tildy remained standing by him, uncertain about what to do, and then when she saw the youth suddenly arch his back and wince with pain, she hurried from the barn and back to the house.

Arthur Winterton and the wool merchant were sitting at the table, the gin bottle already half emptied, arguing about prices. Winterton scowled at Tildy's entrance. 'I thought I told you to help out in the barn, girl . . .' he began, but Tildy cut him short.

'Hark to me, Master Winterton. Young Jem is feeling badly, and I reckon it could be something serious that's the matter with him.'

'Oh you does, does you. Be you a bloody doctor then, that you knows what ails the bugger?' the farmer jeered. 'By the Christ, but we'em living in queer times arn't us, when a bloody gang-woman reckons herself to be a doctor. What say you, Jacob?'

Tildy gave the merchant no chance to answer. 'Look Master Winterton,' she said forcefully, 'I make no claim to be a doctor. But I've nursed the sick, and I've seen enough of ailments to be able to tell when one is serious. And I'm telling you now that young Jem is ill. I can't tell you what it is that's wrong with him, but I can tell you that it needs a doctor to come to him.'

Arthur Winterton's face darkened, and he gritted out ominously, 'Who the fucking hell does you think you am, to be telling me what's needed for me own son? I reckon youm getting above your bloody station, girl, and I also reckon that a taste o' the whip 'ud do you a power o' good. What say you, Jacob?'

This time the merchant was quick to reply. With shrewd perception he had recognized Tildy's depth of anxiety and instinctively judged her to be a woman possessing considerable common sense and intelligence. 'I say that you'd do well to pay heed to what the wench is telling you, Arthur. Ne'er mind this talk of the whip. Let's go and have a look at the lad ourselves.'

Arthur Winterton, pig-headed though he was, had sufficient respect for the merchant's judgement to pause and consider for a few moments. 'Alright then, Jacob,' he answered, 'let's you and me goo and have a look at him. But mind my words,' he pointed a thick spatulate finger into Tildy's face, 'if youm wasting my time, girl, you'll be crying salt tears afore another meal introduces itself to your belly.'

Tildy ejaculated an audible exclamation of disgust, and

hurried back to the barn with the two men at her heels.

Her fears were realized as she entered the great double doors and saw the cluster of men beside the weighing scales. Jem was lying on his back in the middle of that cluster and Tildy pushed through and looked down in horror.

Jem's features were suffused and the facial muscles drawn back in a hideous rigid grin, the jaw locked and blood frothing between the teeth. His body was spasmed into a backward curving arch so exaggerated that only the back of his head and his heels were in contact with the ground, and choking sounds came from his throat. Even as Tildy looked his arched body abruptly sagged and collapsed, then writhed again and arched high, and she saw that now the tip of his tongue was trapped between his teeth and nearly bitten through by the force with which his jaws had snapped together in this fresh paroxysm.

She went down on her knees beside his straining body, but was helpless to do anything to help him.

Old Gilbert Tongue, the shepherd, pushed through the watchers and knelt beside Tildy. From his waist pouch he took his horn spoon and tried to insert its handle between the youth's clenched teeth so that he could lever the jaws open and release the badly lacerated tongue.

While he struggled without success to achieve this, he muttered angrily, ''Tis the fucking lockjaw. 'Tis the fucking lockjaw,' over and over again.

Tildy's heart sank within her as she heard him, because she knew that when this dreaded disease took hold, normally death was its faithful companion.

This time the spasm lasted for over a minute before the body once more collapsed, and the boy lay in exhausted distress, moaning and half-senseless. Tildy stared wildly upwards and a sudden unreasoning anger engulfed her. 'Now will you send for a doctor?' she shouted at Arthur Winterton. 'Or do you want to take the whip to my back before you do?'

The big man ignored her outburst, and as Tildy stared at him she suddenly realized that his eyes held an anguish of distress. Shock and wonderment at this unexpected display of emotion caused her to fall silent, and Arthur Winterton bent low and lifted his son's body and cradled him against his chest as if he were a small child. Followed by the others the farmer carried his son with an effortless ease to the house, and upstairs to the bedroom. Gently he laid him on the narrow bed next to the bed of Tobias, and sank down on his knees, eyes intent on Jem's tormented face.

Tildy, realizing the futility of badgering the farmer to take any action at this moment in time, did so herself, driving the others from the room and downstairs, and once there sending old Gilbert to saddle a horse and ride to Redditch for the doctor.

Jacob Sarney told her diffidently, 'I'm going to have to finish the weighing and packing, Missy.'

She nodded brusquely. 'I understand that, Master.'

The man smiled at her reassuringly. 'Try not to fret yourself about the boy. I'm sure he'll be alright.'

'I pray to God he will be,' she answered fervently, and the man patted her shoulder.

'Ahr, I guessed you was powerful fond of him, girl. Anyway, I'll see to the weigh-count meself. Your master needn't concern himself with it. I'll keep a just tally.'

'Many thanks, Master,' she muttered, then went to heat some water and as soon as it was warm took a bowlful upstairs to wash and cleanse the blood from Jem's face. With the help of Arthur Winterton she undressed the youth and put him into the bed. Once satisfied that Jem was resting as comfortably as possible, she asked Arthur Winterton, 'Can I get you anything, Master Winterton?'

Eyes fixed on his son, the big man shook his head. 'No, girl, nothing.'

Downstairs again, Tildy busied herself with the multitudinous tasks of the house, trying not to allow into her mind the fearful thoughts pressing their way into her consciousness. But the struggle to keep those thoughts at bay rapidly became an unequal one, and she was forced to surrender to their assaults.

The curse doll! It presented itself vividly in her mind's eye. The human hair glued to its scalp, had been the same colour as Jem's hair, and the thorns embedded in it had marked roughly the places where Jem had complained of pain in his body . . .

'Was it meant for Jem?' she wondered. 'And can it really be witchcraft? But why should any witch want to hurt young Jem? He's a sweet, kindly boy, and wouldn't do harm to anything or anybody.' Her mind sought for rational explanation to explain Jem's sudden affliction. 'It can't be witchcraft! There's no such thing. It can't be the fault of that doll that he's been struck down like this. No child's toy made from clay could hold any power to harm people.' With a tremendous effort she thrust the notion from her. 'When the doctor comes I shall ask him what's caused this thing to happen, and until then, I'll not think any more about it.'

Keeping that resolve firmly fixed she buried herself in work.

Chapter Sixteen

Maddy came back with a willow basket full of fresh cresses and little Davy, excited by the adventure, rushed to tell his mother of the wonders he had seen by the riverside. Distraught as she was by Jem's sudden illness, she tried her best to match the child's delight in his stories of kingfishers and an otter, and the fish that for brief moments had actually wriggled in his fingers before escaping, but Maddy could see that something was troubling her friend, and at length sent little Davy and Annie off to play in the orchard.

'What's up, Tildy?' she asked as soon as they were alone.

As Tildy related what had happened to young Jem, Maddy's rosy face paled. 'Lord save us,' she breathed fearfully, 'it's the curse doll brought this to him. Lord save us all! Who'll be next, I wonder?'

Tildy was saved from replying by a frantic shout from the staircase.

'Tildy, come up here! Quick!'

It was Arthur Winterton's voice, and both women hurried to obey the summons.

In the bedroom young Jem was now lying on the floor by the side of his bed, with the coverlet and sheet still half-wrapped around his lower body. He was on his side, his spine arched backwards like a bow-stave drawn to its limit, his face hideously distorted and almost purple, while from his throat issued a continuous strangled moaning.

'What happened to him? Why is he lying so?' Tildy's horror caused her voice to rise in a near-shriek, and behind her in the doorway Maddy threw her apron up over her face and slumped back against the passage wall screaming hysterically.

Blood was bubbling and frothing from Jem's mouth, and Tildy wrung her hands in distress at her own impotence to do anything to aid the stricken youth, and Arthur Winterton likewise could only stand and curse in despair.

'He just come straight off the bed, God damn and blast it! He come like a bloody jack-in-the-box. One minute he was alaying theer almost peaceful, then the next he just jerked back into a bloody bending like he is now, and come jumping straight off the bloody bed. What can we do for him, girl? What can we do to help him?'

Even in the midst of her own distress Tildy was touched by compassion for this big brutal man whose massive strength was powerless to aid his son, and who was now betraying a love for that son which Tildy had never known he possessed.

Mercifully the attack abated and Jem's body collapsed once more, and the hideous purpling of his face lessened to a dull reddened flush.

'Help me put him back on the bed,' Tildy directed the farmer, and momentarily marvelled at this reversal of roles between them. She giving orders now, and the master obeying without question. 'I'll needs clean his mouth out. Can you fetch me some water and rag from the kitchen?'

Winterton nodded and went without hesitation, while Tildy tried to open Jem's mouth so that she could evaluate the damage he had done to his tongue and inner cheeks. To her dismay she found that although the arching spasm had ceased, the youth's jaws and body still retained a locked rigidity which prevented her from examining the inside of his mouth. So she was forced to content herself with feeling along his legs and arms to ascertain if he had broken any bones in his headlong fall from the bed. She remembered stories of people racked by lockjaw actually having their thighbones broken by the terrible force with which their leg muscles retracted and cramped when the spasms struck.

Maddy Thomas was still slumped against the passage wall with her apron up over her head, but thankfully her screams had ceased and now she merely moaned and snivelled. Tildy went to the girl and shook hard, then pulled the apron away and told her sharply, 'Get you downstairs, Maddy, and get the cabbage and potatoes ready for supper. Go on. And stop bloody skrawking! You'll upset Davy and Annie if they see you acting so.'

'I can't help it, Tildy,' the girl whined miserably, 'I arn't tough like you be. I'm frightened, so I am.'

Pity for her friend flooded Tildy's heart, but when she spoke her voice was hard and cold. ''Tis no use being frightened. That won't serve any useful purpose. Get on downstairs and do what I've told you. And see to Davy and Annie as well. I'll have to stay here for a while. Go now, before I get angry with you.' She gave the other girl a shove along the passageway, and to her relief Maddy went as bidden.

For all her outward display of cool control, inwardly Tildy wanted nothing more than to go away into some quiet corner and weep herself. She was equally frightened and distressed by the harrowing sights and sounds of Jem's attacks, and it was only by drawing deeply on her reserves of stubborn courage that she was able to maintain her façade of coolness. But even her courage could not prevent the trembling of her hands, which visibly agitated the water in the small bowl when she took it from Arthur Winterton.

Once more she gently sponged and cleansed the bloodied face of the youth, and tried to make his as comfortable as possible in his bed.

Arthur Winterton had sunk down upon Tobias' bed, his eyes locked on his younger son, and when Tildy went to leave the room he pleaded, 'Doon't go, girl. Stay here wi' me. I'll feel easier in my mind iffen youm here.'

Although she had no liking for the man, despising his ignorant brutality, his drunkenness, his physical grossness, yet at this moment Tildy's heart filled with pity for him, and she nodded in silent assent, and seated herself beside him on Tobias' hard cot to keep vigil over the suffering youth.

The big man began to talk disjointedly, almost as if he were speaking to himself, 'It makes no rhyme nor reason this happening to young Jem. The only normal kid I'se got. Why didn't it happen to Annie, or Toby, that's what I can't understand?' His tone was one of a blank incomprehension. 'Why did it have to be our Jem, instead of one o' the other 'uns, whom already damaged in the yed? It doon't make any rhyme nor reason . . . My missus birthed ten kids, and all but three om 'um ne'er lasted more nor a couple or three years at the outside. All on 'um died except the three still wi' me. And only our Jem was unflawed, and now he's been struck like this. There's no sense in it. No sense in it at all.'

Tildy sat listening to his ramblings, her mind racing as she puzzled on the implications of what the man was saying.

It was Doctor Charles Taylor, physician and surgeon, who came back with old Gilbert, driving his own smart carriage and pair of high-mettled horses. An old man who together with his dandified son, Hugh, had the largest medical practice in the two parishes of Tardebigge and Ipsley, Charles Taylor invariably wore the powdered tie-wig which was the badge of his profession, and well-cut black cutaway tailcoat and knee-breeches, with a ruffled white cambric shirt, white stockings and highly polished high–low boots. A tall black top-hat topped off his ensemble. His plump face was remarkably unlined for his age, and was as rubicond as the fine tawny port wine he drank in such large quantities, while the ampleness of his paunch bore witness to his love of a fine table.

That he had come in person on this call was a tribute to the standing of Arthur Winterton locally, because Charles Taylor only ever attended on the most important and richest inhabitants of the two parishes.

Gravely he examined the sick youth, asking no questions until he saw the nearly healed punctures on Jem's palm that had been made by the sheep-shears.

'When did this happen,' he asked Arthur Winterton.

The farmer shrugged. 'I doon't know.'

'If you please, Sir,' Tildy put in, 'it was during the sheep-shearing nine or ten days since.'

Taylor pursed his lips judiciously. 'Did much blood flow?' he wanted to know. 'Were the points deep-bedded in the flesh?'

'A fair depth, I think,' Tildy told him, 'but there wasn't a deal of blood considering.'

'Just so, just so,' the doctor murmured. During his long years of practice in both rural and town conditions he had amassed a vast experience of wounds of all types, and their after-effects. 'Were the punctures washed and cleansed, girl? Was any sort of salve put on them?'

Tildy shook her glossy head. 'Not to my knowledge, Sir. But the shears were well greased and wrapped before being put away,' she added as an afterthought, and the old doctor ejaculated disgustedly, 'Bah! Utter nonsense! Damned superstitious nonsense! There are times when I consider you yokels to be still living in the Dark Ages, be damned if I don't!'

'But the wounds are free from infection, Sir,' Tildy was stung into arguing. 'You can see that they are nearly fully healed. Mayhap the greasing of the shears did have some good result.'

For the first time since he had entered the room the doctor now regarded Tildy closely, and a gleam of recognition came into his eyes. 'I know you, do I not, young woman,' he stated. 'I seem to recall your face'.

'If you please, Sir, I was employed by your son to be sick nurse to your cousin, Mrs Dugdale of Bordesley Hall, some time past.'

Full recognition dawned and the old man said frostily. 'Yes, I know you now, young woman, and if my memory don't deceive me, you were too free with your tongue towards your betters at that time also. So be good enough to hold it now until I ask you to speak.'

Arthur Winterton's scant reserve of patience was being

sorely tried by this exchange, and he interjected, 'God-dammit, Taylor, let's get on wi' the business you was brung here for, and stop wasting time arguing wi' bloody servants can't we.'

The irascible old man ignored him, and instead lectured Tildy. 'This youth is labouring under a dual affliction. He has what is vulgarly known as the lockjaw, which is Trismus, and also Opisthotonos, or Tetanic Recurvation, more commonly known as Tetanus. Now in my experience this can result as a consequence of the infliction of a deep puncture wound, and no matter that the wound is apparently healthy I have seen this consequence many times during my years of practice.' He paused as if to evaluate what impression this display of professional expertise had had on this beautiful young woman, and satisfied by the dawning expression of respect in her face, went on in a kindlier tone: 'Unfortunately, Winterton, the boy is gravely afflicted, and to speak frankly the prognosis is not favourable. However, be assured that I shall exert my utmost endeavours to effect a cure.' He smiled with a grim irony. 'The boy will need constant nursing, and although this young woman is far too insolent towards her betters, nevertheless if my memory serves me correctly, my son held her in high regard as a sick nurse. So my advice to you is to utilize her in that respect, while the boy's illness runs its course.'

Arthur Winterton signified his agreement with the suggestion.

'Good!' Charles Taylor became briskly authoritative. 'Listen well both of you, for there is much to be done, and it must be done well and without any further loss of time . . .'

Chapter Seventeen

More than twenty-four hours had passed since the coming of Charles Taylor, and during that time Tildy had not slept or left the side of Jem Winterton except to snatch a bite of food, or to relieve her bodily needs. The old doctor himself had not left the house, and was now sleeping fully clothed on Tobias Winterton's bed, snoring loudly, mouth open, his porcelain false teeth fallen away from his shrivelled gums.

Jem himself was comatose, his breathing rapid and laboured, his head and body wet with sweat, his face livid-hued. The terrible spasms had reoccurred at irregular intervals through the night and day, and each attack had left the youth weaker.

Tildy, sitting on a stool beside the bed, feared for the worst. She had helped the doctor to administer doses of opium to the patient at three-hourly intervals, also purges. castor oil given orally, and clysters of sulphate of magnesia in pint infusions of senna administered rectally by means of bladder and tube. Together she and Taylor had constantly fomented Jem's jaws, throat and chest with decoctions of tobacco, and had applied poultices of tobacco shreds to the lower jaw and throat.

Five times Tildy had changed the soiled bedding and bathed the boy to cleanse away the foul-stenched discharge induced by the enemas, and now, fast nearing bodily and mental exhaustion, she fought to keep her eyes open and her attention fixed on the patient.

A tapping sounded on the door and Tildy went to open it. Maddy Thomas held out a small crock bowl towards her. 'Here, Tildy, I'se brung you some tay, I pinched some leaves from the Master's caddy,' she whispered and winked, 'Theer's a drop o' the old bugger's brandy in it as well.'

Tildy smiled her thanks and gratefully sipped the hot steaming liquid.

'How's Jem?' Maddy asked, concern showing in her expression.

Tildy shook her head sadly. 'Not so good, Maddy.' Then in her turn whispered, 'Is Davy alright, and the Master and Tobias?'

'Davy's playing wi' Annie in the orchard, and Toby's out working. He reckons it's best for him to keep busy at this time, to try and keep his mind off what's happening.'

Tildy nodded understandingly. 'And the Master, what's he about?'

On the doctor's insistence Arthur Winterton had been excluded from the sick room, for although he clamoured to help them, his anxiety for the boy rendered him a liability rather than an asset.

Maddy's plump face was both solemn and mystified at the same time. 'He's still sitting in his armchair, staring down at the table-top. He arn't moved nor spoke, nor slept since he left this room last night. I'se never seen him like this afore, Tildy, it's like he's in a trance, like he's bin bewitched.'

'Oh Maddy, have done with this talk of witchcraft, for the love of God have done with it,' Tildy remonstrated wearily. 'Haven't I already told you what the doctor said had caused the lockjaw? It was the puncture with the shears, Maddy. It has naught to do with witchcraft. You ask old Gilbert, he'll tell you that the shearers always go in danger of getting attacked by the lockjaw.'

Maddy's features assumed a mulish obstinacy. 'I doon't care what old Gilbert says, Tildy. I saw that curse doll, didn't I. I saw wheer the thorns was put in it. Them bloody thorns was pushed into the jaws, warn't they. And young Jem's got the lockjaw, arn't he. You can't deny that fact, can you.'

Tildy was too tired to argue. 'Alright Maddy. Believe whatever you want to believe. I just don't care at this time, I've too much to be going on with as it is. All I really want to do now is to lie down and sleep.'

Her friend was instantly contrite. 'I'm sorry, Tildy. I arn't wishing to upset you, really I arn't.' She smiled and stroked Tildy's face with her fingers. 'Does you want some more tay?'

Tildy nodded assent, and whispered jokingly, 'I like the stuff, but it does make me pee an awful lot.'

The other woman chuckled lewdly. 'I could tell you summat as makes me want to pee a sight more than tay does arter I'se had a dose of it.' She nudged Tildy's ribs archly. 'Mind you, it doon't stop me wanting it.'

The next instant Tildy heard a peculiar snapping impact from the room behind her, accompanied by a brief choking cry and she immediately pushed Maddy away from the door. 'Leave the tea for now.' She pressed the empty bowl into the girl's hands and closed the door in her frightened face, then turned knowing what she would find.

Jem's body was again arched upwards beneath the bedcovers, his face purple, muscles and tendons strained in stark relief, veins and arteries pulsing like writhing serpents. His breathing a harsh tortured rasping, and sweat pouring from every pore.

'Doctor Taylor! Doctor Taylor! Wake up! For Christ's sake rouse yourself!'

Tildy roughly shook the sleeping man into wakefulness, and blearily he stumbled to his feet, cursing his stiff joints, and pushing his false teeth back into position as he bent over the sick youth.

'Well, that's a mercy at any rate, he's not trapped his tongue this time,' Taylor muttered. 'Where's my wig?'

Wordlessly Tildy picked it up from the pillow of Tobias' bed and handed it to the old man, who spent a couple of minutes carefully arranging it on his bald head. Then he sniffed loudly, and frowned. 'The air is foul in here, girl. You'd best get a window open. How you people can live in such a stink is beyond me,' he finished pettishly.

Tildy experienced strong indignation, 'I asked you to let me open the windows hours since, Doctor Taylor, and you refused me permission.'

He waved her away. 'Get on with it, girl, and hold your tongue.'

'Damned old fool!' Tildy muttered beneath her breath, and thankfully opened the casement to feel the cool sweet air of the late evening flood in to replace the stinking staleness of the room's atmosphere.

When she looked back at the bed her heart sank as she saw the grave expression on the old man's face, and she moved to stand opposite him as he lowered his head and placed his ear against the straining rib-cage of the writhing body. When he straightened upright Taylor sighed gustily and told Tildy, 'I fear he is sinking fast beyond recall, girl. His heart will not stand many more such spasms.'

Tears of distress stung her eyes. 'But is there nothing more we can do for him, Sir? Are there no other treatments we can try?'

He regarded her with genuine sympathy. 'You hold the boy in great affection, do you not.' It was statement, not question, and Tildy nodded vigorously.

'I do indeed, Sir. He is a gentle, kind soul and has not a bad bone in his body. It is not fair that he should be so afflicted when so many evil ones go through life in full health and vigour. There's no right nor justice in it.'

The old man smiled mirthlessly. 'In the practise of my profession, Crawford, I have long since ceased to expect any apparent right or justice in the inflictions visited on mankind. Only God knows the purpose of them, or why one should suffer and another not.'

'Then God should put his house in order!' Tildy blurted out angrily, and the old man chuckled with genuine amusement.

'Don't let Parson Clayton hear you say that, girl.'

Before Tildy could answer, Jem abruptly subsided in the bed, as the spasm lessened its hold, and lay with eyes dazedly wandering, muttering incoherently in a semi-delirium.

Taylor laid his hands on the youth's forehead, and clucked his tongue. 'The fever is increasing in strength. You'd best sponge him down with cold water, girl. If it does nothing else, it will at least soothe him a little.'

While she was engaged in this, Doctor Taylor paced slowly up and down the room, apparently deep in thought. Then came to a standstill directly behind Tildy as she sat on her stool and rested his liver-flecked hands on her shoulders.

'There is perhaps one chance of saving the boy. How strong-stomached are you, girl? Because I'll need you to assist me.'

She looked up at him over her shoulder. 'I will do whatever you need of me, Sir, if there is a chance of saving Jem's life.'

His fingers momentarily squeezed her flesh. 'Good girl!' he told her. 'Now, who else in the household is possessed of strong nerve and stomach, and strong arms as well, because I intend to amputate the boy's arm.'

'To cut his arm off?' she exclaimed with horror.

Again his fingers squeezed her flesh. 'It is his only chance of life, Crawford. To divide the disorder from its source. His vital fluid has diminished so much that death even now has him in its grasp. The only chance of cheating death is to amputate. If there was anything else to be done, then I would do it. But alas, there is nothing that will serve.'

Tears fell from Tildy's eyes as she stared down at Jem, visualizing him as a one-armed cripple.

As if reading her thoughts, Taylor told her gently, 'Better for him to lose an arm, than to lose his life, girl. And unless I amputate, and quickly, that he will most surely do.' Releasing her shoulders his manner became brisk and businesslike. 'I shall go and speak with Master Winterton, and obtain the other helpers I need. I want you to lie on the other bed and rest while I'm gone. The boy will do well enough for now. He'll not suffer another attack for a while. Come now, lie down and rest.'

Tildy allowed herself to be led to the other bed, and

thankful for this opportunity to close her aching eyes, lay down on its hard mattress to fall asleep almost at once.

When Doctor Taylor woke Tildy darkness had fallen and a strong wind had risen, its gusts moaning around the eaves of the ancient house and rattling the ill-fitting casements of the windows.

She peered up at the old man and then looked across at the other bed. In the wavering light of the candle the doctor carried she saw that it was empty. Cold dread struck through her. 'Where's Jem?' she questioned fearfully. 'He's not died, has he?'

'No, girl.' The doctor spoke softly. 'But I'll not hide from you the fact that he is very near to death. I am going to operate immediately. Pray God it will not be too late. Come with me.'

The kitchen was lit by half a dozen smoking lanterns, their light tinging the complexions of the people there with a sickly yellowish pallor. Jem was laying on his back on the great table, clad only in a pair of long under-drawers. His breathing was rapid and stertorous and the sheen of sweat on his head and body shone dully in the lamplight.

On a bench next to the table the doctor's medical chest was opened and from it Charles Taylor lifted an old frock coat the front and folds of which were thick with the encrustations of dried blood, pus and body fluids. He removed his well-cut black tailcoat and donned the frock coat in its place. Next he took varied instruments from the chest and laid them on the bench in a grim line. Long-bladed and short-bladed scalpels, forceps, a small hand-saw, pieces of sponge, a small tin bowl, curved needles and lengths of waxed thread, these latter he threaded through the lapel buttonhole of his frockcoat so that they hung like streamers before his chest.

These preparations completed, Charles Taylor issued his instructions.

'You will hold the patient's head firmly, Master

Winterton. You fellows take a leg each and keep them pressed down to the table.'

Old Gilbert and Purple-face Joe took their stations.

'You, girl, take this lantern and direct its light upon this arm so.' Susy apprehensively obeyed.

'You Tobias, will hold down your brother's other arm and shoulder, and be ready to exert your utmost strength to keep him fixed and still. And you,' Taylor pointed to Sim, 'will put your weight on the patient's hips. And mind well what I say, all of you, on no account allow the boy to struggle free, and close your ears to any cries or pleadings he might give utterance to.

'You, Crawford, will act as my assistant and you, girl,' he told Maddy Thomas, 'you will stand by the bench here and be ready to hand to me anything I might need from these articles I have laid out. If all of you attend well to your duties, then this business will not take long to complete, and the boy's pain will quickly be at an end.'

It was Jem's right arm that was to be amputated, and Taylor demonstrated what he wished Tildy to do. 'Now Crawford, you will take the upper arm in your hands so, and exert a firm pressure to stretch the skin and integument, pull it backwards towards the shoulder. As I cut two flaps, you will hold the upper flap back to enable me to see clearly what I am about, and then take hold of the lower flap also and hold that back as well while I saw the bone through. I shall use a screw tourniquet on the upper arm to prevent any great effusions of blood, and we'll tie a leather pad between his teeth for him to bite on.'

He regarded the semi-conscious youth with satisfaction. 'I doubt he'll feel any great degree of pain; he's under the influence of the opium doses.' Next he spoke to all of them. 'Now remember what I have told you. Pay careful heed to what you are about, and in very short order the business will be done.'

Quickly the doctor tied a leather pad securely between Jem's teeth, and strapped the brass screw tourniquet onto the youth's muscular upper arm, then tightened it to constrict the blood flow. 'All of you take your positions.

Crawford, lay hands on and stretch towards the shoulder.'

As all moved to comply, Charles Taylor lifted the long-bladed scalpel from the bench, gripped Jem's elbow with his left hand and lifted it, nodded to Tildy who was standing face to face with him, then transfixed the youth's upper arm between biceps and bone with the blade, and with a deft slice cut a semi-circular flap of flesh.

'Hold it up and back, Crawford,' he instructed quietly, and Tildy's fingers gripped the hot raw bleeding flesh and held it up and away from the ivory whiteness of the bone. A quick twist and slice and the lower flap was done. A circular slash and the bone was free and completely exposed.

Susy's lantern shook and wavered and Taylor cursed her, 'Hold still, damn you. Hold that glim still!'

He laid down the knife and took up the small handsaw and began to cut through the white glistening bone. A powerful wave of nausea hit Tildy, and her sight swam as her stomach heaved, but she fought to control her senses and continued to obey her previous instructions. A moan and a heavy thud told Tildy that Maddy Thomas had fainted and fallen, but she kept her own eyes firmly fixed on the saw-blade. As the serrated teeth cut into the bone Jem's eyes widened, he screamed and his body heaved upwards. 'Hold him still, damn you. Hold him still,' the doctor shouted angrily and the men exerted all their force to hold the youth's plunging body. Then the saw-blade cut through the last layer of bone, and Charles Taylor casually pitched the severed arm to the floor. He swabbed the raw surfaces with the sponges and used small forceps to pull out the ends of the severed arteries and quickly ligatured them, before unscrewing the brass key of the tourniquet. Bloody serous fluids oozed from the wound as the doctor deftly sewed the flaps of flesh together over the stump of bone, then slapped a poultice made from bread and warm water over the sutures and padded and bandaged the stump.

Jem had sunk back, his face an agonized grey, wet mask between his father's great work-scarred hands. Both Arthur and Tobias Winterton's expressions showed anxiety as they gazed at the youth, but the other men's faces were stolid and unmoved and momentarily Tildy found herself envying their apparent indifference to the sight and smell of blood and mutilation. She herself felt sick and weak, and her innards seemed to be trembling violently, as were her hands now that reaction to the operation had struck home to her.

Charles Taylor used a piece of filthy rag from his medical chest to wipe the blood and fluids from his hands then used the same rag to cursorily cleanse the blood-stained instruments before replacing them in the chest.

'You may take the boy back to his own bed now,' he told the older Winterton, and the big farmer carefully lifted the youth and bore him away in his mighty arms. The old doctor regarded Tildy with considerable respect. 'You have done well, Crawford. Do you feel able to maintain a watch over the boy for the rest of the night?'

She nodded. 'I think so, Sir.'

'Good.' Taylor smiled, and then instructed her, 'The boy may well sleep for some considerable time, but if he should wake then you may give him small-beer to drink if he complains of thirst, and if he can keep that in his stomach then feed him beef tea to restore his strength. You can mix a glass or two of port wine with the tea, that will help replace the blood he has lost.'

An audible groan from the side of the bench reminded them of Maddy Thomas' presence and Tildy hastened to raise her friend up and make sure that her fall when she fainted had not caused her any injury.

Maddy sat slumped on the bench, the colour slowly returning to her face. The doctor took his leave, telling Tildy that he would return the following day.

'What if Jem should suffer more attacks, Sir? What shall I do then?' Tildy asked him as he left.

The man's plump pink features were solemn, and he told her in a low-pitched voice, 'If the spasm is severe in its nature, Crawford, then I fear that there will be little that either you or I can do. The operation will have failed to divide the affliction from its source.'

'And Jem will die?' Tildy sought confirmation of her

worst fears, and received that confirmation when the doctor nodded.

'Almost certainly he will, Crawford, unless there is an intervention of the Divine Will.'

When Charles Taylor's carriage had rolled away from the yard, Tildy set Maddy Thomas to prepare the beef tea and as soon as the kitchen emptied as her workmates sought their beds she scrubbed and mopped the blood-stains from table and floor.

Tobias Winterton picked up his brother's severed arm, and with tears running down his cheeks went with it from the house.

'Wheer's he going wi' that?'Maddy wondered aloud, and Tildy could only shrug in ignorance.

Once she had finished her cleaning, she went upstairs to the patient's bedroom.

Arthur Winterton was seated on Tobias' bed, his face drawn and gaunt in the dull light of the lantern. He frowned at Tildy as she entered, and whispered hoarsely, 'Get to your bed, girl. I'll look to the boy.' When she hesitated he went on, 'I'll call you if anything should happen. But he seems to be peaceful now.'

Jem was lying absolutely still, only the barely discernible rise and fall of the coverlet over his chest showing that he still breathed.

Feeling utterly spent herself, and knowing that there was nothing she could do for Jem at this time, Tildy did not argue with the man. 'Very well, Master. But if he should wake, then call me, won't you.'

Winterton grunted an affirmation and Tildy left him alone to his vigil.

The hours passed with a terrible slowness and Arthur Winterton's lids became heavier and heavier, then closed of their own volition. He awoke with a start in the grey of early dawn, and shivered with the chill of the air.

Jem lay still, his face white and bloodless, his mouth agape, his sightless eyes wide and empty, and the big man vented a long wailing cry as he realized that while he slept death had claimed his son.

Chapter Eighteen

It was a Saturday, and although no statute had been enacted, Saturday was the market day for Redditch town and from before dawn people with goods and produce for sale had been arriving to take up their stands. By ancient usage the market traders erected their stalls along the road stretching from St Stephen's Chapel crossroads eastwards towards the Old Lock-up.

Tildy, Maddy, little Davy and Annie were sitting in the back of the cart driven by Tobias Winterton, baskets of eggs and butter covered with clean white cloths beside them, and a dozen hens, lashed together by the legs in clusters of three, clucking mournfully in concert with the two trussed sheep that also shared the constricted space.

The cart creaked past the stinking Big Pool and approached the castellated Lock-up as the first rays of the rising sun gilded its parapet. Tobias looked back and down at Tildy.

'Wheer does you want to get off?' he wanted to know.

Tildy shrugged. 'Anywhere that suits you to drop us.' She could not help feeling some irritation at the way he was still treating her with a sullen hostility. 'Whooaaa, whoooaaa.' He brought the carthorse to a halt by the side of the Lock-up.

'You'd best get down here then,' he told her, and made no effort to aid the two young women as they unloaded the baskets of butter and eggs, and the tied chickens.

Tildy beckoned to little Davy. 'Come now, Honey.' She lifted his small body over the tailgate. 'Now stand here like a good boy while I help Annie. Come on, Annie, love.'

The Mongol girl's face was badly swollen on one side of her jaw, and she had a huge swathe of bandage wrapped around her head to cover the swelling, which was caused by a badly decayed tooth. Snuffling with distress she allowed Tildy to help her fat ungainly body to climb down onto the road. Tildy briefly hugged the girl to her. 'Now don't you cry any more, Sweetheart. We'll soon have that nasty tooth taken away, and then you won't be feeling any more hurt from it, will you?'

Tobias Winterton's eyes momentarily softened as he saw Tildy hug the girl and heard her soothing tones, but when he spoke it was still with harshness in his voice. 'When 'ull you be ready to goo back home?

Tildy's resentment of his surly manner surfaced briefly. 'When we've done all that's needful,' she answered tartly.

His handsome features scowled down at her. 'And how long is bloody needful?' he demanded.

'How can I know how long?' she demanded exasperatedly. 'I can't say how soon we'll be able to sell this lot. And then I've got to shop for some calico cloth, and thread and needles and buttons. Then I've got to find the tooth-jack and get poor Annie's tooth drawn. And your Dad wants me to go to Mister Bott's on the Lower Green there and pick up that watch he left to be mended.'

Maddy Thomas grumbled loudly, ''Tis alright for you, Toby. All you'se got to do is to drop them bloody sheep off at the butcher's, and pick up the new barrel from Cooper Freeman, and them youm done wi' chores, arn't you. You can goo and sit on your arse in the bloody alehouse and leave all the bloody shopping and such to me and Tildy. Your Dad's told us to get tay, and sugar as well, and two sacks o' salt.'

'I doon't care what he's told you to get,' Tobias rejoined angrily, 'I can't waste time hanging about bloody Redditch for you two. Theer's too much needs doing back home. If you arn't ready to goo when I'se done me errands, then you'll just have to bloody walk home.'

'Oh will we,' Maddy flared. 'Well my bucko, if you thinks I'm agoing to walk back to soddin' Ipsley carrying two sacks o' bloody salt on me back, then you can think agen.'

'Oh bugger you!' the young man swore petulantly, and shouted to the horse to move on. The cart lurched away, and Maddy shook her fist at it.

'And bugger you an' all!' Her rosy face flaming with temper, she told Tildy, 'I'm fair fed up wi' that bugger these days, Tildy. He's become a real nasty miserable sod, so he has. He's getting to be more like his bloody Dad every day, I'll take me oath on it. For two pins I'd leave this lot lay here and bugger off back to Studley.'

Tildy, although sharing the other's girl's resentment, tried to be charitable. 'He's still upset about young Jem, Maddy, that's why he's like he is these days.'

Two weeks had passed since Jem's death and all three adults of the small party still suffered after-effects of one sort or another because of that death. For Tildy it was purely and simply a sadness that such a fine youth had been taken. For Tobias it was a grief compounded by a bitter anger against the fate that had robbed him of a brother he loved. For Maddy Thomas it was a source of fear. Despite everything that Tildy said to her concerning the cause of Jem's death, the girl remained convinced that it had been brought about by witchcraft, and was living in dread of any further evil being wished upon the Winterton household. Now she quickly crossed herself. 'Don't keep on talking about Jem, Tildy. It'll only bring more trouble to us.'

Tildy sighed and shook her head resignedly. 'Oh Maddy, I wish you'd get it into your head that it wasn't witchcraft or anything like that. The poor lad got the lockjaw from the shears. Doctor Taylor assured me of that. And he's a man who knows all about such things, isn't he. It was a terrible accident, Maddy. That's all, only an accident.'

The other girl's expression became mulishly obstinate. 'He can say what he likes, Tildy, but I knows better.'

Tildy accepted the futility of further argument. 'Alright, Maddy, let's leave it. Come now, let's find a good spot for selling.'

Together they mauled the heavy baskets and the squawking chickens up into the market-place and found a clear space between two stalls where they could lay out their wares for sale. At this hour only a few early shoppers, mainly housewives in white aprons, mob-caps and shawls, were wandering the market. The main business would come later when the needle mills and workshops discharged their masses. Tildy looked around speculatively, as by her side Annie wept and complained constantly of the pain in her jaw, and little Davy, seeing his beloved playmate so distressed started to weep in sympathy.

'I think I'll go and find the tooth-jack, Maddy, and get this poor soul attended to. It's best I get her tooth drawn now, while it's still quiet.'

Maddy grinned and quipped, 'It's best you get it done now while the bloody tooth-jack's still sober enough to see what he's about. The bugger's always blind drunk by breakfast time.'

Tildy smiled agreement, and told Davy, 'Now Honey, you must stay here with Maddy while I take Annie with me to get her made better.'

'I want to come with you, Mammy,' the child wailed in protest. 'I want to come with you and Annie.'

Tildy shook her head in firm negation, mindful of how the screams of some of the tooth-jack's customers could frighten small children. 'No, you're to stay here, and that's an end to it.'

His small face pouted, but he recognized his mother's tone, and knew that when she spoke like this, no amount of tantrum or coaxing would sway her.

'If you're good, then I'll buy you some ginger-snap.' She softened her refusal to take him with this piece of bribery, and he crowed with delight. 'And Annie as well, Mam. Some ginger-snap for Annie as well?'

Maddy chuckled fondly, 'Oh you're a good little soul, bless your little heart.' She swept him into her arms and smothered his face with kisses, laughing as he struggled and wriggled to be free.

Tildy seized the opportunity to escape without further argument, and taking Annie by the hand led her away through the stalls.

She found the tooth-jack enjoying his breakfast of meat pies and gin in the tap room of the Unicorn Inn. He was a fat man whose red-faced joviality contrasted oddly with the gruesome looking ropes of decayed teeth festooned about his body to serve both as a badge of his profession and an illustration of his vast experience of tooth-drawing. Even his ancient tricorn hat had strings of black, brown, green, yellow fangs dangling from its brim.

There were a few other men in the room, mostly local artisans wearing their square box-like hats fashioned from heavy brown paper and aprons rolled about their hips. Tildy explained her need to the tooth-jack, and he grinned at her, disclosing a mouthful of teeth every bit as colourful as those strung around him.

'I'll be with you just as soon as I finishes me brekfust, my maid.'

'How much do you charge?' Tildy enquired.

'Tuppence the tooth,' he informed, 'and worth every penny. Though I says it meself, I'm the best tooth-puller in the Midlands, bar none. Why, I'se pulled teeth from the yeds o' more lords nor ladies than I can recall the names on.'

Tildy put her arm around the whimpering Annie, who had been staring with a fearful fascination at the dangling ropes of teeth. 'There now, Honey, don't fret. This gentleman is going to take away that nasty tooth for you.'

The man laughed at Annie's woebegone face. 'That's right, my maid. Theer's no call for you to goo blarting your eyes out. I'll have the bugger shifted afore you can blink.' He crammed the last of the meat pies into his capacious mouth and chewed gustily, then wiped his greasy dirty hands on his equally greasy and dirty breeches. He swallowed hard and took a long gulp from his glass of gin, then belched in satisfaction. 'That's better,' he gusted, and winked at Tildy. 'Theer's naught to bate a good beef pie for brekfust, my maid. It sets a man up for his day's work.

Now you just bring this 'un outside wheer the light's better to see by, and I'll have a look at her.' He spoke to the room at large, and if any o' you gennulmen wants to avail yourselves o' my services, I'm now opening for business.'

Outside the tap room door was a flight of stone steps leading down to the courtyard of the inn, and at the bottom of these the tooth-jack seated Annie.

'Now open your gob, my maid, and let the dog see the rabbit.'

The girl began to wail loudly as he pried open her jaw and peered within, and her wailings attracted the attention of the loungers in the yard. Within seconds a small audience had gathered, and inevitably the more callous among them were quick to jeer at the frightened girl.

Tildy's first impulse was to round on them angrily, but she knew that to react to their baiting would only encourage them to further provocations, so she held her temper in check, and merely asked the tooth-jack, 'Do you want me to help you with her?'

He chuckled wheezily. 'No, my maid. That wun't be needful.' He fumbled in his pocket and brought out a rusty pair of pincers. Annie's wails became high-pitched and she tried to jerk her head free of his restraining fingers.

'Damn you, be still!' he shouted suddenly, and as she froze into momentary immobility he plunged the head of the pincers into her gaping mouth, his hand clamped, twisted and jerked, Annie screamed, and with a triumphant chuckle the tooth-jack waved the pincers in the air, their jaws locked on the offending tooth.

The crowd applauded jeeringly, and the fat man bowed mockingly back to them. then held out his free hand towards Tildy. 'That's tuppence you owes me, my maid.'

She handed him the coins, then comforted the sobbing girl, wiping away the blood on her lips and stroking her face.

'Hush now, Annie. It's all done with, Sweetheart. Hush now, the pain will soon pass.'

'Just make a wad out of a bit o' rag and let her put it over the hole and bite down on it. That 'ull soon curb the bleeding,' the tooth-jack instructed Tildy, and she nodded.

'Many thanks, I'll do that now.'

The fat man addressed the audience: 'Do you see how quick it's over. One twist and it's done. That's why I'm reckoned the best tooth-puller in the bloody Midlands. I'se ne'er bin known to draw the wrong 'un yet.'

'No, and you'se ne'er bin known to grow a new 'un either, to replace them you'se pulled. When you can do that then I'll let you pull these buggers.' A respectably dressed, middle-aged man in the front of the small crowd displayed his horribly decayed teeth.

The tooth-jack immediately pulled a handful of teeth from his pocket and held them under the man's nose. 'Look at them well and close,' he challenged, 'don't they all look sound and strong?'

After a pause the man agreed, 'That they does.'

'Well then, my good sir, if you'se got the rhino to pay with, I can grow these in your jaw. I can pull them o' yourn out, and pop these in to replace 'um. Arter a few days when the flesh takes hold on 'um, they'll be so fast held that you'll be able to ate a bloody horse wi' um, bones and all.'

Tildy stared at the displayed teeth, wondering how the tooth-jack had obtained them.

One of the crowd answered her unspoken question. 'They'm from dead men, they am.'

Instant repulsion assailed her, but her curiosity still held her there, and she remained at the steps, cuddling Annie while the snuffling girl bit miserably upon the wad of rag Tildy had fashioned and placed across the cavity left by the drawn tooth.

The tooth-jack scoffed at those in the group who appeared to share Tildy's repulsion. 'It doon't matter a toss wheer these come from. They'm good and sound, and that's all that matters. And theer's one thing that's certain sure, theer arn't going to be nobody coming to your door to ask for their bloody teeth back, is there.'

'No, but their bloody ghosts might,' someone said with apparent fearfulness.

The tooth-jack roared with laughter, and shouted, 'Well even if they does they arn't agoing to be able to carry 'um away, be they. I arn't met the ghost yet who carries a bag wi' him.'

The man with the badly decayed teeth licked his lips, seemingly racked by indecision, then asked, 'How much?'

'A tanner apiece, and bloody cheap at the price,' the tooth-jack announced. 'And don't forget, that for that price you gets a tooth drawn and a new 'un back.' He paused, his shrewd eyes examining the man before him. 'Tell the truth now, Cully, 'as you bin able to ate a bite o' meat, or a piece o' hard cheese wi' them bloody teeth o' yourn for these many years past? I'll wager that you arn't.' He gave the other no chance to reply. 'But just you think how good a beefsteak 'ull taste to you arter you'se got your new teeth. Just imagine chewing a ripe piece o' good hard cheese. Just imagine biting into a sweet fresh apple. And just imagine not ever having to be tormented wi' the bloody toothache ever agen in your life. By the Christ, it 'ud be worth a king's ransom to you, 'udden't it now?'

The man nodded.

'O' course it 'ull be. Now, say the word, and you can be ateing all them things within the week. Tearing your meat like a bloody lion. What do you say?'

Decayed Teeth looked crestfallen. 'I arn't got enough money.'

'How much has you got?' Tooth Jack demanded.

The man fumbled in his pockets and drew out a few coins. 'Tenpence ha'penny.'

The tooth-jack grinned and made an expansive gesture with his hands. 'I'll tell you what. You seems a decent sort o' man, so I'll do you a favour. I'll give you two new 'uns for your tenpence ha'penny. Two front 'uns, one at the top and one at the bottom. You'll at least be able to bite summat, if it's only your wife's neck.'

The crowd laughed at his sally, and Tildy joined in their laughter, although experiencing a touch of queasiness at the thought of dead men's teeth biting her own neck.

'Come now, let's have an answer,' the tooth-jack urged. 'Is it yes or no?'

The other man stood scratching his chin while the crowd, eager to be entertained by his sufferings, urged him to accept the offer.

'Goo on, do it.'

'Just think on how handsome you'll be wi' new teeth.'

Ne'er mind your missus's neck, you'll have your picking o' sweethearts then.'

'Here, man, I'll gi' thee a ha'penny towards the price.'

Tildy, mindful that she had errands to do, yet could not draw away, repelled yet fascinated by the prospect of seeing the tooth-jack replace bad teeth with good.

'I'll tell you what, Master tooth-jack,' Decayed Teeth eventually said, 'if you'll do it for ninepence, then I'm your man.'

'Done!' The tooth-jack laughed uproariously, and bellowed, 'Come one, come all, and see a modern miracle performed by yours truly, Albert Sykes, the finest tooth-puller in the Midlands.' He held out his open palm towards his customer. 'Come now, Sir, select your new teeth. These be upper fronts, and these be lower fronts.'

The man indicated two long-rooted specimens, and Sykes complimented him fulsomely.

'By God, but youm a man o' good taste, Sir, and a shrewd man o' business.' He addressed the audience at large: 'Does you see what this gentleman has done, my lords, he's picked out the two finest examples of upper and lower fronts that I'se ever come across in all the years I'se practised my profession. And I'll tell you true, I'd reserved them two fine teeth for His Grace, the Earl o' Plymouth hisself.' He assumed a doubtful expression. 'I arn't really sure that I can let you have them two, Master.'

'You'se made a bargain, now stick to it,' Decayed Teeth protested vigorously. 'You told me I could have me pick, so doon't try gammoning me now. Them's the two I chose, and them's the two I wants. I'se got as much right to 'um as any bloody earl.'

The crowd applauded this spirited assertion, and the

tooth-jack held both arms high in surrender.

'Alright, alright, my good sir, you shall have these two, and be damned to the Earl o' Plymouth. So give us the ninepence, and let's get to it.'

All the watchers immediately began to push in for a closer view, and the tooth-jack told them, 'Hold hard, my friends, I knows you all wants to see this miracle o' modern surgery, but I must have room to work. Come now, good Sir, get you higher up the steps here, and then everybody 'ull be able to see.'

Decayed Teeth now seemed to be enjoying the limelight, and he readily acceded to the tooth-jack's wish, and mounted halfway up the tap room steps and sat down facing the crowd. The tooth-jack pulled his patient's lips apart and made a great show of examining the teeth and gums.

'Now you must keep real still,' he instructed the patient, 'and keep your mouth wide. I'll have this done afore you can blink.'

Then he carefully took the two replacement teeth and held them between his own lips, produced the rusty pincers from his pocket and brandished them high, gripped the other man's open jaw with his left hand and with a practised dexterity plucked two teeth from their sockets. The patient bawled out in shock and pain, as with equal swiftness the tooth-jack dropped the pincers back into his pocket, spat the replacement teeth into his hand and plugged them into the two bleeding cavities. Producing a scrap of filthy rag he wiped the blood from the patient's mouth and with an air of professional pride displayed his handiwork to the crowd.

'Theer now, my lords, look at them, arn't they beauties! Arn't they the finest gnashers anybody could have. They'm a thing o' beauty, arn't they just. Show 'um off, good Sir', he urged. 'Give the good people a big smile and let 'um see how beautiful your new teeth be.'

Still half-dazed with shock and pain his customer tentatively touched his mouth, then bared his bloody teeth and gums in a grotesque travesty of a smile, the two implanted teeth showing with a startling whiteness in contrast to their blackened neighbours.

Tildy's fingers went to her own mouth as she gazed, and she was simultaneously torn with the desires to chuckle with delighted amusement, to be physically sick, and to turn away with repulsion.

'Now doon't bite wi' them new 'uns for a week at least,' the tooth-jack instructed. 'If they doon't get set in as hard as bloody rocks, then you'll only ha' yourself to blame, and I'll not be held responsible.'

Annie tugged at Tildy's arm. 'Where's Davy? I want Davy.'

Tildy smiled at the girl. 'Alright dear. We'll go back to Davy. But first we must go to the shops and buy some cloth to make shirts for your Dad and Toby and buy some other things as well.'

Taking the girl's hand she led her away from the Unicorn.

'How much for the butter?' The mob-capped housewife asked Maddy.

'A shilling and fourpence the pound. And the cheese is eight pence the pound.'

'That seems dear.' The woman's faded eyes evaluated the muslin-wrapped lumps, then moved to the trussed hens, and her head jerked dismissively. 'Them fowls looks to be dreadful scraggy as well.'

Maddy scowled up at her. 'Look Missus, I arn't their bloody owner. They belongs to my master, Arthur Winterton. If you'se got complaints about the goods he's sent me here wi', then goo and see him about it.'

'Saucy hussy!' the woman sniffed indignantly, and flounced away in a huff.

Maddy lifted her hand in a lewd gesture to the woman's retreating back and called to Davy who was playing in the dust nearby, 'Come here by me, Davy, and don't be wandering off.'

It was now ten o'clock in the morning and Maddy Thomas' normally equable temper was being sorely ruffled by her failure to sell any of the goods she had brought to the market. Times were hard in the town, and all the stallholders were by now grumbling about the poor trade they were doing that day, but they at least were able to drop their prices and thus sell something. Maddy, however, was bound by Arthur Winterton's instructions. He told her what prices she must ask, and without his prior permission she dare not alter those prices. The trouble was that if she returned to the farm with the goods unsold then she knew that she would have to face the farmer's ungovernable temper. A prospect that made her quail in anticipation. Now she stared miserably about her in search of Tildy.

'What's keeping you so long, my duck?' she muttered beneath her breath. 'At least if you was here I'd have company.' She leaned forwards and felt the cloth coverings of the butter. The sun was becoming hot now, and she was worried about the danger of the butter melting. She rearranged the white cloth covering over the baskets and moved them into the scant shade afforded by the vegetable stall to her left side.

A burly man dressed like a Needle Pointer in a red flannel shirt, leather waistcoat, cord breeches, rolled apron round his hips, square brown paper hat perched rakishly on his frowsty hair leaned down to prod the trussed hens with brutal fingers.

'What you asking for this bleedin' skin and bone, my wench?'

Even at this hour his breath reeked of beer and gin, and Maddy, who was well aware of the Needle Pointers' reputation for violent outbursts, answered quietly, 'Half-a-crown apiece, Master. They makes fine roasting.'

His hard eyes scanned her plump breasts. 'Not half as fine as you'd make, my pretty.'

She preened before his admiration, and answered cheekily, 'Ahr, but you'd not get a fine bird like me for half-a-crown.'

He laughed and told her, 'If I could, I'd buy a bloody dozen of you, my duck.'

Again his brutal hands mauled the squawking hens. 'I'll tell you what, I'll gi' you four bob for two on 'um,' he offered.

She shook her head. 'It's more nor I dare do, Master, to drop the price. It's Arthur Winterton who sets it, and I dares'nt let 'um goo for less, or he'd take the skin off me.'

'Now I'd like to see the bugger try and do that iffen I was with you.' The Pointer smiled grimly. 'Mind you, I arn't saying that I udden't like to take summat off you, but it 'udden't be your skin.'

By now Maddy was thoroughly enjoying the conversation. The man was quite good-looking, she thought, and had a bit of a way with him. She also thought that if she continued to flirt with him she would most likely succeed in selling him the hens at the price Arthur Winterton demanded for them.

She licked her lips lasciviously. 'I can't help but wonder what it is you'd like to be taking from me, Master? Because I'm only an innocent young maid so I am.'

The Pointer grinned. 'I'll needs whisper that to you, my pretty. I 'udden't want anybody else to know our business.' He brought his head low so that his mouth was by her ear and began to whisper, and as he whispered Maddy giggled and preened and giggled and preened, playfully slapped him, and giggled some more.

The young half-grown puppy licked Davy's face until the child shouted with laughter, then tail wagging furiously, bounded away. Davy got to his feet and went after the animal, and delighting in the play the puppy dodged and jumped and yapped with excitement. The pair went along the row of stalls and squatting market-wives, and across the front of the chapel, then on to the Green with its humps and hollows where gravel and sand had been dug out. In this magical new place Davy lost all track of time, seeking only to capture his new playmate. At last, right on the edge of one of the shallow pits the child succeeded in grabbing the young dog's hind leg, and in his excitement wrenched it painfully. The dog yelped and turned with snapping jaws, and its sharp teeth bit into Davy's cheek.

The child screamed and fell tumbling down the slope of the pit, his skin grazing against the rough gravelled side, and lay face downwards sobbing bitterly in the rubbish at its bottom.

For a moment the young dog stood with hanging tongue and cocked head gazing puzzledly down, then wagging its tail went bounding away in search of a fresh playmate.

'Now then, now then, what's you blarting for, young 'un? Fell down and hurt yourself, has you?'

The cracked voice caused Davy to turn over and squint upwards through tear-blurred eyes.

'My oath! You'se come a bit of a cropper, arn't you, my little chap. You'd best come on up here and let me take a look at you.'

The cracked voice was kindly, and Davy got painfully to his feet and stumbled up the slope towards it, sobbing afresh at the pain in his gravel-skinned elbows and knees.

'Oh theer now, doon't you take on so, dearie, you'se only lost a bit o' skin by the looks on it. And what's happened here, I wonder.' Fingers gently explored his wounded cheek, wiping away the blood and dust, and tongue clucked with concern. 'Oh my, it looks like you bin bit by summat, little chap . . . You tell me what's happened now, and I'll make it all better for you, wun't I. . .'

Davy blinked to clear his sight and saw a thin, brown, deeply-lined face with dark bright eyes surmounted by a wide-brimmed straw hat. Isolated black fangs glistened as the almost lipless mouth opened, but despite her ugliness Davy felt no fear of the old woman.

Tears forgotten now that he had found a new friend to talk to, Davy told her, 'The dog bited me, and I fell down that big hole there.' He pointed into the shallow pit.

The old woman's tongue clucked sympathetically. 'Well now, what a bad old dog it was to bite you like that. If I see him I'll give him a big smack for it.'

'Oh no, he didn't mean it. We was playing,' Davy protested, and the old woman cackled with laughter at the child's earnestness.

'Well, youm a rum little chap, I'll be buggered if you arn't. Now you must tell old Esther what youm named, and wheer you lives, so she can take you back to your Mammy.'

'My name is Davy, and I live with Mammy and Annie and Maddy.'

'Are they your sisters, Annie and Maddy?'

The child's face screwed up in concentration as he pondered the question, then said gravely. 'Annie plays with me, and I let her play with Sergeant Tom. She likes Sergeant Tom.'

The old woman was greatly taken with the child, finding his manner quaint and appealing. 'And who is Sergeant Tom, my honey?'

'He's my soldier.'

Once more she cackled with laughter. 'Well youm a caution, you am. Now can you tell me wheer you lives.'

'Oh yes,' he nodded confidently. 'We live at Toby's house.'

'And wheer might that be?'

'It's a long way away.'

'Did you have to walk here then, Honey?'

'No,' he shook his head, 'Toby brought me in his cart.'

'From what direction, Sweetheart?'

The child stared about him, then flung out his arm towards the westward side of the Green, which was lined with buildings.

'Does you live over there, in one o' them houses?'

'No!' The childish voice rose high with impatience. 'Not there. We live in Toby's house. It's got lots of rooms and there's lots of animals there.'

Old Esther Smith thought for some moments. She knew that beyond the western edges of the Green the land fell away to the valley floor, and that there were farmsteads and cottages dotted across that valley. 'I reckon you must live in one o' them places down theer and make enquiries as to if anybody knows who you properly be.' She smiled tenderly down at his solemn features. 'What does you reckon to that plan, my chap?'

Davy paused for a moment as if deep in thought, then asked, 'Shall you play with me now?'

'Not now I can't, Davy. Mayhap some other time. But now we must find your Mammy. She'll be worrying wheer you'se gone, I shouldn't wonder. Come now, you take hold o' my hand, and we'll goo and look for your Mammy, shall us.'

Davy took the claw-like hand with an utter trust and went happily with the old woman, prattling to her constantly as they walked across the Green.

Tildy smiled as she saw Maddy flirting with the Needle Pointer. 'Now I can ask her if it's alright for me to take Davy to visit Mother Readman, while she stays with the baskets. She won't grumble if she's got a beau to pay her attention.'

Her eyes searched for her child, and she frowned slightly when she didn't see him. Then shrugged, 'He'll be sitting behind her where I can't see.'

Maddy sighted her friend approaching and pushed the Pointer's head away from her ear. 'Me mate's come, so stop your nonsense now.'

The man straightened, and questioned, 'Well, be you agoing to meet me later then?'

Maddy arched her back so that her breasts jutted provocatively, and teased, 'I might, then agen, I might not, it all depends.'

'Depends on what?'

'On whether you buys these fowl from me.'

The Pointer chuckled. 'I'll tell you what, girl. You bring a couple on 'um wi' you when you comes to meet me. I'll buy 'um arter.'

'After what?' Maddy felt a little piqued.

'Arter we'se had our bit o' pleasuring.'

'You cheeky bugger! What does you take me for?' Maddy was now really piqued.

Before the man could reply Tildy came up to them. 'Where's Davy?'

'Just over theer,' Maddy began, then stopped and

suddenly rose to her feet, eyes anxiously darting from place to place. 'He was here a minute ago, Tildy. Playing just over theer.'

Tildy felt a rush of mingled irritation and anxiety. 'Oh Maddy, you promised you'd look after him,' she snapped. 'Where is he got to? How long is it since you saw him last?'

A guilty flush suddenly flamed in Maddy's cheeks, and Tildy began to panic. 'You don't know how long he's been gone, do you?' she accused angrily. 'How could you have been so bloody careless of him, Maddy?'

The Pointer realized that Tildy was upset and tried to mollify her. 'You'se got no call to worry your yed about the nipper, Missus, he can't be too far away.'

She ignored him, and instead stared up the market place, which by now was well thronged with people, livestock and carts. 'He's so small he could easily get knocked over or fall under a cart wheel. And then there's all sorts o' people come here on a mart day. Just supposing some loony get's hold of him.'

As Tildy voiced her fears Maddy's face blanched. 'Dear God above, Tildy, doon't even think such things,' she burst out, and the next instant was gone, running through the stalls, pushing men, women and animals aside and shouting as she ran. 'Davy? Davy? Davy? Davy?'

Annie Winterton's simple mind grasped that something was amiss and now she started to bawl loudly in distress.

Desperately Tildy fought to control her own rising panic, and to think rationally.

'Listen Missus, is there ought I can do to help?' the Pointer offered, and gratefully Tildy asked him, 'Please, Master, can you stay here and look after the girl and the baskets for me while I go and find my baby?'

'I can do better than that, Missus,' the man told her, 'just you tell me quick now, what he looks like and what he's got on in the way o' clothes.'

'He's about thirty inches high with black curly hair and blue eyes, and he's wearing a brown frock and brown sunhat, and his name is Davy Crawford.'

'Right!' The Pointer nodded and beckoned to a couple

of loungers who had been listening to the interchange. 'You heard that, lads?'

They nodded.

'Goo and start spreading the words through the mart then, to look out for a lost kid o' that description, and when he's found to have that word spread also.' The Pointer grinned at Tildy. 'You goo and search yourself, Missus, I'll stay here wi' this poor cratur and your baskets. It's best that you bestirs yourself, because you'll never abear just hanging around here for news, will you.'

Tildy was truly grateful for his help and thanked him profusely before hurrying away.

The news that a child was lost spread through the market crowd with surprising rapidity and many people turned aside from their own concerns to join in the search for little Davy.

Tildy went methodically from stall to stall asking if anyone had seen her child, but only one of the squatting market women thought that she had seen a child of his description chasing a dog some time previously.

At the cross roads she came up with Maddy Thomas, who had been along the Evesham Street. Maddy was beside herself with worry. 'Jesus Christ, Tildy, wheer's he at? Wheer's the little cratur got to?' She was nearly weeping.

'Perhaps he's aplaying on the Green, Missus?' a man suggested. 'A lot o' the small 'uns goes theer to play.'

Tildy was struggling to keep calm and to think rationally. 'Could some of you go to the far end and work back towards us, and I'll start from the chapel end.' She looked at Maddy Thomas' distraught face. 'You'd best come with me, Maddy.'

There were now nearly a dozen searchers, and they fanned out across the Green. An elderly woman came out from one of the cottages on its western edge, and shouted, 'What's you looking for?'

'I'm looking for my little boy,' Tildy shouted back, and gave the elderly woman his description. 'Have you seen him?'

'I reckon I might ha' done.' The woman nodded her toothless chin, and pointed. 'Theer was an old 'un, wearing all black wi' a straw bonnet on her yed, went down theer a bit since wi' a babby wi' a brown frock on it. Her was agooing down into the Common theer.'

'Do you know who the woman was?' Tildy questioned.

'Well, I doon't know her to spake to, but her looked like the old witch-'ooman from over by Mappleborough theer.'

'It's old Esther!' Maddy shrieked hysterically. 'Her's stole Davy! The old witch has stole our little Davy. Come on quick. For the love o' God come on quick.'

She started to run towards the narrow alleyway between two rows of cottages that led onto the Common, a stretch of gorse-bushed heath falling away into the valley to the west of the town. Tildy and the other searchers ran after her.

Midway down the slope of the Common, old Esther Smith had halted and was asking little Davy if he could point to where he lived. There were several isolated farms and cottages in sight and the child screwed up his face in concentration.

The old woman quickly realized that the child had no idea, and she told him, 'I reckon we'd best call at the fust house we comes to and ask if anybody knows who you be, little 'un?'

Davy pondered this for some moments, and then said solemnly, 'But we know me, don't we, Auntie Esther. I'm Davy.'

She cackled with laughter. 'I knows youm a proper caution, my chap.'

'Theer they be!' Maddy Thomas shrieked and pointed down the long slope. 'Theer's the witch wi' our Davy! Let's get her! Let's get the evil old bastard!'

Like a pack of hunting hounds sighting their quarry the searchers vented baying howls and went plunging downwards.

'Let's kill her!' Maddy Thomas shrieked as all her fear and hatred of the old hag exploded from her. 'Let's kill the witch!'

Old Esther Smith turned and saw the contorted, hate-filled faces as the pounding feet drew nearer and nearer, and fear budded, then abruptly blossomed into terror as she realized that they were crazed with hunger for her blood. In the grip of that terror she turned and fled down the slope towards the thickets of gorse and bushes, and Davy ran after her, crying out for her to come back to him, for he also was afraid of the oncoming mob.

Tildy outstripped all of the others when she saw her child turn and run, and reached him and snatched up his small body and sank down on to her knees, clasping him tight to her heaving breasts. He shrieked and struggled against her restraining arms until he knew who she was, and then sobbed and clung to her, while she kissed and cuddled him, oblivious to those others running past her bawling threats and imprecations.

'Is he alright, Tildy? Has that fucking old witch done him harm?' Maddy Thomas, face pouring with sweat and panting gustily leant over to examine the child. 'Jesus Christ! Look theer, on the poor little cratur's face! The evil old cow's bit him by the looks on it. And just look at his legs and arms, they'm tore to bloody shreds.'

Despite her own overwrought emotions Tildy was able to comment sarcastically, 'I wouldn't call a few grazes being tore to shreds, Maddy.'

Her friend was unabashed. 'And his poor little face, did that old 'ooman bite you, Davy? Did her?'

Davy had drawn comfort from his mother's embrace, and was no longer sobbing. Now he shook his head solemnly. 'No, she didn't bite me, the dog done that.'

'The dog?' Maddy shrieked, and stared at Tildy with horror. 'That warn't no dog, Tildy. That was the old bastard's familiar, that was. 'Tis well known in Studley that old Esther can conjure up the Black Dog of Arden.'

'Stop talking such nonsense, Maddy,' Tildy said sharply. 'You'll have the child frighted to death with your stupid fancies.'

'Bugger me, Tildy, I doon't for the life o' me see how you can doubt that her's a black witch. No mortal 'ooman of her age could ha' run like she did.'

Tildy shook her head impatiently. 'For God's sake be quiet, Maddy, while I talk to Davy.' With gentle questioning she drew his recollections of what had happened from him, and became satisfied that the old woman had only tried to help the child. 'There now, Maddy, you've heard what Davy has said. Old Esther was only trying to return him to me.'

Maddy Thomas rose to her feet and spat on the ground in disgust. 'How could her have been trying to do that when her was taking him in the opposite direction to wheer we lives? Youm being wilful blind, Tildy. The poor little cratur can only tell you what her's conjured him to say.' She pointed to where the mob were fruitlessly beating the gorse thickets in search of the old woman. 'And look theer now! Does you mean to tell me that any mortal 'ooman could ha' gone from view like her's just done.'

Old Esther Smith had indeed disappeared among the thickets, and a slight shiver of unease passed through Tildy's body. 'Can she really be a witch?' she wondered inwardly. Aloud she said sharply, 'Leave it lay now, Maddy. For pity's sake, leave it. Let's just be thankful that Davy is alright and back with us safe and sound, and let old Esther alone.'

By now the others in the group were tiring of their sport, and were straggling back up the slope towards the two women.

'Many thanks for helping me to find my baby,' Tildy told them, 'I'm truly grateful to you.'

'That's alright, Missus,' a stocky man told her, and scratched his tousled head in mystification. 'It's bloody funny wheer that old bitch went to though, arn' it. Just vanished, her did. Vanished into thin air.'

'That's because her's a black witch!' Maddy Thomas spat out. 'And her can take any shape her wants to. She's changed into some other form, that's what her's done. That's why her got away.'

As strength returned to her trembling body Tildy suddenly raised herself up. 'Annie! I've left Annie up in the town. Oh my God, she'll be fretting herself to death.'

She rose and lifted Davy in her arms. 'Come now, Sweetheart, we must go and find Annie. Come on, Maddy, we can't leave Annie up there with that Pointer any longer. It's not fair to the man to take advantage of his good nature so.'

Wearily she trudged up the Common and through the alleyway and crossed the Green. The mart was now in full swing and the crowds had increased. Tildy could not help but wonder at the normality of the busy scene in comparison to what had taken place down on the Common. 'Could old Esther really be a witch? Has she got the power to vanish? That's the second time that I've seen her one instant, and the next instant she's no longer there. It's really strange.'

From behind her Maddy called, 'You goo on, Tildy, and I'll catch you up. I just want's to pop in the Malt Shovel for a minute.'

'Take your time, there's no great rush. I can see to things,' Tildy told the girl, secretly relieved to have a few minutes of respite from her friend's protestations of old Esther's demonic powers, and went on alone.

'Where's Annie? Where's Annie? I want Annie.' Davy wriggled in her arms.

She reached the space between the stalls where she had left Annie with the Pointer, and her heart sank.

The Pointer had gone, and with him had gone the trussed fowls, the cheeses, the butter, and the articles she had bought from the shops. Only Annie was left, sitting by the side of the empty baskets, tears trickling down her swollen cheeks.

Chapter Nineteen

'What'll we do? What'll we do, Tildy?' For perhaps the fiftieth time Maddy wailed the question, and Tildy was forced to bite her tongue to stop herself from screaming.

They were sitting in Mother Readman's kitchen and had been in its gloomy stale-smelling confines for more than two hours.

'Now stop fretting yourself, girl,' Mother Readman told Maddy gruffly, 'I'se got some people out theer amaking enquiries about that cove who pinched your goods, and as soon as they finds out anything, then we'll be the fust to hear of it.'

'Arthur Winterton 'ull bloody well kill us,' Maddy moaned, rocking backwards and forwards on her stool in distress. 'He'll flay us wi' that bloody whip of his, so he 'ull.'

'Doon't talk so d'arft, girl. It warn't your fault,' Mother Readman snapped. 'How was you to know that cove was a bloody thief?'

But Maddy refused to be comforted and threw her apron over her head and sobbed bitterly.

Tildy sat with hands entwined upon her lap, watching little Davy and Annie, who were absorbed in some game of their own invention at the great table in the centre of the room. She envied their ability to exist only in the present moment, with no thought for what had gone or what was still to come.

'Who had the stalls next to your spot then, Tildy?' Mother Readman wanted to know, and Tildy shrugged.

'They were strangers to me, Mother, from Birmingham by the sound of them.'

The old woman's massive tallowy face scowled contemptuously. 'I'll wager that they'm involved somehow. All them Brummagem bastards am the same. Fly coves, who'd take the teeth from out o' your yed when you was wearing.'

Despite her worries, Tildy could not help but smile at the old woman's rampant prejudices. 'They seemed decent folk enough, Mother. When I told them what happened it was them who sent for the constable to come.'

'Tchaa!' the old woman's floppy mob-cap flapped around her pendulous cheeks as she tossed her head in scorn. 'Fat lot o' good that is, sending for that thick-skulled mawkin! Couldn't catch a pig in an entry, that bugger couldn't!'

Suddenly she lifted a finger to her lips and with a silent speed that belied her massive bulk she was gone from her chair and crossed to the far end of the room where the passage led to the front of her premises. The door to the passage was closed and Mother Readman paused for a second with her ear cocked as if she listened, then abruptly she slammed the door open and darted through into the dark passage.

Her disappearance was immediately followed by a shout of pain and the next instant Mother Readman reappeared in the kitchen dragging with her a dilapidated scarecrow of a man, with shoulder-length grey hair, a ragged soldier's coat on his shirtless torso, broken boots on his bare feet and a pair of ragged pantaloons through the rents of which his skinny legs showed clearly. In one hand he carried a huge tam-o'-shanter bonnet which he was waving in the air and with his other hand he was vainly endeavouring to detach Mother Readman's fearsome grip on his ear.

'Unhand me, woman! Unhand me before I make a ghost of you! Unhand me, I say.' The accents of his gin-hoarse voice were those of an educated man.

Tildy saw and heard him, and burst into delighted laughter. 'Why it's Master Montmorency!' she exclaimed, and as he heard her the scarecrow grinned hugely, displaying his stubs of rotting teeth.

'Is it you, Matilda?'

'Yes it is, you filthy old vagabond!' Mother Readman bawled and shook him by his ear while he cried out for mercy.

Maddy's apron came down and she stared with utter bemusement at the new arrival, as did little Davy and Annie.

'Oh don't hurt him, Mother,' Tildy begged the formidable old woman. 'Leave him go for my sake.'

'Does you hear that, you old bag o' bones? Does you hear that sweet maid pleading for you, you old rat-bag?' With each question Mother Readman twisted the trapped ear until the man cried out in pain. 'It's lucky for you that Tildy's here, or I'd tear the liver and lights out o' your stinking body and make you eat the buggers.' With a final twist Mother Readman released the ear, and pointed to the bench at the inglenook fire which faced the stools the girls were seated on flanking Mother Readman's massive throne-like chair. 'Set your rotten carcass down theer, Montmorency, and don't you dare move t'il I tells you so.'

With a haughty gesture the scarecrow scorned this threat, and turning to Tildy bowed elaborately, flourishing his tam-o-shanter. 'Welcome, thrice welcome, and thrice times thrice welcome, oh beauteous Matilda.' He straightened his skeletal body to its full six feet height and declaimed:

'Is she not more than painting can express,
Or youthful poets fancy when they love?'

Then he winked at Tildy. 'Nicholas Rowe, *The Fair Penitent*, Act Three, Scene One.' He spotted Maddy's amazed expression, and bowed to her also. 'Allow me to introduce myself, Ma'am. Marmaduke Montmorency, your servant, Ma'am. Once an ornament to the Thespian profession, now, tragically, a man scourged by life's misfortunes.' He again struck a pose and declaimed sonorously:

'As if Misfortune made the throne her seat,
And none could be unhappy but the great.'

Then he made a great show of flicking the dust from the bench with his tam-o'-shanter and seated himself with the air of a grandee.

Mother Readman laughed hugely. 'Just see the old bugger, Tildy. He don't change, does he.'

Wiping tears of laughter from her eyes Tildy had to agree.

Mother Readman, settled herself on to her creaking chair and demanded of the newcomer, 'Wheer the bloody hell 'as you bin, Montmorency? I sent word for you to come here nigh on two hours since.'

He inclined his head graciously. 'Just so, Ma'am. Just so. You did indeed send heralds forth from this palace to summon me to your august presence.'

'Then what's kept you so long?' she scowled warningly. 'And it had better be a bloody good reason, my bucko.'

He grinned at her, and for a moment resembled a mischievous urchin. 'It is the best of reasons, my good woman. I was engaged upon your business. Your heralds told me what had happened, and I immediately fell to work.' He lifted his filthy, black-nailed hand on high.

'How doth the little busy bee
Improve each shining hour,
And gather honey all the day,
From every opening flower.

Isaac Watts, died 1748. A scribbler of hymns, but not a bad fellow for all of that.'

''Ull you give over wi' your bloody nonsense, Montmorency,' Mother Readman shouted, 'and tell me what you'se found out.'

His bloodshot eyes were sympathetic as he spoke to Tildy. 'No one seems to know that fellow who stole your goods, Matilda. It seems that he had a woman who helped him to carry them off. But no one is really sure that they can remember either of them. Alas, my dear lady, your birds are flown.'

'Does that mean that our stuff's gone for good then?' Maddy Thomas put in, and Marmaduke Montmorency nodded gravely. 'I fear so, young woman.'

'Oh Christ!' Maddy burst into noisy tears and once more threw her apron up over her face and head.

Tildy's own courage sank as she visualized what this could mean for her and Maddy.

'I arn't aggoing back to that bloody farm,' Maddy affirmed tearfully. 'I arn't getting near bloody Arthur Winterton. I'll goo back home to Studley, so I will.'

'Now doon't talk daft, girl,' Mother Readman admonished, 'if you leaves your master's service like that he can get you put in the Bridewell. And another thing, if you runs off from him now, then he's certain sure going to think that you'se had a part in robbing his goods, arn't he, that stands to reason, that does.'

'What should we do then, Mother? Should we go back to the farm and risk his temper?' Tildy asked, and the old woman's chins wobbled as she nodded and replied, 'O course you should goo back, Tildy. You arn't got no other choice really, has you.'

Reluctantly Tildy was forced to agree.

Chapter Twenty

It was mid-afternoon when the small party got back to the Winterton Farm, and Susy met them in the yard.

'What's up?' She regarded their miserable faces with perplexity. 'You looks like you'se lost a pound and found a penny.'

'It's bloody worse nor that,' Maddy wailed, and burst into fresh floods of tears.

Tildy quickly told the dairy maid about the theft, but did not mention Esther Smith, and the girl's hand went to her mouth as she listened.

'Oh my good God!' she breathed when Tildy had finished. 'Oh my God, old Arthur 'ull goo fucking mad when he hears this. He'll bloody kill you both, so he 'ull.'

Despite her own fears Tildy tried to put a brave face on the situation. 'How can he blame us? We haven't stolen ought from him. Where is he now, I'll go and tell him right off what's happened.'

The dairymaid's cheeky face was solemn. 'He arn't here, Tildy. He's gone off on the drink somewheres. If I was you, my wench, I 'udden't bother waiting here to tell the old sod anything. I'd take to me heels in double-quick order.'

'That's what I bin atelling her,' Maddy burst out. 'I reckon we should goo to me Mam in Studley.'

'I've already explained to you why we must tell Old Arthur ourselves what has happened,' Tildy could not help but speak sharply, because the other woman's fears were threatening to infect her also. 'If we run off, then we'll be judged guilty of stealing the goods. At least this way, we can assert our innocence.'

Susy thought hard for a couple of moments, then said, 'Listen both o' you. Toby come back an hour since and he's up top theer, shifting the potatoes that the gang's lifting. Goo up and see him afore the old man gets back. Toby 'ull stick up for you, I'm sure.'

Tildy could see the sense in that suggestion. 'Alright then, we can do that. But let's get these kids settled first.'

'I'll see to Davy and Annie.' Susy urged, 'You two get on up to Toby right away.'

'Yes Tildy, come on.' Maddy desperately seized at this chance to find someone to shield them from Arthur Winterton's fury. 'We can tell Toby everything. We can tell him how it was old Esther's fault that the stuff was pinched. If her hadn't tried to steal Davy then nought o' this would have happened. It's all because that old witch cursed this place that all this has happened anyway. It's all her fault.'

Susy pounced instantly. 'What does you mean? Come on Maddy, tell me about this curse.'

Despite all Tildy's attempts to stop her, Maddy poured out the whole story of Esther Smith's brutal eviction from the kitchen, her curses, and the finding of the curse doll, and the chase and subsequent mysterious disappearance of the old woman on the Common.

By the time that Maddy's voluble account finally came to its ending, Susy's usual cheeky gaiety had left her, and it was a fearful and subdued woman who asked Tildy, 'Is it right what Maddy says? Did it all happen like that?'

Tildy shrugged helplessly. 'Well, yes, it did happen, but I can't really believe that old Esther has powers.'

'Well I can believe that her has. I'se bin told such things about her afore, Tildy.' The dairymaid's eyes were shadowed and apprehensive, and without another word she suddenly turned from them and ran out of the yard.

'Susy? Susy, where are you going?' Tildy shouted after her, and the girl called back as she ran, 'I'm going to tell Toby.'

Tildy shook her head in defeat, knowing that tired as she was from the events of the day, she would not have enough strength left in her legs to overtake the dairymaid. She swung to berate Maddy Thomas for what she had done, but one sight of the girl's wretched expression stilled Tildy's anger, and sighing, she said only, 'Come on, let's make a start on the chores, Maddy. Or we'll have even more troubles heaping on to us.'

As soon as she had fed Davy and Annie, Tildy asked Maddy, 'Where's the Godfrey's cordial?'

'I've got it in my box,' Maddy told her. 'But what does you want it for, Tildy? You always says that you don't like dosing kids wi' it.'

Tildy's face was grim. 'Tonight I want them both sleeping soundly,' and inwardly told herself, 'I don't want my Davy frightened by hearing me rowing with Arthur Winterton. Or worse . . .'

Chapter Twenty-One

Francis Priest, landlord of the Marlborough Arms inn at Studley village, had known Arthur Winterton since they were both boys together, and despite the always uncertain temper of the farmer the two men had remained friends from boyhood.

Now Priest stood in his snug bar looking down at the snoring Winterton sprawled across the table, a half-empty bottle of gin at his elbow, his hat fallen to the floor, and two empty bottles standing by it in mute testimony to the amount the big farmer had drunk that day. Shaking his head sadly Priest went from the room and closed the door gently behind him.

'Passed out, has he?' In the bar-parlour another drinking crony of Winterton, William Shayler, Constable of Studley Parish, was sitting in company with two local farmers.

The landlord nodded. 'He's well gone. I reckon I'd best send him home in my cart. He'll not be able to sit a horse 'til tomorrow.'

Shayler offered; 'Tell you what, Francis, old Arthur's sold me a sack o' new potatoes. If you like, I'll take him home in your cart meself, and I can bring the sack back wi' me then.'

Priest accepted, then said, 'But you'll take another glass afore you goo, wun't you, Will. I'll join you in one, I could do wi' a drink meself.'

The four men sat smoking and drinking in a companionable silence for some time until one of the farmers remarked, 'Winterton's going downhill very rapid, arn't he.'

'That's true.' The Constable sucked pensively at the long churchwarden pipe he favoured. 'I reckon when he lost his boy, then it knocked all the stuffing out on him.'

'I'm surprised to hear you say that, Will,' the farmer said, 'from what I'se allus known o' Winterton he didn't give a bugger for anybody or anything. He's got the name o' being a bloody tyrant to his people, and to his own kin as well.'

Priest and Shayler exchanged a long look, and it was the landlord who replied, 'How long has you bin in this parish, Josh? About seven year?'

'Ahr, about that,' the man agreed.

'Well then, youm still a bloody foreigner in these parts, my bucko, you arn't bin here long enough to know why old Arthur is like he is.'

The farmer bridled. 'I'se bin here long enough to know what people tells me about him.'

'Now doon't take offence, Josh,' the landlord placated. 'There warn't none intended. Only me and Will here has known Arthur Winterton all our lives, and we knew him when he was a real rollicking blade. But he married the wrong wench, and although it were no fault of her own, the poor wench left Arthur wi' a load o' trouble on his hands.'

'Oh I knows he's got a mongol daughter,' the farmer interrupted, 'but there's many the family who'se got loonies birthed among 'um, and they doon't turn tyrant because of it'.

'It arn't the daughter who'se the trouble, Josh,' Priest told him, 'but the son, Tobias . . .' Before he could enlarge further upon that a shout from the snug interrupted him, and he told Shayler, 'Come, Will. Sounds like Arthur's stirring himself. Let's get him in the cart.'

In the farmhouse kitchen a heated altercation was raging between Tildy on the one hand and Tobias, Maddy, Susy and old Gilbert on the other.

'Theer's only one way to break a witch's curse, and that's to draw her blood wi' a blackthorn root or a nail that's bin rusted in Holy Water,' old Gilbert asserted positively.

'I'll draw the old bugger's blood alright,' Tobias

promised bitterly. 'I'll draw the bloody life from her for murdering our Jem like she did.'

Tildy was experiencing a sense of increasing desperation. 'How can you all go on in this way?' she demanded. 'It wasn't old Esther who killed Jem, he took the lockjaw from the shears. Doctor Taylor told you what caused it.'

'Them shears was alright,' old Gilbert shouted. 'I greased 'um real well. The lad took no harm from 'um, and that's a fact, that is.' He glared at Tildy. 'I'm awondering why youm so powerful fond o' that bloody witch? Her stole your babby this day, and youm still sticking up for her. What makes you so fond on her? Be you one of her bloody coven? Be you a bloody witch yourself?'

Tildy felt like slapping the old man's face she was so enraged by his blind stupidity. But realizing that to lose her own temper would only serve to worsen matters, she tried to answer calmly, 'There are no such things as black witches in this day and age. Old Esther is just a silly, harmless old woman, who mayhap believes herself that she has powers, but that's only her own foolishness. And she didn't steal my Davy either. She was only trying to help him.'

'That arn't what Maddy says,' the old man riposted.

'I don't care what Maddy says,' Tildy became heated despite her intentions. 'It was Maddy's fault that Davy wandered off in the first place. If she hadn't been so taken with that thieving bugger, then none of this would have happened.'

Maddy flushed with guilt, then reacted viciously. 'Doon't you try and lay blame on me to shield your friend the witch,' she spat out, and turned to Tobias. 'What's we wasting time arguing wi' this bloody witch-lover for, Toby. Let's goo and deal with old Esther now, afore she can bring more harm on to us.'

The young man went out of the room and clumped up the stairs, leaving the rest eyeing each other angrily. When he returned he was carrying a long-barrelled fowling gun.

Fear clutched at Tildy. 'What do you intend doing with that?'

He scowled at her, his eyes like those of a rabid animal.

'I'm agoing to rid this world of that black witch,' he growled. 'She'll murder no more young lads.'

'No!' Tildy cried out, and tried to snatch the gun from him, but with almost contemptuous ease he fended her off.

She tried to reason with him. 'Toby, if you kill her they'll hang you. She's murdered no one.'

'Oh yes her has!' Maddy Thomas shrieked.' Her murdered Jem, and her 'ull murder all on us if we doon't get rid on her fust.'

Tobias went towards the outer door, and Tildy sprang in front of him and placed her back against the rough panelling.

'Get out o' my way, you slut,' he warned, 'or I'll do you an injury.'

'No, I'll not let you hurt a harmless old woman.' Tildy stood her ground stubbornly.

'Then be it on your own yed,' Tobias Winterton hissed, and reached for her with his free right hand.

Tildy ducked and hurled herself at him, her hands finding and clutching his gun. The others came to Tobias' aid, but Tildy fought like a wildcat and in their eagerness to subdue her they hampered each other. Locked in a heaving tangle, gasping and cursing, they blundered across the room, knocking benches flying.

'What in Hell's name's happening here?' William Shayler's bull-like bellow brought the unequal struggle to an abrupt halt, and his strong hands wrenched the protagonists apart.

Tildy's nose was bleeding and her neck bore long scarlet streaks left by the fingernails of Maddy Thomas.

Shayler's shrewd eyes measured the situation, and he asked Tobias, 'Is this what it looks like, Toby? All on you agen this young 'ooman? That arn't fair odds, is it.'

The rabid gleam had left the young man's eyes, and now he only stared sullenly at the constable, but made no answer.

The struggle had left Tildy feeling spent, and she slumped down on to one of the benches that were still upright, gasping for breath, and using a piece of rag to try and staunch the bleeding from her nose.

'Does you want to tell me what's happened here, young 'ooman?' Shayler's hard features were emotionless as he stared at her.

Tildy's thoughts raced. She did not wish to get any of the others into trouble, but at the same time she was desperately worried about what might happen to old Esther Smith if she now kept silent. To gain time, she questioned th newcomer. 'Who are you?'

He frowned. 'I'm the constable o' Studley Parish, wench. William Shayler's me name. Now, be you agoing to tell me what's been happening here?'

Tildy's eyes flickered from one to another and each stared stonily back at her. She found it hard to believe that these women and men whom she had thought of as friends should now be looking at her as if she were their enemy. To disabuse them of that notion, she shook her head at the constable. 'We were only funning, but I lost me temper. That's all that happened.'

Shayler was no fool, and although he knew that he must accept what she told him, he made his disbelief plain to see. 'So be it, young 'ooman. But I wants your name, just in case you might have need o' me at some time in the future.

'It's Matilda Crawford,' she mumbled.

'Right then, Matilda Crawford, if youm ever in need o' me, then come or send to Studley.' His hard eyes measured the others in the room. 'Let's have no more funning o' this kind.'

He turned to Tobias; 'What was you intending to use that gun for, Toby?'

The young man grinned mirthlessly. 'Why, to shoot vermin wi', o' course, Master Shayler. What else?'

'What else?' the constable muttered aloud. 'What else indeed?' Then he shook his head doubtfully. 'Ah well, ne'er mind it, I've brought your feyther back. He's outside in the cart, as drunk as a Bobowler. We'll have to carry him to his bed. And whiles I'm here I'll pick up that bag o' spuds I bought from him.'

Tobias Winterton nodded. 'Alright, Master Shayler.

We'll get me Dad to his bed, and then I'll sort out the spuds for you. Gilbert, Susy, give us a hand.'

Tildy and Maddy Thomas were left alone in the kitchen. Tildy rose to her feet and went out into the scullery to wash her face and hands and neck. While she was doing so Maddy Thomas came to stand and watch her.

'Tildy?' she began hesitantly, 'Tildy, I'm sorry for scratching your neck like that. I doon't know what got into me. I'm real sorry, Tildy. It was like a bloody madness come over me. Like I was possessed by summat.'

Tildy sighed wearily. 'Dear God, Maddy, don't start up again about witches and conjuring and curses. I've had enough of such things this day to last me a lifetime.'

The other woman's normally rosy face was now pale and drawn. 'Does you forgive me, Tildy?' There was a pleading in her voice and despite Tildy's resentment of the way in which Maddy had turned on her, she softened.

'Yes Maddy, I forgive you. Let's put this behind us and be friends.'

Maddy began to weep and she came to Tildy and threw her arms around her, like a child seeking comfort. 'Oh Tildy, I'm that fritted,' she hiccuped the words, 'summat evil is in this house. I can feel it. Summat bad is gooing to happen here.'

Tildy vented a harsh, mirthless chuckle. 'That's truly said, my wench. The bad is going to happen to us when Old Arthur sobers up enough to know that we've lost his goods for him.' She hugged the other woman. 'But don't you be fritted, Maddy. I'll tell old Arthur exactly what happened. I'll speak to him for both of us, if that's what you want.' Tildy inwardly marvelled at how matter of factly she was facing that daunting prospect. Naturally she was afraid of the farmer's wrath, yet she knew that when the time came, she would stand her ground and speak the truth. She smiled ironically as she thought, 'I must be a brave coward.'

Her bravery was put to the test when some time after William Shayler had left the farm Tobias came into the kitchen where Maddy and Tildy were preparing the evening meal and brusquely ordered, 'Come on into the yard, Crawford. I wants a word wi' you in private.'

She laid aside the knife she was using to chop the supper cabbage, and drawing deep breaths to still the tremorous feeling in her stomach she followed him outside, aware that Maddy Thomas' frightened eyes were locked on to her back.

Tobias Winterton was visibly trembling with suppressed passion, and his eyes held a strange and frightening expression – an expression that Tildy had seen before in the eyes of a dangerous madman. It took all her courage to simply stand still and face him.

'Now you listen well, you bloody whore,' he hissed venomously, 'because this is the only warning I'm agoing to gi' you. If you ever crosses me agen I'll swing for you. Has you got that, whore, I'll swing for you.'

Tildy was stung to reply by the sheer injustice of his threat. 'I'm no whore,' she flared back, 'and if you try to hurt that poor old woman, then I will stand in your way again.'

His handsome face was a twisted mask of hatred and his voice fell almost to a whisper. 'Youm a whore, Crawford. You was with that bloody Welshman, Oriel Evans. You lay on your back and opened your legs for him up on that haycock field.'

Tildy flushed hotly with shame and embarrassment and she could find no answer to that truth.

Tobias Winterton spat on to the filthy cobblestones. 'That's what I thinks to you, Crawford,' he ejaculated, then jerked his head towards the kitchen door. 'Now get back in theer and attend to your duties.'

Tildy could have stood her ground in defiance of his fury, but was unable to face his bitter contempt, and with a feeling of utter dejection she went wordlessly back into the house.

When Maddy tried to talk to her, Tildy said gently, 'Please let me be, Maddy. For pity's sake just let me be.'

She picked up the heavy-bladed knife and began to shred the huge cabbage on the table before her, and as she cut through its thick green leaves she dwelt on Tobias Winterton's bitter words. 'But why should I have felt ashamed and degraded by what he said to me?' She sought desperately for understanding of her own reactions. 'I made love to Oriel Evans in a moment of madness. Does that really make me a whore? Why should I feel shamed about it, when men may make love to any woman they choose, and have no finger of scorn pointed at them? For a man it's a matter of pride to have had many women, and they are applauded and admired by other men for doing so. Why should we women have to feel that we are whores if we make love to a man we're not wed to?' Tildy felt a rising anger at herself because she did feel that sense of shame. 'Why must I?' she demanded vehemently. 'My body is mine, to do with it what I choose. I know that is the truth. So why must I then allow Tobias Winterton to make me feel that I am a whore just because I have exercised that right of possession over my own body?' Tears of vexation at her own deeply ingrained inability to enjoy her rightful freedom filled her eyes, and she was forced to lay aside the knife for fear of chopping her own hand with its sharp blade.

Lifting the corner of her apron she wiped the tears from her cheeks as Maddy Thomas came from the brew-house.

'What's the matter, Tildy? Did that bloody Toby hit you?' the young woman questioned anxiously.

Tildy shook her head.

'Then why am you crying, my duck? Am you feared of what old Arthur might do to us?'

Again Tildy shook her head, then hastily qualified. 'Well yes, of course I'm a bit feared of what he might do, Maddy. But I'm not crying because of that.'

'Then what am you crying for?' Maddy beseeched plaintively.

Tildy shook her head helplessly. 'I think I was crying, because I can never free myself from my own conscience.'

Maddy only stared at her with a blank incomprehension, and in the midst of her own unhappiness Tildy smiled tearfully. 'Jesus Christ, Maddy! I'm a bloody mess. Arn't I just.'

Chapter Twenty-Two

After a restless, almost sleepless night, Tildy and Maddy rose in the darkness before dawn and went downstairs to prepare breakfast.

During the meal in the lamplit kitchen the two women experienced that peculiar phenomenon of the ostracism of the condemned. None of the other farm servants would meet their eyes, or exchange the briefest of words with them. Tildy had suffered this experience before in her life, but for Maddy it was incomprehensible, and unable to contain herself, she challenged Susy and old Gilbert. 'What's up wi' you two, has the bloody cat got your tongues?'

Susy flushed and mumbled unintelligibly, but old Gilbert only kept his eyes down and stolidly shovelled porridge into his capacious mouth. The rest of the servants behaved likewise, and Tildy signalled to her friend to join her in the scullery.

'Look Maddy, pay no mind to them,' she said gently, 'they'll not speak to us because they're afraid.'

'But why am they fritted?' Maddy asked puzzledly. 'It's me and you that's got to answer to old Arthur, not them buggers.'

'I know, but it's just the way most people are. I've had it happen to me before. I think that somehow they feel that if they shows friendship to us at this time, then somehow or other they'll be drawn into our troubles.'

They heard Tobias' voice come from the kitchen; 'Wheer's them two?' Followed by old Gilbert telling him, 'They'm out back.'

'Right,' Tobias' voice sounded strained. 'Gilbert, Joe, Sim, you stay wi' me. The rest on you get up to the top loft, me Dad's up theer now.'

There was a scraping of benches being pushed back from the table and then the clumping of booted feet up the wooden staircase.

In the scullery, lit only by a smoking rushlight, the two women exchanged looks of foreboding, and Maddy seemed near to tears, while Tildy felt the constriction of fear strike through her throat and chest.

Tobias Winterton entered the scullery followed by the three men he had named and for a few moments stood in silence, staring at Tildy. The note of strain they had heard in his voice was mirrored in his face and he looked far older than his years. 'Youm to come wi' me, both on you,' he said finally. 'Me Dad's waiting for you in the top loft.'

Maddy moaned audibly, and began to sob noisily, and perversely her friend's distress galvanized Tildy's courage.

'For why is he in that top loft?' Although she voiced the question Tildy already knew the reason. The top loft was the whipping room, where Arthur Winterton dealt out punishment to his erring servants and family when he considered that their misdemeanours warranted more than a blow or a kick.

'You knows well why he's up theer. So doon't waste my time wi' stupid questions,' Tobias spoke roughly, but Tildy sensed that that roughness was forced. In his eyes there was none of the hatred and contempt he had shown towards her the previous night. Their expression was troubled and more like that of the young man she had known when she first came to work at the farm.

'Does he man to beat us then?' Tildy demanded, and Tobias could only bluster in reply.

'If you wun't come quiet, then we'll take you up theer by force.'

'Tildy, let's goo up and see the Master and tell him what happened yesterday,' Maddy begged tearfully. 'He wun't beat us once he knows the truth on it. They'll only hurt us more if we doon't goo up quiet.'

For the sake of the other girl, Tildy assented. 'Alright, there's no need to force us. We'll come up and see the master.'

The whipping room ran almost the entire length of the house and was directly beneath the roof rafters. A dirty, rat-infested, musty-smelling loft piled high across most of its floor with the accumulated bric-à-brac of centuries. But the centre of the room was clear except for a long thick plank which had been nailed diagonally to floor and roof beam. The plank had two thick crosspieces bolted to it and both crosspieces had lengths of rope fastened to their extremities.

This was the whipping post where the victim would be tied face downwards on the plank, arms secured to the top crosspiece and legs to the bottom crosspiece.

The staircase leading up into the loft was so narrow that only one body at a time could mount it, and so in single file with Tobias leading, the group entered the room. Maddy was in front of Tildy, and as she entered the loft she wailed loudly and threw her apron up over her face. When Tildy saw what was waiting for them, she also felt like wailing out in fear. Standing beneath the hanging lamp, Arthur Winterton resembled some savage from a previous age, his hair a shaggy mass, his shirt open to the waist to display his hairy-matted chest, his heavily stubbled face bestial in its rage. He was flexing a long thin cane between his big brutal hands and his breath was a harsh wheezing in his thick throat.

The rest of the servants were huddled together on the edge of the pool of lamplight, and Tildy saw them only as a shadowed mass topped with pale blobs of faces.

'Trice that thievin' bitch up,' Arthur Winterton growled and pointed his long cane at Maddy Thomas.

The girl screamed piercingly as old Gilbert and Plum-face Joe dragged her towards the whipping post, and despite her frantic struggles lashed her down upon the plank.

Tildy could not believe what she was seeing and wanted

to cry out in protest yet seemed held voiceless and motionless by some unseen power as Arthur Winterton's fingers hooked into the top of Maddy's dress and ripped it down and open so that the white skin of her upper body was exposed.

'So, you thought to rob me, did you, you thieving scum?' Arthur Winterton's growl was like some ferocious devil in Tildy's ears. 'Well by the time I'se finished wi' you both, you'll ne'er want to rob anybody ever agen.'

Maddy's screams tore through the air, and her body heaved and twisted, but the thick ropes held her fast. Her eyes locked on to Tildy's, and her face was that of a helpless terrified creature of the wild; and in that instant the power that had held Tildy lost its force and she sprang at Arthur Winterton.

'Let her go!' she shouted furiously. 'Let her go, you bloody madman! We robbed nothing from you. You have no right to beat us. We've done nothing wrong! Let her go!'

Lost in his own dark passions Arthur Winterton brought the long thin cane slashing down across the soft skin beneath him, and it bit deeply. Maddy shrieked and heaved and again the cane came down.

Then Tildy was on him, trying to wrest the cane from his hand, and he bellowed, 'Get this hell-bitch off me!' and the men grabbed her and dragged her back, and although she fought like a raging fury, hurled her on to the floor and pinioned her helplessly against its rough boards, while Maddy's shrieks and cries resounded through her being. Then in her turn she was lifted and trussed and the gown torn from her body and the cane swished to cut white hot streaks across her flesh and the blinding agonies caused her to scream and heave and sob.

Then it was over, and only she and Maddy and Susy were left in the room.

Susy untied the ropes and helped her to rise from the plank. 'I'll bathe your back for you, Tildy, and I've got some salve to put on it that 'ull help take the pain away. Come now, let's goo back downstairs. It's all over now, Tildy. It's all over.'

Tears of pain and humiliation streamed down Tildy's cheeks, and angrily she brushed aside Susy's hands. 'Don't touch me,' she choked out, 'I don't need or want any help from you.' She brushed the tears from her eyes and went to where Maddy, sobbing with all the hiccuping grief of a child, was lying in a foetal position on the floor.

With great tenderness Tildy coaxed the girl, 'Come now, Honey. It's done with. It's all over. You come with me now. I'll look after you.'

'Come down to the kitchen, Tildy,' Susy urged, 'I'll tend to your backs for you.'

Despite her bodily pain and outraged emotions Tildy realized that she herself was behaving unjustly in taking out her anger on the other woman.

'Listen Susy, I'm not blaming you for what's happened here, and I'm grateful for your offer to help us. But I want nothing from this place. Not even a drink of water. I'm going from here right now, and I'm taking Maddy with me.'

The dairymaid stared at her bemusedly. 'But how about your work, Tildy? You arn't done your chores, has you.'

Tildy stared at her in utter amazement, and then, abruptly, her overstrained nerves betrayed her and she dissolved into helpless hysterical, sobbing laughter.

Chapter Twenty-Three

Arthur Winterton was seated in his chair at the head of the table when Tildy came downstairs with her pathetically small bundle of possessions and leading little Davy by the hand. The farmer's bloodshot eyes fixed on the bundle, and then he grunted, 'Wheer does you think youm gooing, Crawford?'

Tildy looked at him with loathing. 'I'm leaving here.' Then her eyes widened with surprise as Maddy Thomas came into the room carrying a jug of cider and some eggs which she placed in front of Winterton. 'What are you doing, Maddy? Where's your bundle?'

'She's attending to her duties,' Winterton answered for the girl. 'And if you know what's good for you, Crawford, you'd best get on wi' your own work.'

Tildy ignored him and instead said to Maddy Thomas, 'Fetch your things, Maddy, and let's get out from this house.'

The other woman only stared at the floor with frightened eyes, biting her lower lip, and shaking her head.

'What's the matter with you, Maddy? You've no need to be feared of him, because if he offers to lay a hand on either of us, then I'll lay charges against him.'

The beating had had a cathartic effect on Tildy, purging her fear of the farmer, and although her back burned like fire, the pain only served to fuel her resentment of Winterton and harden her resolve to submit to no more humiliations at his hands.

Suddenly Maddy threw her apron up over her face and rushed out of the room and upstairs, weeping noisily as she went. Tildy would have gone after her, but Winterton rose from his chair and blocked her way.

'What have you done to her?' Tildy demanded, and Arthur Winterton smiled jeeringly.

'I'se reminded her which side her bread's buttered on, Crawford. Her's one o' my bondagers, and if her leaves my service wi'out my consenting to her discharge then I can have her committed to the Bridewell. So, she stays here until next Michaelmas, unless I decides to get rid on her afore that. Just like you 'ull. So get to work.'

Tildy knew that it was futile to argue further. 'I'm not one of your bondagers, Master Winterton, you'll not keep me here by holding any Bridewell over my head.'

A hint of puzzlement gleamed in his eyes. 'Look Crawford, I had the right to punish you for what you did wi' my goods.'

'No! You had no right to beat us,' she told him vehemently. 'We didn't steal your goods. The Constable at Redditch can tell you that.'

'Whether you stole 'um or not doon't signify. They'm still gone, arn't they. And they was put in your charge, warn't they. You can think yourself lucky that I only tickled your backs for you. If I'd chose to, I could have had you charged and whipped and then locked away, and you knows that that's a fact. I reckon I'se let you off real lightly.'

Tildy could only shake her head in frustration. 'He really believes what he's saying,' she told herself, 'he really does think that he's acted leniently towards us.' Aloud, she said quietly, 'I'm gong from here,' and moved towards the outer door.

Winterton made as if to take hold of her arm, and she snapped, 'No, Master Winterton, don't lay so much as a finger on me. Because if you do, then I swear on my baby's life, that I'll wait until you lie asleep, and I'll take a knife and kill you.'

Momentarily he was taken aback by the savagery in her face and voice, and beside her little Davy, frightened by this startling change in his mother's normal gentle-voiced manner, burst into tears.

'Goo then, and be damned to you,' the big man growled. 'Youm more bloody trouble than youm worth, you saucy bitch.'

Tildy made no reply, only hurried from the house and down the lane towards the Icknield Street, dragging her tearful child with her.

Once out on the trackway she slowed her pace, telling Davy, 'I can't carry you, Honey, Mammy's hurt her back and you're too heavy to carry until it gets better.'

The child's fit of weeping passed, and he wanted to know, 'Where are we going, Mam?'

Tildy shook her head, and smiled ruefully. 'Do you know, my sweetheart, I'm not really sure.'

She considered her predicament. She had no money, no prospects of employment, only the gown she was wearing, now that her other one had been ripped almost in two by Arthur Winterton, and her back throbbed more painfully by the minute. Yet, paradoxically, her spirits rose as she walked slowly on. 'I'm free of that maniac, and although my back's sore, it won't be the death of me.' She smiled fondly down at little Davy, striding out manfully beside her, clutching his wooden soldier in his free hand. 'And as long as I have you with me, my son, then nothing else really matters,' she thought.

When they had travelled about a mile, Tildy called a halt and seated herself on the grassy bank bordering the track. While Davy played with his toy she tried to decide what she should do. 'I could go back to Mother Readman's. But it's not fair to be taking advantage of her so. She's got little enough of her own, without my burdening her with two more mouths to feed.' Another factor which made her reluctant to return to her old friend's house was the danger that living there entailed for Davy. Tildy looked at him now, and marvelled in the change that these few weeks of living in clean air and eating good wholesome food had wrought in the child. 'If it's at all possible, then I'll keep him away from the Silver Square. But where can we live?'

Lost in her thoughts she did not see the approaching

figure until little Davy exclaimed delightedly, 'Look Mammy, it's Auntie Esther come.'

The old crone was carrying a willow basket piled high with different types of leaves and roots and twigs she had gathered.

When Davy called to her she came to a standstill and her bright dark eyes beneath the broad rim of her straw bonnet twinkled with pleasure. 'Well, if it arn't my little chap. And is this your Mam?'

Tildy nodded and smiled. 'It is, Mrs Smith. And I've not had the chance to thank you yet for helping my boy like you did, when he got lost.'

'Ahr, and it near cost me sore, didn't it?' Momentary bitterness shaded the wrinkled brown face. 'But I knows you, doon't I, young 'ooman. 'Tis a pity your boy couldn't tell me proper who he was, then I could ha' brung him direct to you. Be you still working for Arthur Winterton?'

'No.' Tildy grimaced as a sharp pain lanced across her injured back. 'No, I left that house this morn, and I'll not be going back there.'

'Served you badly has he, Arthur Winterton?' The old crone had noticed Tildy's grimace of pain. 'Had you triced up on that whipping post did he, like a lot of other poor souls has bin triced up.'

'Yes, he whipped me, and Maddy Thomas as well,' Tildy confirmed, and flushed with the remembrance of her humiliation.

'Is your back paining you, young 'ooman?' the old crone asked, and when Tildy nodded, said, 'You 'ud best come along wi' me and let me tend it for you. If you doon't have it seen to it might goo bad ways.'

'I've no money to pay you with,' Tildy told her, and the old woman frowned.

'I'm not asking you for money, am I, young 'ooman,' and then cackled with laughter at Tildy's obvious embarrassment, 'but if youm set on giving me summat for tending your back, I can always find a bit o' work for you to do for me. Come on now, time's awasting.'

Without a backward glance she set off southwards along

the track, and after a moment's hesitation, Tildy rose and followed.

Esther Smith's cottage was an ancient single-storied, mud-walled hummock on the edge of the wild heathland known as the Mappleborough Green, which ran along the edges of low-lying, thick-wooded hills some three miles east of the town of Redditch. When Tildy had come there before it had been at night, and the cottage and heath had seemed a place of ominous mysteries. Today, bathed in sunlight and with the singing of birds filling the air the cottage with its unkempt thatched roof had a certain picturesque charm that appealed to Tildy. Its interior was as Tildy remembered it. Clean and fragrant with the many bunches of dried herbs hanging on its limewashed walls and from its roof rafters. One entire end wall was filled by a great stone inglenook and it was sparsely furnished with a small square table flanked by wooden stools, two chests against one wall beside a storage barrel and a bucket. Shelves fixed to the walls carried utensils and food pots, and a doored wooden partition bisected the interior. Although the floor was only of hard-packed earth, yet it was as smooth as flagstones, and rush mats were strewn across it.

'Set you down theer,' Esther Smith instructed and took off her straw bonnet to reveal her stringy grey hair dressed in coiled plaits around her ears, 'and loose your bodice down so I can see your back.' She cackled with laughter as she saw the instant doubt in Tildy's eyes. 'You needn't worrit about any man coming in and seeing your tits, my duck. Me husband died a while since, and I arn't got anybody coming to court me.'

Little Davy tugged on Tildy's hand, seeking attention, and the old crone bared her blackened fangs of teeth in a fond smile. ''Ud you like a bit o' sugar-cone, my little chap?'

The child assented eagerly, and she rummaged in one of the food pots then handed him a large piece of coarse greyish sugar.

'If you goes around the back, my chap, you'll find some

puppy dogs to play wi',' Esther Smith told him, and reassured Tildy, 'He'll take no harm, young 'ooman.'

The child went off happily, and Esther Smith gave her full attention to Tildy's injuries. She clucked her tongue commiseratingly when she saw the long raised red weals the cane had left on the younger woman's skin. Then, from the pots on the shelves she took various ingredients and mixed them into an ointment which she gently rubbed into the weals.

'Theer now, that'll do the business, my duck. Arter a while you wunt have no more soreness, and in a couple o' days you'll be as good as new.'

'Many thanks, Mrs Smith.' Tildy was truly grateful, and could already feel a not unpleasant tingling as the ointment began its healing work.

'Now, you'll ate a bowl o' soup wi' me, you and your babby,' the old crone insisted, overriding Tildy's protests, and using flint and steel kindled a small fire of twigs in the grate of the inglenook, over which she placed a small iron pot containing the soup. 'That wun't take long to heat up.'

While they waited for the food to be ready the two women chatted easily, and little by little the old woman drew from Tildy the full account of all that had happened during her sojourn at the Winterton farm.

'Now I'll set you to rights, Tildy Crawford.' The old crone's head shook slightly on her scrawny wrinkled neck. 'I never set no curse doll near that house. I arn't a black witch, for all that some says I am. I uses my powers to aid folk, not to harm 'um. I know I lost me temper ar Arthur Winterton, but it was words only. I conjured naught agen him and his, even though I could ha' done so.' Her piercing black eyes locked onto Tildy's, and the younger woman found herself believing all that the old crone was telling her. 'To spake the truth to you, Tildy, theer's no need for me ever to conjure agen the Winterton's. That family is already damned. Theer's an evil force lurking among 'um, that 'ull destroy 'um some day. I'se felt it, and seen it.'

Despite the warmth of the room Tildy felt a cold shiver

pass through her, and impelled by an unconscious volition, she asked, 'Is there madness in their blood, Mrs Smith? Because at times I feared that Tobias and his father both were mad.'

The old crone's isolated blackened teeth glistened in an admiring smile. 'That's it, young 'ooman. I reckon you'se got a touch o' the power yourself to ha' seen that. I'll tell you straight, that young Tobias is the wust on 'um. Folk reckon that he's a good man. But I knows better. His dad is a nasty piece o' work, but the young 'un has got evil in him, Tildy,' her cracked voice sank to a whisper, 'real evil, he's got in him.'

For long long seconds Tildy gazed as if mesmerized into the black eyes before her, until the spell was broken by Davy running in through the door.

'Look Mammy, look at my dog.' In his arms he cradled a small black mongrel puppy.

'No, my honey, it's Mrs Smith's dog, not yours,' Tildy remonstrated fondly.

The old crone cackled with laughter. 'It shall be yourn if you wants it, my little chap.'

'Can I keep him, Mam? Can I? Can I?' the child begged excitedly.

Although she hated to spoil his happiness, Tildy was forced to shake her head. 'No, Sweetheart, you can't have him to keep. I have to find somewhere for us to live first, and then seek work. Mayhap then you can have a dog.'

His small face became crestfallen, and Esther Smith stroked his thick black curls with her clawlike hand. 'Why don't you ask your Mam if you and her can both live here wi' me, my little chap. Then you could have the dog for your own, couldn't you.'

His eyes shone with delight. 'Can we, Mammy? Can we? Can we live here with Auntie Esther?'

This completely unexpected turn of events left Tildy momentarily nonplussed, and before she could even formulate any reply, the old woman said. 'It 'ud be a good thing for the little chap to live here, Tildy Crawford, and it 'ud be a good thing for you as well. It's peaceful here, and the air is good and clean, not like up in the town theer. This little 'un 'ud learn much here, and so 'ud you. You'd learn things here that can't be got from books and suchlike. I'se took a liking for you both, and when you goes to your work, why the little chap 'ud stay here wi' me, and keep me company.' She ruffled Davy's curls. 'I reckon you'd like that, 'udden't you, my little chap. You'd like to keep me company and have your puppy to play wi'.'

A curious sense of pre-destined happenings coming to pass invaded Tildy's mind and with an inner wonderment she found herself warmly accepting the old crone's offer.

Esther Smith's bright black eyes twinkled in amusement, and she asked, 'You arn't feared then o' what folk 'ull say about you?'

Tildy shook her head. 'No, I've never been feared of what people will say about me,' then asked in her turn, 'but what could they say, anyway?'

The old woman cackled with laughter. 'Why, Tildy, they'll say that youm become a witch, like me. They'll say that we both rides through the night on broomsticks.'

Tildy's own laughter bubbled from her. 'I wish I could ride a broomstick, Mrs Smith, it would save me a deal of sore feet.'

'Can I ride a broomstick as well, Mammy. Can I? Can?' little Davy begged, and the women's eyes met above his head, and their laughter mingled and echoed among the rafters.

Chapter Twenty-Four

In the pre-dawn darkness the gang was mustering around the entrance to St Stephen's Chapel, on the steps of which stood Jeremiah Borth and one of his assistants. The assistant carried a bull's-eye lantern which he shone into the face of each woman and child as they reported to the Overseer, to have their names checked against the list in Borth's pocket-ledger. The air was chill and many of the smaller children were already whining and whimpering at the prospect of the long trudge and hard toil which lay before them.

Tildy swallowed nervously as she approached the two men standing on the steps, uncertain of how she would be received by Jeremiah Borth. The beam of the lantern caused her to blink in momentary dazzlement as it struck her eyes and she heard Borth's voice.

'Well, well, well, if it arn't the lovely Tildy Crawford come avisiting. And what can we do for you here, my wench?'

Although his tone was jeering, Tildy could detect no hostility in it, and she told him, 'I'm seeking work, Master Borth.' She waited now for him to scathingly reject her, in revenge for their previous clashes. But to her surprise he merely nodded brusquely, 'Alright, girl. Get wi' the rest on 'um. We'll be leaving shortly.'

Feeling a distinct sense of relief she obeyed his instruction and moved to join the crowd.'

'Is that you, Tildy?' Sarah Farr came up to her. 'What the bleedin' hell be you adoing here? You arn't finished wi' working for Winterton, am you?'

'I left there a week since,' Tildy confirmed, and cut short the woman's spate of fresh questions with a shake of her head. 'No Sarah, it's over and done with. I'll tell you all about it some time, but for now I'd sooner leave it lay.'

'Am you living back at Mother Readman's?' the other woman persisted.

'No, I'm staying with a friend at Mappleborough. It's a lot healthier for little Davy there.'

Sarah Farr winked and nudged Tildy. 'Who'se the friend, Tildy? Is it a chap?'

Tildy shook her head smilingly. 'No, it's not a man. If you must know, I'm staying with old Esther Smith.

'Jesus Christ!' Sarah Farr's gaunt features showed her shock. 'But her's a bloody witch!'

Tildy laughed with genuine amusement. 'No she's not, Sarah. She's just a poor lonely old woman, and she's proven a good friend to me.'

'You wunt be calling her that when her turns you into a bloody toad or summat.' Sarah Farr's words were only half in jest.

'Come on then, let's be having you,' Borth shouted, and Tildy asked her friend, 'Where are we working?'

'A place called Hill House Farm on the other side o' Tardebigge Canal. A good four mile from here as the crow flies.' Sarah Farr scowled glumly. 'It's a bloody long walk for the kids. Mind you, they'm mostly on the pea-picking, which arn't too heavy for 'um. Us women am mostly raising the early taters. Bloody hard collar, that is.'

With Borth and his assistant at their head, the gang, numbering almost fifty souls, moved from the Green and westwards down the Unicorn Hill in a straggling column.

'How is Borth treating you now?' Tildy asked as she walked side by side with Sarah Farr, halfway down the column.

'Well, the bugger still drives us hard, but he's straight enough in paying out, and most weeks we gets a couple o' pence more than we'd get from the parish.' She lowered her voice to a conspiratorial whisper. 'There's a few o' the wenches gets most o' the easy jobs though. Them that does a bit of extra on the side for Borth and his mates, if you knows what I mean.' She winked hugely, and Tildy nodded her understanding.

'That's how Bella Parks has got back on the gang.' Sarah Farr pointed towards the head of the column. 'See her theer wi' her eldest nipper. They do say that Borth spends more nights with her than with his own missus nowadays.'

'Poor Bella,' Tildy remarked with genuine sympathy.

Sarah Farr grinned. 'Oh you can save your pity, Tildy. Her seems well satisfied wi' the arrangement.' Again she winked hugely. 'If you knows what I mean.'

'But it's still wrong, Sarah, that a woman should be virtually forced into acting the whore just to put a bit of bread into her kids' bellies.' All Tildy's resentment of the injustices meted out to the women of the poor rose once more to the surface, but inevitably once more she was forced to acknowledge her own helplessness to rectify those injustices when Sarah Farr said, 'Well, at least he don't serve her badly, from what she's told me, Tildy. He treats her better than her own man did when he was alive. You knows yourself that theer's an awful lot o' married women who'se husbands uses 'um like whores and wuss. But what can the poor wenches do? It's a man's world, arn't it, my duck.'

'That's all too true, Sarah,' Tildy agreed grimly, 'that's all too true. But some day, God willing, it might change.'

'Oh yes it 'ull change alright, but pigs 'ull be flying afore it does.' Sarah Farr sighed sadly, and they continued their journey in silence.

By break of dawn they were in the potato field, and under Borth's directions most of the women paired off, while a few of them and all the children went on to the pea field. Borth's assistant went with the latter, but Borth himself remained with the potato gang. A farm cart drawn by a spavined old horse came lurching on to the land, and its smock-clad driver distributed its load of long-helved forks and rough sacks among the women, one fork and a pile of sacks to each pair. The pairs spaced themselves along the deep-ridged furrows, and the work began.

Tildy and Sarah Farr toiled together. Sarah Farr dug out the ridges spilling the roots and earth into the furrow, where Tildy, on her knees, grubbed out the potatoes with her bare hands and rubbed the dirt from their skins before placing them in the sacks. The land was damp from the rain of the previous evening, and very soon Tildy's sacking overskirt was thick with wet clay, and the chill dampness saturated her petticoats and penetrated to her skin. Periodically the two women changed places, and each time Tildy rose to her feet to take the fork she found that the kneeling had cramped her back and leg muscles so badly that for some minutes she could only ply the tool with a slow and painful clumsiness that only eased when the effort of digging the heavy clay soil brought an increased flow of blood pumping through her constricted arteries.

The women worked in a silence broken only by the occasional word passed between them, and the audible grunts that the effort of lifting and moving the heavily loaded sacks forced from their throats.

Jeremiah Borth paced slowly backwards and forwards along the lines of women, his sharp eyes evaluating their workrate, and occasionally he would halt beside a labouring pair and stand silently regarding them, inwardly enjoying the obvious nervousness his nearness engendered. But at this hour of the day he made no attempt to drive them to greater effort. That would come later when their flagging energies and tired muscles forced them to slow their pace.

He came to a standstill next to where Tildy was wielding her fork and a spasm of lust tightened his groin as he saw her firm high breasts pushing out against the thin fabric of her bodice. His tongue ran slowly along his lips as he imagined how her shapely body would feel lying naked under him and mentally he vowed: 'I'll have you one fine day, Tildy Crawford. I sweat to God, I 'ull.' Aloud he said conversationally, 'What's brung you back to the gang then, Tildy? Did you have a falling out wi' the Wintertons?'

Although she disliked and despised the man intensely, Tildy knew that to openly display her feelings would only bring fresh troubles upon her head, so she answered in a carefully neutral tone, 'Yes, you could say that, Master Borth.'

'Which one on 'um tried to shag you, the young 'un, or the old 'un?'

His brutal question brought a deep flush spreading up from her throat, and he chuckled lewdly as he saw its effect. 'Was it both on 'um then?'

Tildy fought to hide her resentment of his crudity, not wanting to give him the satisfaction of openly reacting to his deliberate baiting. And she succeeded so well that she was able to force a smile as she told him, 'Neither, if you must know. They both acted like gentlemen towards me.'

'Did they now.' He found himself admiring her spirit, and for a brief instant the long and deeply buried kindlier side of his nature asserted itself. 'Well, so long as you does your work, Tildy, I'll not hold the trouble you gi' me before agen you.'

For the first time since he had halted beside her Tildy met his eyes squarely. 'I'm grateful for that, Master Borth.' She meant what she said, and unaccustomedly disconcerted by the unexpectedness of his own momentary softening, Borth could only nod brusquely and walk on.

Sarah Farr looked up grinning and whispered hoarsely, 'Bugger me, Tildy, what's got into the bastard? He spoke to you like you was bloody gentry at the last, didn't he?'

Tildy's answering smile was tinged with bitterness. 'Well, I'll go as far as to say that for once in his life he spoke to me as if I were a human being, and not some sort of animal, Sarah.'

'The next thing you knows he'll be whispering sweet words into your earhole, and buying you fairings, my duck,' the older woman joked.

'The next thing we'll know is his stick over our backs if we stops from working!' Tildy's mood lightened and she chuckled. 'At least you've got one comfort, Sarah, from where you are now, you can only rise in the world.'

'That's true, and I reckon it's about my time to do just that, arn't it.'

Suiting action to words the woman rose to her feet, and with a smile Tildy handed over the fork and sank down on to her knees in the furrow.

Chapter Twenty-Five

July, August and September were the months of harvest and the gang went from farm to farm, and Tildy went with them, stooking and binding corn, gathering oats and barley and rye, picking peas, harvesting beans, pulling browned bolled flax and hemp, gathering hops, handhoeing and lifting turnips and carrots and parsnips. All through the long weeks she rose before dawn and trudged away from the isolated cottage, to return after dark, weary beyond belief, yet strangely contented.

Old Esther Smith had spoken truly when she said that Tildy and little Davy would learn much from her. The old crone possessed an immense store of knowledge about herbs and plants and the uses they could be put to. She knew the ways of the wild animals that dwelt in the fields and heath and woodlands, and was imbued with all the ancient folklore of her race. During Tildy's brief respites from labouring with the gang she wandered with Davy and old Esther through the secret pathways and hidden places of the countryside and at times during those wanderings felt that the three of them were penetrating the fringes of mysterious worlds that lay beyond the ken of mortal folk.

Sometimes in the dark hours of the night she would sit with the old woman in the firelight and, while the wind moaned softly around the thick walls of the tiny cottage, listen enthralled to tales of witches and warlocks, of seers and sorcerers, ghosts and spirits, and the unseen powers of good and evil that waged unceasing warfare for the possession of the souls of mankind.

Between the two women there had developed a strong bond of love and respect and a shared devotion to little Davy, who in return loved both of them. Each night in the sweet-smelling bed she shared with old Esther, Tildy uttered silent thanks to her own private Deity that she had found this haven in which for as long as it might continue to shelter her, she could gather her strength and courage to face whatever other tribulations that life might have in store for her.

October blustered in with cold easterly winds and heavy rains, and Tildy went to her daily drudgery wearing an old coat and hat that had belonged to Esther Smith's husband, and wore the dead man's heavy hobnailed boots on her feet. Although the main harvests had been gathered, there was still work for the gang, for now the main potato crop was ready to be raised, and the big mangold-wurzels, used for cattlefeed, to be lifted. The children were put to 'twitching' whenever the days were dry enough for the ploughs, and like scavengers they roamed the new-cut furrows gathering the white roots of couch grass and other weeds, and when the days were too wet for the plough, then the children would take willow baskets and collect and clear stones from the earth. For the youngest and strongest of the women, of whom Tildy was one, there was also the work that she came to hate above all else, the carting and spreading of manure. The rancid stench of rooted matter and human and animal excreta impregnated her clothes, and no matter how hard she scrubbed her body and how frequently she washed her hair it seemed to her that the vile smell still clung to her.

The harsh weather brought great hardship in its wake. Many of the gang, already debilitated by excessive work and poor diets, lacked the physical resources to combat their constant exposure to the cold and wet and fell ill with racking coughs, feverish colds and rheumatism.

Tildy herself remained free of these afflictions, a fact she attributed to the ministrations of old Esther, who insisted on dosing her daily with strong teas of wild basil, and tiny wafers made from the dried juices of wild lettuce, and when her joints and muscles were stiffened and sore, applying hot poultices of wild thyme to soothe them. The old woman treated Tildy's bruises with ointments made from chopped parsley and salt, the cuts on her fingers with nettle poultices, and when the skin on her hands cracked from her labour the old woman made decoctions of oak bark and bathed the cracks with it.

So, despite all the harshness of work and weather Tildy was confident that she would endure and survive. Then, midway through the last week in October, she lost the companionship of her workmate, Sarah Farr.

Lowan's Hill Farm was situated on the high spur of ground that faced Redditch to the north-west across the broad shallow valley that carried the Red Ditch stream to join with the River Arrow in the Old Abbey meadows. From dawn until the now fast approaching dusk eight of the gang women had been working in the highest field on the spur, exposed to the icy winds and driving rain, topping and tailing turnips in preparation for storage. The crop had been sown in long straight drills and the women moved between these drills, bending constantly to wrench the heavy globes from the clinging earth with their left hands and then straightening to hold the clayed vegetables outstretched before them by the leafy tops while chopping off the tails and tops with the thick-bladed cutting implements they carried in their right hands.

The wet had long since soaked through Tildy's layers of clothing and the icy blasts of wind had chilled her to the bone, and now she toiled in a state of benumbed misery, conscious only of the weariness of her body as she bent and wrenched and lifted and chopped, and bent and wrenched and lifted and chopped, and bent and wrenched and lifted and chopped in a seemingly endless mind-deadening monotonous purgatory.

She was aware periodically of Sarah Farr's racking fits of coughing in the drill adjoining the one she was working in, but knowing that there was nothing she could do to ease the other woman's bodily sufferings, could only stoically endure the harrowing sounds. They had been alloted a certain number of drills to clear, and Jeremiah Borth would accept no excuse for their failure to complete the task before nightfall. All that Tildy could do to aid Sarah Farr was to finish her own drills as quickly as she was able, and then help Sarah Farr to finish hers. With this in mind, Tildy tried to summon fresh reserves of energy and to drive herself on to work more quickly.

Dusk had fallen when Tildy chopped the last turnip in her drill, and she trudged slowly back towards where Sarah Farr was bending low, tugging weakly at a tenacious earth-clinging root.

As Tildy neared the other woman Sarah Farr succeeded in wrenching the turnip free of the imprisoning earth. She straightened and brought the heavy-bladed cutter down. The root tail fell away, the heavy blade rose and as it came chopping down a terrible fit of coughing exploded from Sarah Farr's throat, shaking her entire body and deflecting her aimed blow. The blade bit deep into the back of her left hand, severing bones, sinews, flesh; the turnip fell to the soggy ground, and Sarah Farr's racking cough became a choking scream as she stared down at her bloody, mangled hand. Tildy cried out in horror, and broke into a run, hampered by her long soaking wet skirt and the clods of clay that clung to her heavy boots. Before she could reach Sarah Farr the woman's eyes rolled upwards in her chalk-white face and she slumped to the earth in a faint.

Tildy gagged with sudden nausea as she bent over the fallen woman and lifted the injured hand. Shards of ivory-white bone glistened in the blood-jetting wound and it looked at first sight as if only shreds of flesh and skin held the hand together.

Shouts echoed across the dark field as the other women hurried to join Tildy, and while she waited for them to reach her, she tore off strips from the bottom of her petticoat and used them to bandage Sarah Farr's hand, and to fashion a crude tourniquet around the woman's arm in an effort to staunch the loss of blood.

Tildy stared desperately around her and through the gloom saw that at the edge of the field there were piled some old hurdles. She yelled to the oncoming women to fetch a hurdle with them, and when they did so, instructed them to lay Sarah Farr's limp body on top of it. Lifting the makeshift stretcher between them they struggled across the muddy ground towards the glimmering lights of the farmhouse some quarter of a mile distant.

By the light of the kitchen's oil-lamp Tildy was able to examine her friend's injury more thoroughly. 'We'll needs get her to a doctor,' she told Jeremiah Borth.

The Overseer grunted morosely. 'I wanted that field finished tonight, God damn it.' He turned to Ballard, the farmer of Lowans Hill. 'Has you got a spare cart, Master Ballard?'

'Theer's only the muck-cart here at present, and that's half full,' the man told him.

'She wunt take any harm from a bit o' muck,' Borth grunted sourly. 'We can shove the hurdle atop of it.'

The farmer's fat red face was doubtful. 'Well, it arn't really convenient for you to take the cart just now. I was agoin to have one o' my men finish loading it.'

Sarah Farr's head moved and she moaned piteously as consciousness began to return.

'For God's sake let's get her to a doctor, and not waste any more time,' Tildy burst out angrily. 'Her suffering is more important than a load of muck, isn't it?'

A trifle shame-faced, the farmer grudgingly acceded. 'Alright then, Master Borth. You can use the cart. But get it back here as soon as youm able to.'

Once the moaning woman had been carried out and loaded on to the back of the stinking cart, Borth told Tildy and the other women who had been with her, 'You lot get back up theer and finish that field off. I'll take her to the doctor.'

Tildy could hardly credit what she heard. 'Someone of us must go with the poor wench,' she protested, 'if only to steady her on the hurdle.'

The other women muttered in support of what she said,

and Borth scowled, and lifted his peaked cap so that he could rub his shaven head, then exasperatedly told Tildy, 'By the Christ! It's allus you who stirs things up, arn't it!' He paused and stared hard at her for some seconds.

Tildy stamped her booted foot impatiently. 'We're wasting time here, Master Borth.' She pointed to one of the women. 'You walk behind the cart and keep Sarah steady on the hurdle. I'll lead.'

She went to the horse's head and taking the lead rein slapped its muddy flank. 'Get up, then! Get up!'

The rest of the women followed the creaking cart and Jeremiah Borth stood silently and watched them leave. By his side Ballard remarked resentfully, 'That dark-yedded 'un needs taking down a peg or two. She doon't show the proper respect towards her betters.'

He gaped in surprise as his companion suddenly roared with laughter.

'What's so funny about me asaying that, Master Borth?' he demanded aggrievedly.

The Overseer shook his head as his laughter slowly stilled. 'No matter, Master Ballard, no matter. I'll goo and round up the rest o' my people. We'll finish the turnip field fust thing tomorrow morn.'

It was long past midnight when Tildy finally made her way across the heath towards old Esther's cottage. Tired and depressed she slowly trudged the last few hundred yards that separated her from warmth, food and shelter. Mercifully the wind had dropped and the rain ceased and in her present mood she was grateful for even such small mercies.

She had taken Sarah Farr to the house of Doctor Charles Taylor, and the old man had done what he could to save the woman's injured hand, but had been forced to amputate the fore- and second fingers and Tildy knew that it would be many weeks before Sarah Farr would be able to work again.

'Still, at least Doctor Taylor said that he would speak to the Vestry for Sarah, so she'll get the Relief from the Parish.' Tildy drew some comfort from that.

The dogs that guarded the cottage barked furiously as Tildy neared the building and she called out to them so that they would recognize her voice. In answer to her shout the cottage door opened and old Esther appeared, silhouetted by the fitful glow of the rushlight.

'Am you alright, Tildy?' Her cracked voice quavered anxiously, and Tildy hastened to reassure her and to explain her late return.

'Will Shayler's bin here,' the old woman informed her. 'Theer's bin a young wench set on, and badly served, this night. And the men have bin out searching for the bugger who done it. When you never come back to your usual time I was sore feared that summat might have happened to you as well.'

While Tildy thankfully took off her boots and wet clothing, and washed herself in the bucket of warm water near to the inglenook fire, old Esther bustled about preparing a bowl of hot broth for Tildy's supper, and talking volubly. 'The constable from Ipsley, Edward Ashwin, him who'se got the Ipsley flour mill, he's out wi' men as well, and Cooper from Beoley. The poor little wench was one o' the Nolan girls from Clarke's Green. Her's in service at Beoley Hall, and her 'ud bin home to visit her Mam, who'se bin took sick. It was when her was acrossing Machbarrow Hill that the bugger jumped out on her.'

'Is she hurt badly?' Tildy asked with concern.

'Well, the bugger had his way wi' her, and the poor little maid was virgin. But he beat her cruel as well, so it 'ull be a long time afore her's properly right agen.'

'Did she know what the man was?'

'No. She says he was awearing a hood, so she couldn't see his face. But I reckon it'll be the same bugger who had a goo at that other wench awhiles past.'

'But I thought they reckoned that that was a tramper,' Tildy objected.

'No, that was no tramper,' old Esther scathingly dismissed the suggestion, 'No tramper could have got away like he did wi' strong young lads at his heels. It's got to be a local to manage that, who knows the country hereabouts. And ask yourself, Tildy, what 'ud a tramper be doing out on the Machbarrow Hill on a night like this 'un, all cold and wet. A tramper 'ud be snugged up in a byre or barn, not wandering abroad over a bleak place like Machbarrow Hill. Theer's naught to be got up theer that 'ud be any use for a tramper, is there.' The bright dark eyes gleamed with certainty. 'Nooo, the bugger is a local, that's as sure as God makes little apples, that is. Someone who saw that little maid, and knew her, and knew wheer she'd be heading.' She placed the big steaming bowl of broth on the small table. 'Come now, ate this, my Honey. This 'ull stick to your ribs alright.'

Tildy gratefully spooned the hot savoury mess into her mouth and its warmth filled her stomach and spread through her body, bringing with it an overwhelming sleepiness, so that she could barely keep her heavy eyelids open, and old Esther's voice sounded increasingly muffled and far away. Her head drooped forwards and she fell asleep, still clutching the wooden spoon in her hand. The old woman gently roused her and led her to the bed, and as if Tildy were a small child guided her down upon the coarse sheets and tucked the coverlet around her.

Tildy lay breathing evenly, and old Esther stared down at her peaceful face, smiling fondly. 'Youm a good little wench, Tildy,' she whispered, 'and I couldn't think more on you if you was me own flesh and blood. You and your babby am my kin now.'

Very quietly the old woman crept out from the bedroom and seated herself by the inglenook fire. There she sat gazing into the glowing mass of wood and turf, muttering to herself at intervals, and rocking her body in slow gentle rhythm as the hours passed.

In the bed Tildy stirred restlessly as frightening dreams invaded her sleep. In those dreams she was crossing a wild and desolate moor and far behind her a hooded man was coming in pursuit. She tried to run but could not, and always the hooded man drew nearer and nearer. Tildy fought to move her leaden limbs but they seemed entangled in invisible webs and no matter how desperately she struggled her pace became slower and slower and slower and inexorably the hooded man gained on her, until she heard his harsh breathing in her ears and felt his fingers clutching her shoulder. She turned and in blind terror tore at his black hood, and came awake with an anguished scream as she saw his face.

'Tildy? Tildy? What ails you, Honey?' Old Esther's arms enfolded her, and Tildy's terror lessened, and she panted, 'I was dreaming, Esther. I was dreaming about the hooded man. I saw his face, Esther. I knew him.'

'It's the Powers that's showed you him, Tildy. They've done it. I sensed 'um here this night, Tildy. I been sat at the fire, and I could feel 'um all round me. Who is the man, my Honey? Give me his name.'

Tildy's mind was clearing fast as full wakefulness came to her and all her rationality rejected what the dream had shown her. 'It's was only a dream, Esther. That's all it was. Only a silly childish dream. It means nothing.'

'Doon't say that, girl,' the old crone snapped angrily. 'Arn't I told you that the Powers be real? That they'm all around us. I knew from the very fust minute you come to live here wi' me, that you had the "gift". I knew that sooner or later the Powers would show you things that am hidden to other folk. That's the way they fust come to me, Tildy, in me dreams. Just like they'se come to you this night. And I was like you that fust time. I was too fritted to believe.'

Tildy could only shake her head. 'No, Esther, it can't be. It can't be.' Conflicting emotions battled for domination within her. Fear, belief, disbelief, acceptance, rejection; her head was spinning from the impact of their combined assault.

'Who was the man you saw, Tildy? Who was he? Give me his name,' the old woman's cracked voice badgered ceaselessly, 'Tell me, Tildy. Tell me. Tell me. Tell me,' until driven beyond endurance Tildy shouted wildly, 'It was Tobias . . . Tobias Winterton . . . He was the man I saw . . . Tobias Winterton . . .' Then unable to control her strained emotions any longer, Tildy burst into tears, and sobbed out, 'I fear I'm going mad, Esther. I fear I'm going mad . . .'

The old crone rocked Tildy in her arms as if she were a child, crooning to her. 'It's alright, my Honey. It's alright. You arn't mad. It's alright, old Esther's wi' you. Youm safe here. Youm safe here wi' me. It's alright, my Honey. It's alright.'

Tildy clung to the old woman as if she were the mother she had never known, and drew peace and comfort from her cradling arms, and the dawning of the day found them sleeping, still locked in that embrace.

Chapter Twenty-Six

Jeremiah Borth stood in the middle of the turnip field watching Tildy walking down the drill towards him. The six women busily topping and tailing the vegetables watched surreptitiously, their ears straining to catch what would pass between the man and the young woman.

'What time does you call this?' he demanded sourly as Tildy came to a halt facing him.

'I'm sorry for coming late.' Tildy's face was white and drawn, her eyes troubled and her manner strangely distracted. 'I overslept. It was very late when I got back home last night, what with taking Sarah home after the doctor had tended her, and then bringing the horse and cart back here.'

'It was your choice to goo wi' Sarah Farr, and you doon't get paid for bloody over-sleeping, you lazy cow. You gets paid for being here to time, like the rest on 'um, not for laying stinking in your bed.' He waited expectantly, as if anticipating a flash of rebellion from this normally fiery woman, and his hard eyes showed puzzlement when she only stood with downcast eyes and made no answer.

The silence lengthened, until finally he told her brusquely, 'Get to work, and doon't take a break until you'se made up for your lost time. If I catches you standing still before I tells you you can, I'll be taking me stick to your arse.'

Submissively she obeyed, and now the man was really puzzled. 'This arn't like you, my wench,' he thought. 'What could have happened last night to make you like this, I wonder?'

Disappointed at being cheated of witnessing a clash between the two, the other women also exchanged puzzled looks, and low voiced exchanges.

'Her's bloody quiet, arn't her?'

'It arn't like Tildy Crawford to stand being spoke to like that.'

'Perhaps her's feeling badly. Her doon't look well, does her.'

Tildy deliberately moved further along the field out of earshot of the others and set to work. While her body mechanically performed the labour, her mind was engaged elsewhere.

When they had woken that morning old Esther had immediately tried to persuade Tildy to go to the constable and tell him that Tobias Winterton was the man who had attacked the girl.

Tildy had rejected the idea with horror. How could she lay such charges against anyone on the strength of a nightmarish dream? Anyone who heard her saying such things would instantly class her as a madwoman.

'And rightly so,' Tildy told herself now, 'and I must be made to even consider the possibility that my dreams could show me the guilty man. Old Esther is making me as daft as she is with her stories of strange powers.'

Bend, wrench, straighten, chop. Bend, wrench, straighten, chop. She drove her body harder and harder as if by doing so she could rid her mind of the thoughts that tormented her. But relentlessly they held their grip and intensified their attacks.

'Old Esther's been right before with her predictions, hasn't she. And not only to me, but for many many others as well. Look how she warned Maddy Thomas about her babby. And how about that woman in the Silver Street, and the one from Headless Cross. There's no doubt that she does foresee things at times.

'Just supposing she is right, and that Tobias Winterton is the man who'se been attacking those girls? Supposing he was to attack another poor wench, mayhap even end by killing her, how would I feel then? Knowing that perhaps I might have prevented it by doing what old Esther wants, and going to the constable?' She shook her head sharply. 'And suppose old Esther just wants to cause trouble for the Wintertons? After all Arthur Winterton did ill-treat her. Perhaps she still wishes to even the score, and she's just trying to use me to that end?' All Tildy's instinct rebelled against these latter notions. 'No! Esther wouldn't use me in such a way. There's no real harm in her, that I know by now. and I truly believe that she cares for me and Davy as if we were her own kinfolk. She'd never do anything that might bring harm to either of us, I'm certain of that.' She sighed deeply. 'What should I do? Dear God above, what should I do? Is there anybody or anything that could tell me that?'

Slowly the day wore on and Tildy continued to be beset by her tormenting thoughts. The gang were spread out across the farm performing a variety of tasks and Jeremiah Borth continually patrolled the various areas of labour. Periodically his thoughts also returned to Tildy Crawford's behaviour, so out of her character as he knew it. During the time she had been back with the gang he had made no sexual advances towards her, although his desire for her had not lessened. But he had realized long since that she would never grant him any sexual favours, no matter what type of approach he made, and so had resigned himself to failure in that aspect of his life. Although this peeved him at times, yet as the weeks had passed he had found himself reluctantly admiring her courageous spirit, and also appreciating the fact that she was a conscientious and willing worker.

During the course of the day he became increasingly curious as to what had caused this sudden change in her. So, when he returned to the turnip field early in the afternoon he went to where Tildy was still toiling alone.

His practised eyes measured the amount of work she had completed, and he told her, 'You can take a break now, Tildy Crawford. You looks to have made up for the time you lost.'

She nodded without looking at him, and would have

walked to where she had left her small canvas bag of food and the tiny keg of cider, but he called her back to him.

'I wants a word afore you goes.'

She halted and faced him, and again he was struck by how white and tired-looking her features were, and her withdrawn, distracted manner.

'Am you feeling alright, girl?' he asked. 'Am you feeling badly?'

She shook her bonneted head. 'No, I'm not feeling badly. I'm perfectly well, thank you.' Her voice sounded flat and expressionless.

He was shocked to find a desire burgeoning within him to do something to restore her normal vitality and spirit, and for some moments only stood staring silently at her while he tried to come to terms with this unaccustomed emotion.

'Can I go and eat now?' she asked, and he nodded brusquely, then on sudden impulse held up his hand to stay her.

'Does you know the Green Lane, down by Studley village?' he questioned, and went on without giving her a chance to reply, 'Anyway, you can find it easy enough. Abel Morral's got a needle mill down theer, and it's on this near side o' the village. Theer's a farm further up the lane kept by Widow Spencer. I'se arranged to send a small gang theer tomorrow to lift the last of her carrots. I wants you to take 'um down theer, and oversee the work for me. I'll pay you a bit extra for it, and it 'ull be easier collar than this for you. I doon't expect you to pull carrots yourself all the time, it's better that you keeps the kids working and keeps an accurate tally. You should have it done in a couple o' days. Make sure youm theer at fust crack o' light tomorrow morn to meet the kids.' He turned and walked quickly away leaving Tildy staring somewhat bemusedly after him.

The news of the attack on the girl had spread through the entire district in the usual rapid and mysterious manner that such news was spread, and when the day's work had been completed and the gang gathered for the return to Redditch, Tildy was assailed from all directions with questions.

'Did you know that poor cratur, Tildy?'

'Was the constables searching around your house?'

'Arn't you fritted to walk back home by yourself?'

'Is it true that the bugger was nearly copped?'

She answered as best she could, and was thankful to be able to escape from the questioners at the Redditch Green. She called into say hello to Mother Readman, but anxious as she was to return to little Davy, stayed only a few minutes and made no mention of her own preoccupation.

An elderly carter that she knew offered her a lift from Brendon in his vehicle and she was glad of his garrulous company as far as the Dog Inn crossroads on the edge of the lonely heathland that was Mappleborough Green.

Davy and old Esther welcomed her home, and for a brief while Tildy was able to forget her own thoughts while she listened to her child's excited stories about the rabbit that old Esther had caught in her snares, the savoury appetizing scents of its cooking bubbling even now from the chain-hung iron pot above the inglenook fire.

'You'll get taken up for poaching, Esther,' she said, only half-jokingly, for the shadow of the savagely punitive game laws was an ever-present threat hanging above the head of anyone who was not a landowner.

The old crone cackled with laughter, and winked slyly. 'I bin ataking game ever since I left the cradle, my duck, and I'm too long in the tooth to be copped at it now.'

Later, with Davy sound asleep in his small truckle bed, the old woman returned to the subject of Tobias Winterton, but Tildy wearily told her, 'For pity's sake, Esther, leave it lay. I'm too tired right now to think of anything but my bed.'

In sleep, however, the dreams of a hooded man pursuing her came again to Tildy, and again she woke with a cry of terror as she saw the face of Tobias Winterton.

Bathed in clammy sweat Tildy lay staring into the darkness, while old Esther snored beside her, and as her terror receded her mind grappled with what she had dreamed, seeking rational explanations for the dream's recurrence.

Since leaving the Winterton farm she had seen neither

Arthur nor Tobias Winterton, and had only glimpsed old Gilbert and one of the women fieldworkers once each at a distance. Although some of the gang had worked at the Wintertons' during the main harvests, Tildy had not. She had normally been sent to the farms more distant from Redditch. Although at times she had naturally wondered how the people she had known at the farm were getting on, her attitude was that once she had left that place, then it had no longer any relevance to her life, and indeed, her new life with old Esther had engrossed her to the exclusion of nearly everything else.

'There's no reason for me to keep on dreaming about Tobias Winterton,' she told herself now, 'and even less for me to dream of him in the way that I am. I could understand if I dreamt that Arthur Winterton was attacking me, but not Tobias. I never knew or heard of him offering insult or violence to any woman except for that one time when he was so upset by what happened to young Jem. Any man might have acted as Toby did then, under such circumstances.'

She stirred restlessly, and realizing that she would not be able to sleep anymore that night rose from the bed carefully, so as not to disturb old Esther, and went softly into the other room to prepare herself for going to her work.

Chapter Twenty-Seven

The morning was grey and drizzly but the wind had shifted its quarter and brought milder temperatures with it. Widow Spencer's farmstead bordered the lane and she herself was waiting with Tildy in the muddy farmyard for the straggle of children as they arrived in charge of an older girl.

Tildy's heart filled with pity as she looked at the small peaked faces and red-chapped hands of the youngest children, some of whom were not much older than her own child, and for a moment or two her eyes filled with tears as she imagined her Davy standing there, clothed in virtual rags, runny-nosed, dirty and neglected-looking as most of these children were.

'By the Christ, but they're a pitiful sight, arn't they,' she remarked, low-voiced, to the woman beside her.

The middle-aged Widow Spencer was tall and raw-boned, and clad like a labouring woman in sacking skirts and a man's ragged coat, and a roughly fashioned hood-like headcovering made of canvas.

Her dour, weather-beaten features showed her surprise at Tildy's statement. 'Why does you say that, Mrs Crawford?'

'Well, look at the way they're clad, for one thing' Tildy illustrated.

'They doon't look any different to how I looked at their age,' the widow observed grimly. 'They ben't gentry childer, be they. How else should you expect the little buggers to look? They'm agoing to be pulling carrots, not learning how to dance a bloody minuet. They ought to be grateful that they'se got work to goo to.'

'I suppose you're right,' Tildy accepted to save useless argument. It was a trait among her own class that she constantly met with, that they expected their children to follow their parents' path in life, and sizeable numbers of those parents actively resented any child who might evince any desire to deviate from that path, or show any capabilities that they could utilize to aspire to something better in life for themselves than their parents had known or experienced.

Silently Tildy vowed, 'You'll never have to stand with these poor little mites if I can do ought to prevent it, Davy. I don't want you to tread the same path that I've trodden. I want you to live like a free-born man, not a parish pauper at the beck and call of any Jack-in-office with a profit ledger in the place where his heart should be.'

The widow issued out sacks for the crop to be collected in and led the small procession to the carrot field.

The carrots were sown in long drills and their green leafy tops waved slightly in the breeze like the plumes of helmets.

The widow saw Tildy's frown of doubt and divined the reason for it. 'You'll not need forks to dig 'um out from the drills' she said, 'the ground's soft wi' the rain. Any size o' kid 'ull pull 'um up with ease.'

Tildy's doubts on that score remained despite the assurance. 'Pull them up they might, Widow Spencer, but they'll find it sore hard work, I think.'

'Well that's what I'm paying for,' the woman told her gruffly, 'and I wants 'um to break off the tops, and put 'um aside for me cattle to ate. They can be heaped at the drills' ends.'

Tildy nodded silently.

'I'll leave you to it then,' the woman continued. 'Remember, I wants hard work from these little sods, not skylarking. Master Borth has contracted to finish this field in two days, and if it arn't done by then you'll all on you be forfeiting part o' your wages, for I'll not end a loser by it, you may be sure on that. I'm paying you bloody paupers too much as it is, by my way o' thinking.'

Tildy nodded, and said sarcastically, 'What else could you rightfully expect from overpaid pauper kids, Widow Spencer, except a deal of hard work,' then turned away to give the children their instructions.

The widow stared uncertainly at Tildy's back for a moment or two, then turned away herself.

When Tildy looked at the extent of the carrot crop her heart sank. Even to her admittedly experience it looked to be far too much for badly-fed children to clear in the alloted time.

By nightfall less than a third of the crop had been cleared and even that amount had only been achieved by Tildy herself foregoing any but the briefest of rest-breaks and working herself to a virtual standstill.

As she passed Abel Morral's needle mill on her way home she found herself looking almost with envy at the lighted windows from behind the dirty cracked panes of which came the sounds of wheels trundling and pulleys whirring, leather belting slapping and serried ranks of punches and hammers and files tapping and rasping in metallic concert.

'At least they're dry and warm inside there,' she thought, ruefully looking down at her wet, clay-heavy skirt and boots. Then she thought of the Lye Wash Shop at the Fountain needle mills where she had slaved in filthy grease, and steam and wet, and her incipient envy left her abruptly. 'At least I'm working in clean dirt now,' she smiled wryly, 'although there's a deal too much on it for comfort.'

Old Esther had asked Tildy to bring salt back with her, and she decided to go into Studley Village and buy a small sack of it.

At a small shop in the straggling main street she found what she sought, and was leaving when a familiar voice halted her.

'Tildy, is it you?'

She found herself looking into the rosy beaming face of Maddy Thomas. The two girls hugged and kissed each other with a genuine pleasure at meeting again.

'You mun come back and have a dish o' tay wi' me, and a bite to ate,' Maddy insisted, and practically dragged Tildy along the road with her, all the time talking excitedly. 'It's lovely seeing you agen, Tildy, I arn't half missed you, and my little Davy. How is he, Tildy, how is the little duck?'

'He's thriving, thank God,' Tildy was able to tell her before Maddy rushed on.

'I left bloody Winterton's at Michaelmas, Tildy. So did most on us, and bloody glad to leave, I'll tell you true. The place has gone to rack and ruin, so it has. Old Arthur is out on his bloody mind wi' the drink night and day, and Toby, well, he's, he's . . .' she hesitated, as if searching for words, 'he's acting real strange, Tildy. He arn't a bit like he used to be. He's become as free wi' his fists and boots as that old bastard of a feyther of his. And he's took to the drink as well. And when he's in his cups, then God help any poor maid who gets next him, because he'll have his hand up her skirts and his prick into her afore she can say Jack Robinson. Theer's times he acted like a wild beast towards me and Susy, Tildy. I'll tell you no lie. the bugger put the fear o' Christ into me more nor a few times, I'll tell you. I was real glad when Michaelmas come round this year and me bonding had finished. I'm working as maidservant to John Tilsey down by Toms Town theer, and it's a bloody paradise arter Winterton's. Mind you, they'm bloody Methodys, and powerful fond o' ranting prayers and singing hymns all day, but at least I'mm laying safe in me bed o' nights. And I can get home nearly every day to see my kid and me Mam.'

The mention of Tobias Winterton and Maddy's description of the changes in him threw Tildy's thoughts into turmoil, and she longed to get away by herself so that she could assimilate what she had been told. But reluctant to hurt her old friend's feelings, Tildy did not wish to suddenly hurry off and appear rejecting of the other girl's offer of hospitality.

She stopped speaking to draw breath and Tildy seized

her opportunity. 'How far do we have to go now, Maddy? Because I'm really tired, and could do with getting home myself.'

'We'em here, Tildy.'

A terrace of low-roofed cottages was set a little way back from the road, and Maddy pointed towards the nearer end one.

'It's just theer. Me Dad's gone off down Worcester way apple-picking, and most on the kids has gone wi' him. So theer's only me Mam and the little 'uns at present. You come on in and rest a spell afore you goes home.'

Maddy's mother was an older plumper version of the girl herself, and her manner equally warm and welcoming, and Tildy sat contentedly enough sipping hot tea from a cracked crock bowl and listening to Maddy's gossip about her new employers, and the low state the Winterton Farm had come to.

At last, Maddy's recital faltered, and she asked Tildy what she was working at, and where she now lived.

'I'm back working with Jeremiah Borth's gang,' she told them, 'and I'm living at Mappleborough, with Esther Smith.'

Both women stared at her with shock and dawning horror in their eyes.

'But her's a witch!' Maddy's mother exclaimed. 'Her's a black witch! Doon't you know that, girl?'

'She's no witch,' Tildy tried to tell them, 'she's only a lonely old woman who dabbles in fortune-telling and such-like. There's no harm in her, and she's proven a good friend to me and my Davy.'

The mother and daughter exchanged a fearful glance and the older woman crossed herself nervously. Tildy sighed with mingled sadness and exasperation, and old Esther's words came back to her; 'It's true what you told me, Esther,' Tildy acknowledged inwardly, 'people will think me a witch also because I live with you.'

She rose to her feet. 'Thank you for the tea, Mrs Thomas,' she said politely, 'and it's been lovely seeing you again, Maddy. I must get back home now.'

The two women remained seated and did not answer her, only stared with mute hostility as she quietly left the cottage.

The incident had depressed Tildy, and as she walked the lonely miles to Mappleborough Green she tried to come to terms with the fact that a woman she had counted a dear friend could no longer be considered so.

The clouds that had earlier blanketed the land had rifted and scattered and the moon was in its last quarter, the thin crescent casting a faint light across the wild heath she was traversing. A sense of foreboding began to pervade Tildy, and although she tried to dismiss it as a silly nervous fancy invoked by the loneliness and the memory of the hooded attacker of her dreams, still she unconsciously quickened her pace and started to peer about her, and make detours to avoid any clumps of gorse and shrubs that were large enough to conceal someone in hiding. A weak wind skittered intermittently, momentarily setting the tall stems of couch grass dancing and rustling the dying leaves on the trees and shrubs.

Half a mile from old Esther's cottage a high-pitched scream echoed from the dark woodlands that shrouded the low-lying hills to her right-hand side, causing Tildy to start in fright and setting her nerves jangling. She experienced an eerie sensation that someone or something was watching her, and darting nervous glances into the surrounding darkness, she hurried her pace until she was almost running across the rough ground.

Her foot caught in a tangle of low-lying bramble and she fell forwards. On hands and knees she swore to herself as she struggled free of the thorned tendrils and searched for her canvas bag which had gone flying as she stumbled. She found it and bent to pick it up, and as she did so her peripheral vision glimpsed a moving figure coming rapidly towards her. Tildy straightened, breathing in rapid, gasping intakes and peered hard in the direction of the figure. At first she saw nothing, then she almost cried out in fright as the solid black silhouette reappeared. Moving diagonally across the ground as if to intercept her path.

'God help me!' Tildy gasped aloud, and lifting her long skirts and bunching them high on her slender legs, she started to run. Fear pumped adrenalin through her body, and added strength and speed to her flight, and she thought she heard a shout from the dark figure, but dared not look to see where it was, only went pounding on towards old Esther's cottage. She came in sight of its dull lights glimmering from the two small windows at its front and at the same instant thought she heard the thudding of boots behind her.

'Help me, God! Help me!' she begged inwardly, and gasping for breath, forced her weakening legs and body onwards.

Slowly the lights drew nearer, but now her legs were racked with agonizing cramps and her body, already overtaxed by the labours of the day, near exhaustion. It was as though she were reliving her nightmares, as she struggled to hurl herself onwards and drag breath into her heaving lungs, and her muscles failed to respond to her demands and she moved slower and slower and slower, and could hear the thudding boots behind her coming nearer and nearer and nearer.

Now she was only a score of yards from the cottage, but the harsh panting of her nightmares was in her ears and the thudding boots at her heels, and then she tripped and went sprawling, and emitted a high-pitched despairing scream as she fell. Helplessly she lay face downwards, her skin crawling in anticipation of the brutal fingers digging deep.

She heard shouts and the frantic barking of the dogs and feet hurrying towards her, and shrieked as hands grasped her shoulders, and she twisted her body and struck out wildly, but was instantly pinned down against the earth.

'Tildy! Tildy! Tildy!' Esther Smith's high cracked voice sounded in her ears. 'Tildy, Tildy, it's me!'

Tildy sagged helplessly and sobbed with relief, and the pinning hands released their hold, and she and Esther Smith were clutched in each other's arms.

Anger began to smoulder within Tildy, anger that ignited into a white-hot fury directed against her pursuer, and she swore to herself: 'I'll kill him for this. I swear on my baby's life, Ill kill him for this.' So all-consuming was this lust to kill, that when the tall figure of a man loomed over the two women Tildy struggled to rise and hurl herself at him, and it took all old Esther's wiry strength to hold Tildy's exhausted body back.

'No Tildy, no. This is Will Shayler. He's bin awaiting wi' me in the cottage for you to come back home.' The old woman's shouted explanations gradually penetrated Tildy's distraught mind, and the madness of rage left her and she was able to recognize the constable of Studley parish.

Chapter Twenty-Eight

It was two hours later, and Tildy was calm now, and her body refreshed by food and warmth.

She, old Esther and Will Shayler were seated around the fire quietly discussing the happenings of the night. Neither Esther Smith nor Will Shayler had seen Tildy's pursuer, and although the constable had searched the surroundings and had retraced Tildy's path across the heath he had sighted nothing suspicious.

Tildy herself was beginning to wonder if she had imagined the whole episode, if in some way she had experienced a waking nightmare.

'Could I have deluded myself into believing that someone was chasing me? Could it have all been in my imagination, what with feeling tired and depressed as I was, and having the memories of my dreams, and thinking of that poor little wench who was set upon?' she wondered aloud.

'I suppose it could be possible, Tildy Crawford,' Will Shayler answered, 'but from all accounts youm a level-yedded 'ooman, not some flighty young maid. So it arn't probable that you imagined what happened out theer tonight.'

Tildy examined the man's face in the shifting flickering firelight. She judged him to be in his middle forties, square-jawed, rugged-featured, thick-set; he looked a tough customer. Curiously she asked, 'What brought you here tonight, Master Shayler?'

For a few seconds he sat as if giving deep thought to her question. Then answered, 'I'm agoing to be straight wi' you, Tildy. I come here because old Esther sent for me to come, on account o' them dreams you bin having.'

Tildy could not believe she had heard him correctly, and queried, 'My dreams?'

He nodded gravely. 'That's just so, Young 'ooman. Your dreams about Tobias Winterton being the man I'm seeking.' When she would have spoken he held up his hand. 'No, hear me out, Tildy. I'se known Esther here all me life, and I know that her arn't a black witch. But I believes in her powers as a wise-woman. Her's told me things afore which has helped me to catch wrongdoers.'

This time Tildy refused to be silenced. 'But you cannot condemn a man because I dreamed that he was chasing me. That would be a madness. Esther is my good friend, but in this thing I believe that she is letting her dislike of the Wintertons influence her too much.'

'Youm a foreigner here, Tildy,' the man said quietly, 'you doon't know the history o' the Wintertons.'

'What does that have to do with my dreams?' Tildy demanded heatedly.

''Ull you stop argufying and harken to Will Shayler for a minute,' old Esther scolded, 'and then you'll see what him and me are adriving at.'

'Very well, I'll listen, but I'll not necessarily agree,' Tildy assented ungraciously.

The constable's hard features were grim, and his manner exuded a calm conviction which Tildy could not help but be impressed by.

'Arthur Winterton has always been known as a rough and violent man, Tildy, and so was his feyther and his grandfeyther afore him. But there's never bin any madness in the family. Not until Arthur Winterton took a wife. Her finished her days locked up as a raving lunatic in one o' the madhouses at Henley.' He stopped speaking and leaned forward to emphasize what he said next. 'What I'm agoing to tell you now must remained locked up in your own mind, Tildy Crawford, and you must not spake of it to any living soul, because none on it can ever be proven for judgement by the law. Do you swear to stay silent?'

Tildy nodded in awed fascination. 'I so swear,' she murmured.

'So be it,' Shayler accepted, and his voice dropped to a near whisper. 'Arter Arthur Winterton's wedding, all seemed well wi' 'um both. Then his missus had a couple o' childer. This was before she had Tobias. Her started acting strange, and throwing fits o' terrible tantrums. And it was woe betide anybody who come near her then, because her 'ud fly at 'um like her was a wild beast.

'Naturally Arthur took his belt to her, but it didn't matter how much he beat her, she still kept throwing these fits. She'd even try to attack Arthur himself when one of her passions was on her, and her' 'ud use whatever her could lay her hands on to try and harm him; pokers, knives, pitchforks, anything.'

The memory of her own violent marriage prompted Tildy. 'But surely it was a natural thing for the poor woman to try and defend herself. I've experienced Arthur Winterton's violence myself, Master Shayler. I can't blame any poor soul who fought him back.'

'Hush, Tildy!' old Esther exclaimed. 'Hush and listen.'

The constable smiled mirthlessly. 'Yes, Tildy, I'll agree wi' what you say. I couldn't blame her for fighting back neither. But in all fairness to Arthur Winterton, it warn't him who mostly started their rows. He was besotted wi' the wench. Fairly worshipped the ground her walked on, so he did. That's why, when the two childer was found drownded in the river, and his missus lying senseless on the bank wi' her skirts soaking wet, Arthur Winterton 'udden't believe that her had drownded them kids deliberate, but would only believe what her told him. That they'd fallen in and she'd tried to drag 'um out and had suddenly fainted, and the poor little souls had died by accident.'

'But perhaps she spoke the truth!' Tildy protested vigorously.

'If she spoke the truth, Tildy, how was it that the kids drownded in the shallows, wheer the water warn't above six inches at the deepest part?'

'But tiny children have been known to drown in a few inches of water,' Tildy argued, and now it was old Esther who answered her.

'They warn't tiny, Tildy. One on 'um was five years old, and the other four, and it was me who layed 'um out, Tildy. Me and old Molly Rankin. I saw bruises on one o' the poor little cratur's throat. The sort o' bruises that a strangling grip might leave.'

The constable took up the story. 'From then on things just went from bad to worse over the years for the Wintertons. 'Til at the death Sally Winterton had to be put away, as much for her own sake as for anybody else's.'

For some time all were silent, as Tildy thought over what she had been told. The memory of Arthur Winterton's ramblings about young Jem being his only unflawed child came back to her, and also the remembrance of Tobias' unbalanced reaction to her friendship with Oriel Evans. Eventually she turned to William Shayler and stated quietly.

'You believe that Tobias Winterton has inherited his mother's madness, don't you, Master Shayler.'

The man nodded solemly. 'I do. And I also believe, Tildy Crawford, that despite leaving no trace, it was Tobias Winterton who came chasing after you this night. I believe that you stand in grave peril of your life, young 'ooman, as long as that madman remains free.'

Tildy drew a long deep breath to steady the sudden pounding of her heart as the constable added. 'I'm not happy about that pauper wench that supposedly run away from the farm a few months since. Young Sally Jukes.'

'You think that Tobias might have harmed her?' Even as she asked the question Tildy foresaw the man's answering nod.

'He could well ha' done. And to be fair, it's only these last days I've bin wondering about it,' Shayler admitted. 'Arter all, runaway servants are a common thing, I could be doing Tobias an injustice, but I still got the feeling that her's laying dead somewheres about here.'

'But if that was so, then surely she would have been

found by now? Even if she was buried some trace of the grave would be seen.'

He shrugged his powerful shoulders. 'There's a deal o' woodlands in these parts, Tildy, and plenty o' places wheer nobody steps foot one year to the next. She could lay theer 'til Doomsday and nobody the wiser.'

Again there was a long silence, then Tildy asked, 'Just supposing, and only supposing mind, that what you say is true, and that Tobias Winterton is a dangerous madman who is a threat to my life, then what can be done about it?'

'Wi'out hard and sure proof, then nothing can be done,' Shayler told her bluntly. 'I can't take a man up just because I suspects him, more's the pity.'

A sensation of sickening helplessness invaded Tildy. 'So that means that he must commit some outrage before anyone will do aught?'

'That's exactly what it means,' Shayler confirmed, with an edge of bitterness in his voice.

With shock Tildy suddenly realized that a part of her had already accepted the fact of Tobias Winterton's guilt, and although with that realization there came an automatic attempt on her part to reject that acceptance, still it remained.

'Then what can I do to protect my Davy and myself from him?' A peculiar feeling of detachment came over her as she asked the question, as though it were only of academic interest.

'You must be on your guard, and try not to walk abroad at night, but stay close where you've others about you.'

'Doon't you fret, my duck,' old Esther told her defiantly. 'The bugger 'ull do you no harm whiles youm here wi' me. I'll conjure our safety.'

Tildy chuckled ruefully. 'It would take a very powerful spell to stop a madman in his tracks, Esther.'

'Who'se talking about spells,' the old crone cackled gleefully, and went to one of the chests standing against the wall, and opening its heavy lid lifted out a rusty bell-mouthed flintlock gun. 'This old blunderbuss is a powerful charm, my duck. It'll blow the maddest madman to bloody Kingdom Come.' She rummaged further through the chest and lifted out a wooden box. 'I've powder here, and plenty of nails and such in the shed out back theer. When we sets the dogs on long leash, and gets this loaded, then if that mad bugger shows his face, he'll think he's afacing Badahoos walls, so he 'ull.'

The peculiar sense of detachment still held Tildy in thrall as she took the fearsome weapon from old Esther's hands, and she wondered at her own lack of emotional response to the fact that she was seriously contemplating the bloody destruction of a young man should he approach the cottage.

William Shayler broke the spell that held her. 'You take care what youm adoing wi' that bloody thing, you two,' he advised. 'By the looks on it, it could blow up in your own face if you puts too much of a charge o' powder in it.'

Tildy shivered violently, and put the gun from her with sudden revulsion.

Shayler put on his wide-brimmed, low-crowned hat. 'I'll needs be off. I'm agoing to make a social call on the Wintertons, and I'll see how the land lays theer. I doon't reckon you'll be troubled agen by anybody this night, but it wunt hurt to bring the dogs to the front door, and mayhap have one on 'um inside here wi' you. And remember, only use a small charge in that bloody gun.' To Tildy he said, 'You goo careful now, girl. And remember, not a word to anyone about what's passed between us this night. You may rest assured that I'm agoing to do all I can to bring the bugger to book afore he can harm any other poor wench. And now I'll bid you both a good night.'

Chapter Twenty-Nine

Again that night the dream of the hooded man assailed Tildy and again she woke bathed in a clammy sweat of terror. She rose from her unquiet bed and went to sit by the fireside, and it was there that old Esther found her dozing uneasily in the grey dawn.

'Tildy, Tildy, go to bed, my honey. I'll watch over you,' the old crone urged gently.

'I must go to my work, I'm late already.' Tildy was stubbornly adamant despite old Esther's protests. 'No, Esther. If I don't work, then we'll not have enough to eat next week.'

'But what if Tobias Winterton comes after you?'

'No, he won't come after me by daylight, if it is him that's doing these things.' Tildy was instinctively sure of that fact. 'Whoever it is only roams by night, Esther.'

'But arn't you feared, girl?' the old woman asked incredulously.

Tildy grimaced. 'Of course I'm feared. But I'm not going to let fear rule me, Esther. Once I let that happen, then I might just as well be laying in my grave, because life won't be worth the living them.'

The older woman sensed that nothing she could say would shake Tildy's resolve. 'So be it then. But at least take this wi' you, so that youm not entirely helpless.'

She proffered a horn-handled clasp knife, and to please her friend Tildy took it and slipped it into the pocket of her gown.

'God guard you, Tildy. I'll be on pins 'til you gets back safe.'

'It doon't look to be gooing over-fast, does it?' Widow Spencer observed sourly when she came to the carrot field while the children were eating their meagre breakfast. 'You'll needs drive these lazy little sods a bloody sight harder if youm to have it done by nightfall.'

Tildy stopped working and glanced at the rain-weeping grey skies, and then at the miserable gang of muddied, wet children. 'What would you have me do to drive them harder, Widow Spencer, take a whip to their backs?' she questioned tartly.

'If needs be, Mrs Crawford,' the woman snapped back.

'That I'll never do,' Tildy retorted spiritedly.

'Then you'll be losing money, wun't you. And I reckon that Master Borth 'ull have summat to say about that, wun't he.' The widow's hatchet face appeared to relish the prospect. 'He'll soon warm their bloody hides for 'um when I tells him how they'se bin skylarking instead o' working. They'll be shedding bitter tears then alright.'

Tildy could only shake her head disgustedly, and bent once more to her work, deliberately ignoring the other woman, who in the face of this contempt could only glare impotently, and stump away muttering, 'I'll have summat to tell Master Borth about you, you saucy bitch. You just wait and see if I wun't.'

Tildy worked her way to the end of the drill, and then straightened her aching back, and was about to call to the children to resume their work, when the words caught in her throat, and a shiver of fear coursed through her.

A solitary horseman was coming through the field gate. He wore a low-crowned top hat, blue riding-coat and breeches and leather kneeboots. Even at a distance of more than fifty yards and despite his unfamiliar clothing Tildy could recognize Tobias Winterton.

The children were making their way towards her and were in between her and the man. Tildy's first impulse was to turn and flee, but she could not bring herself to leave the children alone and unprotected, and screwing up all her courage she advanced to meet him. Her mind desperately searching for some feasible plan of action that would keep both herself and the children safe from harm.

She tried to smile at the children, and telling them, 'Get on with your work now, kids, I'll join you presently,' she steeled herself, and trudged steadily towards the oncoming man, her hand seeking beneath her sacking skirt to find and grasp the horn-handled knife in her pocket.

The man reined in his horse a couple of yards from Tildy, and in her turn she slowed and halted. Beneath the dripping wet brim of his hat Tobias Winterton's face was puffed and blotchy, his eyes red-rimmed and bloodshot.

Tildy could think of nothing to say to him, and stood silently, waiting for him to make the first move, her heart pounding furiously and her mouth dry with fear.

He shifted in his saddle and the leather creaked loudly and Tildy's body started involuntarily.

He smiled sadly and slowly shook his head. 'You've naught to fear from me, Tildy Crawford.' His voice was hoarse and low-pitched.

Tildy fought to still the visible trembling of her body, and to summon every ounce of courage she possessed.

Tobias Winterton stood up in his stirrups and looked around the field, saying as he did so, 'I'se just had a word wi' Widow Spencer. She reckons youm going to be in trouble if this field arn't cleared by nightfall. I doon't like the old cow. Never has done. So I thought I'd gi' you a hand to get it done.' He looked directly down at her and smiled pleasantly. 'I doon't want to see an old friend like you get into trouble, Tildy.' He pointed to the field's boundary where an old rusty plough was lying against the hedgerow. 'Theer now, theer's a bit o' good fortune. I'se got rope in my saddlebag, and I reckon I can fashion a harness o' sorts from it. You get them kids ready wi' their sacks, and I'll soon have these drills stripped out for you.'

Tildy could only stand in speechless bewilderment as the young man rode across to the rusty plough, and taking the rope he had spoken of, fashioned a rough harness to enable his horse to draw the plough.

She watched while he removed the coulter blade and dressed in all his finery took the plough handles and drove the horse and plough along the lines of drills, the plough's mould-boards slicing easily through the soft damp earth undercutting the rows of carrots and tumbling the earthen ridges sideways so that the crops of roots fell free.

He went to the opposite end of the field, turned and came back, and as he passed her once more smiled pleasantly and called out, 'Come on now, Tildy, get them kids collecting. You'll soon have it done now.'

Still locked in a dazed uncertainty of bewilderment, Tildy obeyed.

The advent of the plough speeded the work of clearing dramatically, and while Tildy toiled with her thoughts in hopeless turmoil, still she could recognize a sense of gratitude burgeoning in her towards Tobias Winterton, while at the same time the sheer incongruity that she should feel anything other than fear and hatred of the man whelmed over her.

By late afternoon he had scattered the final drill, and leaving the horse still attached by its rope harness to the plough he came back to where Tildy was busily filling a sack with the crop.

She tensed as he neared her, and her hand went to the knife in her pocket, while her eyes quickly scanned to see that the children were at a safe distance. 'If he tries to attack me, at least they're far enough away to be able to make a run for it themselves.' She tried to draw comfort from the thought, as she steeled herself for whatever might come.

Tobias Winterton came to as standstill some yards from her. His clothes and boots were saturated by rain and thick with mud, and Tildy thought without any sense of irony, 'What a shame! His nice clothes are ruined,' then marvelled that such a thought should occur to her at such a moment.

'Don't be feared, Tildy,' he told her softly, 'I'm going away now, and you'll never see me again in life. I had a long talk with Will Shayler last night. He told me of things that I'd feared, but not really known for sure.' He paused, and a grimace of pain passed across his face. 'But I knows for sure now, Tildy. I've wronged you and others, mayhap today 'ull make some amends for it. I'm leaving you the horse. Do with it what you will. I hope you'll be able to think kindly of me some day. Try to remember, that it warn't really my fault, that I'm what I am.' He smiled with an infinite sadness. 'I just thought of a song me Mam used to sing to me when I was a nipper, Tildy. It used to finish, "and when I'm dead, Love, come and see me, and grow sweet flowers upon my grave." I wish now I'd planted flowers upon her grave, because then she could have looked down from Heaven and seen that I remembered her.'

Without another word he walked away, and Tildy stood watching him cross the shattered ridges strewn with the broken green leaves and disappear through the gateway.

Only then did her tense body sag and begin to shake uncontrollably, and the tears run unchecked down her cheeks.

It was Will Shayler who came to the cottage late that night to tell Tildy and old Esther that Tobias Winterton's drowned lifeless body had been found in the River Arrow by old Gilbert Tongue the shepherd.

'Did he die by his own hand?' old Esther asked, and the constable shrugged.

'Well, he was taken from the water in almost the very same spot that his two brothers drownded all them years ago. So you may draw your own conclusions.'

''Tis a blessing that the bugger's gone,' old Esther stated vehemently. 'Now women may walk safe again.'

'Amen to that!' Shayler agreed. 'I had a long talk wi' him last night. He denied that he'd molested any 'ooman, and truth to tell, he didn't give the impression that he lied. But then, how's a madman to tell the difference between what's true and what arn't? What say you, Tildy?'

She shook her head sadly. 'I don't think he knew himself what he was doing when the madness first came over him. But I do believe that after you spoke to him last night, he remembered what he had done. That's why he drowned himself. Because he knew then for sure in his heart that he carried his mother's madness in his own blood.'

Her memory went back to a day of hot sunshine, and a young man with the looks and figure of a Greek god standing waist deep in clear sparkling waters, the white teeth gleaming in his sun-bronzed laughing face.

'That is how I want always to remember you, Toby,' she murmured, 'and someday soon I'll come and plant sweet flowers upon your grave . . . That I promise . . .'